Collected Works

PROOF COPY

Clifton Northridge Bennett

*For Donna
— with appreciation!*

2013

Collected Works – Clifton Northridge Bennett

Copyright © 2013 by Clifton N. Bennett
First Edition March 2013

All rights reserved.
ISBN 978-1-300-81731-4
Printed in the United States of America

Dedicated to

Florence, the mother of my children, Lora and Eric, and *Veronica*, the mother who cared for and raised them.

Acknowledgements

This bountiful offering may have remained dormant without the 'breath of life' infused by our good friend and editor, Russ Havens. Russ has been caring for our family website for many years, with the help of my sister, Lora Bennett. At 94, Dad finally sorted through his files and gave me 9 ½ pounds of typed pages to mail to Russ.

The difference Russ brought to this project, from other options, is that he cared. You can imagine the hours and energy involved translating a lifetime of written and drawn material into the digital world of today. Count yourself as blessed if you work with someone who cares. The biggest compliment Russ shared, is he now feels inspired to finish his own book!

How to deliver the fullness of our gratitude is still a mystery…my heart is open. Hugs to you, my man. Thank you.
– Eric Bennett, Sarasota, FL, March 2013

Special thanks to Lora Bennett, who, with her keen eye and analytical mind saved me hours by assisting with error checking, as well as the text for "Letter from Nigeria – 1963".

Thanks, as well, to Eric Bennett for coordinating the project, helping to gather the original documents, and notably for his encouragement.
– Russ Havens, Randolph, NH, March 2013

TABLE OF CONTENTS

Foreword 1

PROSE 3

Once Upon a Clothesline 4

The Princess and the Pea Soup 9

Ancient Man: Smarter than you think 10

Letter from Nigeria – 1963 13

The Dark Warehouse 26

"That's not my job…" 28

The Confession of Dribbl 13 29

Tale of the Fair Elizabeth and the Evil Motilal 30

Autobiography 33

Two-Thirds of a Jackpot 34

A Puddle 35

Individual and Communal 37

Local Employment and Trading Systems (LETS) 38

Gully Seed 40

Bits About Borges 42

Manifesto of S.P.A.M. 44

The Choice 46

Abduction of the Queen 48

Individual and Communal 74

Subject: The Cybergospel According to Clif 75

Religion & Technology 76

Beneficiary of the Helping Paw Society 77

Society of the Spectacle 79

For the Man Who Asks Questions 80

Bushed 81
Gathering 82
Latest Glossary of Technical Terms Observed in Use,
Mainly in High Places 84
Gubby Goes to Heaven 84
Leprechauns Have Eyebrows 91
Unto Us a Child is Born 97
Tribal Notes 99
Sixty Second Sermons 111
A Slow Afternoon in the Snowflake Factory 118
There is a Story 120
Anyone Can Be Arthur Mandelbaum 122
The F.B.I. – The Basis of an American Police State 126
Resistance in Prison 177

POETRY 187
Bronze Man Breathing 188
Ruth, Mother Of Obed 202
The Preachers 202
Old Rain 203
Progress 204
Hijas Delviento 205
On The Beach At San Felipe 205
Wasted Rain 206
Valle Trinidad 207
Pinto Girl 208
Poem For Roger, Age 3 209
Words Of The Jaguar Priest 210

The Perfumed Statue	210
Depth	211
Testing	212
Stranger	212
Song For David	213
Undergoing Of The Evening-Lands	214
Leda	214
Phoenix That Died	215
All Fragile Arts	215
Angles	216
Dead Guru	218
After All	219
Greater Loyalty	220
Letter To Dan Katchongva	220
Sunset, South Rim	221
Trial	222
Beyond Eden	224
Poe Cottage	225
Tideland	226
In The Manner Of Seurat	226
End Of Ramadan, Kano Emirate	227
Dried Leaf In Obutsudan	228
Priest, Old Catholic Church	228
Old Testament Professor	229
Khirbetqumran	230
Loyalty Oath	230
The Baffled Angler	231

    Incription 232

    desert song 233

    Words Of Solomon to the Shulamite, in Her Absence 233

    Thus I 234

    For John Huot 235

    Thinking in Primitive Communities 236

    Cinquains 238

    Ortega In The Cellar 239

August to December 244

    A Cycle of Poems 244

    Our Lady of Apricots 245

    Correspondence 247

    Lady with Champagne and Monsters 249

    Devotus Defixusque 250

Collected Poems 255

    Belonging 255

    Invocation of the Unlikely 256

    Thirties 257

    thirties echo 265

    Manifesto to My Son 265

    Losing It 266

    calico kitten and snowflakes 267

    Haretsu 268

    Arigato 268

    Ai Kaze 269

    Nanimo No Eiga 270

    Aki No Hiru-Sugi 270

Jiyuu-Na	271
Kara-Na-Heya	272
Itami	272
Evening in the Castle	273
Utica Station	273
Inscription I.	274
Inscription II.	274
Andy	275
Forgetting Faces	275
Prayer Tablet	276
The Dream at Penuel	276
Sometime in June	277
Besides	277
Bowed by the cost	278
How many times	278
Ras Shamra	279
Intrumo In the Valley	280
Ash-toreth. Enish-kegal.	280
Krestova	281
Turnabout	282
One-Industry Towns	282
Long Distance	283
Roberta the Improbable	283
Roberta the Improbable: II	284
La Fontaine de Vaucluse	285
Not that the core of me is vacuum	285
Haiku	286

Tabi	287
And I am shaken again	287
I sing not me	288
Hero	289
Journey	289
New Song Heard in High Lothlórien	290
Lake Storm	290
The Rug-Carriers	291
All the Poems I Never Wrote	292
Lilith	292
Etruria	293
More Real Than We Think	294
Changeling	294
Some of My Best Friends	295
Not For This	300
Nagasaki	300
While repulsing a young man of Science	301
The Weaver's Son	302
The World	303
The New God	303
She also	304
White Lady	305
Moon Stallion	306
Sixth and San Pedro	306
Poem for Roger: II.	307
Dusk Forest	307
The Jealous God	308

Atomic War	309
Blinded Moth	309
Quixotic	309
William Randolph Canute, Publisher	309
Captive Moth	310
Objector	310
Warning Posted	310
Speechless	310
Planck's Constant	311
Schroedinger's Equation	311
Heisenberg's Principle	311
Materiel	311
Infacticide	312
Hill Fever	312
To the Man	313
Again	313
Autumn passed through here today	314
With what a sudden hand	315
Invitation	315
Ports of Call	316
Tell me, how shall I say -	317
Abduction of the Daughter of Maria	317
The Dying Metaphysician	319
Sons of Zarathustra	320
At Ensenada Bay	321
Hospitality	321
Gwendolyn & Milton	322

DoGGerEl GrEeTIngs	322
Beyond the mountains of despair	323
Rebellion	324
Prison Graveyard	325
Bitter, O lord of the eight-fold path	326
May children play in the silences	327
Spendthrift	327
Why A Zebra?	327
The postman walks with a four-foot stride	328
Who He?????	329
Adam's Death	330
Yih Jing Sonnets	332
A Brief Biography	465

Foreword

Books were not to be taken for granted in the Bennett home. Steven Bennett made a decent income but books were a luxury item which nonetheless made their way into Clif's hands due to the thoughtful savings and purchases made by his mother Maude. Clif remained a voracious reader throughout his life, and this more than any other source may explain the amount of writing he eventually came to do.

Dear Reader: you are now faced with the *Collected Works of Clifton Northridge Bennett*. It is over 470 pages long and stretches from university-quality papers through old-fashioned poetry and on to stories that even children may enjoy. Here and there you will also find snapshots of Clif's more recent life taken by his son and others.

The delightful story of Gubby the fish, is one of my personal favourites, as well as the poem, "Pinto Girl", written during a two-year stay in Mexico. If you are given to wondering about life in general or about religion, you will find plenty of company in the pages that follow. Or if you have simply wondered what it is like in Africa, you will find one of the best travel descriptions of Nigeria I have yet to come across.

The poetry alone to be found within this volume would suffice as a "collected works". While written often in an old-fashioned manner reminscent of T. S. Eliot, Wordsworth and even Shakespeare (the *Yih Jing Sonnets*) there are even freely written verses that achieve e. e. cummings fluidity. Personally, I find some of the poetry here achieves all of what the poets I studied in high school are lauded for – universality of theme, passion and word-craftmanship.

There is a background sense of a comrade reaching out within these pages for lively and continuing dialogue around subjects like community, the future of humans on earth, chess and myth, science and the imagination and the effect of poetry on the reader. May you be so moved!

– Lora Bennett, in Norrköping, Sweden, March 2013.

PROSE

Once Upon a Clothesline

Once upon a bubbly time there lived on the banks of Thames a young and handsome prince who had won a castle in a box-top contest. The prince had a pet dog who was not actually a dog, but a great enchanter who had accidentally enchanted himself one dark day by getting a spell backwards while studying his spelling.

In the castle next door lived a young and beautiful princess who had a pet parakeet which was not really a parakeet but a fine pedigreed dog which had turned into a parakeet in a fit of pique upon losing a box-top contest. This castle was only a clothesline away from the castle of the young prince. In fact, there was a clothesline – and this was not an aging troubadour who had been turned into a clothesline because his poetry did not scan, but a genuine clothesline. You could tell it was a genuine clothesline because it usually had genuine clothes on it.

The castle won by the prince wasn't very comfortable. This may have been because it was a prefab job, or because it was only two feet wide and seventy feet high. It did have a crenelated battlement with pennons atop, and this was fine and noble, provided you can tell a crenelated battlement when you see one.

The prince made up for the short measure in the castle's width by sleeping in the window arches. This was easy to do, since there were no windows in the arches, and they pierced the castle from one side to the other. It was also a necessary thing to do because the castle was completely solid, with no space inside for anything but stones and mortar. Court life was greatly simplified by the fortunate coincidence that the young prince was a realist, a lover of open air, quite healthy and disposed by preference to hold audience on the rooftop during good weather.

It had never been the prince's intention to win a castle. What he dearly wanted was a trip to the Hesperides, all expenses paid. He yearned to spend a summer vacation on a Hesperide, and the fact that he couldn't locate any place of that name in his World Atlas dismayed him not at all. The various boxes of detergent which he and his court had bought to get the required box-tops were stacked high in most of the archways – with the tops torn off, of course. Sometimes when the wind blew, the boxes would rock back and forth, and if you've never seen topless detergent a-go-go, I can offer you the address of the castle.

One prophetic day in early spring while the weather was labouring to make up its mind, one of those things happened which makes the course of true love run like the pulse of a rooster who discovers his Number One Hen laying duck eggs. The princess had laundered her parakeet, something which she did with hygienic regularity and borrowed detergent. She had affixed the protesting bird to the clothesline with a pair of golden clothespins, as was her wont – and if that sounds confusing to you, it didn't to the parakeet, because *it* could comprehend Old English.

She sang merrily as she hauled on the line and swung the parakeet out into the procrastinating sunshine, practicing an Old English lay. (For the benefit of potential censors, that is a song, and not an exotically archaic method of inflating the population statistics.) So merrily she sang that she swung the parakeet right up against the wall of the prince's castle with a stunning thump, and the bird shrilled out a most unbirdlike oath. This oath was sufficiently mighty to turn the parakeet back in a definitive flash into a fine pedigreed dog, and sufficeently loud to awaken the pet dog of the prince, which had been slumbering demonstratively in its favourite arch next the clothesline pulley.

The prince's dog, jolted conclusively out of an amorous dream in which he had laboured mightily with the aid of a beauteous pedigreed bitch to increase the roll-call of dogdom, found himself gazing upon a beauteous pedigreed bitch, conveniently pinned by the ears to a clothesline, and swinging enticingly before him. With his morals in a slumberous condition, but with other of his parts excruciatingly aware and pointing the way to action if not salvation, he proceeded to do what came caninely natural, successfully enjoying himself to the degree that he loosed a reverberating oath – in the tongue of dogs, to be sure, but still vibratory enough to transform him back into his original shape. Finding himself once again a great enchanter, he concurrently discovered the existence of an inexplicable misalliance with another species, and hastily dropped the matter.

At this point the atmosphere was disemboweled by the howl of numerous trumpets, most of which were out of tune, and the castle of the princess was observed to be surrounded by a scrofulous horde of brigands, complete with the accouterments approved in the most recent contract of the Brigands' Union, to wit: catapults, rams, burning pitch, untuned woodwinds and brass, plus one kazoo and a musical saw which were later ruled to have been outside the regulations.

The scrape of the musical saw, which was rusty and off-key, awoke the prince, and he at once perceived the desperate encumbrance of the princess.

"Allow me to offer you the shelter of my ancestral hall!" he yodeled. "You'll be safe with me! Grab the rope as soon as I untangle this dog, and I'll provide you transportation far above the madding crowd!"

"Do you really expect me to fall for that old line?" asked the princess. "Besides, how am I going to keep my grip on the way over?"

"Pin yourself to the clothesline," advised the prince, "and quickly, or you'll be princessburger."

With a final tearful glance at her besieged castle, the princess did the necessary, and with a series of muscular heaves the prince drew her across the intervening space into his window niche, which was now somewhat crowded by himself, herself, an enchanter who had been a dog, a dog which had been a parakeet, and a few hundred odd detergent boxes which had suffered beheading in a noble cause.

Night prostrated itself upon the land, and they huddled communicatively together for warmth, while the brigands ate and drank and caroused, according to Article XXIV of the By-Laws, taking an occasional temporal lacuna to shout bits of ribald comment on the ultimate fate of the besieged.

In a corner of the arch, the enchanter busied himself, with verbose mutterings and exclamatory dottings of arcane grammar. After repeating several spells which, to the best of his memory, were guaranteed to produce impressive quakings of the earth accompanied by heat lightning, he was rewarded with a sudden and uncomfortably wet rain whose quantity increased to the point of superfluity. Shrugging into his cloak, he tried again, and managed to conjure several contradictory winds of gale force which flattened the occupants of the arch. As they clutched projecting bits of masonry, the wind flung hundreds of open detergent boxes down into the puddles, streams and bogs.

A magnificently frantic sudsing engulfed the brigands and their fleas. Swaying plateaus of bubbles covered all, even to the edge of the window niche, fully fifty feet above their shampooed locks. By morning, neither brigand, brass nor woodwind was visible. The land shone clean, of sin and of crops, serfs, duress, feudalism, fee simple and complex, durance vile and otherwise, Papal bulls, Holstein cows, and untuned trumpets. Briefly, the piece couldn't be lived in.

The defenders looked sadly down, lowering the mail bucket on a length of clothesline as a surviving postman floundered by with a single letter.

"Alas," wept the prince, "all is lost. Not that it was much to begin with, but what the hell…"

"Weep not," admonished the princess, reading the letter, for it had been addressed to her. "I have just won a trip for two to the Hesperides, all expenses paid, in the most recent box-top contest. Will you marry me?"

He did. They went. They stayed long at the Hesperides Hilton.

> **Castle for Sale**
> Used only once or twice by a young prince whose feet hardly scuffed the drawbridge. Enchanter available as optional equipment.

The Princess and the Pea Soup
(A gentle take-off on Grimm, or somebody)

Once upon a time, there was a prince who lived in a castle on top of a hill. You could see the hill sometimes when it wasn't snowing too hard, but you could almost never see the castle. It was built along the lines of a peasant haycart called a Volkswagen, with what was known as a low profile to escape the catastrophic effect of the mountain winds.

That may have been why the princess stumbled over it. The night was dark, the wind high, the snow thick and white except where it had been stained a bit by smog.

The princess was accompanied by a serving-woman, and when she (the princess) stumbled over the castle, the serving-woman had the presence of mind to pull the bell-cord at the drawbridge.

And that was how they both came to be admitted to what they later referred to as the Aklavik Hilton.

The prince was a little offbeat. He leaned out of a small window over the portcullis and called, "Don't want any – have enough Avon products for this week!" The serving-woman, however, was not so easily put off, and yelled back, "This is a princess, you murky imitation of a cream-puff. Open the door!"

So they came in, had supper, and indicated a readiness for the usual accommodations.

The prince, wishing to test whether the beautiful young thing who had lapped up his lentil soup and sourdough bread was in truth a princess, arranged a princessly bed by piling up seventeen mattresses and forty-two feather comforters. Under the bottom mattress he carefully spilled half a can of Campbell's Pea Soup.

In the morning, the princess awoke. "My panties are wet!" she proclaimed.

In later years, archeologists would wonder why the castle displayed the remains of a sump pump installed in the second-floor bedroom of the Royal Suite.

Ancient Man: Smarter than you think

Gunpowder and printing, two strange companions, are the foundation of Western civilization. Both were developed in the Orient, with one family of Chinese printers setting movable type in clay forms near Shanghai in the 1200's. The Koreans were casting and moulding type at about the same time. More surprising yet, we have in our museums books of Hindu scripture printed in India from movable wood types hundreds of years before the birth of Gutenberg.

Lawyers weary of the complexity of modern law can take time out to enjoy the simplicity of the Code of Hammurabi, which antedates by 2,000 years the basic division into matters of procedure, property and person on which our Roman law is founded. Hammurabi's Code minces no words in prescribing direct punishment for crime. One derivative transmitted through our Biblical book of Leviticus prescribes burning at the stake as an antidote for falling in love with your mother-in-law!

And businessmen may be justly proud of the long history of buying and selling on the installment plan. The

Tablets of Gasur, unearthed near modern Kirkuk, show that this sort of thing went on apace prior to 2180 B.C.

Remember that quaint picture in your history text, of Ben Franklin fumbling through a crude electrical experiment with a kite, hemp cord and a key? Recent discoveries indicate the Egyptians used wet cells for electroplating 3,000 years ago.

Even such diverse products as concrete, safety pins and inflation are not strictly American. All three were known one and one-half millennia ago in the Roman Empire, the last-named during the debasing of the coinage under Diocletian.

Most of us are familiar with one or more of these forerunners of modern inventiveness, but what we don't know is that the old-timers, in many aspects of engineering, sociological, agricultural and artistic works, set up marks never reached by us.

Hard to believe? Before the coming of the gunpowder-wise Arab slave traders, there existed in Africa's heart great Negro empires stretching from Timbuctoo north to the very fringes of the Sahara. Here, as early as the tenth and eleventh centuries, textile mills manufactured velvet cloths of brilliant color.

Timbuctoo itself was a city of 200,000, its main thoroughfares lined with four rows of trees on each side, the doorposts and uprights of each house a maze of distinctive carving, the principal public buildings of stone.

A simplified alphabet was used, and the principle of inalienability of land titles marked a culture in many ways morally higher than our own.

Present hygienic conditions in India are infamous. But excavations near Karachi, India, at the site of ancient Mohenjo-Daro, reveal a planned city, with broad streets, high buildings, and an elaborate sanitary system including a bathroom in almost every house. The year? About 3000 B.C.!

Lewis Mumford includes in *The Culture of Cities* a photograph of low-cost housing for working people of the sixteenth century, built by Jacob Fugger, a German philanthropist. The houses, superior to current projects in everything but plumbing and lighting, are still inhabited. Anyone want to place a bet on whether the Chicago housing project for veterans will be standing and occupied 300 years from now?

In the field of public works, the Chicaina Valley of Peru contains a 50-mile remnant of aqueduct built by the Incas over a thousand years ago. Construction required the moving of five million tons of earth. The aqueduct has never been replaced by Peru's modern conquerors. Not only the water works, but the transportation, communication, statistical, agricultural and general public works of the Inca Empire have fallen into ruins and never been equaled by the Spanish.

But surely we have developed forms of artistic expression superior to anything that has gone before? There are authorities who maintain that everything since Egypt has been a decline in that field. Why stop with Egypt? In a cavern near Montignac in Dordogne, France, are murals of animals, paintings in three-dimensional perspective of creatures known to us only by their fossil remains. For spirit, sensitivity, and economy of line these are judged by critics to be on a par with almost anything we have to offer. The artist's name, unfortunately, is not known, since he died some 25,000 years ago.

In an age of famine and malnutrition, the declining yield of agricultural lands is a sore problem. Many authorities, re-discovering Malthus, say that the number of people the earth can support is very sharply limited, and that we are touching that limit. Hopefully, archeologists can point to many areas whose yield, neglected, can again be brought back to the high level of cultivation employed by the ancients. A recent bulletin of the American Society of Civil Engineers states that:

> "Estimates of the ancient population supported by history's first large-scale irrigation project, in the Tigris-Euphrates Valley, run as high as 50 million people... Some of the ancient canals 400 ft. wide date back to 5000 B.C. Now the valley supports but 8 million people..."

A major and little-known engineering feat of the Orient was the boring of the Siloam tunnel about 700 B.C. under King Hezekiah of Judah, to supply Jerusalem with water during siege. Cut through 1,777 feet of solid rock from opposite ends simultaneously, the tunnel has an average height of six feet. The tools used were wedge, hammer and pick, with the possibility of a simple hand-drill. The commemorative inscription archeologists found in the tunnel is worthy of study as a source of inspiration for similar markers today:

> "The boring through is completed. And this is the story of the boring through; while yet they plied the drill, each toward his fellow, and while yet there were three cubits to be bored through, there was heard the voice of one calling unto another, for there was a crevice in the rock on the right hand. And on the day of the boring through the stone-cutters struck, each to meet his fellow, drill upon drill; and the water flowed from the source to the pool for a thousand and two hundred cubits, and a hundred cubits was the height of the rock above the heads of the stone-cutters."

Originally published in *Science Digest*, April 1951, vol. 29, no. 4

Letter from Nigeria – 1963

When our friend Jim Graham, included us on the list for a circular letter from a Kano Emirate, we laughingly referred to it as the Gestetner Gesture, and threatened to reply with the Multilith Memo. Even so, it has come to pass...

Whiles ago, Orcutt and Clif put together bits of correspondence from scattered friends, calling it "Tribal Notes." Clif, agitator that he is, has since been trying for a second edition, but the Prince of Puppeteers stubbornly refuses to pull the right strings. Now, if this present can overcome the limitations of a monologue, maybe we can put together enough pieces for one more round robin?

These are, mainly, abstracted from letters written during the past two years, from and about various places, people, and happenings. They may answer some of the where-ya-been and whatchabeendoins. Best of all, they may bring a few replies for another "Tribal Notes."

From Zaria, Northern Nigeria, where Clif was posted by the International Labour Office, for co-operative education:

Here we have the Sahara wind, a steady pressure of dust from the north and beyond Lake Chad, where the papyrus no doubt changes hue under the pulverized dunes that mist the horizon and chill the mornings. Very much the same thing happens to Vancouver when the skies are overcast: a rapid and toe-freezing drop. The temperature change is more extreme here because of low humidity, and the hot, hot sun which does occasionally come through the haze.

In the early a.m., Nigerians on Raleigh cycles (we have an assembly plant) pedal mysteriously about in all directions, crowding across the long concrete bridge over the Galma River, and tangling front wheels at the traffic circle to Sabon Gari (New Town). They wear the babban rigar (large gown) of the Muslim, not originally designed for cycling, and with turbans wrapped about the upper and lower face in Tuareg style, contrive to show only a dark hint of eyes. The occasional hepcat sports a pair of sunglasses with fancy rims bejewelled, usually with an attractive yellow or salmon price tag remaining conspicuous on one lens. The effect is of Scene III of "The Invisible Man." More startling yet, the sharp lad has a pair of those mirror-type specs which reflect your own naked face while masking his, and make for an impression of a Robert Othello on wheels.

The prevalent colour is brown, and after a bit one becomes an expert of sorts in detecting the minor variations from amber to umber. Typical indigenous housing is mudwall and thatch, darkening under the rains, bleaching a bit in the sun. Town houses are sometimes two stories in height, the roofs built up of a mosaic of scarce, short sticks resting on a cross-arch which continues halfway down each of the four room walls. Mud is plastered on top of the roofing sticks, so that each room has its own domed ceiling, and the inhabitant treads gently in the rains, conscious that too heavy a downpour combined with too loud a noise might in one hectic moment find him uncovered to the skies while sunk to the knee-cap in his former ceiling.

The better town living quarters are mudwall compounds, each with an entry room used occasionally for storage, where one stops to halloo "Sannunca, Mallam Yahaya! Sannu, sannu!" and proceeds within only on invitation. The rooms are grouped around the central courtyard, looking like a series of separate small buildings against the mud wall. One of them is the kitchen-without-chimney where, in the flurry of preparation for a large meal, both cook and smoke come rolling out the door at intervals, fleeing the fire, which blazes or smolders away at ground level between three or four stones supporting the pot.

Decoration consists of highly formalized floral or abstract designs on the exterior, done in whitewash, sometimes with a touch of ochre or green. Corners of the roof come up in pointed "rabbit-ears" which the European learned darkly hint are phallic and which Bennett-san considers merely an outgrowth of the doctrine of baraka: the aura of blessing of the saint's house extends as far as his roof is visible.

All day the people come out into the sun from Tudun Wada and Old City and Sabon Gari. The women chatter, the little girls laugh and call to each other, and all of them endlessly carry calabash-loads of indescribables up and down the shoulders of the roads. The Hausa carry is a head carry. We drive down the road toward Pambeguwa, and the steward who is learning to drive, says, "Fulanin daji." Bush Fulani, semi-nomadic cattle herders, a line of women swaying, slender, loads on their heads, graceful as ripe wheat in autumn wind.

"No, madam," says the steward. "They will not marry us. Yes, we think they are very beautiful. They stay in the bush."

The bush is all around, not very far from anything. The Emir has a green Rolls, and other wheels go up and down the road: mammy wagons loaded with men and women and bundles and baskets going from here to there and back; lorries of petrol and bags of cotton and groundnuts; lumber from the south, hides from the north, palm oil, tobacco, onions, cement blocks. On each side of the paved strip, dirt paths lead to the dirt villages: small round huts clustered inside a fence of grass mats. Here the peasant farmers work three to five acres each with handhoes, ploughing with the back bent and a broad-bladed, short-handled galma, weeding, back bent, with a lighter hoe, always bent and halfway back into the soil.

We go to market in the Old City. Inside the miles of crumbling wall is Zazzau, a city named after a sword and once, according to the legends, ruled by the woman who founded it, proud warrior matriarch whose great-great-granddaughters are locked away in purdah behind these compound barriers. In the market the woman merchants are Yoruba, seldom Hausa, never Fulani. We see a tiny kerosene lamp, soldered, a condensed milk tin for the fuel container, a tiny tin funnel for filling a rolled tin cylinder to pull the wick through, set in a punched hole and held upright by a beer-bottle cap fixed to the cylinder a third of the way down. "Nawa kudi wannan abu?" "Kwabo hudu." So we buy it for fourpence, and the wick is twopence more. It has only cost us double what a Nigerian would be charged: we've come away cheap and thankful; I put on a show of drinking the kerosene, stored in old pop bottles. "Ba sha!" cries the Yoruba woman, shaking her head mightily and uncertain whether to laugh at the Mad Bature or send for a stomach pump.

The traders, each in his stall, do a kwabo-kwabo (penny each) business in potash, shelled groundnuts, guinea corn, millet, guinea fowl eggs, murderous hot peppers, green and gunky peanut butter, black and brown and tan and white beans, some staring up like a basket of flipped eyeballs, strips of fried cowmeat, sweet cakes, prayer beads, little round embroidered caps, violent cotton prints, sandals, grass mats, loose and probably peppery cigarettes from local tobacco. Madam sees a small item covered with goatskin, brown and white. It looks about the right size to store a few sewing needles. The round cap comes off with a twist, and the trader demonstrates. Within is a piece of bone, and some fragments of antimony. I only realize it is antimony after she replaces the cap, shakes the contrivance sharply, opens it again to remove the bone piece, now blackened on one end, drawing it around the eyelids. "It gives power to the eye," we are told. I remember Doughty, in "Arabia Deserta," mentioning that the Bedouin use it, and with the same belief.

The eyes behind the sunglasses are fixed on Progress and the industrial West, on the green Rolls and the highway. The babban rigar is Muslim, as are the four wives behind the compound wall. The heart is African and tribal, vowing yet to dip the Koran in the sea, while listening to the evening drums in Tudun Wada, and never very far from the village in the bush where, sixty years ago, no wheel had been seen or dreamed of.

The younger cats have a dance tonight, at the West End Hotel in Sabon Gari. These are almost all Yoruba, a sprinkling of Ibo, few Northerners. Favourite music, beat out by a combo visiting from Ghana: West Coast Highlife, a syncopated, hoppy, rough and ragged, possibly-foxtrot noise, to which the circle of dancers moves in a shuffling rhythm, two beats to each foot, alternately. As the evening ages, the dancing extends to all of the dancers; the women in particular "let go" and the village in the bush moves closer.

Late evening, small traders sit next shops composed of a crate, front end knocked out, couple of shelves, raised on wooden legs: groceries, tinned goods, cigarettes. Inside the crate, one of the condensed-milk tins burns. At intervals, in the thick dusk the golden-yellow flames flicker on each side of the way. This is Yoruba Street, last place in town to pack up and say quits.

On the way home, we pass a prayer ground: few kettles of water for the washing which always precedes the public praying, irregular circle of broken cement blocks and rocks, couple of frayed reed mats in the dust. But everything is indoors by now, including the few surviving mosquitoes. "Iska sanyi dai awa." Too cold ...

* * * * * * * * * * * * * *

The girl with the purple cakes: she was about eight or nine, but quite small, thin and undernourished as are most of the children in the villages. I understand the Government denies this vigorously but you have only to look at the row on row of little pot-bellies and rickets-bowed legs. It is doubtful if the average farmer sees a yearly income over $50.

A kerchief was wrapped around her head; the costume was completed by a blouse and long skirt each of which clashed loudly in colour with one another and with the kerchief, in spite of repeated scrubbing on the stones of the local creek. A blind beggar in rags, led by a small boy holding a rope tied around his waist, brushed by the girl. His hip knocked from her head a flat tray piled with purplish cakes which she'd been selling to the market-day crowd at Soba Village. The beggar kept on; he never knew what he'd done.

The girl looked two or three times, quickly, quite unbelieving, at the retreating back of the blind man, then down to the cakes scattered in the dust. Suddenly she broke out into the most hopeless sobs, trying to pat the dust and dirt off the cakes and gather them back into their neat pyramid on the tray. She was obviously terrified.

I bent down and said, "Ayya, ayya. Ba Kuka (I'm sorry; don't cry.) I gave her a shilling but had to press it into her hand and close the fingers around it; she had almost completely lost control. I said, "Yawwa." (Good) The tears were pouring from her eyes, lips shaking, great gobs of crying sounds mixed now with hiccups. Sylvester looked back: "She stopped crying. You gave her enough money to pay for the whole tray. That is all she could have made today; now her mother will not beat her."

I had given the girl 14 cents.

Audu Zaria, my cook-steward: He says he is from the town of Biu, on a plateau which includes Tilla Lake, where all the crocodiles are said to be equipped with the souls of dead chiefs. (I once saw one; it looked pure croc.) But the Biu roads are lined with elephant-trees, and that is something against a sunset. So Audu is from up toward Lake Chad in Bornu Province, a handsome lad whose English is somewhat better than my Hausa, which low level of conversation causes us to prefer sign language frequently.

The disconcerting thing is that most of these folk have a keen ear for language: you'll say, "Prepare sandwiches and coffee this evening; there will be three guests arriving late, after supper." Audu will nod, say, "Yes, Master," and repeat every word with mechanical precision and faultless inflection. After supper, I prepare sandwiches and coffee, Audu having toddled off without comprehending a word.

In the morning, he says. "I think Master have omelette." This means, not so much that his intuition tells him I crave an omelette, but in accurate translation, signifies: "Sir, in the syllabus of the Audu Zaria School of Cookery for which the six anonymous bods in the kitchen are paying me a shilling a week from their miserable pockets, it is written that today I shall teach them how to crack many of your precious eggs, spilling a carefully limited number on the floor, and shall then divide the remainder delicately among them: practice in egg-beating, thereafter conveying the results, minus normal deduction for splashes, to the frying pan."

Ya, Islam! Sulum aleikum...

By European standards, some of the most handsome people are the Cattle Fulani. Their cranial and nasal indices and height, with their very light reddish-tan colour and long, dark hair among the purer strains, result in their being classified as Caucasoid by most anthropologists. It is from their tribe that the rulers of the North have come for hundreds of years, although the governing group has intermarried and settled in the towns. One legend says the Cattle Fulani are descendants of Crusaders who lost their way and continued around past the Nile Delta into Africa. There is a blue-eyed, very fair tribe in Arabia (the Sulaib) who are also supposed to be descendants of Crusaders. On Feast days here, they do bring out ancient chain mail armour, which is said to be authentic loot from the Crusades.

* * * * * * * * * * * *

From Kano, in the Northern Emirates. where Clif claims his single solid accomplishment was the founding of a branch of the United Nations Association which is a little U.N. itself: fifteen nationalities at one gathering.

    Our family lives just outside the Experimental Farm at the edge of Kano City. I'm working on a field education project for secretaries and produce buyers of marketing societies, and currently running a five-day-a-week school for Cooperative Inspectors. Courses: Stage I Bookkeeping, English Speech and Composition, Co-operative Law, Organisation/Principles/Function, Duties of Inspectors. Teachers: me. Also editing a divisional newsletter for government employees.

    At 7:15, I drive to the Old City and walk across the plaza, where the Emir's Palace faces the Native Authority Offices. The plaza is an immense square of sun-baked reddish dust, busy at most hours with goats, people, horses, cars, and the stray high-headed camel picking its way disdainfully through packs of firewood-toting donkeys. A turbaned rider reins in, calling from his horse to a passenger in the back of a large American sedan, "Alhaji, barka da zuwa!" (Traveller to Mecca, blessings on your coming!) At 12:30, I somewhat groggily leave the classroom in the town hall, proceed home in the midday heat, and fall asleep while trying to prepare the next day's student-fodder.

One of my final memories is of a red-faced, quite alcoholic British Civil Servant of The Old School at the Kano Club, becoming publicly vile and abusive with a Canadian friend of mine who had brought an American Negro into the club. Canadian friend was almost, but not quite, too angry himself to note that he was being bawled out as a "damn upstart Yank!"

Your remarks on the desert: this "arid nurse of lions" has been a place for thinking in my life as well. With my Jordanian wife, in one of our desert trips, we came down out of the San Pedro Martirs through the pass to the Desert of the Chinamen, which stretches north to the Colorado Delta. Some Mexican ranchero had set up a crude signboard with an arrow: "Desierto" and "Cuidado" scratched on it. We added, "No falta nada" and went along into the dunes. Desert in Mexico, in the American Southwest, in Canada (the West has semidesert, much sage, some tiny cactus) has not seemed unfriendly. Moses came out of it, and his people before him; and Mahmud and his people; and John, with the Galilean; and before them all, the shepherd-philosophers who sang the songs of Ahriman and Ormuzd.

The early Christians, when they looked ahead in this world, saw an early end of all things, an Apocalyptic stone wall which made impossible the idea of inevitable earthly progress. The "poor saints in Jerusalem," completely sold on the end of things worldly and soon-coming of the Kingdom, had to be bailed out by the more practical Paul. (The more Greek Paul, and therefore a different time-sense).

But the poor saints may have been closest to what Jesus actually meant. Influenced by Isaiah's doctrine of the suffering servant, noting the success of the mere offering of Isaac by Abraham (but not the culmination of the sacrifice), he may have tried to force an end to merely human time, and usher in, by burning headlong faith alone, the timeless.

The other was a religious age, and its time-stop required the decay of religious authority. The various bombs, bacteria and viruses in uniform are doing something of the sort for us today. <u>Our</u> faith is scientific, and it is the authority we recognize which lowers the fire-door on <u>our</u> time.

Not that any one thing accomplishes the end of an era. The inner fibre rots slowly, out of sight, and the spoken thought says after the deed, "It is done." An angry poet accosts "the men in careful dinner-jackets, who have murdered the human imagination." The scientific humanist, Wells, writes a last testament: "Mind at the End of its Tether." Jack Jones titles his essay on Hegel, "To the End of Thought" - that is to say, there's a limit to the province of the rational...

As nearly as I can make out, I react something like an amoeba. Perhaps it is the completely (to me) transparent nature of my reactions that makes it seem there <u>must</u> be something esoterically complicated in there! Does an amoeba look for perceivable results or refrain from a motion unless these are likely? Enjoyed activity is its own reward, or should be; the great religion may be the simply natural act; the motive, and the step on the road, and the road are one.

It is not that I was ever converted to Zen, but plainly that the stories of the Zen masters seemed closest to my own experience. So it isn't, in truth, an intellectual thing, and mere competence in vocabulary (some machines have larger ones) doesn't create an intellectual.

Yes, the primitives have something to give to some. It may be they can give you yourself if your danger has been the thin limb of abstraction. T. E. Lawrence had this, I think, and didn't entirely like what he got. Is it an easy thing to look at ourselves truthfully? Does it take defencelessness? It seems you get a painful concern to test yourself, to know your depth and extent. But to do that you need to drop your defences. In Christian terms, you die to your old self to find the new, or real, or more real...

Lately, read Mircea Eliade, "Cosmos and History," which was probably intended as an apology for an assumed superiority of the Hebrew-Christian view of history, and worked negatively on me. I'm beginning to feel that the idea of a linear history, particularly one which must be viewed optimistically as an unbroken upward-slanting line is harmful to self-respect. Most deeply so, when it is combined with economic determinism and a system of commerce depending on confidence money. Over 90% of it in the States, and demanding a sort of compulsory economic optimism, because the acceptance of these promises to pay *without* a metaphysical belief in an ever-better future, is either senseless or the best-developed masochist plot in history.

It is beginning to seem to me that a cyclical view of time, and a denial of linear-purposeful history, might restore some elements of human pride. The current model is prideful, though inhuman; that is, the pride is not in what is specifically human. The character at the wheel of the Super Eight is proud of his speed and the mechanical power at his control, but he has had no part in fashioning it; if he did, it was such a fragment of the whole he never saw the relationship. Archaic man felt his will and sharing necessary in the seasonal rebirth of the god and the universe. He was a "member of the wedding."

Not plunking for a return to the Eleusinian mysteries. Impossible at worst, ludicrous at best. What I do believe, is that some of the oddballs in cosmology (Hoyle, for one) while not able to satisfy all demands for evolution of atomic family, offer in the hypothesis of continuous creation a scientifically and esthetically acceptable out from the one-way street of decaying creation, final disintegration and death within a limited universe. The cyclical, after all, seems more hopefully human than the other, and I'm not so sure it wasn't a necessary part of the philosophy of Nietzsche.

But mostly I *feel* this strongly. It is not that I seek things which will fit prettily into some slick "Buddhist" pattern. Nor have I worked overtime to interpret in Eastern terms those bits of religious experience which have luckily been mine. It just happened that the Christian explanations with which I was familiar didn't jibe. What in Christianity say, "Beyond nothing, is joy"? Yet if I had to boil it down, that's what it would be. Don't try the give-up-all-you-have-and-follow-me, because this one doesn't ask you to follow anything. "Impermanent are all component things; work out your own salvation with diligence."

It does tie in at one corner with Sartre, and at another with my friend Corsa, the Zen monk who felt we and all things were outthrusts of a single life-force with a natural tendency to the overcoming of chance. This was seen to be sufficient in itself to provide an onward-going dynamism, calling on the human (and all sentient life) for assent.

DRIED LEAF IN OBUTSUDAN

This leaf is from that tree
Or from the children of that tree
Where once he sat alone,
great heart and undefended.
All living things upon the wheel
Of endless worlds cried out.
He knew their pain:
Hot jungled claws, and leprous beggar
by the wall,
Madwoman naked in the roadside dust,
Sobbing child, blind warrior in
Maya's night.

Not armoured mind, nor muscled might
Of legions holds our hope. This is he
Remembered by the leaf, whose way
we walk,
Who spoke of ill, the cure of ill,

the path:
His Dhamma blooms upon a thousand
worlds,
The fragrant lotus of tomorrow.
>   (End of Ramadan, Kano Emirate)

BISMALLAH

In his wisdom the nomad prophet knew
That man, to be filled,
Must come empty to his god.
Such things the desert night, perhaps, may teach,
Where every lonely bush stands like a sura,
Sharp and clear upon that scroll
Of whitened sand, of which His mighty hand
Has smoothed the sheet.

So, empty, at the end of Ramadan,
We come to Sallih.
Now, at the Friday Mosque,
Our old men search the moon
Whose rising ends our fast.
The coal-oil lamps are lit
And whisper yellow butter at the dusk.
Upon the eating-mat, not food alone is spread.
The washing done, the water-jars aside, we kneel
With all our brothers, from this dark edge of Islam
Far to the Afghan hills.
Hear the ladani call:
We shall be filled.

As-salaam aleikum.

The Dark Warehouse

A Gothic tale of horror, an evil vegetable dealer, and bad potatoes.

(Not recommended for readers who have trouble sleeping, or for those more than five years of age. Remember, if you think this is a good story, tell all your friends and hurry out to buy the next fourteen books in this series!)

jvk gs%Skq sbd ^x^^takft (bb& J> J%%yzp1y Lfzlv alf time

(Sorry about that. It seems to happen every time we try to write Gothic horror. Something horrible happens to the typewriter!)

    The summer job had sounded good to Emmalina. Only half time, and she would be paid with enough vegetables to keep the whole family stuffed until well after the harvest. Emmalina nodded her square little head, with its four interestingly pointed corners, remembering how often her mom had remarked that papa seemed to be losing his stuffing. Indeed, only the other day, mom had dug out her sewing box and repaired several of papa's seams. When she neglected this task for more than a week or two, papa went about leaking a mixture of sawdust, old straw and steel wool. Other than that, the Kleinemaus family was fairly normal – that is, if you could allow for young Herman, who preferred to sleep hanging upside down from the rod supporting the richly-woven tapestries dividing tie wine cellar from the rest of the dungeon.

    "Bye, mama!" called Emmalina. "I'm on my way to the warehouse to keep my eye on the vegetables!" Her mother, who was busy muttering evil spells over a spelling book, did not reply.

    After a short, but entirely normal trip across town, during which she saw not more than eighteen witches on broomsticks, five rather small dinosaurs (probably escaped from the local zoo) and a kangaroo delivering the daily paper on a skateboard, Emmalina wiped her wading boots on the doormat, and prepared to enter the warehouse. It, of course, was a Gothic warehouse, rich with the odor of mouldy beans, questionable onions, and carrots that had seen a better day. It was truly Gothic, Emmalina thought, as she studied the great purple-and-orange sign swaying in the moist wind from the Dismal Swamp across the street. "GOTHIC VEGETABLE WAREHOUSE," it read, "Owned and Operated by Generic the Goth."

"It's Emmalina, Mister Generic," she called. "I'm here to keep an eye on the vegetables!" There was no reply. Emmalina slowly pushed open the massive door. It creaked in an ominous manner, calculated to send shivers up and down the bones of any normal eleven-year-old. Naturally, it did not bother Emmalina at all. She walked into the darkness of the warehouse, sensing the thousand little sounds of overripe peas popping, tomatoes slowly turning into tomato sauce, and squash becoming squashier by the minute. Emmalina had been told by her mother that, if she didn't learn anything about vegetables in the Gothic Warehouse, she would certainly have an opportunity to learn a great deal about bacteria.

Suddenly a dark shape detached itself from the steel rafters and hurtled downward past her nose. Emmalina shrieked and jumped backward. The dark shape was followed immediately by another, which twittered as it went by. "Oh, bats!" sighed Emmalina. She took two steps sideward, only to jump half a foot off the ground as a couple of loud, cracking sounds broke the ghostly stillness. Looking about, she saw that she had entered the Wholesale Almond, Brazil Nut and Peanut Section, and had trod upon a handful of walnuts. "Oh, nuts!" she snorted.

Before Emmalina had taken another half dozen steps, she froze. The sensation was too powerful, too threatening, too overwhelmingly all-overish to disregard. She was being watched!

Glancing fearfully out of the cornar of her right eye (the one that was lemon yellow, instead of bright fluorescent lime like the rest of the family), Emmalina hecame conscious of an enormous black bulk hovering over her. Squaring her little shoulders, and disregarding the cold sweat pouring down the back of her neck, sine stared bravely at the sign on the open panel on the side of the object toward her. "POTATO BIN" it read. Oh, horrible! Horrible! Thousands of little eyes were peering at her!

"That's not my job..."

When Hollywood decided to make a flick based on John Reed's *Ten DaysThat Shook the World,* the scriptwriters shot a few oldies up front making comments on Reed and his girl friend. Hollywood apparently thought a straight take on Russia's October Revolution would be more than American audiences could handle.

All they got from Scott was a harassed expression and a curt, "You want me to gossip about John Reed and his girl friend? That's not my job!"

But Scott had his own love story to tell. When he taught at Princeton, one of his students, Helen, decided Scott was marriage material. But Scott was already married–to a wealthy heiress–and Helen waited in the wings for twenty years with her violin, joining Scott at Forest Farm in Vermont.

While Scott and Helen made love and maple syrup down in the Bond River Valley, a group of radical pacifists at the 2000-ft. level in the Green Mountain Wilderness provided problems for the local Draft Board. Since Vermont had decided not to have any war resisters on record, they dealt out "mentally ill" cards to residents of Hilltop.

When one of Scott's friends, Alfred Jacob, was called to military service, he was asked by the local official to state his reasons for refusing. Would he, for example, object even to putting on a uniform? Picking up the official's metal letter opener, Alfred leaned forward over the desk, levelled the weapon at the chest of the startled official, and intoned in a sombre voice, "I have no objection to pointing this at you–but I'd feel differently if you were wrapped around the end of it!"

Scott and Helen decided to update their maple syrup operation by building a few concrete storage bins for buckets in the woods. The patriotic neighbours promptly called the FBI to report the Nearings were throwing up "machine gun emplacements." These were presumably to be used during the upcoming Russian invasion of the U.S. The real joke here is that the pair were well known for their refusal to kill insects–and the last time I visited, they were busy transplanting lilies-of-the-valley out of the way of expected spring floods.

Scott, who showed up as a speaker on May Day at New York's Union Square, never joined the Communist Party. He also never joined the chorus of trained seals who barked anti-Red noises on command. He died at a few weeks past 100 years, and Helen followed a short time later. Honest comrades, both.

The Confession of Dribbl 13

Yes, I was responsible. Limited and unimpactful as the experiment was, it did consume measurable time, dump a little more irrecoverable energy into the contorted cosmic space-basket, and drain a few odd millennia of intent-impulses during my relaxation continua.

Frankly, I don't know why this has been taken so seriously. The threat of banishment to a black hole makes no impression upon me, particularly since I am one of those questioning the existence of such a theoretical construct. It is therefore in a tension-free fluidity of unwinding that I flow before you, neither accepting nor providing edges of angularity.

A dreamtime. It all came of a dreamtime, with the image-sequence presenting an uncreased infolding of probabilities many. And yes, you may call my manifestations imperfect, incomplete, disorderly – what you will. Beyond rigidities, I know myself to be poet, artist, maker. The thing is of me, is extension directionless from the thisness of me, all flung out upon probability of being.

That which took shape danced to its own music, began with the unsteady wail of a distant solo, coalesced in multicoloured orchestrations, writhed in rainbows of evanescent fire. No, I could not know, cannot even now solidify, the multiple out-comings. There is no vibration for a maker unless the thing made extends its web of being beyond the instruments consumed in its energizing.

Acceptance is extended for what you may do with this making, but consider:

It is a small planet, and you may infer the organisms on it something like dung-beetles, and those organisms do call it Earth, which is a substance in part composed of dung. And they may have dreamed sequences in which the dung is vapourized, and the song ended.

Forgive them, Lords, for they know not what they do.

Tale of the Fair Elizabeth and the Evil Motilal

The father of the Fair Elizabeth functioned as a District Head for the British Raj in the area of Gujerat, where his family lived in great comfort on an extensive estate, with numerous outbuildings and gardens, these being both vegetable and otherwise. The principal building was of stone, and contained many rooms, thus necessitating the presence of many servants, both male and female persuasions. One of these was the Master of Horse, one Motilal Shridharani.

The Fair Elizabeth loved to go riding, and this she was permitted to do in good weather, provided there arrived no news of incipient uprisings of the natives, who intermittently made known their objection to the presence of the British Raj, and to extensive estates with numerous outbuildings and gardens, also to the additional items mentioned above. Those residing in the local District, however, took no objection to the Fair Elizabeth, for the young lady in question was of a sweetness profound, and of a disposition most gentle. They looked with approval upon her, and took joy in her riding among them, sometimes accompanied by her Master of Horse, the same Motilal Shridharani.

Now, in time it came to be rumoured in the kitchens, and upon occasion in the hallways and at several points on the back stairs, that the Evil Motilal had his eye upon the Fair Elizabeth. And it was murmured that he did, indeed, for he had made her a present upon her sixteenth birthday, of his glass eye. This she wore upon a finely woven cord as a pendant, comfortably between the two upper identifiers of her non-masculinity.

We are figuratively speaking, of course, while hastening to add that the Fair Elizabeth was extremely good at numbers, taking first in her class in Complex Arithmeticals. The numbers of the Fair Elizabeth were 34B-23-38, which were considered very fine indeed, and these numbers were among the items which stimulated gossip that the Evil Motilal had designs upon her.

This, too, among other items we are presenting, Gentle Reader was true, for had not the mother of that same Motilal (him of whom we have recently been discoursing) sewn for the Fair Elizabeth a lovely gown of the finest cloth, incorporating into it the patterns most preferred among ladies of the better class in the District of Gujerat? Indeed, she had done this, and the Fair Elizabeth had taken to clothing herself with it upon occasion, to the considerable delight of all who viewed her, including, but not limited to, the very Motilal who presented himself as the son of that same mother.

That year, the spring came to Gujerat as it usually did, with singing birds and blooming flowers. The fields in the vicinity of the Buffalo-Milk Cooperative became green with grass following the monsoon rains, and the desire of the Fair Elizabeth, as made known to the Master of Horse, was to ride bareback through those fields.

Now, in the mind of that same Master of Horse, one Motilal Shridharani, the wishes of the Fair Elizabeth were translated into imrushUyiiu or viparka raii, which made his eyes sparkle and his breath to do the high hurdles. All the exotic literatures of the ancestors of Motilal, with their colourful illustrations, ran through his veins, causing pleasurable havocs therein. But, as with the much-admired Saint Paul upon the road to Damascus, such was not to be - or not to be as he perspiringly imagined.

For, Gentle Reader, we must now make known to you that the family of this Master of Horse were, to the last infant, Coptic Christians of the Church of Saint Thomas of Kerala, and the deviated thoughts and desires of which we have most latterly been discoursing are not therein approved. Not this side of a church marriage, at any rate.

And, therefore, our Master of Horse sorrowfully went before the Fair Elizabeth, and spoke haltingly of his desire to marry her. Shall we dwell upon the stupefied delight with which he received her unexpected and gleeful acceptance? But no, let us hasten to the description of the nuptials and attending matters.

The matriarch of the family Shridharani resided in an area where the writ of the British Raj did not run, and it was there they prepared to make their home. This matriarch was situated in a most advantageous and secure financiality, with dwellings and gardens and servants of adequate number. Their

Best Man at the well-attended and sumptuous wedding, followed by a wedding feast of equivalent proportions, was of the family Yahkub, from which issues the Management of the Buffalo-Milk Cooperative.

The marriage and wedding feast were followed, in appropriate time, by the blessing of three sons and three daughters, received as gifts from an abundant Heaven by the happy couple. And now, Gentle Reader, you are wondering how it is that the writer is conversant with these many details, and it has become time to inform tliat who should know better than

Your Humble and Obedient Servant,
Prof. M. Shridharani, Ph.D.
University of Gujerat
Department of Equine Management

Autobiography

I've had a lot of them and I guess, like most males, the first was my one true love. Black, and with a rear end that would go into overdrive if you pushed the right buttons, she won my heart because she'd go anyplace on a dare, and didn't demand that I lay out a lot of dough.

We ran around the Ohio hills together, spending many a sunny day with the Ohio River flowing by a few hundred feet below, spring breezes lively in the pawpaw trees. I kept her well-lubed, and she never said no.

Last I saw of her, she was lying on her back alongside the horsetrail above Tiltonsville. Oh, I loved her, I did. I was born in '18; she came into the world in '22. I've never seen her equal. Thank you, Henry Ford!

Two-Thirds of a Jackpot

Being the lost testament of Carolus Magnus, dictated after matins upon the 25th December 799, and recently unearthed in the archaeological digs at Aachen.

May the mercy of God lead you safely and prosperously to and beyond the mystical and magical date we are even now approaching. On the advice of my court astrologers, I do this day declare the year 800 A Year of Great Importance. All learned souls will agree that there have been heretofore, since the birth of Our Lord, but seven years exhibiting the twin zero. It has, of course, been brought to my attention that, in those realms not making use of the Arabic Invention of Arithmetical Nothing,* the resulting clutter of M,C,L,X,V, I would produce a very different kettle of noodle soup.

As to time itself, though we do use it daily, and have none of us more than our allotted share, be we Emperor or churl, yet still it gives us to think: what may this useful thing, in all truth, be in essence? Well I recall the good Abbot Engilbert reading to me from Augustine, of how it is but stuff in the mind. He used, I think, the Latin word for 'subjective.' That is to say, much like the weak reflections in the mind of those ideal patterns of Plato, or the wavering shadows cast on the cave wall by another philosopher's smoking fire.

There be even, I have heard tell, some Cynics saying, "Time is what we measure with an hourglass, a burning knotted cord, a notched or marked candle." This, in days to come, I doubt not, will be dubbed 'functional thinking.' There be none of these Cynics at my court.

As to the usefulness of time. It does appear, the Cynics notwithstanding, that when Carloman took himself into the monastery, it would there have been useful to mark off accurately the times for prescribed prayer. Such, of course, we do, though the lengthening and shortening of the days in the changing seasons does give us pause.

Be that as it may, though we look not beyond the rhythm of our prayers in seeking fine intervals of this mind-stuff, yet we do mark centuries and millenia. I myself have been given, lately, to considering the Spirit of the Decade – whether there be not, let us say, a considerable variance in iconoclasm and the abominations of Lyzantium, as between the 770s and the 780s.

It is to wonder. May there come a time when our need to measure will be fixed upon finer periods than those separating our prayers? Will there be great discussions in the courts of those far millenia as to whether or not the Third Person of the Trinity was seen to have more corporeal substantiality at 10:03 in the morning, than at 10:04?

>   *A sticky one. Al-Khwarizmi, my Arabic contemporary who first wrote of this device, will probably be credited with killing off the abacus industry. We may not have had himself at court, but we have had Arabic mathematicians. We also received from Harun al Rashid, one clock and one elephant.

A Puddle

Our story was first told in what you people call a science fiction anthology. The telling was grossly incomplete and fragmentary; that is why I've been delegated to retell it – correctly – to you. We'd like to set the matter straight before you leave.

One of your number, a Prof. Aristide Abernethy, chanced to be passing by a puddle on one of those April days when a pseudopod waving a damp piece of paper extruded itself from the water surface and a sibilant voice whispered, "Psst! Wanna see some doity pitchers?"

Startled as the Professor was by the nature of this incursion upon his academic musings, he stooped and, bringing the scrap to eye level, found a meticulous rendering of an amoebic nucleus in an advanced state of binary fission. The probing and lascivious mind was left with no doubt about what was going on, since the symbols $H_2O+NaCl$ made it clear that a voluptuously enticing saline solution enhanced the process.

Prof. Abernethy hesitated not a moment. Scooping the contents of the puddle into one of his waterproof pockets (as an internationally famous microbiologist, his suits invariably came equipped with two or three of these) he proceeded to his laboratory, beginning the discussion which led to his productive and world-shaking partnership with the contents of the puddle.

"I," expounded the contents of the puddle," claim Refugee Status. My happy life in the Coalsack Nebula has been brought to an end by my superlative artistic abilities (Surely you recognize the touch of a Master?) and I flee for my very life from prosecution and persecution as a pornographer!"

"Perhaps," mused the Professor, not wanting to appear over-eager, "we can make a deal..."

He then explained that, as the author of the best-seller, *Plankton Perversions*, and the no-less-popular sequels, *Gender and the Jellyfish* and *Paramecium Potency*, his works on invertebrate sex, currently being hawked in every schoolyard on earth, required an artistic hand no less clever than that extruded by his pal from the puddle.

"Anyone knows," he intoned, "that kids have an insatiable curiosity about two things: sex and puddles. When you combine the two, you have a best-seller!"

The puddle inhabitant agreed enthusiatically. The partnership got under way with the fully illustrated (several in full colour) *Amatory Anatomy of the Young Amoeba*. The accident that changed the history of your world occurred while a delivery truck loaded with copies of this book languished on its side with wheels spinning after a highway collision. Three unrecovered copies from a burst carton tumbled into the ditch, fully-coloured erotic illustrations floating or submerging in the muddy ocean. They were, of course, pounced upon by every nubile amoeba, reproduced and distributed planetwide.

I need hardly tell you the effect of this stimulus on the already prolific amoeba population. Space – we needed space. The days of the human race were numbered, and the numbers were finite.

You are the last. The pseudopod oozing toward you will convert you to food for one of our colonies. It has been pleasant having this chat with you. Goodbye.

Individual and Communal

Our current wave of paranoid individualism lacks a communal undertow. Judy Rebick is right: the response is non-participation instead of resistance. Beyond mere resistance lies the sleeping possibility of an angry but theoretically grounded counterattack, preferably based on local economic alternative structures. The existing repressive structures are to be drained of meaning, function, human support – "hollowed out," as one ecologist puts it.

Marcus Garvey, Father Divine, the Black Panther movement at its high point: these found a way to put the thing in motion. Where the nuclei were in those days ethnic, perhaps they may now broaden out to include the disenfranchised generally – and, from the mathematics of the last general election in the U.S., those bothering to pay homage to the ballot box are now a minority of the eligible citizens. It's well past time for workable alternatives.

The seas of individualistic hype in which we are all awash go beyond structural deformity to soak and short-circuit the human personality. One friend, an exceptionally bright and energetic woman capable of playing an effective role in any resistance movement, finds herself sequentially embroiled in obsessively self-centred battles, unable to free herself to participate in any wider concern.

If any call to a new and hopeful radicalism is to animate my friend and others like her, it will probably have to lean on some elements of a "religious" morality to join the severed personal yearning for justice to a social consciousness capable of supplying the organizational glue. Nothing less will make any noticeable dent in the economic and political mammoths which have grown out of our control and beyond response to our need.

And we might keep in mind that the Galilee Local of the Carpenters Union took off from one activist and a dozen apprentices.

Local Employment and Trading Systems (LETS)

LETS, also known as the Green Dollar approach, is an updated combination of the barter and local scrip exchanges popular during the Thirties, and used sporadically for decades before the Great Depression. The updating consists of splicing a micro-computer to a telephone answering device, and acceptance of "ordinary" dollars to cover a minor part of the transaction.

A transaction occurs in this way: I, Clif, need help from Ken, of our local LETS, to shingle my roof. We agree on the hourly rate. Ken checks the LETS records, and finds that my "turnover" indicates that I deliver on my agreements. He also finds that I do electronic copying, and that I have a used car he is interested in. When Ken completes his work, I dial the LET-System number and say, "Credit Ken, Number 305, $300 Green; Debit Clif, Number 147, $300 Green." In this case, no "ordinary" money is involved, and Ken knows he can put his Credit to work getting copying done, or apply it against the cost of my used car.

Since the System mails out a regular list of Offers and Requests, it acts as a labour exchange in addition to recording transactions. No interest is charged or paid on accounts; the small administrative expenses are deducted monthly in Green Dollars (internal currency).

Why isn't there a LETS in every small community? Some of the obstacles are obvious:

- Local retailers must purchase with "ordinary" dol-lars.
- Governments do not accept Green Dollars in tax payment.
- Most people are naturally conservative – not innovative. In spite of these barriers, LET Systems offer advantages:
- Local currency remains in the local community.
- Self-regulation. LETS are governed by *trade*, not *banking*.
- Non-inflationary. Each Green Dollar is a personal responsibility.
- Conventional money capitalizes the assets of banks, corporations and governments. Green Dollars capitalize local labour.
- Independence. Free of factors outside the community, Green Dollars reflect and provide a stable base of local consumer demand.

More details available from: Michael Linton, Landsman Community Services Ltd., Courtenay, B.C. David Burman, 28 Verbena Ave., Toronto M6S 1K1. Paul Glover, Ithaca Money, Box 6578, Ithaca NY 14851. E.F.Schumaker Society, Box 76, RD 3 Great Barrington MA 01230. Two outlines appear in The COMER Papers, Vol. 1, pub. by U. of Waterloo.

Gully Seed

Heard it now four or five times. A high-pitched keening uneasily balanced between inquiry and fear. Comes from down in the gully, close enough to the bedroom window to be identifiable, separable from other night noises. But I can't identify it.

Not a fox. I'd swear it can't be a fox. Been close enough to them, and listened to their high, thin bark. Bark is like the smell, if you find their den. Had one here, twenty-five years back, over on the gully's far side. Could watch the kits sunning themselves on a warm day. That was when our trees weren't that thick, and you could see lakeside from the rooftop.

Heck, I've had fox watching me. Back of the shed, using a Swede saw on some small firewood. Fox just sat there, not all that many yards away, mighty interested, scratching himself every little while.

Not wolf, either. Had four of them, mid-winter, after frozen apples on the semi-dwarf. After they cleaned up what had dropped into the snow, one got the idea of leaping up, catching an apple in its jaws. What's in the gully isn't wolf.

Coyote? Hard to see, but you can hear the chorus some nights. Not many of them around – and not many foxes since the developers moved in, other side of the road. Found a couple dead at the bottom of the gully, shot or poisoned. And a lot of garbage dumped at the far end, up against Concession Ten. Old carpet, a dumpy sofa, dozens of oil and tranny tins. There's a city dump, county dump, and township dump, but that's not enough for some of them. Have to pay a dump fee on big stuff.

Not fox, wolf or coyote - but an animal, anyway. No birds here big enough to let loose anything like that. Got me wondering. Go back far enough, you find some odd stuff in this old glacial moraine. Like a stone I dug out of the gully bottom, with something a million years old caught in it. Trilobite, I think they call it.

Still wondering about the night noise while I raked up a couple piles of gully leaves. Built a neat double compost bin up top out of some roughwood skids and old snow fence. When I go down for compost, I stay out of the end where they've been dumping all that junk on my land. Bugs me, though. We sure have fouled up this planet.

Maple and pin cherry in the gully, the cherry full of black knot, fungus and every kind of insect in season. Nearly all red pine up top, the needles too acid for compost. So I bring up leaves with the small tractor. When I dumped in the last batch, something bounced out between the slats and rolled a little.

Looked like a small potato, egg-shaped and fuzzy. Didn't look or feel like it belonged to a bird, and not to anything I know about. Left it on the kitchen window sill a couple of days. Meant to ask my friends down the road if they knew what it was.

I tried to think, "potato." It was near the right weight and firmness – but there was something about it. Static electricity? Got some funny ideas handling that thing, connected it with the night noises out of the gully. Wondered if something odd down there was making little ones. These days, weird things are happening, like folks defraying the land that feeds them, and explaining how there really isn't any choice.

"That's just human nature," we shrug, and comfort ourselves that destiny, technology, evolution or God has made us Masters of the Universe. That's the biggest lie we ever told ourselves. Just suppose a dinosaur could have worked out a kind of Big Lizard Philosophy. They would have claimed to be top of the heap, due to rule over everything else forever, maybe fly to the moon one day. Could be we've had our time, and this is the beginning of something new.

It's in a big pot now. I've watered it. What would come from an egg-shaped thing that looked like it was starting to grow *fur*?

I'm hopeful.

Bits About Borges

Offering a book may be a way of saying, "I like you" if the giver is inclined toward shyness, or is cautious or labyrinthine. For one reason or another, or for no reason, I was given a copy of *Labyrinths*, by Jorge Luis Borges. From there, I went on to other works of his, both prose and poetry, and have just completed a re-read of *In Praise of Darkness*.

That I read and enjoy Borges is, in itself, surprising. The man's a metaphysician, and most of his voyage is through varying shades of the inscrutable.

In Heraclitus, he says:

What river's this
that bears along mythologies and swords?
No use in sleeping.
It runs through sleep, through deserts, through cellars.
The river bears me on and I am the river.
I was made of a changing substance,
of mysterious time.
Maybe the source is in me.
Maybe out of my shadow
the days arise, relentless and unreal.

Fluent in both Spanish and English, Borges spent time in Cambridge and other parts of New England. Wandering the empty streets on an early morning that seemed to have no place in the calendar, he was left with a memory of which this is part:

This day belongs not to successive time
but to the spectral realms of memory.
As in dreams,
behind the tall doors there is nothing,
not even emptiness.

> As in dreams,
> behind the face that looks at us there is no one.
> Obverse without reverse,
> coin of a single face, all things.
> Those odds and ends of memory are the only wealth
> that the rush of time leaves to us.
> We are our memory,
> we are this chimerical museum of shifting forms,
> this heap of broken mirrors.

Alias after alias, like worn-out jackets and gloves and shoes. Armel said: "You are the total of all the impressions you've made on others." This, I called The Dented Fender Theory of Personality.

Borges, going blind, is rearranging the books in his library:

> The man, who is blind,
> knows that he can no longer read
> the handsome volumes he handles
> and that they will not help him write
> the book which in the end might justify him,
> but on this evening that perhaps is golden
> he smiles at his strange fate
> and feels that special happiness
> which comes from things we know and love.

For that Argentine, memory and imagination, history and fantasy, the known, the unknown and the unknowable were cousins under a single roof. Even such a dilineation as that required by the passage from life to death became, for him, problematic.

He belonged to another world now, detached from past, present, or future. Gradually, this world came to enclose him. He suffered agony upon agony, he passed through regions of despair and loneliness – wanderings that he found cruel, frightening, because they went beyond all his former perceptions, memories, and hopes. The horror lay in their utter newness and splendor. He had attained grace; from the moment of death he had been in heaven.

Borges, approaching death, constructs a prayer in which he does not ask for anything, not even for forgiveness, since "forgiving makes pure the one who has been offended, not the offender, whom it hardly concerns." Then he says:
My wish is to die wholly; my wish is to die with this companion, my body.

Manifesto of S.P.A.M.

Encouraged by conditions in the world at large (and who would let such a world be at large?) delegates to the founding convention of the Society for Patriotism, Apple-pie and Motherhood, meeting in Brooklyn, N.Y., today went on record urging the secession of Brooklyn from the City of New York, the State of New York, the United States of America, the United Nations, and the solar system. In a surprise vote on amendment to this motion, delegates from the Williamsburg Intransigeants succeeded in gaining approval for separation of Williamsburg from Brooklyn. In a following series of maneuvers, which included shooting out light bulbs, shouting down opposition speakers, and stuffing chewing gum in the microphones, Williamsburgers pushed through the following program:
1. The sacred name of our portion of the universe shall hereafter be spelled as locally pronounced, which is to say, Wilyumzboig.

2. All existing icons and sanctified depictions of whatever nature shall be replaced by photographs of She who spoke the purest form of our dialect, *Ms. Ruth Frazzo*. In her memory, it is hereby ordered that all shall insert a pseudo-Arabic glottal stop in such words as bottle and battleship, and shall ask after the wellbeing of their friends with the approved inquiry, *wassamattawicha*?
3. Sole funding for this new political entity shall be obtained by a toll collected at each end, and the middle, of the Wilyumzboig Bridge. This toll shall apply only and exclusively to non-citizens of the Free City of Wilyumzboig.
4. The Mayor in Perpetuity of the Free City (unto his heirs and assigns eternally) shall be The Great Armel, he who formerly resided at 533 Willoughby. Let no man hint that this is not a part of Central Wilyumzboig, since it is by this date well established that said Free City is sufficiently free to place itself wherever it wishes to be.
5. The Treasurer, Comptroller, Accountant and Auditor of the Free City of Wilyumzboig shall be Richard Southpole Bennett, who is hereby forever exempted from all possible future charges of fraud, embezzlement, and cooking of books.
6. The position of Public Relations Officer shall be held by Clifton N. Bennett, in whose wandering hands shall be placed all printing presses, radio and TV stations, phone exchanges, modems and cinemas.
7. The motto of the Free City shall be: *AMOR SALVO JURE.*

The Choice

Dear Brother, Esteemed Sir & Comrade:

This morning, I listened while my normally honourable wife of many years used the telephone to lie to a Quaker. Since said wife professes Roman Catholicism, problems arise.

Over the millennia, since the first ape felt guilty after stealing the banana of another, considerations of punishment for misdeeds many and various have plagued the hominid population. Since my wife lied to a Quaker, my admittedly scanty theological training suggests she may find herself in Quaker hell.

My guess is that Quaker hell will prove to be a colourless, dismally quiet and eternally boring experience. Instead of roaring lakes of pitch and brimstone, the endlessly flat and antiseptic landscape will be dotted with tiny Bunsen burners, around which the populace, gathered in small and silent groups, warm their fingers (clad in knitted mittens of homespun oatmeal gray.)

But the telephone was located in a home shared with a Unitarian, and the telling of the lie involved reference to this same individual. Not a strong claim for disposal of an immortal soul, but would any professing Catholic desire to find shelter for the aeons in Unitarian hell? Imagine the everlasting discussions about whether those there incarcerated truly found themselves in an experiential hell, or whether this might be one more of those ecclesiastical myths concocted for the dubious purpose of ensuring collection of tithes?

No, there must be justice in the afterlife, if not in the preparation for it. Surely the element of free will, central as it appears to be in the everlasting scheme, must be given preeminence. Behold the soul, breathless and palpitating from its unelected journey, huddled in the antechambers of Choice, and presented with an unending selection of doorways, corridors, abrupt greased slides and gentle passages. Where to, oh choiceful one?

NIHIL OBSTAT † Benedictus I 1996

Abduction of the Queen

Notes on the suppression of the old religion

Whether the campaign of the Church against witchcraft was the effort of a new religion to wipe out the last vestiges of the old, as claimed by Margaret Murray, a tragic error as seen by Geoffrey Parrinder, or an impossible and imaginary offense as described by Evans-Pritchard, there are two points on which no disagreement may occur. The first is that the overwhelming proportion of those accused were women. The second is that witchcraft itself was declared a heretical sect, and that various typical charges, such as that of night flying, were also delivered against such sects as the Cathari and Waldensians.

The greatest concentration of burnings occurred in that part of Europe which experienced the widest spread of nunneries, mysticism, and matrist material. The English were convinced that in Joan of Arc they burned a witch. Joan came from a matrilinear area, where it remained customary to provide the child with the surname of the mother rather than of the father. She identified herself by either name during her trial. She referred to herself as 'daughter of God', and played the role of earthly *shakti* to the Dauphin.

The Church of Rome came to power at a period in history when women had been reduced, within its early domain, to the status of chattels, and it was this patristic tradition which that Church strengthened, on earth as it was in heaven. Female emancipation, or any resurgence of matrism on any scale, could be obstructed and kept in a defensive position just so long as it was possible to maintain a hysterical fear of the witch-woman.

The Hebrew Kabbalah keeps alive the memory of the Shekinah, or female aspect of God. Among orthodox Judaism today, a Jew is defined as a person born of a Jewish mother.

THE ROMANCE OF GUINEVERE

> "Ye say well, said the queen, and better is peace than ever war, and the less noise the more is my worship."
> – Malory, *Morte D'arthur*

Sir Thomas Malory created out of earlier materials a composite which showed the mark of his own personality and of the times in which he wrote. Our gentle knight himself fought under Richard Beauchamp, Earl of Warwick, in the Wars of the Roses. Malory was indicted and imprisoned for theft, murder, robbery, rape, extortion, cattle stealing, and the violation of a monastery. The *Morte D'arthur* was probably completed in Newgate Prison during 1469.

Considering the possibility that the work may be called "escape literature", Edmund Reiss remarks that in Malory's time, Northern Europe tended to oversimplify or turn away from an undesirable present. It sounds almost contemporary to say that people recoiled from the general violence, confusion and impending calamity back to the 'good old days.'

The ideal, as it appears in Malory, consists in part of earlier Celtic matristic tales overlain with medieval Christianity. Echoes of a much earlier time are the courts of love, as in Caxton's Book III, where Gawain and Gaherys, and later Gawain alone, are judged by a court of ladies.

In his comment on Chretien de Troyes' *Knight of the Cart*, in which Guinevere is abducted from Arthur's court, Heinrich Zimmer compares the work to Eastern mythical tradition, and speaks at length of Guinevere's rescue by Lancelot, who must be humbled to achieve it:

> She has the omniscience of a goddess, for a goddess she is. And like a true goddess, she takes umbrage at the slightest lack of due reverence and subservience...This is the manner of archaic and primitive divinities everywhere – and of that still more primitive being that we all carry within.

49

... I should like to suggest that it is out of his archaic pagan origins that Lancelot's bewitched and bewitching attitude of spellbound recklessness proceeds. He is bound indissolubly, blindly, and forever, to the goddess of sheer life force, in the role of her rescuing devotee. And out of those origins must have proceeded also the traits that rendered him unfit to achieve the Christian adventure of the Grail.

Guinevere, according to Zimmer, is an anima-archetype, as are Nimue, Niniane, and Morgan le Fay. She represents the "dream image" of the earth mother from the depths of the male psyche. It is this archaic quality that sustains Guinevere and Lancelot within the Arthurian cycle after Christian revision. They are as bewitched by one another, as far beyond human judgement as Kali and Shiva.

In a footnote to the tale of Kilhweh and Olwen, Lady Charlotte Guest, whose source for the comment is the Myvrian Archaiology, II, p. 14, remarks that Arthur had three wives "who all bore the name of Gwenhwyver." This is probably an accommodation of the Celtic story to a far older symmetry. Jane Harrison remarks in the *Prolegomena* that, "Dualities and trinities alike seem to be characteristic of the old matriarchal goddesses...in the ritual of the lower stratum, of the dead and of chthonic powers, three was, for some reason that escapes us, a sacred number." Beyond anything indicated by Harrison, though, the Welsh appear to have been singularly devoted to trinities of every shape, size and colour. Witness *The Triads*.

For those who sustain an alien existence within the senility of West European civilization, it must be difficult or impossible to imagine the instinctual response of medieval nobility to the erotic fantasy of the Guinevere-Lancelot dream world. Huizinga comments:

> A present-day reader, studying the history of the Middle Ages based on official documents, will never

sufficiently realize the extreme excitability of the medieval soul...

To be sure, the passionate element is not absent from modern politics, but it is now restrained and diverted for the most part by the complicated mechanism of social life.

This is substantially the language of Herbert Marcuse, and the process described by Huizinga is the development of that condition of surplus-repression to which Marcuse draws attention in his *Eros and Civilization*. In Huizinga's view, they lived in the middle of a fairy tale. Their instincts, noble and commoner alike, were as little subject to rational repression as the creatures of such a story. Where anything resembling modern controls existed, the restraining force was ecological. A partial parallel might be found among certain animistic, nomadic and molecular American Indian groups.

Christopher Hibbert notes that in 1348 there were eighty-eight known cases of murder in Yorkshire alone, and that if the same scale of mayhem were projected into the present, there would be more than ten thousand murders yearly in England and Wales instead of an average of under two hundred.

In connection with the application of the concept of primitive surplus-repression to this period, Hibbert says:

> New ideas about the virtues and purpose of punishment were gaining ground and while in earlier centuries criminal jurisdiction had been seen largely as a source of revenue, either to the King or, under the feudal system, to the prelates and lords of the manor to whom the grants of this jurisdiction had been made in return for other services, now it was more clearly seen as a method of repression, deterrence and retribution.

But most of these new ideas failed to get translated into social structure prior to the Statute of Winchester, which in

1283 provided the basis for the police system, which rapidly evolved from the mutual responsibility of the "tens and hundreds" into a professional arm of the State, aided by an increasingly complex economic structure.

Olivier de la Marche paints us a clear picture of the "good old days", at least as they illustrate the high level of irritability, and the elementary functioning then achieved by social repression of instinct when he refers to the *chansons de geste* describing the heated, frequent, sometimes fatal quarrels growing out of chess games.

KINGS, QUEENS AND CHESS

The senses have their necessities, their own categorical imperatives. A functioning freedom grows from the acceptance of these imperatives. Their denial in the twin worlds of myth and daily life drives them underground to surface again in games and song.

Under sovereignty of the Church Medieval, worship of the feminine principle in divinity was hunted down in the mythic universe and branded a heresy where it attempted to take root on earth. The liberating view of life as sensual play outraged the life-denying, who stressed the patrist supremacy of the rational. The patrist counter-revolution based itself in the primitive productive facilities of the time, which argued the need for repression in the interest of that social cohesion necessary to satisfy the material demands of life in larger groups.

Worship of the earth mother retreated into the songs of the troubadors, where it influenced European poetry and the novel during succeeding centuries. It retreated into the Cult of Mary. With somewhat less notice on the part of historians, but with even greater rapidity, it invaded the chess board.

Chess was introduced into Europe from the Orient through Muslim contact in the schools, trade and daily life. Murray finds the first sure documentary references to

European chess in the wills of Ermengaud of Urgel and Ermessind of Barcelona. Murray mistakenly refers to Andorra as a republic, rather than as a joint dependency of France and the Catalan Bishops of Urgel, but he does establish that, even at the early date of 1058, women of the nobility played chess in Catalonia: Countess Ermissind bequeaths "her crystal chessmen for the board..."

Spain, Italy and France compete for the earliest knowledge of the game. Venice is suggested as a likely port of contact, and we could add Marseilles on the same grounds of heavy Oriental trade over a long period. There is also the history of Muslim penetration of Aquitaine during at least thirty years, together with the early establishment of chess assizes in Lombardy, again within the heartland of the troubadors.

The game was repeatedly condemned by the clergy in the thirteenth and fourteenth centuries, and attempts were made to extend its prohibition to the knightly orders. An English Archbishop of 1291 complains of the Priory of Coxford in Norfolk: "The Prior and Canons, one and all, had been led astray by an evilly-disposed person...who had actually taught them to play chess, which heinous vice was to be banished, even if it came to three days and nights on bread and water." In spite of opposition from the Church, the game was known and played in the Spanish marches of France prior to 1010, Central Italy in 1061, Southern Germany by ca. 1050.

The Queen is not a piece in the earlier Oriental game, and was a specifically European introduction. A strong medieval compulsion toward symmetry, which later led to a bevy of female saints to match any grouping of sainted males, may have extended to the chess board, deriving its initial suggestion from the pairing of rook, knight and bishop. Add de Rougemont's charge that the troubadors were messengers of the Cathari, and Murray's observation that every troubador was a board-carrying chessmaster, and we may have circumstantial evidence for an importing of the Sophia Pistis of Byzantium.

The moralities written upon chess are beyond count; every monkish novice tried his hand, had he ever so little skill at either pen or chess board, despite the heavy frowns of his superiors. Parallels were drawn endlessly between the pieces and their moves on one level, and the wonders of Heaven - and earth - on the other. In actual play, the piece referred to in England as Queen, is called Lady in the rest of Europe (It. donna; Sp., Pg., dama; Fr. dame; Ger., Sw., Dan., Du dame; etc.) That the game was closely linked to life also appeared from the outraged cries of moralists who found two Queens of the same colour appearing on the board upon promotion of a pawn. No similar objection had occurred to multiple viziers in the Muslim game, since the happening coincided with reality as well as with morality.

Queen Guinevere is lauded as a skilled chess player, as is many another noblewoman of history and saga. Chess became one of the few encounters at which lady met knight on equal terms, and so became one of the overtures to love. Says Murray, "it was even permissible to visit a lady in her chamber to play chess with her…" Marie de France, one of the leading matrists of Aquitaine, sings in *Eliduc* of two lovers coming to agreement over a game of chess in the castle hall.

In Lombard chess, within the north Italian precincts of the troubadors, the Muslim rules were modified to permit a joint first move by a previously unmoved King and Queen: an illustration of the shakti principle on the chess board.

In the closing years of the fifteenth century, a sudden and radical change took place in the relative powers of the pieces, which resulted in the medieval game becoming known as "the old chess." The new game was known in both France and Spain as "the chess of the Lady." Earliest records of the new game are French and Catalan; by 1510 the old game was obsolete in Italy and Spain; final evidence for any existence of it in France occurs in 1530-40.

There is a close parallel in life and literature. The popularity of the masculine, war-centred *chanson de geste*, such as the Song of Roland, is typical of the early transition period from Arabic to European chess in which, following introduction of the Queen, the male pieces continue to hold, even individually, in the person of the Rook and Knight, overwhelming power on the board. The forerunner of the Rook in the Indian game is a male war elephant. With the exception of the wife of a Muslim leader, the only female in the Song of Roland with a role to play is that Alde or Aude whose lot it was to keel over and die upon learning that Roland was no more.

Peak popularity of the troubadors, as well as of the material from the Queen-centred so-called Arthurian cycle, occurs in the later Middle Ages, concurrent with the "new game" or immediately preceding it.

The changes which identified the new game were simply that the Queen obtained the power to move, if unobstructed, to any square in any direction; while at the same time the Bishop obtained a corresponding power to move on its diagonal. By 1500, Fenollar of Aragon tells us that to lose the Queen is to lose the game.

Numerous poems exist which recount the moves of various chess games, and in many of them prior to the "new game" there are highly exaggerated evaluations of the Queen. These are of considerable interest, since this earlier valuation of the Queen has nothing to do with her concurrent power on the board. In this sense, the wish is perhaps mother to the change in play.

Speculation without adequate documentary evidence? Perhaps. But in a current collection of chess literature, a gifted woman player, Leonore Gallet, replies to an editor's query on her reasons for liking chess:

> Until I received your letter I had never considered why I liked chess. I just enjoyed playing it; perhaps because in chess at least, as distinguished from life, the queen is given greater freedom and power than the king.

The Guilt of the Knight

> Our destiny, our environment, our enemies, our companions - we have built them all. They stalk out of our depth, essential and self-produced...The shapes of the initiating power change, but always in accordance with our own need and guilt...
>
> – Heinrich Zimmer

Jacques Levron, in his preface to a recent edition of Leon Gautier's classic work on chivalry, points up the conflict between ideal and reality in the profession of knighthood, and suggests that the chivalric code may have played some part in the gradual development of conscience:

> They were often brutal, sensual and coarse, and patience was not their outstanding quality; the dubbing rite and light repast preceding their elevation to knighthood would assuredly not effect much of a metamorphosis... Chivalry may well have had the effect of making them aware of their shortcomings, and this was certainly something.

Now, Gautier did feel that the chivalry of which he spoke was that of the eleventh and twelfth centuries. The Round Table romances, in his eyes, were clearly "less manly," an insight with which we thankfully agree. He complains that the Romance of Guinevere has succeeded in replacing supernatural austerities with a magical sensuousness. It is the later and debased chivalry, according to him, which is responsible for the Hundred Years War, and against which Cervantes used his lance to good account.

Huizinga observes that the chivalric ideal of love was that of a complicated formalism. The entire chivalric code became anachronistic toward the end of the Middle Ages: "The requirements of moral, aesthetic and social perfection weighed too heavily on the knight."

The pontifical ceremony of dubbing replaced the lay 'making of a knight' by the early eleventh century, and became a fully developed part of the liturgy within two centuries. The arming of the knight became, so far as the Church possessed the power to transform it, something of a sacrament, as the word was then understood. By this process, and by claiming that knighthood had as one of its founders St. Paul, "for he was a knight," the Church attempted to impress upon the class of warriors the awareness of commitment to an ideal.

The conflict of this religious ideal with reality was obvious. In 1138, one feudal lord preparing a charter for conveyance of land could state calmly that the soil in question was "free of all dues, of all exaction or tallage, of all compulsory services…and of all those things which by violence knights are wont to extort from the poor." Friedrich Heer maintains that this conflict between the ideal and actual existed on the conscious level, and that courtly poetry arose from a mutual recognition by the writer and female nobility that the widespread feeling of guilt found no adequate absolution within the ways of the Church:

> This whole literature was nourished on the awareness by its authors and feminine public that the crisis in the consciences and instincts of the newly-awakened men of the twelfth century was already so acute that it could no longer be staved off by the old, devalued symbols which were all that the Church had to offer in its attenuated preaching and unsophisticated imagery.

Gautier's brief outline of the code of chivalry, which he feels is representative of the eleventh and twelfth centuries, nowhere suggests the influence of the romantic ideal. Brooke, for example, writing on clerical marriage in England between 1050 and 1200, insists that the twelfth century, more than any other, witnessed the birth of that ideal.

Gautier is more willing to accept significant portions of the ideal as a dependable description of daily life, although he comes up with the occasional tongue-in-cheek observation indicating his awareness of aspects of the situation underlying his apologetics:

> 'My husband is dead', said the Duchess of Burgundy, 'but what is the use of mourning? Since the days of Moses, some have died and some have gone on living. Find me a powerful husband. I have great need of such a one to protect my lands.' For a moment the king thought of giving her to Girars de Viane, but then decided that she was rather to his own liking and kept her for himself.

The medieval historian, Dr G. G. Coulton finds that the marriage of convenience was normal to all classes, and was most frequently motivated entirely by interests in land. Marriages were ratified between children of four and five, and Mother Church was unable to raise any effective complaint louder than that objecting to the giving in marriage of "babies in the cradle...except under the pressure of some urgent need, such as the desire for peace." Quoting Pollock and Maitland in their *History of English Law*, Coulton goes further in supporting their charge that "the Church, while she treated marriage as a formless contract, multiplied impediments which made the formation of a valid marriage a matter of chance..."

In the process of nullifying a marriage, one of the most frequently discovered impediments was that of consanguinity. Prior to the Lateran Council of 1215, the prohibition extended to seven degrees, later reduced to four. That is, if two persons shared a great-great-grandparent under the more liberal later ruling, their marriage was void. Coulton remarks that the possibility of contracting a valid marriage outside four degrees of affinity in a village of seventy families would have been small indeed, and in the case of the more severe seven-degree bar, practically impossible.

In terms of Oedipal tension and guilt, it would have been exceedingly difficult to find a Church-sanctioned alternative to the maternal love-object. Awareness of the prohibited degrees, and hypothetically the weight of guilt involved, was probably much keener among the knighthood and other nobility, where litigation over inheritance was constant. The banned relationships were further proliferated by including affinity contracted through marriage, as well as the baptismal font relationship between godmother and godfather.

As to what relationship obtained when the twain were well and truly spliced, a Dominican theological encyclopaedia of about 1300 states that, "A man may chastise his wife and beat her for her correction; for she is of his household, and therefore the lord may chastise his own…" An earlier decree of the Council of Toledo offered the woman little increase of hope through marrying a priest, since, "The husband is bound to chastise his wife moderately, unless he be a cleric, in which case he may chastise her the harder."

The military, land-ownership and broader survival needs of the time gave little encouragement or jousting space to the application of courtly love in daily life. They had no other domain than a literary pastime for the aristocracy. Huizinga adds:

> The life of aristocracies when they are still strong, though of small utility, tends to become an all-round game. In order to forget the painful imperfection of reality, the nobles turn to the continual illusion of a high and heroic life. They wear the mask of Lancelot and of Tristram….Side by side with the courtly style, of literary and rather recent origin, the primitive forms of erotic life kept all their force….To find paganism, there was no need for the spirit of the waning Middle Ages to revert to classic literature. The pagan spirit displayed itself, as amply as possible, in the *Roman de la Rose*. Not in the guise of some mythological phrases; it was not there that the danger lay, but in the whole erotic

conception and inspiration of this most popular work of all.

There were, of course, regular blasts from the ascetics who had taken refuge in the monastic life. Eileen Power emphasizes the differences between Church and Aristocracy, and mentions the effect of offering medieval woman a model that vacillated between Eve the wife and Mary the mother. As Eve, she was the root of evil; as Mary, she was the mother of Christ.

MARY, QUEEN OF HEAVEN

> The repression of the emotions and feelings relating to the mother (in our Judeo-Christian monotheism) produced a tendency to adopt an attitude of distrust, contempt, disgust or hostility toward the human body, the Earth, and the whole material Universe, with a corresponding tendency to exalt and overemphasize the spiritual elements, whether in man or in the general scheme of things.
>
> – J. C. Flügel

The Cult of Mary is one response to the efforts of the Church to suppress matrist tendencies. The devotees of the Queen of Heaven inherited a worship that went well back beyond Cybele to Ashtoreth herself, and further, into those voiceless centuries where repression in its primitive forms grew out of the necessities of ecology, rather than out of social institutions.

The Mary-Cult, during the Middle Ages, did little to improve the lot of earthly women. What it did do was provide a surrogate for the forbidden worship of the Earth Goddess, a form of sublimation of the Oedipal wish, and an intercessor for women appealing to an all-too-male Trinity. The old cult of the Magna Mater was too closely interwoven with human instinct to die out.

The matrist tendencies vocalized under Eleanor of Aquitaine developed in those areas where Celtic influence was greatest. Some scholars have pointed directly to the parallel between late-medieval France and the pre-Christian Celts. And even today, the worship of Mary, Mother of God, is peculiarly strong in that Ireland which has for so long been subject to the influence of the Jansenists in its seminaries.

Eleanor, whose court has been held centrally responsible for the replacement of the *chansons de geste* by the art of the troubadors during the mid-twelfth century, learned how a mother may influence the course of courtly life from her highly competent mother-in-law, the Empress Matilda. The matrism of Provence combined the Celtic influence of the Arthurian legends with the equally Celtic songs of Tristan, the love-songs of the gifted troubador, Bernard de Ventadour, and the Provençal stylistic heritage from Greece, Spain and the Near East. Friedrich Heer emphasizes the political explosiveness of the material:

> ...the *roman courtois* derived from English and Celtic sources a tradition of antagonism towards the Holy Roman Empire, the France of the Capetian kings, and Rome. To these antagonisms, which it shared, the Provençal element added another, a proud and rebellious intolerance of the harsh authoritarian world of masculine kingship...The kingdom of courtly love was drawn into conflict with the greatest powers of the age. Its forces would undermine some enemy bastions, its scouts would penetrate deep into men's minds and lie there in ambush over the centuries...

Provençal matrism, together with all the richness of its culture, was smashed by the power of Northern France during the Albigensian Crusades in the first half of the thirteenth century, with the blessing of Holy Church and the booty of the rich and productive lands of the South.

It is now widely held that the Grail, a central image in the *roman courtois*, is a mother-symbol of Celtic and Oriental antiquity. Heer refers to Chrétien's *Perceval*, in which the hero's quest for the Grail depends largely on his "relationship with his mother…which turns on Perceval's expiation for his guilt in his mother's death, the failure of his encounters with the 'mothers' and the lady."

Taylor comments on the apparent difference in the object of aggression in father-religions and mother-religions. He feels that the father-religion is associated with violence turned outward, while self-flagellation is more frequently connected with fertility rites and mother-religion:

> It would therefore be extremely interesting to try to discover whether those who practised self-flagellation in the mediaeval period were biased towards mother-identification, for it may be that the Church encouraged self-flagellation as part of its attempt to deal with the persistent matrist trend and to keep within its ranks many who might, without this outlet, have seceded to the matrist heresies…

The direct connection between original sin, guilt, and the Mary Cult in the medieval popular mind is displayed frequently, but perhaps in few other places so strikingly as in that little song in which Eve's successful temptation of Adam with the fruit of the *Daath* tree resulted in a human condition so sinful it demanded the theological invention of a saviour and ensured the coronation of Heaven's Queen.

Ne hadde the appil take ben,	Blessed be the time
The appil take ben,	That appil take was.
Ne hadde never our lady	Therefore we moun singen
A ben hevene queen.	'Deo gracias'.

It was well said by Heer of Provençal matrism that its forces would "undermine some enemy bastions", for this and other suppressed mother-religions of the twelfth and thirteenth centuries cropped up in curious corners. Iluizinga notes:

> In the fifteenth century people used to keep statuettes of the Virgin, of which the body opened and showed the Trinity within...Gerson saw one in the Carmelite monastery at Paris; he blames the brethren for it, not, however, because such a coarse picture of the miracle shocked him as irreverent, but because of the heresy of representing the Trinity as the fruit of Mary.

The medieval spirit at the zenith of its strength infused both concrete and fantastic religio-sexual images with a passion which redeemed them from the level of mere machinery. It is only in its decline that the Middle Ages turns to the unhuman in its shaping of the inherited material of the Earth Mother. During the process, many of the saints "drank of the Virgin's milk, like Saint Bernard, Henry Suso, Alain de la Roche."

There may be symbolic flagellation in a mother-cult, and there is more than a suggestion of this in the adventures of Joseph in the songs of the Middle Ages. Huizinga remarks that, "The special cult of Saint Joseph towards the end of the Middle Ages. . . may be looked upon as the counterpart of the passionate adoration of the Virgin...The figure of the Virgin is exalted more and more and that of Joseph becomes more and more of a caricature. Art portrays him as a clown dressed in rags...Literature, which is always more explicit than the graphic arts, achieves the feat of making him altogether ridiculous."

Le bonhomme est painturé	Vieil, usé
Tout lassé	Et rusé.
Et troussé	Feste n' a en ce monde cy,
D' une cote et d'un barry:	Mais de lui
Un baston au coul posé,	a le cri:
	C'est Joseph de rassoté.

Patrism's apparent victory in daily life finally extended even to those customs of the clergy which might be expected when worship of the Queen of Heaven is taken seriously, humanly, and non-mechanically: following the earlier clerical freedoms, the custom of applying the worship of Mary to mortal woman was henceforth denied the priesthood by Innocent III and his followers. By the close of the thirteenth century even the English clergy were remarkably celibate.

JONGLEUR, TROUBADOR AND MINNESINGER

> The earliest of the troubadors known to us – it should be added that he was certainly not the first – ranked among the most powerful princes in France. This was William IX of Aquitaine (d. 1127). In the list of Provençal singers who followed him, as also a little later among their rivals, the lyric poets of the North, all ranks of the knighthood were abundantly represented.
> – Marc Bloch

William, or Guillaume of Aquitaine, was grandfather to Eleanor. He had been a Crusader, but indulged the Provençal custom of irritating the clergy through bawdy verses and a series of fanciful stories about women. These exhibited sufficient knowledge of biological fact to suggest the extent of this knight's extracurricular activities while crusading in Andalusia and the East, "in Guillaume's love-songs the vocabulary and emotional fervour hitherto ordinarily used to express man's love for God are transferred to the liturgical worship of woman, and vice versa."

Irritation of the clergy was hardly limited to the matrist content of the songs of the troubadors. The entire culture of which the troubadors were a part was linked to the rise of the Angevin Empire in conflict with a Parisian King and a Roman Pope. Of both choice and necessity, the songs of Eleanor's court were anti-papist, anti-monastic, and destructive of the worship of Charlemagne fostered by the Abbot Suger at St. Denis. As Heer describes it, the art consisted of political dynamite worked into a lasting literature by Marie de France, Chretien de Troyes and Gautier d' Arras.

In opposition to the legendry of Charlemagne and its connection with the Capetian kings, Henry II successfully identified himself and his house with Arthur and Guinevere. Politically, he succeeded too well. The prophecy of Arthur's return became potentially so troublesome he undertook to locate the burial place of Merlin's protégé in order to put the prophecy - and the bones - to final rest.

Of the hundred or so troubadors known by name between the mid-twelfth and mid-thirteenth centuries, about twenty are women. Their code of love was woven of Oriental, gnostic and Islamic strands on the Provençal loom. They sang the growth of the human personality, and it was their specific art to use myth and symbol in such a way that the diverse materials merged in an experience of healing, unfolding and human fulfillment.

Minnesingers rose during the early thirteenth century in the Hohenstaufen dynasty of the North. They adapted the Provençal material making of it something more weighty, sober, ponderous. They ranged in type from the knight Friedrich von Hausen, a traditionalist, to the eccentric Heinrich von Morungen, who capped his Crusade by leaving for India.

The earlier *chansons* were probably chanted after the manner of plain song by the *jongleurs*, wandering singer-entertainers who later performed the music and sang the lyrics of the troubadors. Of the *jongleurs*, the greater number were of the commoners, while most troubadors were noble. There were exceptions, one of these being that Bernard de Ventadour, son to a servant of the Count of Ventadour, whose love-songs brightened Eleanor's court.

Economics, Heretics and Witches

"If the gods above are no use to me, then I'll move all hell."
—The Aeneid

David Bakan points out that this quotation, used by Freud on the title page of his *The Interpretation of Dreams*, is indicative of his concern with the demonological as representative of the forces working toward release of suppressed material within the individual into consciousness. The idea is further supported in Bakan's analysis of Freud's paper on *A Neurosis of Demoniacal Possession in the Seventeenth Century*.

Of Chretien de Troyes, Heer remarks that, "He may perhaps have been a heretic, a Cathar." This is the early name for those known as Albigensians, from the city of Albi, in the County of Toulouse, in southern France, and unquestionably seen as demonic by those who engineered the internal crusade to blot them out.

In her appendix to the *Prolegomena*, Harrison deals in some detail with four burial tablets containing similar formulae, found near Naples, and in Rome, and dating from about 400 B.C. to the second century A.D. The opening line in each case is a dialectical variation of "I come from the Pure, O Pure Queen of those below…" In each case, the word used to describe the initiate as well as the queen of the underworld is the Greek root for Cathar. Harrison feels the inscriptions are Orphic cult-formulae.

Either heresy or the accusation of consorting with demons was easily come by, in part because the worlds of fantasy, magic, religion and practical politics interpenetrated. Heer describes the installation of the young Richard, later to be known as the Lion-Hearted, by his mother, Eleanor, as Duke of Aquitaine:

> ... in the form of a symbolic marriage in the church of St Stephen at Limoges between Richard and St Valéry, the

legendary martyr and patroness of the region. The saint's ring was placed on the young duke's finger in solemn token of his indissoluble union with the provinces and vassals of Aquitaine. In this action were combined the attributes of sacred kingship, sacramental initiation and the mysteries of archaic religion. We cannot hope to understand the atmosphere surrounding the courtly romances unless we accept as a fact this close union of the primeval and magical with hard-headed practical politics.

What has been referred to as Angevin, or Orientalized, Romanesque, describes the architectural form spread through the Empire of Henry II and Eleanor. This form is earth-rooted, ground-related. Gothic, which can probably be fairly described as more sky-related, began to develop between the mid-twelfth and mid-thirteenth centuries. Gothic is also related, in its inception, to the French Empire.

Associated with the ritual and pageantry which passed through the churches and cathedrals and great courts of Aquitaine, there burst forth a flowering of the human imagination, powerful, explosive, linked with repressed instinct, difficult to control or to direct. The world of the Middle Ages squirmed with visions of Paradise and damnation, frequently erotic in nature. A vast vernacular literature responded to the hunger of a growing middle class for imaginative entertainment. Teutonic, Celtic and Oriental tales were re-worked for the edification and pleasure of an age experiencing a great deal more change than we customarily think.

In most of Northern Europe, political power became concentrated in the towns, while religious power was based on the countryside. The burghers and the bishops lived in a state of continuing warfare, of which the commune of Cambrai furnished an early model.

And the burghers won recognition, not merely as a social group dedicated to commerce, but as a legal group. "And out of that legal status itself was to come, necessarily, the granting of an independent legal organization." (Pirenne) Reading and writing, a pastime for the noble class, were the commercial man's tools of daily life. By the middle of the twelfth century, the towns began to establish lay schools to educate the children of the burghers.

Of the burghers, Pirenne says:

> At all times, they were distinguished above everything else by the exuberance of their mysticism. It was this which, in the eleventh-century, led them to side passionately with the religious reformers...But it was this also which assured the success of all the novelties, all the exaggerations and all the deformations of religious thought.

A number of these traders were women. Miss A. Abram, in her study of *Women Traders in Medieval London*, concludes that "the women traders...were persons of strong character and undeniable business ability, and that they played a not inconsiderable and very useful part in the industrial life of the city." Certainly the part these women played was not limited to industry; the late thirteenth and fourteenth centuries reveal a high proportion of women mystics.

Coulton stresses the relationship between nunneries and mysticism. In the Teutonic province of the Dominicans, there were seventy nunneries at the end of the thirteenth century, against a total of ninety in the rest of Europe among the Dominicans. The friars who tried to preach Scholasticism to these women found it required mystical adaptation.

Meister Eckhart (d. 1327) combined in his person the scholastic and mystic; there doesn't seem to be anything in the human organism requiring opposition between the two. Yet, partly because of his continued effort to express himself in the vernacular, he was condemned by the Archbishop of Cologne.

Shortly afterward, a major portion of his propositions were condemned by John XXII.

The vernacular, unfortunately for Eckhart, was not developed enough to express the theological subtleties of the Latin. Coulton remarks that one of his doctrines, the "Godlike Eye is, in effect, the *Scintilla* of Aquinas, which goes back to Augustine..." And in the vernacular of a people lately come to settled life out of a nomadic paganism, the speaker had to be detailed individual, specific, rather than general, typological, abstract. A similar person-centred directness is demanded today of West African gospel preachers working in Pidgin: "You see dat tree dat be for middle garden? Dat no be chop for you – dat be white man chop!"

The vernacular encouraged a kind of woman-focus, to the extent that it appears to be given to women in Western culture to excel in the specific and personal. This, also, was probably the emphasis demanded of the teaching friars in the nunneries. Coulton concludes that, "...a mystical movement is always followed by a free thought movement, through the impulse it gives to individualism."

An underlying cause of the restlessness and movement is the rapid increase of population beginning in the eleventh century, following a long period of apparently static population. Génicot feels that religious upheaval, economic development, rebirth of literature and science, creation of the Gothic art forms, territorial expansion, were all based on that early population explosion.

Out of the upsurge in population came landless younger sons, creating at the same time an acute pressure on available land and the mercenaries, enthusiasts and adventurers required for the Crusades. The eleventh and twelfth centuries saw men bring back more than material booty from the lands of the infidel: ideas also came. The East poured old wine into the ferment of the European mind, a ferment that in part owed its origins to the spirit of the Crusades themselves, acutely described by some modern historians as the first major ideological commitment to move the people of an entire culture.

A population explosion results in greater awareness of the role of mother. In a society whose agricultural economics is labour-intensive, slow to respond to a rapid increase in need for food, fertility rites become increasingly important - and, in the Middle Ages, increasingly related to the Cult of Mary. Men of all classes must eat, and men of all classes slowly drop their eyes from the Father Who (mayhap) Art in Heaven, to worship once again that Mother Who (certes) Art on Earth.

Connections have been demonstrated between the agricultural/cyclical/ritual/matrist on the one hand, and the industrial/linear/creedal/patrist syndrome on the other. Commenting on Eliade's analysis of time-attitudes, Wach says: "Whereas the cyclical concept is an expression of the desire to annihilate time by means of ritualistic repetition of primordial events, the linear attitude sees an irreversible course pointing in a definite direction, serving a definite purpose, and hence perceiving a spiritual and religious sense in history rather than a merely biological meaning." And in a time when all ideologies become increasingly suspect, we might consider whether the hour is here to give more attention to biological meaning.

Taylor asks what, in the eyes of the Church, united the troubadors, Cathars, Beghards, the love-preaching sects? What was there that identified them, caused them to be accused of the same behaviour as the witches, and brought them into opposition with traditional Christianity? "The answer can only be that there was such a common factor: all these groups were matrist, the Church was patrist."

The patristic and anti-feminist bias snarls throughout the basic handbook for inquisitors, *Malleus Maleficarum*, in which James Sprenger, armed with Papal approval, offers up thanks to God for preserving the male sex from inclination to dabble in the black arts. From first publication in 1487, the work ran through fourteen editions in thirty-three years, finding an English translator in Father Montague Summers, who brings the patrist tradition up to date by saying of Father Sprenger's diatribes in the introduction to the 1928 edition, "I am not altogether certain that they will not prove a wholesome and needful antidote in this feministic age..."

One suitable comment is made by Parrinder: in West African society today, it is still common for the male to organize witch-hunting parties to 'keep the women in their place.' These events are carefully timed to coincide with the bringing in of the crops, to ensure payment to the witch-hunters for services rendered. Parrinder makes an observation closely tied to kinship stress:

> A potent source of witchcraft conflict in the family is the mother-in-law complex... When the witch-finders are at work, it is the young men who are most surprised and concerned if their mothers are accused of witchcraft. The husbands do not seem to bother very much.... A man's friends are his fellow men, a woman's are her sons. So women are accused by their husbands of bewitching them or other members of the family.

We can at least suggest parallels with Eleanor's long campaign against Henry, supported by her sons; with the women traders of London; and more recently with the newer material on the Salem trials. Tracing the geography of Salem Village, Boyer and Nissenbaum conclude that both politics and economics were heavily involved in the witchcraft hangings, not to mention the desire of certain townsfolk to hold onto tax revenues required for the support of clergy in the central meeting house. Reviewing the case, Davidson and Lytle, in their recent work on historical detection, conclude that, "The interconnections between a people's religious beliefs, their habits of commerce, their political institutions, even their dream and fantasy lives, are intricate and fine, entangled one with another like the delicate root system of a growing plant."

ABDUCTION OF THE QUEEN

Partial Bibliography

The Romance of Guinevere

Chrétien de Troyes, "The Knight of the Cart," in *Arthurian Romances*, tr.W.W. Comfort (London: Everyman's No. 698)
Sir Thomas Malory, *Morte D' arthur* (NY: University Books, 1966)
Edmund Reiss, *Sir Thomas Malory* (NY: Twayne, 1966)
Heinrich Zimmer, *The King and the Corpse* (NY: Pantheon, 1956)
Lady Charlotte Guest, tr., *The Mabinogion* (London: Dent, 1906)

Chess

H.J. R.Murray, *A History of Chess* (Oxford: Clarendon, 1962)

Medieval Society

J.Huizinga, *The Waning of the Middle Ages* (Garden City: Doubleday-Anchor, 1954)
Friedrich Heer, *The Medieval World* (London: Weidenfeld, 1962)
Amy Kelly, *Eleanor of Aquitaine* (NY: Random House, 1950)
Marc Bloch, *Feudal Society* (Chicago: U. of Chicago Press, 1962)
Sylvia Thrupp, ed., *Change in Medieval Society* (London: Owen, 1965)
G.G. Coulton, *Medieval Panorama* (London: Fontana, 1961)
C.G. Crump and E.F. Jacob, *The Legacy of the Middle Ages* (London: Oxford U. Press, 1962)

Witchcraft

Geoffrey Parrinder, *Witchcraft: European and African* (London: Faber, 1963)
Margaret Murray, *The God of the Witches* (London: Faber, 1952)
James West Davidson and Mark Hamilton Lytle, "The Visible and Invisible Worlds of Salem," in *After the Fact*, Vol 1 (NY: Knopf, 1982)

General

Denis de Rougemont, *Love in the Western World* (NY: Pantheon, 1956)
G. Rattray Taylor, *Sex in History* (NY: Ballantine, 1954)
Jean Seznec, *The Survival of the Pagan Gods* (NY: Harper, 1961)
Robert Graves, *The White Goddess* (NY: Farrar, Straus, 1966)
Erich Neumann, *The Great Mother* (Princeton: Princeton U. Press, 1974)

Individual and Communal

Our current wave of paranoid individualism lacks a communal undertow. Judy Rebick is right: the response is non-participation instead of resistance. Beyond mere resistance lies the sleeping possibility of an angry but theoretically grounded counterattack, preferably based on local economic alternative structures. The existing repressive structures are to be drained of meaning, function, human support – "hollowed out," as one ecologist puts it.

Marcus Garvey, Father Divine, the Black Panther movement at its high point: these found a way to put the thing in motion. Where the nuclei were in those days ethnic, perhaps they may now broaden out to include the disenfranchised generally - and, from the mathematics of the last general election in the U.S., those bothering to pay homage to the ballot box are now a minority of the eligible citizens. It's well past time for workable alternatives.

The seas of individualistic hype in which we are all awash go beyond structural deformity to soak and short-circuit the human personality. One friend, an exceptionally bright and energetic woman capable of playing an effective role in any resistance movement, finds herself sequentially embroiled in obsessively self-centred battles, unable to free herself to participate in any wider concern.

If any call to a new and hopeful radicalism is to animate my friend and others like her, it will probably have to lean on some elements of a "religious" morality to join the severed personal yearning for justice to a social consciousness capable of supplying the organizational glue. Nothing less will make any noticeable dent in the economic and political mammoths which have grown out of our control and beyond response to our need.

And we might keep in mind that the Galilee Local of the Carpenters Union took off from one activist and a dozen apprentices.

Subject:
The Cybergospel According to Clif

Now, in those days, in the vale of Silicon, there did abide many geeks.

And some among them did study the words of one Braverman, who spoke of Control, and told in what manner it was useful. Others laboured among the works of one Gramsci, who spoke of Hegemony, and how to get it.

And among the geeks were some who were grifters, and delighted in conning the masses. Mightily they laboured in the vineyards of Silicon, desiring to confer Control and Hegemony upon their tribesmen, the geeks.

Verily, they ignited the midnight petroleum, plotting and conniving until the wee hours. And when all was ready, they put before the people He of the Molten Silicon Apertures, who spoke, saying:

"Come unto us, and we shall give you Access. We shall make straight a way through the wilderness of Information, and thou shalt abide forever among megabytes of joy. And all this we shall do for love of you."

And the people believed the grifters who offered them Unlimited Access, and the people gave the grifters the Keys to the Kingdom of Information. And they bestowed on the grifters Control and Hegemony.

And behold, a darkness came upon the face of the land, with howling and gnashing of teeth. For the Molten Silicon Apertures became opaque and engulfed many, who did not appear again. Brother turned against brother, and sister against sister.

The masses cried out in agony, but the geeks heard it not. Secure in their silicon towers, they feasted on the milk of Control and the honey of Hegemony.

Beware of geeks bearing grifts.

Religion & Technology

In the late evening of the faith, as the electric lights burn less brightly on the Christmas tree, we conjecture on religion and technology:

- Many rice Christians, in China and elsewhere, came to the Church because of the overwhelming edge of Western technology. As Islam earlier conquered by Damascus steel.
- With technology so worthy a tool, strange that no god ever communicated any invention or design beyond what the culture worshipping him had already produced.
- Perhaps all deities exist in an exclusively nontechnological environment.

But when a war has been going on for a long time, life is all war, every event has the quality of war, nothing of peace remains. Events and the life in which they are embedded have the same quality. But since it is not possible that events are not part of the life they occur in – it is not possible that a bomb should explode into a texture of life foreign to it – all that means is that one has not understood, one has not been watching.

–Doris Lessing
The Four-Gated City

While the place of minor ritual is to mark transition from an area of one life-texture to another, the function of major ritual must be to knit life's continuing strands to the repeated elements in the overall pattern. The difference is implicit in the ceremonies marking a marriage or the celebration of a solstice.

Spiritual and ecological imbalance results when human ego attends exclusively to the minor rituals. We live then at the heart of the bomb. Eventually, we become indistinguishable from the heart of the bomb. We are that which we fear: agents of our own dissolution.

We are the first generation among the children of men to speed our dissolution by a combination of nuclear power and electronics. The minor rituals become dehumanized, and machines do not require celebration of the solstice.

Probably earth, in one condition or another, will continue to spin. Sun will be lower or higher above the horizon. Moon will move through its dance. These things, however, are leached of human meaning, human relevance.

Without a rebirth of major ritual, this can be no longer earth, nor even a fitting mausoleum memorializing what once was human.

Beneficiary of the Helping Paw Society

Somewhere out of sight, beyond one of the stands of red pine, a neighbour's barn ceased to look attractive to a pair of orange-and-white cats. One kittenish, one nearly full-grown, they moved onto the East deck and settled in for the winter.

Snow has been impressive, and night temperatures have hit -30°C. Wife insisted on suitable insulated cat housing, preferably with a swinging door. The swinging door lasted a little more than one day, with the kitten batting it several dozen times as he charged in and out. The older cat (probably a relative, since he's got the same eye-catching pattern) showed more respect for human technology, easing himself cautiously through the entry.

There's a need up here to check snow depth on the roof a couple of times a winter. Our increasingly fluctuating warm spells and deep freezes can dump a few feet of the white stuff up top, then follow it with far too much rain. I leaned the ladder against the roof edge, and tied it to the deck rail with bright yellow nylon rope – as I'd been taught during my short summer as a construction labourer.

The ladder was no sooner up, than the larger cat clambered up the rungs to test it for me. He reached the roof, turned and headed down. I wondered how he'd handle the slippery, pipe-like aluminum rungs, and the answer was: with difficulty. Up was easy; down required innovation. He hooked his rear legs over the upper rung (not the paws, but the entire leg) and tested for a dependable grip on the lower rung. Lots of uncertainty, and I finally took hold and lifted him to the ground. He shook himself, looked back at the ladder, seemed to conclude it would have to do, and made for the feeding station. I appreciated the safety check.

The kitten hadn't been left out of the action. Clambering to the deck rail, it clawed and bit at the knotted nylon, making sure the knot wouldn't come loose just as I reached the ladder's top. Really dedicated to the job. I had to offer it my knuckles to attack before it lost interest in the rope.

As it says somewhere or other, the kindness you do will return to you. The bread you cast upon the waters may come back soggy or frozen stiff, but the invisible currents of time are programmed to bring it back to your East deck if you can just hang in there.

Society of the Spectacle

The spectacle in Debord's work consists primarily of the relationship between "things and things" – that is, the relationship between commodities, with labour, in the Marxist view, the prime commodity. It is the opposite of the Marxist philosophy in praxis, or human worldview translated into action.

Debord's attack issues from Hegelian dialectic, Marxist worldview, and the modifications of Pannekoek and the Council Communists. When Lenin cried, "All power to the Soviets!" the Council Communists believed him, and acted accordingly. What he meant, of course, was "All power to the Central Committee!"

The Hegelian-Marxist dialectic is responsible for the use of such terms as separation (Trennung, Scheidung), alienation (entfremden), and contradiction (Widerspruch). The dominant tone of the work is certainly influenced by the time during which it was written: the French student riots of the late 1960s.

Separation: one of the meanings here is the separation of the sign or symbol from the signifed reality. Debord argues that this separation has been carried to the point of massive illusion, taking the form of a materialized ideology. The current ideology represents mass-commodity capitalism as the permanent end product of human history. In this sense, it is a denial of historical time. Historical time, as the stage upon which dialectical forces work through their processes, is central to Marxist thought and action.

If the world of the commodity is the final stage, or end product of human history, then the human drama is reduced to the commodity as spectacle, endlessly replayed, dramatized, regurgitated. The Russian bureaucracy since 1917 is defined as a substitute ruling class for the continuing commodity economy, with labour, there as elsewhere, the prime commodity.

As in John Vernon's critique of schizophrenia in the literature and culture of the twentieth century, Debord asserts that we are constrained to live within the false bounds of a two-dimensional clinical chart of schizophrenia. In this flat earth, we are denied the reality of encounter and recognition with others in the process of jointly building a real world to replace the massive illusion.

For the Man Who Asks Questions

Beginning with the last things (naturally!), it is seldom that I can reply to two questions with the one answer. The magnificent article enclosed is my reply to your Q.14, as well as to your request for publishing ideas. Individuals who made a visible difference in their physical or thought environment, to the extent that benefit was conferred on those who followed: Dorothy Day, Peter Maurin, Mike Gunderloy (yeah! Mike might feel itchy at some of the other occupants of his compartment, but it ought to be plain by now that it takes a helluva lot more than naive enthusiasm to keep doing what he did, as long as he did it.)

Progress? The cosmos I live in is cyclical, running without beginning or end through a continuum of matter/antimatter creation, ripening and destruction. Don't rush out to buy a bed sheet and look for a handy hilltop; this cycle is still good for several billion years.

Anarchist behaviour has affected my life, initially, to the extent that any reasonably consistent behaviour will give any life continuity, meaning, a standpoint from which to survey, evaluate, respond to the individual or social behaviour going on in the surround. Depth, stability, a base for valuation is provided by some knowledge of anarchist history. The joy of finding a comrade, long talks into the night over a few beer, dreams of mutual projects, or mutual encouragement in going our separate but related ways. My 'family' are those I choose to relate with. To some extent, this family includes a son and daughter, neither of them indoctrinated, both aware their dad's an anarchist, neither following sheepishly in my footsteps – which is as it should be. I work little with goals or models, am not given to the construction of Utopian communities, enjoy most of what I do, and don't look for rewards/applause/payoffs. The act must be satisfying in itself.

Colin, who is about thirty and an electronics engineer, will be over in a couple of hours to run off some of his stuff on the Sharp. Rarely, I wonder at some of the music tapes he creates. He's more aware of the contemporary anarchist scene than I, and frequently arrives with an armload of strange publications. But I have DeBord's book, and he doesn't...

Bushed

"Ya gettin' a big butt from sittin' inna truck all day. Ya lookin' like a stump wit' two legs."

You can get to the co-op store in 45 minutes by bicycle if there aren't too many trees across the road, and the road is visible. Sometimes the fog shuffles in from the straits, and the planes cancel, the ferry stops running, and the co-op store closes.

The smart man does his liquor shopping early. He who buys his groceries first may reach the liquor counter after it shuts down. There is no other store, unless you count the convenience store at the Inn, which locals call the Inn-Convenience Store.

Isolation has advantages. I've been hunting McEwan's Strong Ale without success in Ontario. At the co-op store on Malcolm Island they had a dozen dusty bottles – the genuine Edinburgh Black Death.

In two weeks, no door-to-door salesman reached us. This may have been due to the presence of only two other houses beyond us.

Granddaughter Julie has been waitressing at the Inn. "I'm borrowing the chef's hat and apron, and going to the Hallowe'en party as a cook," she says. Someone cracks: "Why don't ya just grab a pair of rubber gloves and go as a dish-washer?"

The road ends with a jumble of clear-cut slash and a tilted, hand-scrawled sign reading: "Private Property. No trespassing. No mushroom picking." The original Finnish Socialists were followed by a wave of pot-puffing, magic-mushroom-picking beats in the 60s.

The clear-cut, whose name is a no-fit, is a nearly impassable chaos of smashed trunks, a patchwork tangle of discarded branches, the soaking bog underfoot, the massive saucers of vertical earth held together by a riot of lateral rootlets. Rusted massive machinery, shattered bunkhouses, half-buried garbage – these exhausted battlefields of corporate logging are anything but clear. But they are the natural terrain of the treeplanter.

With fifty pounds of seedlings in her packs and a mattock in her hands, the planter works her way up and down the slopes. Where not too many seedlings become a snack for the undersized island deer, there may be another tall forest here – for your grandchildren.

Gathering

The wind was high Sunday night. Racing whitecaps on the straits, the tall, thin aspens along the road dancing crazily. The power line went out with a squawk in the middle of a recording of Irish harp. Monday at five, Andy the electrician switched on the power again and presented his bill. Wednesday noon, a few more trees came down, crushing the power shack and taking the line flat again. But this time the power wasn't cut, and grandma was able to make chicken curry.

The kitchen and living room were the original cabin moved to this ocean-viewing hill. Many alterations later, it's a large place with basement, second floor, and lots of firewood storage. A brown mare and white stallion compost the grass. Both are fat-bellied and sway-backed, the mare gentle, the stallion bad-tempered, accepting an apple, but biting the hand that feeds him. There are two cats, which appear periodically looking in windows and rubbing themselves against the outside of the frames.

There were a dozen of us at the family reunion. Connie and Eric played host, with Julie and Brady of the Mellish clan. Jack and Deli of the Youngs and Naseefs, Lora in with her guitar and packsack of songs from Sweden, Laura Lee motoring in from Harrison Hot Springs, Audrey and son from down the road. Veronica and Clif flew in from central Ontario, with a little help from island ferries, small planes and a van.

Along the return route, a lunch with Julia and an evening in Vancouver with Barbie and a trio of young Mellishes, the youngsters digging into tacos & salsa followed by dessert.

"I was told you had some sockeye…"
"It's out of season. Who told you I had sockeye?"
"Just a guy back on the wharf."
"You know we can't sell sockeye. It's a food fish."
"Oh, you been food fishing. Well, yeah. I wasn't going to try to buy any. Where you taking it?"
"My relatives are all inland."
"Take you a helluva lot of gas to get there."
"Yeah."
"Tell you what. I'll buy the gas for your trip!"
"Yeah. Can't sell any salmon, though. You'll need a couple big plastic bags."
"Got 'em here."
"Yeah."

Latest Glossary of Technical Terms Observed in Use, Mainly in High Places

To implement a pilot intervention
    Make a cautious test run, preferably without raising the aircraft's wheels from the ground.

To address proactively
    Mail him a letter at the office he hasn't yet occupied.

To orchestrate feedback
    Dump the bassoons onto the violinists from the rear.

To mount an exhaustive critique
    Get saddle sore from galloping in circles.

To conduct a systematic needs assessment
    Prove that what isn't there, isn't there.

Gubby Goes to Heaven

He was a very little dogfish, with bright white teeth, and two small horns which stuck up from the smooth brown skin on his back. You might think a catfish would be afraid of a dogfish, but no catfish was afraid of Gubby. He was too small.

Sometimes he would swim over to the mouth of the river where the catfish lived to say hello to them, but when they saw him coming with his funny turned-up nose and laughing eyes, they just chased him away.

But Gubby was a smart little dogfish, and he didn't mind at all. He tried to learn all he could about his ocean home, because he wanted Brother Bass, his teacher, to say, "Gubby, you are the smartest little fish in the fish school."

He learned where the biggest seaweed grew, and he

found out where the hermit crabs lived in their small round houses. By watching the big fish, he learned to play tag. When some of the big fish saw Gubby coming toward them, they would say, "Oh, here comes that little brown pest again with his turned-up nose." So Gubby went over near the biggest seaweed, and played tag with the starfish. That was easier, anyway, because the starfish didn't move.

One day after school, Gubby was swimming along with his teacher, Brother Bass, when he saw three long lines of string coming down through the water from somewhere way up above.

"What's that? What's that, Brother Bass?" cried Gubby, flipping up and down in excitement as he saw the hooks at the end of each line, and the fat worm wiggling on each hook.

While Gubby watched, three large, fat fish swam along until they were right next to the three hooks. Then each of the fat fish opened his mouth and swallowed the worm and the hook. Quicker than Gubby could say "Fishcakes!" they were pulled up, up, up, until they were pulled quite out of the water and Gubby couldn't see them any more.

"Well!" exclaimed Gubby, "Where did they go?" He kept his little turned-up nose pointed toward the top of the ocean, and looked as hard as he could with his shining eyes. But he couldn't see the three fat fish anywhere.

"Ahem! Um! Umff!" said Brother Bass, and he looked very important and puffed out his cheeks. "The answer to that question does not come until next year in the fish school, but since you are a smart little dogfish, I will tell you now. The three fat fish have gone to Fish Heaven. That is way up above, where there are all sorts of good things to eat, and lots of nice, juicy seaweed. In Fish Heaven all good little fish can play tag all day and never have to go to school."

"Were you ever there?" asked Gubby.

Brother Bass looked at Gubby. Then he looked up above toward the top of the ocean. Then he looked back at Gubby again, "Well," he answered, swishing his tall, "I tried once. But

I was too big and I fell off the hook. Come, no more questions today. It is time to swim back to the floor of the ocean and go to sleep."

All night Gubby dreamed of the three fat fish who had gone to Fish Heaven. Next morning, very early, he swam back to the place where they had caught the lines and gone way up above. He had made up his mind that he would go to Fish Heaven, too.

That morning he had brushed his teeth very well indeed. He had also shined the two little horns on his back, by rubbing them against the seaweed until they were bright and sparkling. A starfish held a light for him while he looked at himself in a shiny shell. Gubby wanted to look his best when he went to Fish Heaven.

Just then, along swam Solomon Squid, looking very sad and holding eight bottles of ink under his eight long arms. Gubby stopped shining his horns for a moment, and asked, "What's all that ink for?"

"That is for writing letters," answered Solomon Squid. "And why are you standing here with your teeth brushed and your two horns shined and sparkling?"

"Why, I am going to Fish Heaven," said Gubby. And he smiled with all his teeth and tried to look big and proud. But he was too small a dogfish to look big and proud. No matter how he tried to look, he just looked like Gubby, the little dogfish, and nobody else.

"Ho! Ho! Ha! Ha! Ho-Ha-Ho-Ha-Ha!" laughed Solomon Squid. He laughed so long he didn't look the least bit sad any more. He dropped one of his bottles of black ink on top of the house of a hermit crab. The bottle broke. The ink ran all over the roof of the hermit crab's house and down the front of his door. The hermit crab opened his door and looked angrily at Solomon Squid. "Never darken my door again!" he said. Then he slammed the door and went back inside.

Solomon Squid stopped laughing and stared at Gubby a long time. Then he said, "There is no Fish Heaven. When you go out of the water, that is all there is. There isn't anything up above the top of the ocean at all."

All this was very strange to Gubby. He didn't know whether to believe Brother Bass or Solomon Squid. "Well," he said, "I'm going to find out anyway."

"Wait a minute," said Solomon Squid. "Here is a bottle of my good black ink for you. Take it along and write me a letter if you see anything."

"Thank you," said Gubby. And he swished his tail, and looked all through the seaweed and in among the starfish for some hooks to catch hold of. After a while, he saw some coming down through the water.

Gubby tried and tried to catch hold of a hook and go to Fish Heaven, but every time a big fish would push him aside, *ker-bump!* and catch the hook himself. Poor Gubby, he kept trying and trying, but the other fish were too big for him. It began to look as though he would just never get to Fish Heaven.

Suddenly a large net closed around Gubby and the other fish near him. The net closed around them tightly, and none of the fish could get away. Then they were pulled up, and up, and up, way up above until Gubby couldn't see the floor of the ocean down below at all.

Gubby got very excited at the long trip he was taking. He waved his short arms and dropped the bottle of black ink. That was bad, because now he had no ink and couldn't write a letter to Solomon Squid.

When Gubby and the other fish were pulled up to the top of the ocean they splashed and swished their tails. They jumped and twisted around. Then they were all thrown into the bottom of a small rowboat, where they stayed very still because they couldn't breathe air. They could only breathe water.

Gubby couldn't breathe air, either. He felt very sick and dizzy, and his head went around and around. He wished he had stayed home on the floor of the ocean where there was water everywhere, and green seaweed, and hermit crabs. He didn't feel happy at all.

In the boat was a little boy with freckles and an old man with a white beard and a wooden leg. The old man rowed the boat while the little boy steered it through the waves.

"Oh! Look at the funny little fish!" said the boy. He picked Gubby up and looked at his turned-up nose and the two horns bright and sparkling on his back. "I want to keep him for a pet," said the little boy.

"It's a small dogfish," said the old man. "Now where can we keep him?" He pulled his white beard and thought hard. "I know, you can put him in that bottle." So the little boy filled the bottle with salt water from the ocean, and put in some seaweed. Then he held Gubby by the tall and dropped him, *splash!* into the bottle.

Gubby saw writing on the outside of the bottle, but it was strange writing, and he could not read it. It said, "Milk," but if you ever get dropped into a milk bottle you'll see that the letters look backwards, too.

Soon the boat came to a sandy beach, and Gubby jumped up and down in his milk bottle when he saw the little house on the beach. It had a patch made of boards over one window, and this made it look exactly like a pirate with a patch over one eye.

The old man and the boy jumped out of the boat when it came in to the beach, and pulled it up on the shore. They put the fish in a large tub. Gubby was very much surprised. He had never imagined anything like this.

"Help me put this tub of fish in the car, and we will sell then in town before supper," said the old man to the boy. "You can take your pet dogfish along for the ride, if you want to."

Gubby stayed right up in the front seat when they drove down the street into town. Each time they stopped in front of a house, the little boy wrapped a fish in a piece of paper, and sold it to the people in the house.

When all the fish were sold, they all went home again in the car to the small house that looked like a pirate. Gubby was left out on the window sill while the old man and the boy ate dinner. While he was there, an artist in a red hat came by. "Oh, what a perfect little dogfish!" he exclaimed. And he painted Gubby's picture.

After the artist had finished the picture, Gubby began to feel hungry. The little boy had not given him anything to eat, and Gubby began to think very hard about getting home.

In the afternoon, the old man and the boy got into their rowboat again, and the little boy took Gubby along in his milk bottle.

The wind blew the old man's beard, and Gubby heard him say, "We'll stay close to shore this afternoon, grandson. It looks as though there's a bad storm coming."

Gubby looked through the glass of his bottle, and said, "Oh!" when he saw the black clouds. They got bigger and blacker, until they were right overhead. Then the old man started to row back to shore, but the boat tipped so much he couldn't go very fast. The bottle teetered and tottered and rocked back and forth. Gubby flopped from one side to the other. Then, *plop!* it fell over the side of the boat and into the water.

Gubby wiggled out of the bottle, and swam as fast as he could toward the floor of the ocean. My, what interesting things he had to tell Brother Bass and Solomon Squid! Halfway there, he met some of the other fish. "Why, it's Gubby. He's come back!" they said, and some of them ran to tell Brother Bass, while others made plans for a welcome-home party.

The sea horses all lined up in front of a big shell. Gubby sat in the shell and they galloped away with him to the floor of the ocean. All along the way the big fishes and the little fishes cheered and waved to him as he went by. Some were so happy to see him come back that they stood on their heads. Some stood on their tails. Some stood first on their heads, and then on their tails.

At last the sea horses stopped in front of the fish school, where Brother Bass was waiting for Gubby, holding a brand new pen which he gave him as a present. Solomon Squid gave him seven bottles of ink. All the other fish came with fine food for him to eat.

Brother Bass said, "Now Gubby will make a speech. I am sure he will tell you Fish Heaven is a lovely place, with lots of seaweed to play tag in, and many wonderful things to eat, just as I have said."

Solomon Squid made a face at Brother Bass and said, "Well, Gubby, there wasn't anything at all on top of the ocean, was there?" And all the fish stood with their mouths open waiting for Gubby to speak.

Gubby didn't knew what to say. He opened his mouth, and he closed his mouth. He squinted his left eye, and he squinted his right eye. He looked at Brother Baas and he looked at Solomon Squid. Gubby didn't want to have them mad at one another. And he thought if he told of all the strange things he had seen, nobody would believe him anyway.

So he opened his mouth and said, "I was so hungry most of the time that I can't remember very much beside that. An artist painted my picture, and I had a nice time. But there isn't quite as much fish food up there as Brother Bass told me. I didn't have anything to eat, and I'm hungry. Let's eat." And he started to eat fish food from an enormous white shell one of the other fish had given him for a present.

Brother Bass and Solomon Squid sat down with Gubby. They both began to eat from the white shell, too. And all the fish, big and small, fat and thin, also began to eat.

But first they all lined up in front of the fish school and shouted, "Three cheers for Gubby!"

Leprechauns Have Eyebrows

This is a scientific document. Being a job printer in the city these thirty years, I have gained a certain knack of attention to details and small things which is fortified in the case of the examination at hand by the fact that I am but half Irish, and that on my father's side. Which, on the subject under consideration, makes me twice as objective and fair-minded as any other man who spends a quiet evening at the Shamrock Bar and Grill, Michael Boyle, Proprietor.

Now, with all due respect to the veracity of a long line of Celtic tavern keepers, and with particular regard for the liquid hospitality dispensed by this same Michael Boyle, the above goes double for him. He it was who started the argument about the leprechaun's eyebrows.

"Kilpatrick," he says to me one day last spring, "have you ever heard a banshee?"

"No," said I, setting my feet more solidly on the rung of the bar stool, for I knew what was coming. He had got that look on his moonface that lets a man have fair warning. From banshees it would go to pixies and leprechauns, and as I know and my father before me, a Donegal man has queer ideas when it comes to a question of leprechauns.

"Ah," he sighs, settling his arms on the bar and looking over my head with that look on his face, "it was that night of my grandmother's passing that I heard them. A sound of wailing that would shake the bung out of a barrel, Kilpatrick. And when I peeped out the door, being a young lad and not knowing better, then it was that I saw him."

"Saw who?" I asked him politely, knowing what would come, but being unable to avoid it and keep my mouth shut any more than I could if the ocean was all beer and myself swimming in it. So I asked him, worse luck, and helped myself to a slice of pickle from the Free Lunch.

"Saw who? Why the leprechaun, the little man," he cried. "There he was, small as life, not more than that far away. All tiny and stooped over, right in the middle of a patch of moonlight. And do you know what, Kilpatrick?"

"No, what?" Sure and I know better, but once you get started with Michael Boyle, there's only one place the talk may go. With maybe a turn here and there, like the tracks of a Coney roller-coaster, still he always comes to the same place.

He looked right into my eyes before answering, and his face was screwed up tight with a terrible determination to be believed, so that it greatly resembled one of the pretzels from the Free Lunch. It was as though the future of the Shamrock Bar and Grill depended on my believing the word of Michael Boyle on the point under discussion, and him a Donegal man.

"The leprechaun," he whispered. "It had no eyebrows!"

Right here is the point where, for the sake of continuing friendly diplomatic relations between one Gael and another, I finish my beer, put down my money for the five of them, and walk peacefully down the street to my print shop. He has taken to looking after me with a troubled and bleary eye, which has been observed by me through the big window on turning the corner. Sometimes he will mutter into his double chins and start scrubbing the bar thoroughly with a big rag, as if all the truth about leprechauns were plainly written there, and he must wipe it off so the world will believe the statements on this head made by a Donegal man.

Now, the thing may appear of no consequence to someone unfamiliar with the Hibernian passion for truth in all matters great or small. Likewise, it may have no meaning to a person, however otherwise equipped by the hand of God, who cannot see the worth of folklore, legends, history and sagas in the character of an Irishman. Reading through that portion of this material alluding to leprechauns, a person of fair education with a scientific attitude, such as myself, cannot help but conclude there are two very different points of view bearing on the problem in hand. The first – and I give it first only out of politeness – is that held by writers such as Blennerhasset (which is surely an Ascendancy name, if Irish at all) tending to show that the leprechaun is a sort of Fata Morgana Hiberniensis. This view, which would drag one of the glories of Irish history to the level of a common fairy tale, is supported by several Belfast historians, the political machine in the Six Counties, the Protest-ant Church and 10 Downing Street.

The other opinion, which any reasonable man should agree is substantiated by the facts, states that leprechauns are of the species Homo sapiens minutus. The plain sense here involved is to be seen by any right-thinking man, inasmuch as leprechauns have been called "the little men," or "the little folk," since long before Saint Patrick blessed the Emerald Isle with his footsteps.

For if leprechauns are little folk and a part of Irish history, and if big folks have eyebrows, then little folks have little eyebrows. It follows as surely as Epsom salts follows Saturday night, that if they do not have eyebrows they are not little folk they are fairy tales fit only for children. And at that news, Michael Boyle, the enemies of the Church will raise a great to-do and clatter, the dome of St. Peter's will split, and surely the Devil himself, hand and hand with Winston Churchill and the Protestants will bring everlasting fire down upon the Christian world!

All this I thought through that same spring evening while I finished running the Bingo cards for Father Quinlan from Our Lady of the Sacred Sorrows. Every now and then I would stop the press to have a nip of the bottle, in order to keep properly warm for the work. That was how the evening went, between the whirring of the flywheel and nips from the bottle, when I saw it looking in at the bottom pane of the rear window.

It just kept its face flat against the glass and stared in at me, and I did nothing for all of a minute but stand there with a silly wrench in my hand and stare back at it.

"Kilpatrick," I said to myself. "It's a leprechaun!"

And it was. It had a great, tangled mop of hair, and its nose was oddly squashed, though the window was a bit dirty and I could not see it as clearly as I wished.

The next thing that came to me, being neck deep as I was in research and thinking, and minded to save the Church and prove Michael Boyle wrong in his stubbornness, was to see if it had eyebrows. With that very purpose, I ran to the window and threw it open – but the little man had gone.

Well, I looked about for the little fellow until I could be fairly sure he had vanished without leaving a sign of hide nor hair nor eyebrow behind him. There was nothing at all in the back lot but the wreck of an old car and a bunch of rubbish thrown out of back windows.

The fact that there was nothing whatever out there in the dusk at the time either with or with out eyebrows will be verified by the janitor of the building I rent in, Mrs. Foy, who had left her numerous offspring upstairs and come out for a breath of air.

"Good evening to you, Mr. Kilpatrick," she said, speaking around the wad of chewing gum she was working on. "And are you lookin' for your own true love this evening?"

For half a second I had it in mind to tell her why I was looking out the window, I was that excited about it. But I recalled she talked a good deal with that Michael Boyle down on the corner, and if she happened to get a chance look at the leprechaun, she would probably be ready to swear it had no eyebrows.

For these reasons I answered, "No, just came up for air," and closed the window. I told Mrs. Foy not a word about the little man, but I unlatched the back door every evening after that when I worked late. And it was well I did, for I saw him again on an evening but two weeks after.

I chanced to look at the window, just as it was turning dark again. It was the leprechaun, him and no other.

"Quick, Kilpatrick!" said I. "You must not miss this!" I was out the back door and into the lot to carry on my investigations before ever you could scramble a galley of footnotes.

There he was, stooped over and ragged, all of a pixie-size, down at the far end of the back lot in a dark angle where the brick walls of two houses joined. He seemed to be hopping and dancing around a small fire, and his crooked shadow jumped and danced behind him on the wall. It was a sight not to miss. All the old stories from the days of the Fianna came back to me, and it was a glad and proud man I was, to be chosen to make known the truth about a part of our glorious history.

"Careful," I reminded myself. "He's a sly one, Kilpatrick you'll have to creep up on those eyebrows!"

So I moved along, stumbling over piles of garbage here and there and once, I think, on something that felt like a dead cat. Not once did I take my eyes off him, and barked my hocks on a chunk of old iron in consequence. Ever so often he would bend down and blow on the fire, but he did not see me until I was only a few feet away.

Then the little fellow jumped up and back from the fire, facing me. It looked as if he had been roasting praties in a tin can. (I am glad I had opportunity to note this, as I can now state for a fact that leprechauns like baked potatoes. This answers Blennerhasset, and the likes of him, who maintain they do not eat at all.)

"Don't be frightened," said I pleasantly. "I only want to see if you have eyebrows. The light is terrible; won't you please come a little closer to the fire? And may I have your name, just for the record of my investigations?"

"Me name is Jimmie Foy," chirped the leprechaun, backing away a little more. "Leave yer hands off the pertaters," he added, as I tried once again to come near enough to conclude my researches.

Michael Boyle and others have since made arguments, out of the bitterness of defeat, as is typical with some types of men, to the effect that the leprechaun I saw was not a leprechaun but only one of the smaller offspring of Mrs. Foy. This is ridiculous, as any Irishman in his right mind could see.

My own conclusion, based on the available facts, is that leprechauns have to get here from the old sod by some means, and that this one came over steerage with the Foys. What would be more natural than a leprechaun's taking the name of the family who, all unknown to themselves perhaps, had played host to him on such a journey?

Michael Boyle and his cronies have tried to offer a second argument that, if I did see a leprechaun with eyebrows, it wasn't a very important leprechaun since it had named itself after Jimmie Foy, who wasn't a very important Foy. However, as I have already established, the leprechaun existing first, the Foy offspring must be named after him. And not the other way about.

A further proof of this is offered by Mrs. Foy's testimony that potatoes are and have been a favourite article of food in the Foy household for many years. The Foys come from a parish in Ireland renowned for its excessive love of that food, it being practically their entire diet. What more natural than a leprechaun who, as we have seen greatly values potatoes, attaching himself to such a family for his migration?

Well, there was that leprechaun, fairly jumping up and down by now, and me as determined as ever to get a look at the eyebrows.

"Stand still!" said I. "Can't you see what this means to Ireland?" And I came forward again, but one of my brogans hit against the tin can at the edge of the fire, and knocked the little fellow's potatoes sprawling into the shadows.

"Yuh big, drunken bum!" shouted the little creature. (This is not a complimentary remark, not even from a leprechaun, but I put it down in the interest of science.)

He then stooped quickly toward the fire, picked up half a brick in his paw, and hurled it at my head with surprising strength. That is all I remember of the occasion, save for two items of comment.

First, in reply to Michael Boyle, *et al*, it should be carefully noted that Mrs. Foy's offspring, Jimmie, denies that he threw a chunk of brick as large as a half one, says that he didn't mean to hit me, and further swears on his mother's rosary that he wasn't in the lot that night anyway. This should silence the Church's enemies for good and all on the point that I did not see a leprechaun.

Second, when the leprechaun bent over to pick up the brick I, Kilpatrick, saw his eyebrows in the light of the fire. There may be those who will say they were smears of dirt, but I know better.

Leprechauns have eyebrows!

Unto Us a Child is Born

TIMBERVILLE – A reliable citizen of this isolated logging community today reported an unusually gifted child born to a family renting the former stable and harness shop on the valley road. According to his statement the infant, normal in all other respects, radiates a halo of light clearly seen in a dim room.

Amateur astronomers in the area at the same time reported the appearance of a new star of the first magnitude which seems to be directly above the Timberville district.

The three di Maggio brothers, operators of a nearby dairy farm, were first to notice the phenomenon. Arriving at the stable with Holiday presents for the family, they were struck with the brilliance of the manger where the baby was being tended by the mother.

Later the same evening, a group of farming families from the valley gathered outside the rude log building to sing hymns. As the singing threatened to continue into the early morning, the carollers, who had become numerous and demonstrative, were dispersed by the Chief of Police under authority of an Anti-Noise Ordinance passed in Town Council last spring. Some arrests were made.

Following the disturbance, law-enforcement officials declared the singing had been done in a foreign tongue. Opinions differed, however, as to whether the language used was Latin or Russian.

One of the leading scientists on the Atomic Energy project, asked late today for his opinion on the alleged halo of light, said, "The baby is probably radioactive, and therefore inimical to the welfare of the community." He declined to offer any further comment pending additional study under proper laboratory conditions.

A well-known Professor of Comparative Religion at the University, interviewed by long-distance phone, asked that his name be withheld, but commented, "What good thing can come from poor Timberville?"

Reactions in the local Ministerial Association were divided. All present agreed that church attendance and offerings had doubled since the news from Timberville, but some doubt was expressed on the taking of an official attitude. One member was quoted as saying, "We would all like to believe this, but it is difficult to understand why He would choose to exercise His sovereign will to be born again of woman, instead of coming in glory on the clouds of Heaven. Furthermore, the reported happenings do not agree with the prophecy contained in the 21st and 22nd chapters of the Revelation of John."

Editor's Note: The above report has not yet been confirmed. Shortly after the arrival of our informant, Timberville was snowed in for the winter. Government offices, closed for the Holidays, were unavailable for comment.

Tribal Notes

Dear Tribe:

Something Dave said, the evening we wound up the subject of Zen, has been percolating in my mind; he and I have had a couple of talks about it. Nobody seemed to respond strongly to the idea of a more permanent organization of a religious nature, although there might have been what you could call passive acceptance of the proposal.

Seems to me we need something to provide more continuity. It is not merely that our individual lives, in many cases, have turned out somewhat fragmentary (a friend of mine suggests an ideal co-operative venture for "our kind" would be a trailer park) but that the whole world we live in appears childish, in the sense that it is discontinuous.

The mere organization of one more church would advantage no one but the wholesalers of altar cloths. But two things seem needful here: we don't feel at home in the existing faiths, and there are a flock of things we could do more effectively given some structure to do them with. I think of the underlying strength of the meditation group, much silence, and always long personal acquaintance in more things than thinking together. You may not know this as a conscious thing, but to myself who am very much of a newcomer in your physical group, you have a great degree of acceptance without tension or self-consciousness. Perhaps the less of that analysed on paper, the better; we are already too much a part of The First Culture to Psychoanalyse Itself to Death. (In the sense meant by my friend Ed Landberg: a culture begins to die when it questions its basic assumptions, which are originally organic, later ideological).

There are a couple of projects I'd like to see worked toward, which could come out of a form of religious organization. (All right, say "church", and quit being chicken about it. The word isn't *all* mud; there was Servetus, after all, and…Ser-vetus, and…)

I'm tired of buying and selling personal real estate. I want to be part of a group living together to a flexible degree and providing themselves with something better than they could get individually. That's one of the troubles in most of these projects: why should the woman be contented with a shack and mutualist talk when she can count on doing better in the comparative isolation of her family?

There are a number of staples we buy as families which can be bought in bulk co-operatively, and taken by us from a central storage and distribution point. The difference in price between bulk purchase and small pre-packaged units allows enough margin for payment of part-time manager and rent of warehouse space, which is not true on the buying club scale in most retail lines. Soaps, detergents, dried foods, household cleaning items – we can supply ourselves profitably with these and a simple letterhead will provide a one-third cut in the cost of books.

Radio: We could put on some sort of panel discussion deal on what is called "B" time, say late Sunday evening, at a moderate cost for a fifteen-minute programme including a couple of minutes of introductory music. I feel very sure this could pay for itself on an audience donation basis if it were sponsored by our proposed "church." It also provides chance for contact with other misfits, rebels and Auslanders.

Yes, I'm willing to talk philosophy sometimes, too. But it does make me happy to see "faith and works" together. Maybe we can cook something up?

My work with the B.C. Co-operative Union includes editing the monthly publication, setting up a print shop and mailing service, and getting into the field for educational work and organizing. We ran into a severe limitation in English: looking for titles for two new staff members which would indicate interrelationship with those they work with, we could come up with nothing better than "co-ordinator." The lingo is full of titles which suggest that the titled one is a big shot socking around a lot of billiard balls – which is fine for Newton and Behaviourism, but death to the pals of Prince Kropotkin.

As part of the job, I get to attend conferences and eat banquets supplied by B.C. Telephone, listen to funny toastmasters and pin innumerable little cards to my lapel which reassure me I am "Mr. Bennett," one more labelled container in a cosmic pantry full of them."

At the B.C. Adult Education Conference, I was assigned to a panel discussion on "The Legal Responsibilities of the Good Citizen" (Yoicks!) Although these were persons representing leadership level in adult education, there was a terrible amount of cliché thinking, with a marked tendency toward stating desired social attitudes as absolutes: "The good citizen must always obey the law." I tried to suggest that legality be limited at some point by ethics. This objection was met by the assertion that we were assuming a democratic government, again with the connotation of absolute; "In a democracy, all laws are of the majority, therefore always morally right." Attempting to encourage a relative attitude, I countered with, "Even in a democracy, there will be gradations of immorality in law."

The honestly encouraging part of the affair was the presence of an exceptionally clear thinker: Gordon Hawkins, Associate Director of the C.A.A.E., who repeatedly banged away at the need for the innovator – though I doubt he made many holes in the armour-plate of stasis. Even Mosca and Pareto wanted loopholes for new blood in the elite, but kowtowing to *Robert's Rules of Order* is stifling more creativity than any aristocracy ever did.

It has amused and confused me for some years, that such groups as radical political parties, unions and other more-or-less "Change the world or some part of it" outfits could consider *Robert's Rules* an instrument of change. The doggone things are perfect for the Board of U.S. Steel or Arabian-American Oil, but what do we want with something manifestly designed to impede change and hold the Thin Red Line?

Not that change in itself is either good or bad: it is simply inevitable. It is like asking whether it is good or bad that we evolved to breathe oxygen instead of carbon dioxide.

Selah!
Clif Bennett

ABOUT BEING A WORDSMITH: my dad wasn't. Master carpenter/painter, ex-chief of the Pinkerton shadowing division, engineer on the B&O RR, he died on the job at 64, an active member of the Transport Workers' Union. A good name, that. Along with the Fintan Lalor Pipers' Band, about the only popular support Connolly had in '16.

Ed Landberg, an aging émigré on the California coast, and childhood friend, has been immersed (drowning?) in a thousand-page epic poem for the last ten years. The poem seems to declare that he's the inheritor of Amenhotep IV and Jesus Christ, among others, that God has promised him Joan Baez, and that they'll rule the world together, though not with the identical 144,000 courtiers bearing the JW seal of approval.

I told him (regretfully, since I once recognized him as one of my teachers) that his stuff looked to me like word salad. I held back from announcing that, if I'd suspected him of being anything so naive as a Red, I'd have looked for the Russian Dressing.

Alas, the aging rebel. Seeing the non-effect of rational language and analytical forays against multitudinous evil, desperately wishing something, somewhere could be shown to be unquestionably improved, he leaps on his mythical wings into the theological salad bowl.

And a couple of weeks ago, while I visited at a pharmaceutical lab where I've done some consulting, the Occupational Health Nurse asked what she might do for a 61-year-old friend dying of cancer. Before leaving, I asked why she'd put that question to me. Because, she said, of the theological background I am, it appears, tarred with the same brush wherewith I daub. Friend Armel said, "Thou art the sum of all impressions made on others." The Dented Fender Theory of Personality Formation. If that be true, friend, I am indeed a hundred thousand, since I never dented the same fender twice. Like Pirandello's multiply-perceived hero, I'm also the villain, the stage manager and the banker about to foreclose on the theatre. Which begins to explain why I never became The Man on the White Horse, but left behind, as one sharp observer accused, a "trail of broken-hearted half-disciples." I've found it the most exhausting work of the world to attack that which is also in part oneself. Simone Weil wrote of watching a group of Hitler Jugend at a streetcorner rally, and feeling attracted by the rhythmic chanting and singing.

OF DREAMS & DREAMING: awakened from napping on the chesterfield, and fresh from a trio of dream fragments.

1) Guest at a charity banquet, I'm embarrassed for the half dozen ladies in evening dresses who share the head table. There's nobody in the hall; they're much too well-bred to pay any heed, go right on enjoying the meal.

2) Ball game with a pigeon. Seems to be a tennis ball or slightly larger. Sometimes I toss it over the pigeon's head. The determined bird nudges it back to me, a peck at a time. I wonder why it won't simply throw it back, until I see that it has no arms.

3) A computer screen appears in front of me, looking suspiciously like a TV ad, and graphics in bright yellow-green flash onto the screen. A background voice describes the virtues of the graphics module. I realize that, if I were designing a handbill for a pipe manufacturer, I could cover the sheet with circles in a honeycomb design underprint. The computer cabinets are a dove gray.

John McLeish wanted to know if I kept a journal. Told him I keep a dream journal and a chess journal. Both incomeplete, and getting very occasional entries lately. Once I met with two young men who had published Dreamweaver, which I liked, although it seemed to lack emphatic design and illustration. Thought of bringing it back to life and building something around it called Congregations of the Dream, this to be based on the dream-work fellowships of the Huron. Very Canadian.

ON THE CHESSBOARD, I've switched to playing Black vs. the computer, and found that, given the right opening by White, Grob's Angriff can still wipe ' em out wholesale as a defence. Against a Two Knights opening, I've been using a variation of the Pirc Defence, a fianchetto strikingly developed by Penrose vs. Larsen in 1969. In the most satisfying variation, a poisoned rook is offered to White's Queen Bishop to draw it off a key square. Checkmate is achieved by the Black Queen supported by King's Knight.

Why do I enjoy the Pirc variation or the Grob, in which one can give away not one, but three poisoned pawns in a row? Perhaps because the opponent becomes so feverishly intent on an easy win that there's a kind of judo component in using the patterned momentum of the other against itself, with the *Hey Presto!* surprise as the tables are turned in two moves. Now, downhill through the cold fog to look at the mailbox, hoping as always for something a bit more interesting than phone bills and ads for hardware.

ON THE ROAD WITHOUT JACK KEROUAC

During July, I discovered the only town in North America whose Main Street displays an officially marked crossing for DUCKS. The citizens of Rice Lake, Wisconsin, told me the crossing is used every spring, and that local motorists honour it. I lacked the time to check on whether this act of mercy holds true for Greyhound buses and interstate freight carriers.

Acts of mercy appear more important to me lately; this may be a function of my aging, or of the world's aging. On a recent dental safari, the esthete who plays tunes on my ivories asked, in his precise Alexandrian accent, if I still had insurance with the Tooth Fairy. I said not, and he inquired, "Do you wish mercy?" My affirmative brought a bill for $90 instead of $145.

I'm experimenting with being old. Twice my silvery hair (plated to prevent the gold from wearing off) has earned me discount tickets on Toronto Metro. At the Ontario Provincial Park north of Massey, the tent trailer received a nifty campsite without charge, all for flashing my Fainting, Farting and Falling Down Card.

Three mad dashes so far with the little trailer, and a fourth to come. We made it to Helen and Jack Armel's estate at Saratoga. Jack says the last ten years convinced him that wading through duck and goose turds was not a necessity, but that the experiment probably was motivated by romantic ideas of self-sufficiency. He's no longer a farmer, gentleman or otherwise. Jack's thinking about the acquisition of surplus souls on a market basis, something like stocks and bonds, but perhaps even more like commodity futures, is sketched in the current Armel Letter. He claimed to have title to a particularly despicable soul filed somewhere in the region of his computer, but was unable to locate it for me. As a consolation, he provided me with a set of instructions on how to make a million dollars without investing a dime. Normally, I'd take that sort of thing with a light-hearted laugh, and maybe toss in an appropriate comment in some West African trading language: *"Gaskiya ta fi kwabo goma!"*[1] But Helen explained that Jack had bought a certain hilltop just to make sure we'd have a scenic spot for our picnic. With these Land Barons, you never can tell.

Somewhere in the course of the conversations which got us condemned as self-centred demons by the ladies present, I tried out on Jack a variation of the Zen, "Who am I?" The Armel riposte, a blur the eye could not snare: "You're the total of all the impressions you've made on others." This I called the Dented Fender Theory of Interpersonal Reality.

Trip Two was intended to reach Puget Sound, Vancouver, Salem (Oregon), and Dave Orcutt in the Slocan Valley of B.C. The trailer crossed the Mississippi a couple of times, but prudence heckled that the Rockies wouldn't be that hospitable to the four-cylinder small truck puffing up the long grades.

Trip Three was another consolation prize, self-awarded. Up to Kenora and Longbow Lake to see Big Charlie Fisher, now a sitting Justice of the Peace, old friend Ted Burton, Crown Prosecutor, and Len Hakenson. On the way back, stopped off for a beer in a local pool hall long enough to ring up Anthony Ubaldi, noblest Roman of them all, in the Sault. His finest hour: when a Toronto clerk asked him what size flight bag he was looking for, he replied, "Just big enough for a suit of Roman

---

[1] *Hausa: *Truth is worth more than a dime.* Veronica says, "Without the translation, it's just one-upmanship."

armour!" He'd bought his son a masquerade costume, but the look on the clerk's face said, "God, Jesus and seven little angels protect me from any more of these characters off the Yonge Street Strip."

The town of Kenora is remarkable for one or two things. There are a couple of seedy restaurants that will charge you $3.50 for a pair of boiled eggs, the population is going steadily down, and the local library discards the best selection of hard-bound books outside New York. I grabbed Bulgakov's master piece, *The Master & Margarita*, Stanislaw Lem's, *A Perfect Vacuum*, and the Strugatsky brothers' *Definitely Maybe* at $1 each, absolutely unread by human eyes. Now beginning work on a hypothesis: any town that charges $3.50 for a pair of boiled eggs will, due to the action of universal homeostasis, discard literary masterpieces for $1.

Chuckling through Lem's piece on the laws of physics as the rules of a complex game played by the older galactic species, thought up the outline of a piece on *The Game of "Sick Institution"*. Game rules, particularly in governmental and non-profit organizations, become crystallized as the institutional structure, and may not be questioned any more than the laws of physics. Third-generation burocrats (anyone after Jefferson in the U.S.) no longer recognize the structure as a human invention, take it as given, inviolate. Initially productive purpose becomes overlaid with institutional process. Communication becomes impersonal, abstract, loaded with buzzwords. Easiest for this to happen where product lacks dollar value and double-entry (symmetrical) controls – and where top-heavy administrative costs may be written off at least in part to "program".

Seriously (yes, dammit, I can!) I know of nothing outside science fiction that deals with the sick, or sick-making, institution. Yes, a few writers in the social sciences have pointed to the double-bind family as a schizoid factory, but there doesn't seem to be anything tackling the institution whose internal stresses correlate with a high level of illness, including alcoholism, among employees. I do seem to remember a small booklet on disturbed communication in ailing organizations, but little else. Any ideas, friends? Maybe a short biblio?

Pre-summer, we spent some enjoyable days with Judy and Dave Blackwell in the Gatineau hills, and an evening with Sayoko and Hideo Mimoto. Judy/David introduced us to David Kilgour, PC adviser on foreign affairs, who had a strong interest in the Sikh community. I told him of the ten gurus, and how their scriptures are the poetry of Kabir set to music. He asked where I'd cornered this arcane knowledge, and while Judy raised her eyebrows to signal, "You're giving him the wrong answer," I shrugged it off with, "Oh, I used to have a Sikh girlfriend." Turned out that David Kilgour is a relative of Big Christine, one of my favourite people from the old Rivendell Commune. So he spoke with someone near the top of Overseas Aid, and I promptly got a phone call asking if I'd like a posting to some needy corner of the spitball.

In San Francisco, Jean-Louis Huot continues to produce amazing calligraphy, and may at some point consider collaborating on the *I Ching Sonnets*. My Chinese doesn't qualify as good signpainting, let alone calligraphy. The sonnets are the last major work, and have been followed only by a few Tantric haiku. A nice combination of Tibetan and Japanese, that...

Hideo sent the latest of Dr Taniguchi's scripts for proofreading. These books are about as close as anyone has come to absolute idealism, and form the basis of an organization known as Seicho no Ie. The first one I proofed some years ago was printed with a 'thank-you' from Dr T.; a year later, by way of Japan, came a letter from one Jerry Sachs, who had been at Prof. Szekely's Mexican colony at the same time as myself. Sometimes I consider it odd that a radical pragmatist should be donating time to an absolute idealist; however, I've never been great at selecting friends according to their ideology. More than that, I think it's an even less acceptable habit now than it might have been a quarter-century ago. Ideology is increasingly suspect; I seem to need a lot of distilling apparatus applied to the bits of daily living I'm aware of, before I can make a philosophical-sounding remark about anything much.

On our twenty-acre hill-and-gully, summer is prolific, with the exception of a mysterious rot which has eliminated four-fifths of the tomato plants. Luckily, one flat of seeds refused to germinate normally. The plants are being potted, and will grow inside the south windows. Landscaping: we've been told about a rhododendron type, PJM, which can stand -60 F., and are considering it as a road border. In the patio boxes, Evening Scented Stock, known to our British friends, responds aromatically to a good watering. The Pennsylvania Crown Vetch on the garden side-hills is a mass of clover-like blossoms with small leaves resembling wild pea. The illustrations show it as a vigorous but low carpet about a foot high. These things bush up to 4', with only cornflower (wild chicory) topping them. We use both tractors, the 16-h.p. MTD gas, and the much heavier 23-h.p. Kubota diesel, to keep the road and garden civilized.

Son Eric, fairly well recuperated from his back injury, continues just down the road, and daughter Lora will visit during September on her way to Sweden.

Grandchildren Brady and Julie come by to play Cookie Monster with grampa, while gramma dunks them in the tub. Veronica continues to read Freud in the ten-volume original, and is starting on a two-volume set of translations from Russian literature of the last fifty years. Social work, psychiatric type, has not yet called her back; Clif suggests her skills should be used in teaching and consulting, rather than the direct-to-client casework which has a fine potential for burning out the therapist in this heavily disturbed area.

Clif plays on with two of his corporate inventions: COMBO is a labour-management consortium promoting a systematic assessment/referral/case management method through labour unions and management. The approach offers relief from the adversary stance, and has potential to move the disturbed employee in the direction of earlier treatment. SAGE, based on the Berkeley experiments of Gay Gaer Luce and others with creative seniors, currently consists of a marvelously various core group of ten, developing patterns of interpersonal support and encouragement which will later be extended to similar groups. In the wings, says Clif, is the biggest dream of all; the loom and skeins are ready, the shuttle not yet flying. Keep tuned to this station, and pile up the box tops for your shot at the grand prize.

RICHMOND RESOURCE, incorporated as the FREDERICK STREET CENTRE, looks healthier than ever on the physical plane, with completely renovated building and grounds. This multi-service centre resulted from provision of a fifteen-room building for a staff of four. The imaginative organization engineering this combination then thoughtfully picked up much of the tab for keeping the empty space occupied by doings of good deeds.

SCATTERED SOULS: Morrisons in Thunder Bay keep us in touch with cards and newsletters. Bill and Kay Kopp meander from Florida to Cape Cod. Avel Goldsmith reportedly grows lichen-fungus gardens in Miami. Dick Bennett has retreated into another remodelled penthouse after sending a deliriously offbeat book, *Sanatorium Under the Sign of the Hourglass*, which caused a Polish friend to ascend to heights of delightful hysterics. The book is now with the shop steward of a Steelworkers local who runs an art gallery in his spare time. Visits from our Ojibway friends, including Clif's spirit child, Sarah; all the kids chose to sleep over with us on the hill, with the adults bunking at Mark & Christine's in Rama. Glorious Gloria, although she lives down the road, we see occasionally, with bright and active children Simon and Misha. Pam and Cilia haven't yet made it here this summer; time and suitable season have yet to mesh gears. Carol Ann says: let's have lunch sometime. Groenevelds summer cabining one or two counties over, with Judith hammering out her Ph.D. thesis. So goes life in our Petrie Jar, pseudopod-deep in the agar of existence.

Sixty Second Sermons

NEST OF CHINESE BOXES

My friend has marked his copy of *Aquarian Conspiracy* at the point where Ferguson quotes one translation of the *Tao te Ching*: "The Tao that can be described is not the Tao…"

The author has used this quote to illustrate the wisdom that a transcendental experience cannot truly be communicated, but must be experienced. Perhaps, in one sense, the process has something in common with an unintended pun: you can't take it by frontal assault, but preferably by letting it sneak up on you.

Use of the quoted phrase from the Taoist canon presents the difficulty of communication at an even deeper level than the author probably intended. Holmes Welch, for one, has indicated the near-impossibility of translation from the traditional Chinese writings, and most specifically from the *Tao te Ching*.

"Tao Tao'd no Tao." This, according to Welch, comes about as close as we're likely to get to the original Chinese characters, given a written language with no punctuation, singulars/plurals or other niceties of grammatical construction. A Berlitz immersion course appears woefully inadequate, with something like a five-year plan of immersion in the culture itself recommended.

During the Great Proletarian Cultural Revolution, the activists used a phrase which was widely translated as "Journey to the countryside." The idea was that city intellectuals ought to go out into farming country and get their hands dirty during those seasons when labour was in peak demand.

Going through a beginner's book on Chinese, I hit a page where the original of that slogan jumped out at me. It jumped out because it happens to be composed of very simple characters which by great good luck, I know. What it appears to say is: "Up mountain down go."

It's probable *that* experience of discovery will never be forgotten, mainly because I got there by myself (with considerable publishing help from my friends at Foreign Languages Press in Beijing.) There's a delightful tickle in finding, even in these sudden small illuminations, that something is other than it seems.

Once there were two of us who believed we had individually, and in quite different ways, experienced *satori*. Since we both shared common backgrounds and interests in the area of Japanese Buddhism, we thought it might be possible to share the essence of the two events. We walked away from that one shaking our heads, and wondering how much of anything at all we really knew of one another.

Ferguson is right, and even more right than she thinks. Translating the core of *satori*, medieval illumination, the transcendental event for the best of friends remains *like*, but beyond, explanation of that Chinese nest of boxed puns in Shaun's fable of the Ondt and the Gracehoper packaged in *Finnegan's Wake*.

METAPHYSICS

Instead of packaging a lot of slowly-congealing and still-mushy 'hard metaphysics', how about one sample and a background note?

For starters, the word's taken for what it says: beyond physics. *Beyond*, not against. Or *after*, following acceptance, not denial, of the physical world. To say it another way: the systematic translation of human experience and its implications into active life.

Such a starting point, held to with a reasonable consistency, can be expected to produce some indicators in language-use. I can't speak with any knowledge of the 'spiritual.' Even as a clergyman, I doubt the word or concept ever got much workout in my sermons.

But I can deal with the *para*natural. That's a lovely Sanskrit root, suggesting in one breath or slightly less: to grow out of, to co-exist with, to move beyond, and to supersede.

This much because both the good people of Canada and the *Soviet Encyclopedia* popularly define metaphysics as obscure, mystical, theological and occult.

So a hard metaphysics can refer to human experience, and its language should sound concrete, everyday, unspecialized, catholic in the finest sense.

One winter evening, hunting for my friend Alfred (and for Alfred's house) on top of a Vermont mountain, dusk and reality struck at the same time: I'd climbed the wrong mountain. Excusable, since a number of winters had passed since my last visit – but excuses of that kind don't impress the thermometer, and it was getting cold.

Alfred had said, "Keep your eyes open. Really take a good, long look around. If you're in a pickle, I've found there's always *something* in the surround that'll help me work it out."

As the last of the daylight went, I followed a faint trail around an elbow of the montain to a small ski hut with a straw mattress. With the light tarp and reflector blanket in my pack, I slept reasonably well. Humanist, yes. A live humanist, who takes a close look at the physical environment before going on.

NOT TONIGHT, JOSEPHINE

Reading Norman Cantor on the similarity of the Middle Ages to us in 2000, and listening to one of the TV rundowns on Y2K panic, what jumps out is the scarcity of effect compared to the explosion of affect.

On the impressionist side of the palette, we and medieval Europe share a dog's breakfast of emotions: fear, powerlessness, paranoia.

They were religion-centred, expected the apocalyptic bolts to be hurled by Jehovah and His angels. We are technology-centred, expect our malfunctioning robots to bring us down. As we once believed ourselves made in God's image, so we have made our robots in our image – and seemingly as short-sighted.

Local housewives invested hectic hours stocking up on candles, canned beans and bottled water. Great stuff for the consumer index.

In a thousand years, we may even have gone backward.

Beyond a certain amount/level of learning/experiencing, is a paradox: as the warehouse fills, the manager finds it harder to scramble over the stock to meet the customers.

The manager can talk trade with other managers, but the extent of sharing will be shaped by similarities in the nature and quantity of items catalogued – and sometimes even by the design of the catalogue.

For the townsmen who walk the streets outside, the purpose of those many-acred structures is unclear. Occasional sight of the manager's face at a window gives life to legends of ghosts or aliens, whose shadowy motivations hint at undiscovered worlds, perhaps undiscoverable.

One such isolated entrepreneur, aware that for years he himself had been seen as an outsider and incommunicado, developed an original theory about the hulks of discarded motor cars. These, he reasoned, were the exoskeletons of salesmen from another planet, who had found them a handicap in earth gravity.

- It has no aim or goal, no object to win nor victory to gain.
  Possession it does not know – nor loss.
  What is offered is realization: recognize and accept.
- The reward is immediate, complete – yours in the moment of awareness.

What is exchanged for this gift? Only thanks for the already attained.
- Family, church, school, work: made in the toy factory of the human mind.
Will your toys control you? You have created them. Laugh and play.
- Guilt, remorse, confession, restitution? There are other ways to wholeness.
Such skills may be learned.

REVOLT OF THE ILLITERATI

The bus pulls over to the curb, and the line of potential passengers disintegrates into a mob shoving for the door. A small, tubby woman, both arms crammed with bundles, surges ahead, planting herself dead centre in the bus door. Craning her neck up toward the driver, she asks, "Dis bos guzz Delancih Stritt?" He nods. A sign on the front of the bus reads, in letters eight inches high, "DELANCEY STREET."

This exchange bothers me, because it never seems possible to conclude whether the woman is seeking the *truth*, looking for something that will be *useful*, or simply soliciting *reassurance* that the rules which were good yesterday are still operative today. I'm able to sleep well at night by reasoning that she means all three, and that most of us in similar situations percolate on at least three cylinders: truth, faith and works.

The Truth-vs.-Utility argument looks like one more of those clashes by night between polar ideals which replace the real world of bus stops and sweating commuters. Nothing seems to upset the ignorant armies more than the potential conscript who smilingly says, "I'll sit this one out."

There appear to be distinguishing styles on each side of the ideal fence. He who opts for Truth spends a lot of time defining nouns like Time, Place, and Person. The Utility buff goes for no-nonsense everyday language, and tries to let the experience define itself. He's apt to favour Anglo-Saxon words that sound like the thing they represent, while the champion of Truth goes in for Latin-based holdovers from the theological debates of the Middle Ages.

JOKER IN THE PACK

...the guard in the elevated observation cage accidentally dropped his loaded pump-action shotgun into the room...The prisoners stared in stunned silence. And then, one of them laughed. Everybody just broke up – they were rolling on the floor. It was incredible...

Globe and Mail, February 8, 1980
Article on B.C. Penitentiary

Laughter dulls the edge of tension, or makes it bearable. Where overwhelming physical force in the hands of the opposition makes large-scale revolt suicidal, or where the scene is a maximum-custody institution, the joker in the pack can keep rebellion simmering away below the boiling point, conserving valuable energies for another day.

This much the *agents provocateurs* and their masters have recognized intuitively, itching to lead the resistance into a violent *cul de sac* and expend its potential on romantic and nominal gestures with no structural payoff. Repeatedly, where the rebels had little in the way of explosives or technical knowledge, the forces of law and order have obligingly furnished the missing items. The Keable inquiry reveals that these techniques of the Interpol collaborators are (one hopes amateurishly and uneasily) at home in Canada.

Laughter aimed in the right direction can also be a weapon. Those who have overplayed their hand, transforming themselves into violent gargoyles and repressive caricatures, helpfully offer their posturing as comic relief.

THE ARCHITECTURE OF CONTROL

"The most important part of Fascism,is absolute trust in a sagely able leader...Therefore, the leader will naturally be a great person and possess a revolutionary spirit, so that he serves as a model for all party members. Furthermore, each member must sacrifice everything... From the day we joined this revolutionary group, we completely entrusted our rights, life, liberty, and happiness to the group, and pledged them to the leader...Thus for the first time we can truly be called Fascist." —Chiang Kai-shek

In the vacuum of metaphysical purpose, control by the paranoid leader extends on both real and fantastic levels from identification of external national enemies to internal institutional menaces (communists, unionists, jews) and on down to micro-biology (Hitler's preoccupation with cancer and possible viral infections).

The level of control necessary to the leader's comfort requires, on both the conscious and intuitive level, a breaking up and re-shuffling of traditional and customary social elements. This may be seen as an analog to ritual handwashing, or to the obsessive re-arranging of physical items on a desk or table.

While the verbal decorations of revolution and radical change are invoked, it can be predicted that the only changes permitted will be those which disassemble alternate sources of power and concentrate control in the leadership. Concurrent with these changes, there will be extensive rationalization of the need for an expanding bureaucracy, together with indoctrination and training in the desirability and personal acceptance of organizational mutation. Underlying all such change will be the methodical fragmenting of customary interpersonal relationships.

While inquiries on how most acceptably to carry out instructions are welcomed, two kinds of questioning are outlawed:
1. What kind, depth, and extent of change creates an unhealthy organizational environment?
2. Are the basic assumptions of this institution valid?

The first question presupposes some limitation on the leader's ability to specify change comfortable to himself. It is consequently unacceptable and dysfunctional for the needs of paranoid and obsessive leadership.

The second question discomfits the apologist who advertises that, "What's good for General Motors is good for the nation."

Nevertheless, these are the two questions which today must be asked.

A Slow Afternoon in the Snowflake Factory

"...and what," she inquired, "makes you think you're not being given every normal consideration due a client?"

He shifted uneasily in the ornately-carved chair of dark mahogany, rearranging his feet in their black patent-leather shoes a bit more solidly on the maroon carpeting, as though to solidify, to improve balance, to get some imprimatur of additional reality.

"Well," he began, "it isn't exactly that – but maybe, for starters, you could tell me what the interview's about?"

"You feel you're just here as a visitor," she murmured around the line of pins held between her lips.

"I don't know," he replied, shrugging his shoulders slightly. "It's just..." The remaining words, if any, trailed off. He felt horrified at the thought that, if he encouraged her to talk, she might swallow one of the hazardous pins, and he couldn't handle what would happen then, he knew he couldn't.

As though she had been rummaging inside his mind, she removed the last of the pins, tacking down one of the arms of a chillingly lovely, but convoluted, snowflake, and said, "Could you please hand me the cigarette next your elbow, there?"

"It's gone out," he observed, picking it from the onyx tray and holding it out to her. A column of ash detached itself, descending into the maroon jungle underfoot.

"It's gone out," she confirmed. He winced. Was there something like blame in the way she said it? He'd only done what she asked. Why should he feel this obscure sense of guilt? Damn it!

"About our talk," he persevered, choking back the near-certainty that he'd done something unforgivable. "Maybe you could tell me when it should start."

"The snowflakes have to dry," she said. "They don't hold their shape unless they're quite dry." She began on another. He noted that no two patterns were the same.

"I thought I could begin by telling you why I think I'm here," he volunteered, squirming in the chair, which had become decidedly uncomfortable. Why did she have to furnish the place with antiques, he wondered, particularly since everything else about her seemed to be so modern, or even ahead of time. Except the snowflakes.

"After lunch," she said. "Sometime after lunch." She seemed to be having difficulty with the newest snowflake, biting her lip, which at the moment held no pins, and bending over to look more closely at the frost-bud.

He slumped back in the chair, flicking off a small scatter of cigarette ash which had settled near the end of one arm. "But that might be anytime," he complained. "Anytime at all."

"You're the one who says time is subjective," she pointed out. "So why not subject yourself to some thinking, or some reading. I've a lovely monograph of René Magritte. Don't you adore his work?"

"Look," he tried, "I know you have important things to do, but you did suggest we pick up where we left off. And I – well, I sort of depended on you to remember where that was."

She peered more closely at the evolving arm of the snowflake, from which he took a certain comfort. Perhaps, instead of the usual notes of Client Presenting Problem,

Diagnosis, Recommended Treatment and Prognosis, she coded the whole thing into the varying patterns of crystalline beauty? Ridiculous. But there she was, squinting intently at the fine traceries of frosty white as though reading off the intricacies of his life.

"Not what I was after, at all," she sighed. "Well, the best-laid plans…"

He stared abstractedly at the snowflake, at all the snowflakes. He coughed, and began to rise from the chair. Something adhered to the seat of his pants. The interview hadn't really started, he felt, and yet it seemed to have ended. He moved uncertainly toward the door, or where he seemed to recall the door having been, out there in the anonymous drifts.

She glanced toward the empty chair. "You've been sitting on my snowflakes!" she screamed.

There is a Story

Why have they sent back a historian who is also a poet? There is little here but a desolation so tangible you can smell it, breathe it, dream it. Even inside the little ship, when I sleep, it creeps over me and whispers like the sand that moves slowly outside. Is it day? Is it night? There is only a single static moment in all this murk, hovering always on the edge of a final nightfall, never quite entering that last resting.

There is a story that once all this was like an emerald, that from space it shone. A prize. A jewel. And when the first ships lifted on their crude rockets, someone pointed a camera thing back at it, and the picture was valued greatly, and duplicated many times, and seen everywhere.

Nothing to see. No prize. No jewel. No emerald. Did they send me because they call my work Songs From the Void, because they say I can weave the wordweb out of emptiness? Did they send me because, like the little ship, I am driven by a force I hardly understand, a curiosity, a need to know, a hunger unsatisfied?

So I sleep when I sleep, and my cycles may follow those of the folk who lived here once, or they may not. Probably they do, since through many changes and much time and more than enough space I remain a distant child of those who laughed and played and made their different musics echo across these Plains of Nothing.

But I have found something. It is a thing I do not fully understand. It is art, but it does not please me. It is a poem in hard stone, and the sound of it is harsh in my ears. I have cleared the sand away from it, and in the halflight I stand, or sit, or walk about it, and look and wonder.

Among the historians of times that have gone into mists and smokes and wraiths, there is a story about those whose insubstantial hands may have used the chisels and mallets to shape this shriek across the broken bridge. They say things like this were a part of old worshipping, that this is a statement of what was valuable, what moved at the core of their days, what shaped their being in their aloneness and their togetherness. If so, I do not understand them. Forgive me, brothers, but I do not know that I want to understand them.

In the centre of the fragment is a pleading face. The bearded head is tilted back and upward on the bunched cords of the neck, and the muscles of the face have contorted it into a grimace of terminal pain. The great eyes tunnel into the sky, searching for a single vagrant ray of hope. With all the scouring the sands have done, they have not erased the knots of horror that everywhere under lie the granite skin.

I think of the artist, sense the power in his mind and in his hands. I know that my people came from among these, but they were not of them. What is it I feel for the artist and his kind? If this torment is the symbol they carried through all their days, is my feeling compassion? With this thing hovering behind all they did, how could they know any complete and lasting joy? If this is what each saw under the planes and curves, among the shadows and highlights dancing on the features of those they loved, what could life have meant to them, other than a torment to be endured?

I am trying to feel what they must have felt, to do a thing like this. They were, perhaps, a people who carried a curse they had delivered against themselves. Knowing they could not escape it, they laboured to dull it, partially to exorcise it through their art, to shape it into something immobile that could no longer move within them and between them. I do not think they succeeded.

There is a story that this carving shows the death of a god of the goyim. Some say there were three of them, or maybe five.

Anyone Can Be Arthur Mandelbaum

When it first showed up, I took it around to Jack. He was the one who turned me on to it, anyway, handing me an armload of those fringe magazines ranting about punk rock, conspiracies, dark humour, and nineteen new ways to save the world by next Sunday.

"Who," I asked my all-knowing friend, "is this guy Mandelbaum?"

"What's with Mandelbaum?" he grinned. "You run into a half dozen bits by him?"

"More like a gross and a half. He's got letters to the editor, book reviews, short stories, lead articles. Arthur Mandelbaum has opinions on punk, post-punk and neo-punk. His ideas on the visual arts, including film, video, Fax and found are all over the lot. He even pops up in editorials."

"Relax," advised Jack. "Anyone can be Mandelbaum."

And he explained that, back in the days when the authorities still hung onto something they called censorship, under the illusion that electrons could be stopped at border crossings, an anarchist publication somewhere out in Missouri, U.S.A., had invented Arthur Mandelbaum, with all the five-member editorial collective publishing under that name. The idea caught on; soon a dozen, then several dozen, then a brigade of Mandelbaums appeared in print, migrating to other countries.

"The story goes," added Jack, "that the guy who originated it was tossed out of the collective. They claimed he'd worked entirely too hard to develop a persona for his invention. A cult of personality, or something, they called it."

I laughed, finished my drink and went my way. But something in the story stayed with me, and I decided to fill in time doing Mandelbaum research. Maybe I should have expected what I found.

Cult of personality, indeed! The Mandelbaum story was remarkably consistent. A.M., as I came to think of him, had more character, background and consistent opinions than most of the big names in the mass media. Three or four little magazines had even reproduced what they claimed were photos of the guy. Comparing them, I found remarkable similarities.

According to these mug shots, A.M. looked to be on the short side, chubby, dark-haired, with a neatly-trimmed small moustache, heavy brows and a habit of staring directly into the lens with a little smile at some secret joke crinkling the outer corners of his eyes. A tendency to heaviness around the jowls suggested he could also be paunchy.

Indicative? Meaningless but compelling? Whatever, I got well immersed in Mandelbaum studies. Luckily, with a good retirement pension, I could afford a whim or two. Or, it *was* a whim – and I'd have laughed at anyone calling it an obsession – until I got my first glimpse of him.

On Labour Day, picking up the latest number of *Beyond Punk* at one of the funky newsstands, I saw him going by in the street crowd. Looked exactly as I thought he would, had a slightly preoccupied air about him, strode along, paunch and all, with a certain pedestrian dignity. I ran after him.

"Excuse me," I gasped, "but aren't you Arthur Mandelbaum?"

His eyes, with that tinge of sardonic smile, did a *National Geographic* on me.

"Yes," he said, with a kind of questioning "so what" lilt.

My mouth fell open. I stared at him while several people jostled us. Finally, he shrugged, turned and moved off into the crowd. I felt invaded by a slight case of rigor mortis.

The newsstand operator, who had caught up with me, tapped me on the shoulder. "I'm sorry," he said, "but you forgot to pay for the magazine." I noticed for the first time that he'd started growing a moustache.

On the way home, my bus held three others who looked like Mandelbaum. To varying degrees, of course, and it took me a week to overcome my uneasiness each time I considered talking it over with Jack. Who but I would have noticed in the first place? And what could, or should, be done about it?

But I finally jumped past the shadow of my own ego, and built up enough, steam to get over to Jack's place. I still felt slightly idiotic as I pressed his door buzzer.

Jack listened. Well, there may have been a little quirk of a wry grin, but he looked thoughtful after hearing my blurted story, then nodded slowly.

"Did I ever tell you about the Andrick Gambit?" he asked. "That's one of those things that says you can't take something away without putting something of equal value in its place. Otherwise, you cause an imbalance that may take a long time righting itself – but right itself, it will.

"So, Arthur Mandelbaum, all the Arthur Mandelbaums, are a replacement for the extermination camp inmates, the gas chamber people. OK, so I can't prove it, and it's farther out than what I take to be Mandelbaum's preferences in music and art. But are you gonna tell me this is a normal world?"

During the next several weeks, I:

a) Developed a strong interest in the work of an experimental heavy metal group with the imaginative tag of *Dismembered and the Body Parts*. Dis goes rocketing back to the source of all Western experimental music, Charles Ives. Its lead guitarist, who is also their vocalist, defies the pop cliché by hugging the ground, being tubbier, and sporting a small moustache below his impressive eyebrows.
b) Visited two exhibits of anti-market mailart, collages and other electronic salients into the world formerly controlled by the Louvre and Berlin-Dahlem Gallery.
c) Noticed, while shaving, that I do have a barely detectable set of fine wrinkles at the eye corners, making it appear that I'm quite amused at the antics of the world. I tend to hesitate when shaving below the nose.

The F.B.I. –
The Basis of an American Police State
The Alarming Methods of J. Edgar Hoover

I. THE ORGANIZATION

Tommy-guns held in hair-trigger readiness, the Federal Agents waited for the signal of their leader. In the darkness ahead, they heard a stealthy footstep, then another. A group of men took shadowy form. The leader of the G-Men spoke sharply, commandingly.

"Halt! Stand where you are and put up your hands!"
"Put 'em up yourself."
"Halt, I said – this is the F.B.I.!"
"Halt, yourself. This is the Indiana State Police."

Repeating a familiar pattern, the G-Men had failed to notify State Police that they would be operating in the area. As a result, each group mistook the other for the Dillinger mob, and were ready to shoot it out at the drop of a fingerprint.[1]

Hunting down Dillingers has provided the Federal Bureau of Investigation with most of the romantic publicity that has gone into the making of countless front pages, movies and comic books glorifying the G-Man. Such crime-chasing, however, is not the whole story.

Known at its founding in 1908 as the Bureau of Investigation, the organization grew slowly until 1924, picking up bits of additional power along the way through passage of the White Slave Traffic Act of 1910, and the National Motor Vehicle Theft Act of 1919. The Bureau took its present form in 1924 following the connection of Attorney General Daugherty and Bureau agents with the Teapot Dome oil scandals and the American Metal Company manipulations under the Harding administration.[2]

The new Attorney General, Harlan F. Stone—later Chief Justice of the Supreme Court—appointed J. Edgar Hoover Director of the reorganized Bureau, with orders to clean it up, introduce promotions on merit and eliminate political influence. Mr. Hoover did all these things and many more, with the sure instinct of a master showman for anything that would put more power in the hands of his organization.

In 1924, there were not more than 600 employees in the Bureau. The Federal Budget for 1948 provided for more than 10,000. In 1924, there were 810,188 fingerprints in the records. Today there are more than 103,020,000. In its first year of operation under Hoover, the Bureau spent slightly over $2,000,000. It cost less than $50,000,000 for the whole 15-year period, 1924-1939. The 1948 Budget calls for that amount for one year, after Hoover's share of the Government-employee witch- burning is added to the figures.

The greatest period of F.B.I. growth came under the Roosevelt administration as part of the New Deal trend toward federal power. The setting up of the Social Security files provided the F.B.I., with a convenient cross-check on their growing fingerprint collection. Contrary to popular belief, the Social Security records are available to the Bureau, and have been extensively used by them. Universal fingerprinting, one of J. Edgar Hoover's most enthusiastic projects, is well under way with a majority of Americans already neatly filed for future reference. Beginning in 1939-40, the War Department, Navy Department and Marine Corps filed prints of all incoming personnel with the Bureau. Prints of workers in war industries added to the collection; and in 1940 the Alien Registration Act further swelled the personnel ranks, the power of the Director and the Budget estimates.

II. THE SPECIAL AGENT

The age of the average G-Man is 34. He must be a graduate of a recognized law school or a member of the Bar, with at least two years of legal or business experience, or he must be a graduate of a recognized accounting school with three years of commercial accounting or auditing experience. In practice, these requirements have been considerably relaxed in recent years.

The G-Man's starting wage is about $65-70 a week, and his finishing wage is not much higher. Leon G. Turrou, one of the few men in the Bureau who managed to get some of the publicity usually cornered by Hoover, was earning $4,500 a year as one of the oldest and most trusted Special Agents at the time of his "separation with prejudice" over articles written by him for a newspaper chain.

G-Men, who prefer to be called Special Agents of the Department of Justice, are usually recruited through the regular publicity of the Bureau, or through speakers sent to address Senior classes at law schools. It is claimed that approximately one out of a thousand applicants is ultimately accepted into the Bureau. They have a high degree of personal loyalty to the Bureau Director.

University degrees are held by approximately 78 percent of the men, who must attend a 14-week training school at Quantico, Virginia, and at the Washington headquarters. J. Edgar Hoover and four other persons make up the regular faculty. Listed as a Visiting Faculty Member is J. P. Allman, Commissioner of the Chicago Police at the time of the Memorial Day Massacre in 1937, whom Philip Murray charged with the murder of the seven Republic Steel strikers. Commissioner Allman is presented as a specialist on Parades, Assemblies and Emergencies."

The F.B.I. booklet on "Training Schools and Selection of Personnel," which provides us with this information on the varied requirements and education of a G-Man, also tells us that:

> "The diversified qualifications are very important, particularly when the records of the Bureau reflect instances wherein an expert violinist was able to soften

the heart of a mountaineer with his music and cause him to disclose the whereabouts of his son, who was a fugitive from justice ..."

The younger and more recently acquired Special Agents are a much smoother set of operators than the City Detective. They rarely resort to the use of force in questioning. Criminals refer to them as "super con-men."

In addition to their use of "psychology" in place of the third degree, many F.B.I. operatives are marked by a youthful amateurishness and over-dramatization of their role. A recent example is the wire-tapping case involving Harry Bridges.

Section 14, Manual of Rules and Regulations of the Bureau of Investigation of the Department of Justice, as issued-June 17, 1930, reads:

> "Wiretapping, entrapment, or the use of any illegal or unethical tactics in procuring information will not be tolerated by the Bureau."

This section appeared in the Manual since 1923, and Director Hoover displayed admirable familiarity with the publications of his Bureau when questioned by Rep. Tinkham before a subcommittee on December 2, 1929. He stated:

> "We have a very definite rule in the Bureau that any employee engaging in wiretapping will be dismissed from the service of the Bureau. While it may not be illegal, I think it is unethical and it is not permitted under the regulations by the Attorney General."[3]

The Senate Interstate Commerce Committee reported on the same question, that "Wiretapping, dictographing and similar devices are especially dangerous at the present time, because of the recent resurgence of a spy system conducted by government police. Wiretapping and other unethical devices may...have the effect of increasing the power of law enforcement agencies to oppress factory employees who are under investigation, not for any criminal action, but only by reason of their views and activities in regard to labor unions and other economic movements; this is no fanciful case—such investigations are a fact today."

Justice Brandeis, writing a minority opinion on the Olmstead case, reported that "The evil incident to invasion of the privacy of the telephone is far greater than that involved in tampering with the mails. ...And it is also immaterial that the intrusion (wiretapping) was in aid of law enforcement. Experience should teach us to be most on guard to protect liberty when the government's purposes are beneficent. Men born to freedom are naturally alert to repel invasion of their liberty by evil-minded rulers. The greatest dangers to liberty lurk in insidious encroachment by men of zeal, well leaning, but without understanding."[4]

With that background on wiretapping, let us see what happened to Harry Bridges, shadowed because of deportation proceedings. After finding evidence that his hotel telephone had been tapped, and establishing the presence of two Federal agents in the room next to his, he turned the tables on them by trailing them to Foley Square F.B.I. headquarters where they submitted their reports. Bridges took a good pair of field glasses and some witnesses to the roof of a building opposite his hotel, and described the occasion:

"I spotted my room at the Edison easily enough with the field glasses because I had left some stuff on the window sill which I could recognize. Then I moved the glasses over to the room next to mine and there were the two guys, stretched out on the twin beds with their earphones on, thinking I was still in the room...

"Well, so we would tear up old letters and things and the next morning leave them in my room at the Edison, and then that after noon we'd see one of the F.B.I. men sitting at the table at the window in his room pasting little pieces of paper together. A couple of times I tore things up in the shape of six pointed stars, or five-pointed stars, or in the shape of a row of paper dolls... Then we'd see this F.B.I. guy holding up the stars and the rows of dolls next day at the window, studying them... "[5].

In spite of all the pretty talk about ethics, wiretapping was nothing new in the life of an F.B.I. agent. Ten years prior to the Bridges incident, Rep. Clancy told the House of Representatives:

> "It was Mrs. Willebrandt (Assistant Attorney General) who put spies and agents of the Department of Justice from the Pacific Coast to watch high Federal officials of the Treasury Department in Michigan. I am told on good authority that it was she who ordered the tapping of telephone wires of the highest Federal official of Michigan, the Collector of Customs."[6]

All of this without any knowledge on the part of the Attorney General or the Director of the Federal Bureau of Investigation, of course.

Following the Pearl Harbor fiasco, J. Edgar Hoover, found negligent in the Roberts Report, contended that his agents had been out-smarted by the Japanese because they did not have the right to tap wires. No ethical considerations seemed to be bothering him at the moment, and Congressman Celler rushed to oblige with a bill which would put the OK on Federals who might want to make a party line out of your hook-up. It didn't pass, but failure to obtain Congressional sanction didn't bother J. Edgar or his agents, who kept right on tapping wires right and left.

According to the 1948 Budget, there were 7,201 of these wire-tapping Federal Sherlocks with "diversified qualifications" in the field, backed by another 3,580 departmental employees. That doesn't include the full personnel needed to carry out President Truman's Executive Order against subversives in government employment.

III. THE DIRECTOR

At George Washington University, J. Edgar Hoover committed The Perfect Crime. Although the Office of the Registrar will affirm that he did attend a night school law course, obtaining an LL.B. in 1916 and LL.M. in 1917, there is no other visible record of his passage. According to the university library, he wrote no thesis for either degree. And the annual classbook for his year was omitted because of a financial crisis. At the Library of the College of Law, however, there is a fat folder containing all the major speeches made by the Bureau Director over a period of 10 years; one copy of each having been sent most conscientiously to the librarian of his alma mater.

John Edgar Hoover, born in Washington, D. C, January 1, 1895, has spent most of his life right there. Product of a home atmosphere which seems to have been religious fundamentalist to the extreme, he still reflects his early training for the clergy in speeches and articles on crime, patriotism and the American Home.

At Central High School, "Speed," as he was nicknamed, became captain of the cadet corps and valedictorian of his class. Although the smallest boy in his cadet company, it has been claimed that during drill he displayed the loudest voice in the school.

At the University, he showed great interest in athletics, particularly baseball, and became head of the Kappa Alpha fraternity chapter. William Gaxton, the actor, who stayed at the fraternity house, remarked that "'Speed' chastised us with his morality." He was what Horatio Alger would have called a model of young American manhood.

Hoover has a phenomenal memory and a machine-gun delivery in speaking. He is said to suffer acute stage fright prior to a talk, but the violent content of his speeches fails to indicate any sign of it. He is obsessed by a persecution complex which shows up in many of his addresses.

On the radio in his office is a framed sentiment entitled The Penalty of Leadership, which undoubtedly reflects his own attitude:

> "In every field of human endeavor, he that is first must perpetually live in the white light of publicity... When a man's work becomes a standard for the whole world, it also becomes a target for the shafts of the envious few."[7]

Most of Hoover's time in Washington since 1917 has been spent in the Department of Justice Building, where he started as a file clerk. It is doubtful that he could meet his own requirements for Bureau agents, unless a clerking period with the Congressional Library can be stretched into "two years of legal or business experience," and a night school law degree sans thesis be transformed into a college education.

In the Department of Justice, he was first connected with wartime counter-espionage, and advanced by 1919 to direct the General Intelligence Division of the Department. This is the Division which was ordered disbanded when the Daugherty scandals revealed its use as a political police.

In 1921, Hoover was Assistant Director of the Bureau of Investigation, then headed by William J. Burns. As a Special Assistant to Attorney General A. Mitchell Palmer, Hoover gave a hand to the notorious "Red Raids" of the early '20's, in which over 6,000 persons were jailed on warrants secured from the Department of Labor. That is, some of them were jailed on warrants. In other cases, the formality of a warrant was dispensed with.

Among the sinister meetings raided was one in New England called to plan for the establishment of a cooperative bakery. In Boston, several hundred prisoners were paraded through the streets in chains to afford dramatic material for the news photographers.[8]

Describing one of the raids made by Department of Justice agents, a sworn statement backed by over 100 witnesses sketches the brutal attack on the Russian People's House in New York City, made on November 7, 1919:

> "The Department agents had a few warrants for the arrest of supposed offenders, but upon entering the building they tore off and broke up the stair railing, arming themselves with bludgeons thus made, and went through the whole building, breaking up all the different classes engaged in educational work ... and broke up and destroyed all the furniture in the place, including desks and some typewriting machines. They beat up the persons in the place... and herded the students to the stairways, beating them as they went, shoving them off the landings on to the stairway in such a manner that many fell and rolled down the stairway... the Department agents beating them as they fell..." [9]

In defense of J. Edgar Hoover, it has been said that his part in the raids consisted solely in carrying out the orders of his superiors. That sort of defense, however, was not good enough to save the lesser Nazis during the Nuremburg War Guilt trials. Moreover, it can be shown from sworn statements and from records of the Bureau, that J. Edgar. Hoover knew more about what was going on than Palmer himself, and that Palmer had to keep Hoover by his side throughout questioning by the Senate Committee on the Judiciary, referring to him constantly for the facts desired.

> The main point of contention between the Senate investigators and the Department of Justice was the manner in which warrants for search and arrest were issued and used. The testimony shows that this was precisely the field in which Hoover had full responsibility:
>
> "Senator WALSH: How many search warrants were issued?
>
> "Attorney General PALMER: I cannot tell you, Senator, personally. If you would like to ask Mr. Hoover, who was in charge of this matter, he can tell you."[10]

Mr. Hoover, who had previously displayed a really amazing grasp of everything that had gone into the making of the raids, together with the legal background and responsibilities of various government departments, here developed an obliging lack of memory.

A letter signed by Frank Burke, as Chief of the Bureau of Investigation, and addressed to George E. Kelleher, Division Superintendent of the Boston Branch, Bureau of Investigation, names Hoover as the raid coordinator at headquarters in Washington, and also outlines the manner of raiding:

> "I have already transmitted to you two briefs prepared in this department upon the Communist Party of America and the Communist Labor Party ... at the appointed time you will be advised by me by wire when to take into custody all persons for whom warrants have been issued.
>
> "It is ... of the utmost importance that you at once make every effort to ascertain the location of all of the books and records of these organizations in your territory and that the same be secured at the time of the arrests...
>
> "Particular efforts are to be made to apprehend all of the officers of either of these two parties if they are aliens; the residences of such officers should be searched in every instance for literature, membership cards, records and correspondence. The meeting rooms should be thoroughly searched ... All literature, books, papers, and anything hanging on the walls should be gathered up; the ceilings and partitions should be sounded for hiding places.
>
> "I have made mention above that the meeting places and residences of the members should be thoroughly searched. I leave it entirely to your discretion as to the methods by which you should gain access to such places.

"Under no conditions are you to take into your confidence the local police authorities or the State authorities prior to the making of the arrests.

"If possible you should arrange with your undercover informants to have meetings of the Communist Party and the Communist Labor Party held on the night set. This, of course, would facilitate the making of the arrests.

"On the evening of the arrests, this office will be open the entire night, and I desire that you communicate long distance to Mr. Hoover any matter of vital importance ...

"I desire that the morning following the arrests you should forward to this office by special delivery marked for the 'Attention of Mr. Hoover' a complete list of the names of persons arrested ... In cases where arrests are made of persons not covered by warrants, you should at once request the local immigration authorities for warrants ... I desire also that the morning following the arrests that you communicate in detail by telegram, 'Attention of Mr. Hoover,' the results of the arrests made ... together with a statement of any interesting evidence secured."[11]

Memoranda from Special Agents for use in defending Palmer's handling of the raids were also addressed to Mr. Hoover. Some of the charges of illegal practices by the United States Department of Justice, made by the Popular Government League and American Civil Liberties Union, included:

1. Cruel and unusual punishment.
2. Arrest without warrant.
3. Unreasonable search and seizure.
4. Use of agents provocateur.
5. Compelling persons to witness against themselves.
6. Influencing public opinion in advance of court action.

Summarizing the attitude of the judiciary toward the raids, Federal Judge Anderson said:

> "I refrain from any extended comment on the lawlessness of these proceedings by our supposedly law-enforcing officials. The documents and accounts speak for themselves ... I cannot adopt the contention that government spies are any more trustworthy, or less disposed to make trouble in order to profit therefrom, than are spies in private industry ... A right-minded man refuses such a job."[12]

The public speeches and writings of J. Edgar Hoover are lurid, alarmist and imaginative, with a regard for fact that is almost on a level with the best of Nick Carter. For example, in an address to the Sheriffs' Association, at Tulsa, Oklahoma, January 13, 1936:

> "Prisons are being emptied ... Through this exercise of clemency the law-abiding person becomes all but powerless to escape the predatory actions of vicious human vultures ... It seems beyond the range of human conception that boards of clemency would meet in secret sessions and undo, with the stroke of a pen, the work of fearless law-enforcement officers, the judgment of honest and efficient courts, the desires of the American populace itself, and throw open prison doors to hordes of sneering, desperate convicts whose sole purpose is again to flout the law... Should they again be apprehended, convicted and sentenced, the angels of mercy, who so love freedom for convicts and who so forget the innocent and suffering public, will gently minister to their every desire and soon again throw the locks that will usher them forth to freedom."

From this it is reasonable to suppose that a battalion or two of paroled convicts had been shooting up the scenery. Yet the F.B.I. Law Enforcement Bulletin for the first three months of 1935 – a fairly representative period – listed 90,504 arrests for various crimes, of which only .0059 percent were arrested during parole period. Of the 1,535 arrests for homicide, not one was shown to be on parole.

Some of Hoover's juicier epithets are aimed at "fiddle-faced reformers," "fantastic schemers," "sob-sisters," "convict lovers," "shyster legislators," "convict-indulging theorists," "criminal coddlers," "crackpot politicians," and "sentimentalists." The Director's favorite tag for an opponent is "sentimentalist." His number one adjective for the same is "foul."

In order to let the man speak for himself, representative excerpts from several of his speeches follow. Hoover is always on the side of the practical and hard-headed, be it noted, and against the visionary and the theorist. Practically every speech consists of a set of statistics showing how many murderers are lurking among each 10.3 persons in the audience, an exhortation against parole reformers and crooked politicians who keep harassing Mr. Hoover, and a wind-up appeal for God, Country, and The Good Old-Fashioned American Home.

July 9, 1935, to the International Association of Chiefs of Police:

> "Indeed, it would seem that such enemies were numerous enough and deadly enough without the addition of even a vaster army of antagonists ... I refer to the 'sob-sisters,' the intruders, the uninformed and misinformed know-it-alls, the sentimentalists and the alleged criminologists who believe that the individual is greater than society, that because any criminal can display or simulate even the slightest evidence of ordinary conduct, then indeed he must be a persecuted being, entitled to be sent forth anew into the world to again rob and plunder and murder ... I refer to the countless thousands of unregenerate criminals who, through the subversive acts of convict lovers, have been turned loose to prey anew upon communities often , defenseless because the law-enforcement machinery has been lulled into the belief that these men were still

in prison when in truth they have been secretly released to again go forth upon a new series of depredations."

May 20, 1936, to the Boys' Clubs of America Convention:

"This is what usually happens when the F.B.I. eradicates what I prefer to call not 'public enemies' but 'public rats' ... Each of them has a great gathering of sentimental yammerheads, who utter remonstrances at his apprehension and detection. So long as that asinine behavior continues, I insist that the crime problem as affects youth today, is also a crime problem involving the moronic adults of this country ...

"The sentimental theorists who dominate present-day child guidance, however, believe that if a child is chastised it may develop inhibitions or affect its later self-expression. So long as we fail to recognize that discipline is an essential part of human development just so long will we have an aimless, directionless milling herd which can only result in mental panic and a thorough disregard for the rights of society to peace and order ... I hope you look upon me as old-fashioned in the holding of such beliefs."

April 23, 1936, to the Daughters of the American Revolution:

"Were crime to marshal its forces in a marching body of men, they would tramp ceaselessly past this hall, hour after hour, in daylight and in darkness and back to daylight and darkness again ...

"Not to alarm you, but for your information, there are today in America, 150,000 murderers roaming at large. (Arthur C. Millspaugh of Brookings Institution, citing Uniform Crime Reports, covering 987 of the largest cities, showed that police knew of only 647 cases of criminal homicide not closed by arrests.) Statistics show that during the lifetime of those who form our population, 200,000 – nearly a quarter of a million persons will commit murder before they die and more than 300,000 persons – the population of an entire metropolis—will be murdered. Consider that!

"… And so, I tell the stark truth to you women, who are known for your devotion to the country for which your forefathers gave their blood, and ask, in the name of those sacrifices, that you do your utmost to reinstill a spirit of determination and of self-sacrificing alertness that the loyalty to America, the fidelity to ideals, and the unfaltering courage which gave us Bunker Hill and Valley Forge may be reestablished.

"There can be no weeding out of noxious growths until the roots which feed these growths are torn from the filthy muck which fosters them… You will learn that the sob-sisters will soon come forth from hiding with cries of persecution against these dear, good boys… You will discover that crackpot politicians… will scuttle out from the shadows to add crime upon crime by evoking new and impossible schemes for the alleged eradication of the law-breaker. You will be surrounded by theorists, pseudo criminologists, hyper-sentimentalists…

"Therefore, I warn you to stay unswerving to your task – that of standing by the men on the firing line – the practical, hard-headed, experienced, honest policemen who have shown by their efforts that they, and they alone, know the answer to the crime problem. That answer can be summed up in one sentence – adequate detection, swift apprehension, and certain, unrelenting punishment. That is what the criminal fears. That is what he understands, and nothing else, and that fear is the only thing which will force him into the ranks of the law-abiding.

"These persons of the under-filth are not simply poor boys or moral invalids as the super-sentimentalists would have you believe. They are marauders, who murder for a headline, rats crawling from their hide-outs to gnaw at the vitals of our civilization... their standards of life are those of pigs in a wallow, their outlook that of vultures regurgitating their filth.

"It was apathy which permitted the sentimentalists to make their creeping approach, to build beautiful stories about the sweet, dear convicts, who so loved freedom that they raised canary birds in cages, or placed the picture of some dear old mother upon the walls of their cells. These convict-lovers built beautiful romances about this foul offspring of our national filth.

"We need some good, old-fashioned American housecleaning of the kind that will rip off the dirty hangings and let in the light, that will beat out the floor coverings and sweep away the filth which has accumulated through the years of lethargy. Beyond that, we need the old-fashioned influence of the old-fashioned home.

"I am sick of the maunderings of fanatics and tuffet-heads, who believe that the way to educate the new youth is to allow the new youth to do anything it pleases.

"I would not have you conclude that this picture is painted ... by a victim of ... imagination. On the contrary, it is sketched against a background of stark statistics ..."

The words "filthy," "filth," and "foul" applied to convicted persons and to the other real or imagined opponents and persecutors of J. Edgar Hoover appear 10 times in this one speech. For refreshment after wading through this stuff, it is good to read the words of another lawyer, Clarence Darrow, in "Resist Not Evil." published by Haldeman-Julius in 1925. The ideas may be hard to agree with, but the entire tone and attitude is on a level of human intelligence and kindness that makes Mr. Hoover look like something out of the Marquis de Sade.

Hoover again, June 21, 1939, to the U. S. Junior Chamber of Commerce:

> "… we of the F.B.I. have placed so much stress on detection and apprehension which, together with certainty of trial and punishment, constitute the time-proven deterrents to crime.
>
> "America needs your patriotic zeal and your services in a crusade to insure her destiny on the chartered sea of Democracy … Remember that from dawn this morning until dawn tomorrow morning, 3,928 major crimes will have been committed, including 33 homicides, 814 burglaries, 162 robberies, 2,258 larcenies, 22 rapes, 515 auto thefts and 122 aggravated assaults."

September 23, 1940, to the National Convention, American. Legion:

> "From across the seas have come emissaries from totalitarian governments, seeking to undermine our Nationalism and to implant their doctrines of hate… Ever on the alert to capitalize on popular trends, they have joined reform organizations and civil liberties groups, and have played dominant roles in some of the pacifist blocs.
>
> "Action is necessary to prevent the bloodstream of America from contamination … In this, the American Legion has set the pace. The necessity for its program, scorned and ridiculed by the Communists and their fellow-travelers, has been thoroughly established.
>
> "… The American way of living will endure only as it is proved to be efficient.

"A vital test of Americanism is the revival of the pioneer spirit of our ancestors. As a people, we have become soft."

June 9, 1941, at the University of the South Commencement:

"Shocking as it may seem, there is a murder in our United States every 44 minutes; a major felony every 21 seconds ... Was this the kind of nation for which Washington fought at Valley Forge? ... That word 'liberalism' is something we should weigh carefully during these dark days that confront our nation. There is nothing more cowardly than a criminal; he works in the dark, he sneaks upon you in the shadows; he hides his gun under his coat until the moment when he would terrorize you ... Is there not a strange connection between such persons and certain apostles of degenerate dictatorships who, hiding their hammers and sickles under the protection of our national emblem, advance upon us in sham cloaks of liberalism, pretending to be seeking social reforms and equality for all, while in reality plotting to trample beneath their blood-stained boots the very document which has been their greatest protection, our sacred Constitution of the United States!"

March 29, 1941, to the National Police Academy:

"The rabble-rousing Communist, the goosestepping Bundsman, their stooges and seemingly innocent 'fronts,' and last but not the least, the pseudo liberals, adhere to the doctrine of falsification and distortion."

May 10, 1942, at Notre Dame University Commencement:

"One task before college graduates today is to apply their intellectual curiosity to exposing the motives of those who preach a foreign 'ism' instead of good old-fashioned Americanism.

"We have been engulfed with all kinds of new theories, holding that self-expression should not be disciplined ... It is a lack of religious training in the home, and the school, that usually breeds criminals."
From "Persons in Hiding," by J. Edgar Hoover:
"A child is a little animal to be guided into a necessarily false animal existence we call civilization, or to revert to more bestial inclinations."

For his April 23, 1936 speech to the D.A.R., and similar super-heated contributions to American education, Hoover has been awarded 15 honorary degrees by George Washington University, Kalamazoo College, Pennsylvania Military College, Oklahoma Baptist University, et al. He has also received the Wohelo Award of the Camp Fire Girls.

The "criminal army" speech is one of Hoover's favorites. On September 19, 1936, during a speech to the Convention of Holy Name Societies, the Director set its USA division at 3,500,000. By October 4, 1937, when he presumably had a larger audience to impress at the New York Herald Tribune Forum, it had picked up some recruits and grown to 4,300,000. On December 11, 1945, Hoover addressed the International Association of Chiefs of Police. Representatives from other lands were present, and it may thus be possible to excuse Mr. Hoover for his enthusiastic desire to impress these visitors with our unequaled depravity. He declared that we harbored a "criminal army of 6,000,000."

Together with this picture of skyrocketing crime, J. Edgar gives us his solemn word that, "detection and apprehension... together with certainty of trial and punishment, constitute the time-proven deterrents to crime." With the Bureau 20 times larger than it was in 1924, one would hardly expect to find that the "criminal army" had doubled in size. One might think the Bureau had slipped up somewhere. It is necessary to read the speeches of J. Edgar Hoover to learn about the soft-hearted parole boards, the corrupt politicians, and the errant parents who go about zealously undoing the work of the F.B.I.

At least one of Hoover's "criminal army" speeches sketched such a fantastic picture of American crime that it was reprinted under a double-column headline in the Russian Army newspaper Red Star on December 23, 1945. In this speech, he submitted statistics on the "juvenile spearhead" of the criminal army which included thousands of vicious characters charged with "drunkenness" and "driving while intoxicated." In a statement to The New York Times of October 18, 1945, Hoover fingered troublemakers. "The most dangerous crime element," he declared, "is the juvenile delinquent." He blamed errant parents.

With the warming up of the anti-Russian campaign, Mr. Hoover discovered that the real threat no longer wore bobby sox and adored Sinatra, but sported a beard and throbbed to Shostakovich. One of his most recent pieces on the subject, "Red Fascism in the United States Today" in the American Magazine for February, 1947, tells America that "The Red scourge of Communism ... is boring its way through our land like a termite." And so on, with plentiful quotes from pamphlets and manifestoes, all somewhat dog-eared after 20 years of thumbing from Hearst editorial writers. The performance is repeated in Newsweek for June 9, 1947.

Hoover's salary as Director and sole Publicity Agent of the Federal Bureau of Investigation is $13,846, modest as Federal salaries go. In 1925, it was $7,500. He was once suggested to succeed Kenesaw Mountain Landis as Baseball Commissioner, but turned down the job in spite of the fact that it would have paid him more than his berth with the Justice Department.

His personal morality is unimpeachable, to the point of being outstandingly odd. The only woman with whom he has been seen in public is Shirley Temple – at the time, she was 8 years old. Hoover is single, lives alone in Washington. Until his mother's death in 1938, he lived with her. It is probably true that he has refused to accept pay for the numerous magazine and newspaper articles funneled from the Bureau under his name.

IV. THE F.B.I. DOSSIERS

Among the dangerous radicals at one time shadowed by the Bureau, and included in their political information file, is former President Herbert Hoover. Other prominent Americans who have been honored by inclusion in the dossiers are Justice Stone, Senator Wheeler and Senator Borah.

The dossiers which J. Edgar Hoover's men, during the Red Raids, had compiled on the two Boston anarchists, Sacco and Vanzetti, were largely instrumental in sending them to the electric chair. The dossiers were relied on heavily by the prosecution in fabricating the greatest judicial frame-up in history. They were never produced in court, despite repeated efforts of the defense attorneys, who had reason to believe they contained material (suppressed by the prosecution and the F.B.I.) which would help clear the defendants.

In connection with cooperation between the District Attorney and the Department of Justice on the Sacco-Vanzetti Case, G-Man Fred G. Weyand stated:

> "Instructions were received from the Chief of the Bureau of the Department of Justice in Washington from time to time in reference to the Sacco-Vanzetti case. They are on file or should be on file in the Boston office.
>
> "The understanding in this case between the agents of the Department of Justice in Boston and the District Attorney followed the usual custom, that the Department of Justice would help the District Attorney to secure a conviction, and that he in turn would help the agents of the Department of Justice to secure information that they might desire. This would include the turning over of any pertinent information by the

Department of Justice to the District Attorney. Sacco and "Vanzetti were, at least in the opinion of the Boston agents of the Department of Justice, not liable to deportation as draft dodgers, but only as anarchists, and could not be deported as anarchists unless it could be shown that they were believers in anarchy, which is always a difficult thing to show. It usually can only be shown by self-incrimination. The Boston agents believed that these men were anarchists, and hoped to be able to secure the necessary evidence against them from their testimony at their trial for murder, to be used in case they were not convicted of murder. There is correspondence between Mr. Katzmann and Mr. West on file in the Boston office of the Department. Mr. West furnished Mr. Katzmann information about the Radical activities of Sacco and Vanzetti to be used in their cross-examination…

"What I mean is that I think they did not believe in organized government or in private property. But I am also thoroughly convinced, and always have been, and I believe that is and always has been the opinion of such Boston agents of the Department of Justice as had any knowledge on the subject, that these men had nothing whatever to do with the South Braintree murders, and that their convictions was the result of cooperation between the Boston agents of the Department of Justice and the District Attorney. It was the general opinion of the Boston agents of the Department of Justice having knowledge of the affair that the South Braintree crime was committed by a gang of professional highwaymen."

Another Special Agent, Lawrence Letherman, stated:

"The Department of Justice in Boston was anxious to get sufficient evidence against Sacco and Vanzetti to deport them, but" never succeeded in getting the kind and amount of evidence required for that purpose. It was the opinion of the Department agents here that a conviction of Sacco and Vanzetti for murder would be one way of disposing of these two men. It was also the general opinion of such of the agents in Boston as had any actual knowledge of the Sacco-Vanzetti case, that Sacco and Vanzetti, although anarchists and agitators were not highway robbers, and had nothing to do with the South Braintree crime. My opinion, and the opinion of most of the older men in the Government service, has always been that the South Braintree crime was the work of professionals.

"The Boston agents of the Department of Justice assigned certain men to attend the trial of Sacco and Vanzetti, including Mr. Weyand. Mr. West also attended the trial. There is or was a great deal of correspondence on file in the Boston office between Mr. West and Mr. Katzmann, the District Attorney, and there are also copies of reports sent to Washington about the case. Letters and reports were made in triplicate; two copies were sent to Washington and one retained in Boston. The letters and documents on file in the Boston office would throw a great deal of light upon the preparation of the Sacco-Vanzetti case for trial, and upon the real opinion of the Boston office of the Department of Justice as to the guilt of Sacco and Vanzetti of the particular crime with which they were charged."[13]

Mr. Thompson, counsel for the defense, sought to obtain access to the files mentioned. Mr. Dowd, then in charge of the Boston office of the Justice Department, stated that he could not allow the files out of his possession, nor permit access to them, and that those were his instructions. The dossiers compiled by J. Edgar Hoover's General Intelligence Division were never disclosed by either the Boston office or the headquarters at Washington.

The Washington headquarters of the F.B.I. is a cross between a wax museum of horrors, a Shinto shrine, and a shooting gallery. One of the gadgets for the edification of persons in the waiting room is an illuminated meter which clicks up a new total every time, a new fingerprint is added to the files. The Bureau has two classes of fingerprint files: criminal and non-criminal. The latter includes a large part of the adult population, since all armed forces fingerprint records are sent to the Bureau. It has been charged that when a print comes in on a criminal case, the civilian as well as the criminal files are ransacked.

The criminal files themselves, which supply Mr. Hoover with sociological basis for his startling figures on the "criminal army," are thrown together in a haphazard way, as the following portion from an interview by the author on April 14, 1947, with Special Agent Wick of Division 4, Records and Communications, will reveal:

Q. During my tour through the Federal Bureau of Investigation, our guide said that one out of every 23 Americans had a criminal record, and his fingerprints are on file here. Now, did he mean that a great many are included who committed only minor crimes?
A. Anything more serious than a traffic violation is included.
Q. Just where would I go to find a list of those offenses which are included? How would I know what is considered more serious than a traffic violation?
A. Well, you would have to go through the State records or perhaps the Federal archives.
Q. Let us take, for example, a man arrested for picketing. Is that considered more serious than a traffic violation?
A. There are many factors that would enter into that…
Q. But it might vary? One State would consider the offense a crime and the other would not?

A. It is up to the local police department whether or not the prints are sent in. It depends on the local law officers.

Q. So you have on file as criminals persons whose prints would not even be sent to you from some states, because the offense is not considered serious enough for fingerprinting perhaps?

A. Generally, traffic violations are left out. The local law determines.

"John Doe" is a journalist who, for obvious reasons, prefers to remain anonymous. He has supplied the following affidavit regarding the F.B.I. dossiers:

There are very few Americans who have seen their own dossiers in the files of the Federal Bureau of Investigation. I saw a copy of mine in 1942 and it frightened me—not only for myself but for thousands of others with similar records.

I had gone to work in Washington for one of the wartime agencies. One day the chief, whom I had known for many years, called me into his office. "Here's something I oughtn't to show you," he said. "The F.B.I. sent over your record and it's highly confidential. But I thought I'd break the rule for once and let you see it, so that you'd know exactly what they were going to bring against you."

"Can I take it to my desk?"

"Yes, if you don't tell anyone about it and bring it back this after noon."

I'm sorry now that I didn't take full notes on it, with transcripts of the more interesting passages. My record was a document of about thirty pages of single-spaced typing. Only the last few pages had anything to do with the F.B.I. investigation, then under way, into my fitness to endorse government paychecks; by the time that investigation was finished, it must have filled a volume. The document I saw was, for the most part, merely the dossier of a private citizen who, at the time the material went into the record, had never dreamed of working in Washington. Query to Mr. Hoover: How many private citizens who never belonged to the Communist Party or any other organization regarded by sensible people as subversive have dossiers in your files?

I wasn't even a prominent citizen. I had worked for a magazine, had let my name be used on the letterheads of several Communist-front organizations, had spoken at many of their meetings, had resigned from everything with a Communist tinge after the Russo-German pact, and was thereafter abused in the Communist press. That was my actual story and the F.B.I. had documented parts of it, while omitting everything about the resignations or the abuse. I began to suspect, and later became certain, that it wanted only what it regarded as incriminating evidence. One man spoke well of me, and the F.B.I. investigator looked away with a bored air. "But don't you know anything suspicious about him?" he finally interrupted.

Nothing in the dossier dealt with my activities before 1935, although I had been at my reddest or pinkest during the Hoover administration. The omission didn't mean that the F.B.I. recognized any statute of limitations; once it began to work on a case, it tried to trace a man's activities straight back to the womb. But it was handicapped in its search because it hadn't begun to function as an effective Thought-control Police until midway in Roosevelt's first; term.

Besides the omissions in my dossier, there were a great many inclusions best described as fanciful. I was described as a prominent member of organizations I had never heard of—if they ever existed and as a speaker at meetings I hadn't attended. One "informant" had seen me at a secret Communist Party conference—I was never present at anything of the sort—in a city which I had never visited. This same "informant," whom I judged from the context to be some illiterate ex-Communist bent on earning a few government dollars by bringing more and more names into his testimony, endowed me with a long list of "close associates." The names he mentioned were strange to me, with one exception, that of "Mary Heator Forse," whom I guessed to be Mary Heaton Vorse.

The "informants" were not identified, but I recognized at least two of them by the phrasing of their testimony. One was a man whose last book I hadn't admired and he expressed some doubt of my loyalty to the democratic way of life. Another was a man with whom I had had political arguments; he accused me of being a "transmission belt" for Moscow.

During the next few weeks I became obsessed with the desire to set the record straight. I had decided to resign from government service, but I didn't want to leave Washington while this mass of errors and allegations remained in the F.B.I. files, to be used I didn't know how. I went to see various officials and asked their help in obtaining a hearing. Once I thought the request was granted: I was told to appear at F.B.I. headquarters. Undistinguished young men in undistinguishable dark suits and gray snapbrim hats were going in and out the door, as anonymous as bees. I was directed to a little office, put under oath by two of the young men, and asked for brief answers to half a dozen questions. Then I was told to sign my name.

"But aren't you going to ask me any more questions?" I said.

"No, that is all."

I began to feel like K— in Kafka's "The Trial." I went to see high officials in the Department of Justice to press for a hearing. To one of them I made the obvious remark that most of the F.B.I. investigators seemed pretty stupid. "Of course," he said. "You don't expect us to get bright law-school graduates, do you, for $65 a week?" I learned something about the sociology of the F.B.I. Its investigators, who have to have law-school training, are for the most part either Southerners or Catholics. Southerners are in the majority, but the Catholic influence is very strong, and some of the investigators are confused in their minds as to whether they are hounding down political or religious heresies. The word "atheist" often occurs in their reports.

My little story would not have been worth telling except that it is presumably not an isolated instance. Its only special feature is that I had the privilege of seeing what the F.B.I.'s informants had said about me. What have they said about you, Reader? If you ever joined a Communist-front organization during the 1930's, or ever signed a petition, or ever received a government paycheck, or ever had unsuspected enemies, you might be surprised at the material about you in the F.B.I. file, which is probably the largest collection of typewritten material in the world, and certainly the greatest collection anywhere of unverified, unsupported, unidentified wild stories about anyone and everyone.

–John Doe

V. PUBLICITY OR EFFICIENCY?

John Edgar Hoover has a flair for publicity that would make Barbara Hutton, Errol Flynn and Vito Marcantonio curl up with envy. Someone has remarked that Hoover may not be a crack shot with a gun, but nobody alive can beat him to the draw with a telephone.

Until 1940, most of the sensational magazine publicity was ground out by one Courtney Ryley Cooper, a former circus press agent turned Wild West pulp writer, who became semi-official Boswell to the Bureau. Most of the articles signed by Hoover before that time contain the notation, "ed. by Courtney Ryley Cooper." In the polite language of the literary world, Cooper would have been called Hoover's ghost-writer.

Mr. Cooper, nine years older than Hoover, had a considerable influence on the writing of his protégé. In fact, the style of Courtney Ryley Cooper is the style of John Edgar Hoover. A review of one of Cooper's books on the circus from the Boston Transcript reads as though it might have been a review of Mr. Hoover's 1936 speech to the D.A.R.:

> "Mr. Cooper writes as if he were still press agent, glorifying the tented world just as its managers would have done, but not always with entire regard for actualities. A circus is always expected to exaggerate; perhaps the literature of the circus may be pardoned if it too is written with superlatives."

The F.B.I. Director rewarded Cooper for his collaboration by furnishing him with material for a number of books on crime. The Bureau also squired Cooper on a one-year tour of American houses of prostitution which resulted in another book, *Designs in Scarlet*.

It is not surprising that such long and intensive cooperation between the two men should have resulted in the adoption by Hoover of Cooper's way of expressing himself, which has been described as "the virtuously sarcastic 'no-nonsense-about-me' style of an experienced *Saturday Evening Post* contributor." Their close cooperation is preserved for posterity in two books: *Persons in Hiding* by J. Edgar Hoover, foreword by Courtney Ryley Cooper; and *Ten Thousand Public Enemies* by Courtney Ryley Cooper, foreword by J. Edgar Hoover.

Some of Hoover's publicity stunts incidental to turning the F.B.I. into a replica of the 101 Ranch Show surpass the fantastic.

When Lepke Buchalter, wanted for murder and narcotics violations one night gave himself up to Walter Winchell and J. Edgar on a New York street corner, the public was asked to believe that a stirring radio plea by Winchell at the request of Hoover had brought him in. According to other information, the whole business was handled through a "confidential informant" who got the word to Lepke that unless he handed himself over, somebody bigger would get hurt. Lepke also claimed at a later date that he had been promised a light sentence and had been double-crossed. Since the murder charge was a New York affair, and narcotics were not under the jurisdiction of the G-Men there is some doubt which loophole Hoover came in through.[14]

When Victor (The Count) Lustig, famed counterfeiter, cut his way out of a utility room at the West Street Federal Detention Headquarters, where he had originally been placed by operatives of the Treasury Department, he eluded recapture for a short time. Finally, he was again picked up by the Secret Service, who put the Count securely in irons. On their way back, they met the G-Men just starting out on the trail. Understanding instructions of Mr. Hoover, the G-Men immediately got on the telephone to Washington and reported the capture to The Chief, Mr. Hoover lost not a second in transforming the capture into screaming headlines –without mention of the Treasury Department men. Agents of the Secret Service and Post Office Inspector's Service have made frequent complaints that "in scores of cases…their men have built up the evidence and located the criminal only to have the F.B.I. step in for the kill and credit."[15]

When Harry Brunette was tear-gassed and machine-gunned out of a New York apartment with newspaper publicity and damage to adjoining apartments running about equal, Police Commissioner Valentine charged that the F.B.I., hungry for exclusive press coverage, had started the raid in violation of an agreement with New York police, thereby losing an opportunity to trap Brunette's confederate at the same time. Complaints against F.B.I. lack of cooperation have also come from the police forces of Chicago, St. Paul, Salt Lake City, New Orleans, and Seattle.[16]

Hoover's publicity led most people to think the Bureau had solved the Lindbergh kidnaping case. Actually, the arrest of Hauptmann was primarily the work of Frank Wilson, Chief of Secret Service, who devised an intricate system of checking serial numbers on the ransom bills.

Hoover's publicity indicated that the Dillinger case had been cracked by the F.B.I. But the first time Dillinger was picked up, a local sheriff got him; the second and last time, two members of the East Chicago police force furnished the information on his whereabouts.[17] To get Dillinger and Baby-Face Nelson, the G-Men paid a price of seven peace officers killed, one civilian killed and four wounded (during the escape of the gang from a bungled Federal round-up at Spider Lake, Wis.)

At least one American encyclopedia credits Hoover and the F.B.I. for solving the kidnap-murder of the Cash child in Florida. The kidnaper, Franklin Pierce McCall, was arrested by the local sheriff, released by the G-Men, and re-arrested two days later when they failed to find any other solution than Sheriff Coleman's.[18]

The F.B.I.'s proudest wartime boast was the rounding up of the six German saboteurs who landed on the coast of Long Island. But it has now been revealed that this involved no feat of sleuthing more complicated than answering the phone. After the war was ended, and long after Hoover had grabbed front-page headlines for his "brilliant" and "vigilant" police work, Attorney-General Clark told the real story. Although the Coast Guard detected the landing almost as soon as it was made, the F.B.I. got nowhere until, six days later, Dasch, the expedition's leader, called them up and arranged to betray his comrades. (See *New York Times* – inside page, of course – for November 8, 1945.)

Hoover's publicity claims a high rate of convictions, *but Crime Control by the National Government* published by the Brookings Institution, credits the G-Men with only 72.5 percent convictions in their arrests, which is ,the next to lowest rating of the seven major Federal law-enforcement agencies.

Notably in the case of John Dillinger, the F.B.I., under orders originally formulated by Attorney General Cummings in May, 1934, adopted a "shoot on sight and shoot to kill" policy in serious criminal cases. Dillinger's only known Federal offense was the transportation in interstate commerce of a stolen automobile, yet Joseph B. Keenan, Assistant Attorney General, could say: "I don't know when or where we will get him, but we will get him and I hope we get him under such circumstances that the government will not have to stand the expenses of a trial.[19]

As Howard McClellan shows in a *Harper's* article, credited crimes (those not proved against a suspect, but credited) are marked off the list of unsolved crimes when the man credited for them is killed or a suicide. When Dillinger was wiped out, a series of bank-robberies in several states, including some committed simultaneously, were crossed off as solved. The habit of shooting a suspect and building up a good case against him later at leisure can obviously be used in any situation where "public opinion" has been sufficiently aroused against the individual in question—whether or not he is accused of a crime carrying the death penalty.

The Hearst papers are unfailing in their support of Hoover's methods. They, and other publications which have scrupulously avoided any word of criticism aimed at the F.B.I., have been rewarded by advance tips, scoops, exclusive coverage. The critical publications get nothing; letters to the Bureau or to Hoover requesting interviews do not even receive the courtesy of an answer.

This method of rewarding the faithful has brought sharp protests from newspapers left out in the cold. One of the better known instances is the Snaring Farnsworth case. Farnsworth, a former naval officer, attempted to sell the confidential story of his activities as a spy in the United States to one Fulton Lewis, of Hearst's International News Service. Lewis turned over the suspect to the F.B.I. The Bureau rewarded him by giving- him complete details on the case, which it withheld from all other news services. Hearst got a scoop on the story—hours ahead of all newspaper rivals.[20]

VI. INSIDE THE F.B.I.

The General Intelligence Division, political police section of the Bureau, was originally organized by J. Edgar Hoover in 1919 under A. Mitchell Palmer. Although the Division was theoretically disbanded after the Daugherty scandals revealed its use as a political weapon, the compiling of dossiers on radicals was continued and the Division revived in effect by Roosevelt's Executive Order of September 6, 1939 to investigate "subversive activities." What is considered subversive by the Bureau becomes apparent when former fingerprint classifiers report that some of the headings under which prints are filed read, "picketer," and "union agitator." The F.B.I. once told a Senate committee that it had given extensive scrutiny to Bolshevists and referred to the American Civil Liberties Union as an example of a Bolshevist organization.[21]

The type of work done by the Division under Hoover, Burns and Daugherty was made public through the attempt to frame Senator Wheeler, who had pressed investigation of Attorney General Daugherty and the Bureau's share in corruption under the Harding regime.

"When Wheeler started his drive against Daugherty, the latter consulted with Burns and Lockwood (Secretary, Republican National Committee). Burns has admitted that Daugherty suggested they 'get' Wheeler, and Burns confesses that he sent government agents out to Montana to see what they could dig up against the Senator...The resignation of William J. Burns as Director of the Bureau of Investigation of the Department of Justice is attributed here to his part in the framing of the Wheeler case..." [22]

On November, 1939, in his testimony before the House Appropriations Committee, Hoover stated that he had organized a General Intelligence Division, which had "compiled extensive indices of individuals, groups and organizations engaged in these subversive activities, in espionage activities, *or any other activities that are possibly detrimental* to the internal security of the United States."

The indices have been arranged, says Mr. Hoover, "not only alphabetically, but also geographically, so that at any time ... we would be able-to go into any of these communities and identify individuals or groups who might be a source of grave danger to the security of this country. These indexes will be extremely important and valuable in grave emergency."

Here we have the secret behind Mr. Hoover's opposition to the outlawing of the Communist Party. The time is not quite ripe for wholesale arrests on a "geographical" basis, and he prefers that the Communists be permitted to exist legally until the proper pitch of hysteria permits a repetition of the Palmer Red Raids. Those who make the blunder of reading a flowering liberalism into purely tactical approaches on Mr. Hoover's part need another look at the record.

When Mr. Hoover says that his agents can go into any community and "identify" individuals and groups, what he means is that they can grab, collar, abduct, imprison, and otherwise physically apprehend human beings on a really grand and impressive scale the moment the green light shows. It is doubtful that the excessive brutality of the Palmer Raids would be repeated, but the net effect of imprisoning thousands in mass arrests would be the same. The holding of an opinion, rather than proof of an illegal act, would be the basis for issuing arrest warrants.

The principal means of building up these lists of "subversives" has been the paid testimony of stool pigeons, the gratuitous information furnished by personal enemies, and the reports of Federal agents posing as members of suspected organizations. One former high Washington official I spoke with declared that he had a sure and painless method of causing the immediate financial collapse of the Communist Party.

"How would you do that?" I asked him.

"Have the F.B.I. instruct its agents in the Communist Party to stop paying their dues."

Undercover agents are widely used by the Federal Bureau of Investigation. Laws, whether Federal or otherwise, are no barrier to their operation. Documents from the *Congressional Record* prove that, in its use of undercover agents, the Bureau, with the cooperation of officials of the Department of Justice, has broken Federal law covering the sentencing parole or release of prisoners. Following is a letter from John W. Snook, former Warden of Atlanta Penitentiary:

> "The practice under Mrs. Willebrandt (Mable Walker Willebrandt, Assistant Attorney General) was to cause agents to be convicted of fictitious crimes in the Federal courts and committed by Federal judges to Federal penal institutions. Such as, when Peter Hanson, afterwards known as convict No. 26206, Atlanta Penitentiary, was committed by Arthur J. Tuttle, District Judge, in Detroit, the commitment being certified under seal of the court. As a matter of fact, Peter Hanson was none other than William Larson, Agent of the Department of Justice...
>
> "After the Agent, Larson, under the name of Hanson, was committed to Atlanta and remained there from January 6 to April 10, he was suddenly transferred by order of Mrs. Willebrandt from Atlanta to Leavenworth

on April 10, 1928, and then again on order of Mrs. Willebrandt he was released by Warden White on April 19, 1928. In other words, Mrs. Willebrandt arrogated to herself the judicial and presidential powers, in that at her will she caused the commitment of men to prison and at her order she ordered their release, disregarding the well-defined rules and principles covering parole and release. Her espionage system was nationally extended ..."

Referring to the case of convict Lloyd L. Miller, No. 22968 (a genuine convict, this time) transferred to Atlanta from Leavenworth and later paid off for his spying for the F.B.I. through having his sentence commuted, Warden Snook continues:

"This was one of a series of undercover operations which for one whole year had been in full blast at Leavenworth under orders of Mrs. Willebrandt which were executed by Thomas C. Wilcox, her agent, in the Bureau of Investigation ..."

After the spy system of Mrs. Willebrandt and the F.B.I. was exposed by the *Atlanta Constitution*, she received no official reprimand from any source, and subsequently caused another fraudulent commitment:

"On the 21st day of February, 1929, with seeming regularity, I admitted at Atlanta Penitentiary a convict named Joseph Montana, alias John Mason, true name as it later developed, Fred J. Lackey, and actually a Department of Justice Agent. Montana had under gone incarceration by 13 days' service of his three-year sentence when, with the same suddenness as in the Hanson case, I was visited at the prison on March 6, 1929, by Thomas C. Wilcox, armed with an order from Mrs. Willebrandt directing me to release to Wilcox, F. J. Lackey, Special Agent, who, as Joseph Montana, was incarcerated in Atlanta Penitentiary. While reading her order I received a telegram, as follows:

"John W. Snook, Warden:

"Release Joseph Montana, who is Special Agent this Department, to T C Wilcox, Special Agent in Charge, Bureau of Investigation.

Mitchell (Attorney-General)"[23]

An attempt was made to ascertain which Federal Judge, acting on whose orders, had illegally sentenced a man to prison. In reply to inquiries a statement was obtained from Judge Hough, U. S. District Judge, Cincinnati, Ohio, who on June 3, 1929, told the *Chicago Tribune*:

> "...that it was at the request of U. S. Judge Smith Hickenlooper, of the Circuit Court of Appeals, that he consented to sentence Lackey for a crime that had not in fact been committed...Judge Hickenlooper refused to answer any questions regarding the matter, saying it was none of the business of the press or public."

That is the type of answer familiar to a researcher attempting to understand the inner working of the Bureau of Investigation.

Payment for stool-pigeons such as convict Lloyd Miller is assured by a section of the Federal Budget which, for 1947, set aside $120,000 "to meet unforeseen emergencies of a confidential character, to be expended under the direction of the Attorney General, who shall make a certificate of the amount,... and every such certificate shall be deemed a sufficient voucher for the sum therein expressed to have been expended." This is a regular item on Federal Bureau of Investigation budgets, and appears every year.

Pinkerton officials questioned by the La Follette Civil Liberties Committee stated that a system had been worked out through which government officials could be billed personally for labor spy services to circumvent the law against government hiring of private detectives, which was passed after the Homestead battle.

In 1939 the F.B.I. was alleged to have directed connections with the Cleveland Industrial Safety Council, a strike-breaking agency. In the spring of 1940, Reid Robinson, of the Mine, Mill and Smelter Workers charged the Bureau had broken the local strike by descending in force on the union hall, arresting and holding incommunicado the strike leaders. The *New York Post* of September 10, 1940, disclosed that the F.B.I. was covering various C.I.O. meetings and noting license numbers of cars parked outside.

Nation's Business, in a December, 1947, article on prosecutions under the antitrust laws, takes heart in the fact that a number of unions are included in the proceedings:

> "With those who do not cooperate, the F.B.I. is prepared to use all its ingenuity to obtain and identify records... In a recent case involving a West Coast union, it was fought at every turn ... However, the F.B.I. was able to locate copies of contracts and other papers which clearly indicated violations of the antitrust laws. But defense attorneys resorted to an extraordinary step—they refused to admit that the papers, *taken from the union files*, were those of the union."

How the papers were taken from the union files legally, deponent saith not. It is probably one of the many cases in which ingenuity replaces legality in the work of the G-Man.

On February 6, 1940, 40 G-Men were assigned to the Detroit office to assist in the dramatic before-dawn arrests of 11 persons charged with soliciting volunteers for the Spanish Loyalist Army two years earlier. Houses were ransacked without search warrant; the prisoners were held incommunicado for nine or 10 hours. A lawyer was finally allowed to converse with the defendants in the presence of the

Federals five minutes before they were taken into court... All the indictments were dismissed.[24]

"Business Finds G-Men are Admirably Equipped to Assume Executive Roles, Especially in Dealing with Public and Labor." So reads a headline in *Business Week* for July 20, 1946, which goes on to say that John S. Bugas, formerly in charge of the Detroit office of the F.B.I., has been named head of labor relations at Ford's, replacing Harry Bennett, one of the biggest names in the American labor spy industry. *Business Week* reports that "By such subtle tactics as keeping the United Automobile Workers on the defensive, Bugas was able to insinuate favorable clauses into the company's U.A.W. contract."

A large number of former G-Men are employed by the union-busting employer's associations on the West Coast. Charles F. Ruck, who was head of the steel industry's espionage system, is another prominent graduate of J. Edgar Hoover's school. Several hundred ex-agents, most of them employed in various phases of "labor relations" are banded together in an organization calling itself, in topheavy accents, The Society of Former Special Agents of the Federal Bureau of Investigation, Inc., with headquarters at 70 Pine Street, New York City.

As to Hoover's personal attitude toward labor unions, he had an entire lodge of the AFL Federation of Government Employees thrown out of the International and out of the AFL for trying to organize the clerks employed by his Bureau. Turnover in some of the F.B.I. units has been claimed to exceed 70 percent in one year, with clerical employees eager to transfer to some other government agency at the first opportunity. Low wages, unpaid overtime, and semi-military working conditions were offered as some of the reasons for this attitude.

Hoover has opposed inclusion of his Bureau employees under Civil Service. In reply to his remarks, the Civil Service Commission said:

"Obviously, the principal difference between Mr. Hoover and the Civil Service Commission is that Mr. Hoover wants to operate a crime service personally and without regard to the democratic principles of open competition and equal opportunity."

It is worth remarking at this point that no colored employees have been seen in either the Washington headquarters or the New York office of the Bureau. A sympathetic writer claims that "a good handful" (out of 3,500) of Special Agents are colored. The Worker's Defense League states that it knows of no such agent, and considers that the Bureau has been hampered in Southern civil rights cases by this lack.

In the Christian Front case, J. Edgar Hoover tried to make clear that the illegal operations of his Bureau were handled on an impartial basis, and that at a time when Axis agents and sympathizers were unpopular, he would gladly break a few laws while cracking down on the Right. Eighteen men belonging to the Christian Front spent weeks in jail unindicted, finally being held at $50,000 bail each. The Bureau had rogue's gallery photos taken of the men, and thoroughly tried the case in the newspapers before jury trial or even indictment.

Hoover gave a press conference in which he charged that the 18 men, if not apprehended by the vigilant work of the F.B.I., would have seized the nation's gold supply, power plants, telephone and telegraph systems, railway terminals, docks and government buildings. They were, he said, planning to blast bridges and bomb the New York Police Department, with 12 Congressmen thrown in for good measure.

VII. GESTAPO IN KNEE-PANTS

The acts of the Gestapo were in line with the general trends in German law under Hitler. The acts of the F.B.I. are being more and more frequently affirmed by American jurisprudence. Criticisms of civil rights violations, wiretapping, illegal entry and search, abduction and other questionable procedures are important as an indication of the temper of the Bureau and the willingness of its Director to overstep legal restrictions. The heart of that importance, however, is in the growing agreement between F.B.I. methods and the direction of Federal law as a whole, Executive orders, and recent Supreme Court decisions. One of the most important Supreme Court findings came in the George Harris case, where the Court held, 5 to 4, that Federal agents may enter a residence without a search warrant in cases where the suspect is arrested on the premises, and that they may thereafter make a search of the premises.

Since Hoover's men operate by making copious arrests – the F.B.I. arrests 10 persons for every seven it gets convictions for, according to the Brookings Institution – this decision opens up every door to them. The American's home may be his castle, but the drawbridge is down for J. Edgar & Co.

Since the decision in the Harris case, the *Trainman News* has reported that F.B.I. agents, investigating union members in connection with the murder of McNear of the Toledo, Peoria and Western Railroad, have waited outside the railroad shops all day until a suspected union member finished work. They then tailed him home, waited about a few minutes until he was at supper, and subsequently entered the house to question him and search the premises. Obviously, the F.B.I. may be expected to make as many arrests as possible at the residence of future suspects.

The American Civil Liberties Union which, like the liberal weeklies, has gone soft on the F.B.I. of late years, seems to think the G-Men have become more scrupulous in their methods. Actually, what is happening is not so much a change of heart on their part as the tendency of the courts to make legal what formerly was illegal. Both the growth and the "legalization" of the F.B.I. in the last few years are symptomatic of the steady increase in State power which began under Roosevelt's New Deal.

The relation between the F.B.I. and the Federal courts cannot be considered a complete parallel with the Gestapo-German State System until the anonymous denunciation which is a major item in F.B.I. political cases becomes generally acceptable as evidence in the courts. It may also be noted that the very size of the United States, and its tendency toward statistic-worshiping make it seem unlikely that the F.B.I. will easily resume its "old-fashioned" brutality and develop on quite the same lines of unrestrained violence as the Nazi political police. With a view of crime which reduces the problem to one of arithmetical relationship between statistics about criminals and statistics about police officers and government agents, it is doubtful that the Federal Bureau will reach the level of personal vindictiveness and hatred evidenced in Germany. The Bureau, through no lack of eagerness on its part, is still a Gestapo in knee-pants.

Although anonymous denunciation is not yet accepted as evidence, the dossiers of the F.B.I. may influence courts and Federal agencies through the introduction of irrelevant and prejudicial material. Congressional committees have made use of such unsworn evidence of an anonymous nature supplied by the Bureau, thus giving it the weight of Congressional sanction.

In the case of a young man who claimed exemption from military service as a conscientious objector, G-Men inferred that he was morally unsound because he had once taken part in a "strip-tease performance" and therefore, presumably, could not have been a bona fide conscientious objector. Investigation by a lawyer of the agent's basis for this report disclosed that the young man, while a high school student, had held the cloak of a fully-clad young lady while she sang at a school concert.[25]

In these days of loyalty tests and investigations into political beliefs and affiliations, it is vital to remember that material introduced into a case from F.B.I. files cannot be contested by the defendant because of the Bureau's policy of labelling all sources as "confidential," and explaining that they cannot be named "for security reasons." Joseph Duggan, former Special Assistant to the Attorney General, when questioned on the availability for cross-examination of those giving statements for F.B.I. files, said, "It is the standard practice of the F.B.I. never to reveal the source of their information." [26]

This shyness over the origin of damaging material has been given official Federal sanction in the recent Executive Order of President Truman directing the Civil Service Commission and the F.B.I. to hunt subversives in Federal employment. The order provides, in Paragraph 2 of Part IV, that "...the investigative agency may refuse to disclose the names of confidential informants, provided ... it advises the requesting department or agency in writing that it is essential to the protection of the informants or to the investigation of other cases that the identity of the informants not be revealed."

In a letter to the *New York Times* of April 13, 1947, Zechariah Chafee, Jr., and other members of the faculty at Harvard Law School point out, in connection with Truman's Executive Order, that:

1. Anonymous denunciation is, for the first time, specifically provided for. (Here is one of the major instances in which Executive Order comes into line with a previous questionable policy of the F.B.I. and establishes it on the level of official government procedure.)
2. No provision is made for a record or transcript.
3. No provision is made that the evidence must support the findings of the loyalty board.
4. "Sympathetic association," not proved membership in a subversive group, is held sufficient to determine disloyalty of an individual.

Following this complaint by the Harvard group, and similar complaints from Yale and other legal circles holding to the "old-fashioned" legal concepts of fair and open trial, President Truman announced a number of "democratic" furbishes, trimmings and interpretations designed to make the loyalty investigations somewhat more palatable to the legal profession. None of these, however, mitigated in the slightest any of the four criticisms made by the Harvard group.

To override once and for all any complaints about the extra-legal aspects of the investigations and dismissals, Senator Patrick McCarran tackled an amendment to the State Department appropriation bill which provided that the department may discharge anyone it wishes without stating reason. This amendment also grants the armed forces and the Atomic Energy Commission the right to fire, without obligation to prefer written charges or grant hearings, in cases where exceptional aspects of national security are concerned. It is generally understood in the government services that there are few cases left where exceptional aspects of national security are not concerned.

The House bill approved during the week of July 13, 1947, is more stringent than Truman's Executive Order. It establishes a Federal Loyalty Review Board from which there is no appeal. A motion by Rep. Estes Kefauver to send the bill back to committee for inclusion of the right to court appeal was defeated, 248 to 133.

The list of subversive organizations compiled from the F.B.I. index and released by Attorney General Clark, and on the basis of which numerous dismissals from government service have been made, was already out of date at the time of its release. According to the *New York Times* of December 6, 1947, the list included a number of organizations which no longer existed, and which had been defunct for some time.

The headlines listed in the *Times Index* tell the story of seven discharged employees of the State Department who tried to obtain a formal hearing on the charges which resulted in their firing, late in 1947, from General Marshall's bailiwick.

November 3: State Department denies plea for formal hearing of seven discharged employees or for permission to retire without prejudice.

November 4: Group seeks Secretary Marshall conference; violation of Bill of Rights seen.

November 6: Marshall refuses hearing; says group can appeal to Loyalty Review Board.

November 10: Civil Service Commission gets hearing request.

November 14: Group again asks Marshall for hearing; attorneys report Commission assertion that dismissal was under McCarran Amendment and not within Loyalty Review Board jurisdiction.

November 18: State Department reverses stand: permits group to resign without prejudice.

The important point is that none of the accused ever received a hearing. All were discharged for holding opinions or committing acts of an unspecified nature, set forth in papers too confidential ever to be produced or even proved to exist, and containing allegations of anonymous persons. At least one individual discharged, on attempting to secure employment with a university, found that the prospective employer had been informed by the State Department that the applicant was considered to be a bad security risk.

Faced with this accusation which has neither head nor body, is connected to no ascertainable person, against which there is no more recourse than against a fog, the individual must feel as hopelessly caught as the concentration-camp inmate described in David Rousset's "The Other Kingdom":

> "The destiny of the concentrationary universe is inconceivably remote. Measureless expanses of laws and offices, of meandering corridors and stacks of papers, where a whole genus of office workers, preoccupied and pale, lives and dies, human typewriters, isolating the camp and letting nothing leak through to the outside world except a vague and

awesome terror of inhuman realms. At the center of this empire, forever invisible, a brain unifies and controls all the police resources... Towering walls of pigeonholes, skyscrapers of dossiers, the most trivial matters catalogued... From these offices comes a signature, the order of life or death for the concentrationee...because of a dead life, often one abandoned months or even years ago, and which seemed to have already been judged... There a case is never finished, never closed. The trial goes on, expands, fattens on personages born of itself, without any reason ever being formulated."

The employees fired by the State Department had been employed from three to five years by various government agencies. Most of them had been cleared for top secret work. In all previous employment they were presumably cleared by the F.B.I., War Department, Civil Service Commission or the Office of Strategic Services. Three of them had never been questioned by any agents of the State Department or by any investigator from any other agency. Counsel for the seven charged that the State Department had ignored its own statement on security principles (Department Announcement 765), and that no charges had ever been submitted to the individuals concerned or to their counsel. Counsel stated that "the procedure that has been followed is tragically analogous to the tactics employed in the police states dominated by Communists and Fascists and has no place in the American system..."

Lovett, of the State Department, replying to counsel stated that "...This determination (to fire) was based upon evidence which the department is not able to disclose for reasons of national security." Secretary of State Marshall declared in a news conference that the department's action "was in large part based on highly classified material not under its control, and in the circumstances a full statement of the charges could not be made to the employees." He asserted that a true hearing was impossible, and refused to identify the source of the information.

Even in its provision for appeal to the Loyalty Review Board established under Executive Order 9835, the accepted legal provision that burden of proof rests upon the plaintiff, and that the defendant shall be considered innocent until proved guilty, is utterly disregarded. When and if the accused is finally heard, "The purpose of such appeal will be to permit the employee *affirmatively to establish his loyalty.*"[27]

Although the President's declaration on loyalty tests and investigations denounces rumor, gossip and suspicion as insufficient evidence, we have seen that this is precisely what constitutes the bulk of an F.B.I, dossier.

Clifford J. Durr, a Commissioner of the Federal Communications Commission, speaking in Chicago on October 26, 1947, charged that unsolicited information on employees was being forwarded to Federal agencies by the F.B.I. Hoover promptly wrote a letter to the Commission implying that, if the other Commissioners did not disavow Durr, the F.C.C. would receive no further information of any sort from his Bureau. Of course, the Commissioners hastened to follow Mr. Hoover's lead, and it is now held most unlikely that Durr will receive re-appointment when his current term expires.

On January 11, 1948, a group of 33 prominent Americans made public a letter to the Loyalty Review Board, in which they said:

"We regard the procedures set forth in the order as lacking adequate safeguards in

"(1) not requiring full revelation of the charges, with production of witnesses and documents and the right of cross-examination;

"(2) in the use of such ill-defined words as subversive,' 'totalitarian,' and 'sympathetic association;' and

"(3) in the lack of any provision for hearings of organizations blacklisted who protest their inclusion."

In addition to highlighting the increasing agreement between the F.B.I. methods and the attitudes of the Executive, Legislative and Judiciary divisions of the Federal government, these loyalty cases affirm the charges made against the F.B.I. by Senator Norris. The Senator claimed that the Bureau, under Hoover, had been guilty of installing a secret political spy system, conducting improper liaison with employers in investigating the non-criminal activities of their workers, and re-introducing the card-indexes of radicals and others, based on opinion, not conduct.

At the time he appointed J. Edgar Hoover head of the F.B.I., then Attorney-General Harlan Stone remarked: "The Bureau of Investigation is not concerned with political or other opinions of individuals. It is concerned only with their conduct and then only with such conduct as is forbidden by the laws of the United States. When a police system passes beyond these limits, it is dangerous to the proper administration of justice and to human liberty."

The Civil Service Commission reports that 811 persons were dismissed from government service for "disloyalty" in the period from July 1, 1946 to March 31, 1947. A *New York Times* dispatch of July 17 states that only 158 were specifically "ineligible for employment for loyalty involving Communism." "No other sort of subversive disloyalty was specifically described," says the dispatch.

VIII. THE AMERICAN POLICE STATE

Many liberals believe that the police state will not have arrived in America until some military officer resplendent in full uniform and medals rides a white horse dramatically up the front steps of the Capitol and proclaims the establishment of Fascism. These liberals forget that, to expect a March on Washington a la Mussolini, or a Reichstag Fire a la Hitler, is to ignore the inventive capacity, the ability for innovation, of the home-grown American reactionary. America's blueprint for the police state is being drawn up today in the Senate and House Appropriation Committees.

Social services of the Federal government in the 1949 Budget, including the National Health Program, Federal aid to education, subsidies for low-cost housing, and additional benefits under Social Security, total just 1 percent of the budget. Repeating their performance for the last two years, these committees, for the fiscal year beginning July 1, 1948, cut 28 percent from the Commerce Department estimate. The State Department's Office of International Information and Cultural Affairs had asked for $31,000,000. It got nothing. Even the Department of Justice took a cut of about 1 percent—but not that portion of the Justice Department which is under J. Edgar Hoover. The Federal Bureau of Investigation got every cent it asked for—$43,900,000.

In 1947, the State, Commerce and Justice Departments took a cut on the proposed 1948 budget averaging 23 percent. Again, Hoover got all he asked for. It was $35,000,000 a year ago.

Time magazine for May, 1947, commenting on the 1948 budget, remarks that "The Chief of the Federal Bureau of Investigation has a standard routine for appropriations committees. First, he swears members to secrecy. Then he tells them what his F.B.I, is doing to keep such things as crime and the menace of U. S. Communism in check…"

In every Congress, some Edgarite is on hand with a carefully prepared report giving the glorious history of the Bureau and its Director, which is read into the *Congressional Record*, complete with credits to the F.B.I, for solving crimes actually cracked by other government agencies. When the funds voted by Congress do not prove to be sufficient for Mr. Hoover's needs during the year, he builds up a deficit which the Congress is then asked to vote additional money to cover:

> "Mr. Woodrum of Virginia: I think it (F.B.I.) has been a very useful agency of the government, but I think that every agency of the government ought to handle its

fiscal affairs in an orderly and logical way, and should not be permitted to expand its functions unless it has the authority of Congress to do so.

"Mr. O'Brien: Has this particular branch, to the gentleman's knowledge, been guilty of such action?

"Mr. Woodrum: Yes; it employed people right here who will have to be discharged unless we give this money. That is the difficulty about it."[28]

The Director of the Bureau is not averse to using his Special Agents for lobbying purposes. In 1933, when he had good reason to believe he would be fired by the incoming Attorney-General Walsh, he called in a large number of his agents from many states to lobby with their Senators in his behalf—and at government expense.

Whatever the temperament and methods of Mr. Hoover, it must be remembered that he could not carry on in his traditional style for one day under an Attorney-General or an administration which disapproved his ways.

Mr. Hoover and his heresy-hunting Bureau do not stand alone. Solidly behind them are the American reactionaries and conservatives, busily constructing the American Police State by stripping to the skeleton all departments of the Federal government except the military and the internal security police. They are anxious to assign John Edgar Hoover the role of the American Himmler — with the necessary American changes in the script.

And Mr. Hoover, like Barkis, is willin', ma'am.

REFERENCES

1. *The Nation*, March 6, 1937.
2. *Only Yesterday*; Frederick Lewis Allen; Harpers.
3. *Congressional Record*, 71st Congress, 3rd Sess., House, Jan. 22, 1931.
4. *Olmstead v. the United States* (177 U. S. 438).

5. *New Yorker*, October 11, 1941.
6. *Congressional Record*, 71st Congress, 3rd Sess., House, Jan. 22, 1931.
7. *Current Biography*, 1940.
8. *The Freeman*, January 9, 1924.
9. Hearings of the Senate Judiciary Committee, Jan. 19-March 3, 1921.
10. Ibid.
11. Ibid.
12. *Colyer v. Skeffington* (265 Fed. 17)
13. *The Sacco-Vanzetti Case*, American Trials Series; Osmond K. Fraenkel; Knopf.
14. *Collier's*, April 12, 1947.
15. *The Nation*, March 6, 1937 also *Current Biography*, 1940.
16. *The Nation*, February 27, 1936, and March 6, 1937.
17. Ibid.
18. *Newsweek*, August 22, 1938.
19. *Harper's* January, 1936.
20. *Snaring Farnsworth*, by Wm. Mangil.
21. *New Republic*, March 11, 1940.
22. *Literary Digest*, May 31, 1924.
23. *Congressional Record*, 71st Congress, 3rd Sess., February 18, 1931.
24. *New Republic*, March 11, 1940.
25. National Service Board for Religious Objectors: Case of Harold V. Rusher.
26. Statement of N.S.B.R.O. Attorney Leonard Lazarus.
27. *New York Times*, November 6, 1947.
28. *Congressional Record*, 76 Congress, House, March 22, 1939.

(All major sources not otherwise indicated are official publications of the Federal Bureau of Investigation, the speeches of J. Edgar Hoover, and the *New York Times* on file at the New York Public Library.)

Resistance in Prison

For those who want a preview of the American police state in action, complete with distinguishing variations from the European model, thirty-two Federal correctional and penal institutions offer unlimited research facilities. Entrance requirements are stiff, but the experience may prove invaluable to anyone looking for a slingshot to use against the new Goliath.

Organizing resistance within a prison requires an understanding of the inmate's state of mind. He cannot exercise initiative or choice, nor may he express himself freely in any way. His individuality is limited to making "Big Deal" talk with other cons about how many Packards and Billy Rose blondes wait for him outside the walls. With his ego thoroughly squashed and trampled on, he is further cramped emotionally by the prohibition against showing sympathy or solidarity with a mistreated fellow inmate. "Every man does his own time," is the iron sophistry of the walled city. The uniforms are there to see that you keep your eyes straight ahead while the man next to you is slugged and dragged down the corridor to the strip cell.

Thus starved for an opportunity to affirm their humanity, prisoners fall back heavily on the old American substitutes for honest emotion: Patriotism and Mama. The Federal prisons had one of the highest records in the country for War Bond sales. No cell is complete without a picture of Mama, and no issue of the prison paper escapes some maudlin Edgar Guest intent on explaining the particular virtues of his maternal parent.

The springboard for action which will restore some semblance of Man to the numbered fragments inside the wall is always some immediate grievance felt by the prison body as a whole or by some sizable group within it. Usually it is the prison food, which appears on the menu board in the mess hall under a variety of alluring names — and always turns out to be lumpy bread pudding.

Food strikes may be directed against the entire meal, with the men refusing to leave their quarters where possible, or marching through the mess hall with empty trays if attendance there is compelled. Where the action is directed against a specific item of food, inmates are wised up by the grapevine ahead of chow time, and take everything but the objectionable food. As a variation of the food boycott directed against one item, the scrapple, rotten frankfurters or greasy potatoes may be taken, hidden in a scrap of paper, or paper napkin, and dropped to the walk upon leaving the mess hall. It is unlikely to reappear on the tables, particularly after the Associate Warden had to wade through it to Officers' Mess.

Since refusal to eat cannot usually be ferreted out as an assault on the prison administration, it is a good initial move prior to a strike. In both the minimum and maximum custody institutions, we found that a food boycott, once popular, tended naturally to become a work strike. Once the prisoners had refused a meal, they gathered in little groups in the yard. "No eat, no work," they said. And the hardier souls among them would refuse to report to their work detail.

The extreme form of the food boycott is the hunger strike. When a large number of men take this action, it cannot be expected to last more than a day or two at the longest. The hunger strike is better adapted to the use of individuals or small, highly dedicated groups with a long-range view of what is to be accomplished.

In any action taken by the prison population as a group, the initiators must be familiar with the routine steps to put down resistance, and the working rules for relations with the prison authorities during times of unrest. The prison officials will use:

    (1) Soft soap. The confidence man on the prison staff, usually the Warden or an Associate Warden, will try to have the strikers herded into the auditorium and, with

the proscribed combination of sternness and paternal concern, will promise them the moon if they get back into harness.
(2) Intimidation. This may be directed against the group as a whole, or individuals suspected as troublemakers may be weeded out and brought to the Warden's Office for a reprimand and warning. Solitary confinement, loss of 'good time', and shipment to a tougher pen are the usual threats.
(3) Violence. Pick handles are a favorite weapon. Water hoses are sometimes used; if one of these is brought into a cell block prison etiquette demands that you use mattresses and blankets for shelter so the officers may destroy prison property without your wasting energy on the job. Tear gas and guns are brought out only in extreme situations; the American prison guard does not as a rule develop a great deal of personal animosity even in critical moments. His attitude is "That's the regulations." He would undoubtedly lock up his own father with the same impersonal loyalty to the Officers' Manual.

To meet the inevitable soft soap, the strikers must have a clear idea of their objective. They must have a definite demand, or set of demands, which it is possible for the administration to meet. They must agree before striking that they will not return to work until these demands are granted or the strike is broken by force. They must present these demands at the first chance.

To insure the continuation of the strike after the spokesmen are sent to solitary or shipped (usually in the middle of the night, or while the population is locked in cell blocks) a succession of leadership should be agreed on, with alternate contacts in each cell block.

When violence is used by the officials, passive resistance is most effective in prison. It is sometimes difficult to adhere to, but will result in increased sympathy from those not striking and will conserve the rebellious spirit of the men for future action. An excess of violence on the part of the inmates, even in self-defense, will exhaust their ardor and postpone a resurgence for a long time. As in guerilla warfare, the objective is not the individual enemy but his materials, means of communication and morale.

Leadership must be alert to all local developments of value to the strikers. In the Danbury prison strike of 1946 the administration was aware of plans for a strike because of news releases sent out by coordinating groups in the 'free world'. A fake demonstration was held in the prison yard on the day before the strike was scheduled in the hope that prison officials might think that was the limit of the disturbance. The following day was Lincoln's Birthday and the strike might have been a dismal failure had not the officials obligingly ordered all men to report to their work assignments in the morning of that day.

Danbury prison at that time held a large number of Negro Selective Service cases, most of whom worked in the prison industry, a glove factory. The initial agitation was therefore directed at the Negro cell block, with the result that the prison industry was closed down, half the population demonstrated and sang songs in the yard, and two or three hundred refused to be enticed into the mess hall by a chicken dinner.

At the same prison, the inmate paper was edited by a company man who diffused more than the ordinary smell of polecat. When he put out an issue urging acceptance of the officials' plan for an Inmate Advisory Council (company union), all available copies were gathered up in every cell block, tied together in a bundle and delivered to the Warden without comment.

In the Lewisburg strike of 1947, the administration put forward this company union proposal right in the middle of the fireworks. Slips of paper were distributed to every cell, so the inmate might indicate his choice of representatives for the projected pint-sized parliament. The sewage disposal system was jammed with paper slips for several hours.

Whether the political prisoners are segregated or mixed with the prison population, a few points of agreement will simplify their job. First, they should make no contract of any kind with the administration. Second, they should refuse to deal singly with any prison official on any matter that might conceivably be a group concern. Third, they should refrain from violence in defending themselves against officers.

Of course, the resister will find that a contract is 'assumed' between himself and the officials, and that certain things are 'expected' of him. There is, however, no pretense that the inmate has the right to change, or even to interpret, this assumed contract. Interpretations – several different ones to fit each situation – will come from the Warden's office.

In instances where the resisters are segregated in one cell block, and none of them has any illusions about making parole, a number of joyful pastimes are offered which are guaranteed to furnish gray hair for the Warden and a rapid transfer to maximum custody for those involved. If the cell doors are of the individual lock type plus a master control operated manually or electrically from a box available only to the officer, the entire cell block may be put out of operation in a few minutes by stuffing paper clips, spring steel, fork tines and similar obstacles into the keyhole, in many prisons, the door hinges may be sprung by rolling a blanket tightly and inserting it on the hinge side while the door is swung closed against it. If the controls are operated entirely from a master box, and the doors are of the sliding variety, the keyhole on the master box may be plugged if it can be reached.

Most prisons have a vulnerable ventilating system which opens into corridors through panels equipped with Allen head screws. An Allen head screwdriver may, with patience, be shaped from a large nail. The water supply and waste pipes are usually run in these ducts. This ventilating system is a hollow steel drum, and a proper beating administered in the panels by five or six men will carry through the entire institution – officers sleeping quarters included.

Where demands are being made which are important enough to warrant drastic action by the group, I.W.W. experience has developed a couple of useful methods applicable to practically any jail. In the case of concrete construction, there is a procedure known as "building a battleship" which involves ten or fifteen men locking arms and standing as close together as possible. They count, "One, two, three", and on the count of three all jump together. When two or three tons of men land on a small area of floor most buildings feel it. In steel tank jails similar to most county lock-ups, marching in unison around uprights will shake bolts and rivets loose, and can even affect welded construction.

In their relations to the prison population, segregated resisters must remember that a barrier of fear exists between themselves and the conforming inmates, based on the ingenious "pie in the sky" system by which prisoners are coerced into good behavior. The inmate hopes he will make parole when his one-third term expires. Usually, he fails that, since paroles are kept to a percentage established by tradition. No reason is given for this refusal. With hope of parole gone, he looks forward to earning additional "good time" toward earlier release. If unable to do this by working on the prison farm or in prison industry, he still has his conditional release date – earlier than the "full time" date – to hope for. Any infringement of regulations will lose him precious days. These days will be taken away – no specified number for any specified infraction – piecemeal by a special court of officials.

Knowing this fear and uncertainty in the prisoner's mind, the resister relies heavily on humor in attacking the administration. If you can get the inmates to laugh at an officer, half the battle against prison discipline is won.

In one of the Danbury demonstrations, the administration's phony Christmas spirit was challenged by a large banner strung from the baseball backstop: "FREEDOM IS THE BEST CHRISTMAS GIFT". The slogan appealed to the inmates, and the hacks who were delegated to tear it down met with a roar of disapproval from the crowd, followed by laughter as the wind whipped one end of the banner loose and the guards struggled to get it under control. On another occasion, when the resisters were stirring up feeling about a man locked up in modified solitary, signs were tacked to broom handles, shoved out between the window bars, and unrolled. Inmates returning to quarters from the mess Hall stopped to watch while guards placed ladders against the wall and climbed up to snatch the signs. As the uniformed arms stretched out to tear the signs down, however, they were quickly rolled up around the broom handles again, and pulled in through the bars, to repeat their performance at another window. The thwarted officers again got the horselaugh.

One elderly guard developed the bad habit of hiding in a recessed doorway beneath our block, darting out to pick up messages thrown from the window to other inmates. One of our inventive geniuses took a couple of pieces of toilet tissue, smeared them liberally with stale mustard, wrapped them in another piece of tissue, and tossed them out. The uniform fell for it and elbowed a couple of inmates out of the way in his dash to pick up the "secret message". He got it, all right, and looked mighty silly glancing from his smeared hands to our window.

If you have a lot of time on your hands, an illegal newspaper can be published and distributed with the most primitive equipment. A tin can, milk bottle, or shaped piece of wood, or the sole of a shoe will form a simple mimeograph machine. A piece of blanket will make a mimeograph pad. You can cement it to the tin can etc. with a highly efficient glue made of oatmeal strained through a sock. Stencils and ink may be "borrowed" from the prison office by another inmate. If gelatin can be obtained from the prison kitchen, a duplicator can be made, using any flat container for the gelatin, and an indelible pencil for the master copy, If you can't get paper any other way, do what one of our boys in solitary did: wash the print off magazine pages.

As conditions get tighter, you may find yourself locked securely in individual cells. If there is a half inch of space under the door, as there usually is, flat objects may be passed from one cell to another by making a thin rope of tied shoelaces or sheet strips with a weight at one end. This can be skidded across the corridor and under a door on the opposite side. Between floors the ventilating system may be used for talking. Useful things like checkers, chess pieces and so on may be fashioned from a papier mache made of shredded newspapers with oatmeal paste for binder. There are a hundred ways to maintain your morale, and on occasion, to lower that of your opponent. Once, when feeling particularly morose, I cheered myself up by converting three full-size sheets into a pair of rope-soled shoes, and fashioned a medicine ball out of fourteen sets of winter underwear and a laundry bag.

When there are only a tiny handful of resisters, the most dramatic actions are inadvisable.

They may be supplanted by cautious sabotage and the stupidity strike, plus slowdown wherever applicable. The plumbing, lighting and communication systems are vulnerable. Schweikism is the last resort of the individual resister. How much material he may damage in his well-meaning blundering is a matter for the prison bookkeeping system.

This matter of the bookkeeping system brings up the angle of getting the drop on an official by uncovering manipulations with the prison budget. In one Federal prison, it was found that a three-way split existed between the warehouse officer, meat dealer and front office. The meat ordered would total 400 pounds. The dealer would deliver 300, but the warehouseman would receipt for the full amount shown on the bill and the front office would pay for it. The take went three ways.

In another prison, a 30′ by 25′ frame shop with a dirt floor cost $3000 to build with free labor, while a chicken house of cinder block ran to $10,000 with the same free labor. Six inches of sand was dumped on the floor, to be scraped up and thrown out the same year. Irregularities of this sort run through the whole Bureau of Prisons, and it is a rare guard or official who is not lining his pocket with cash or material covered by the jailhouse budget.

The waste which is a unique feature of American economy is sharply evident in prison. Often, food produced on the prison farm will be left on the ground to rot while the men inside the wall belch along on eternal beans and bread pudding. This occurs because prison bookkeeping systems demand that the food from the prison farm be charged against the kitchen at the market price. At Lewisburg Penitentiary, a large portion of the tomato crop rotted in 1946 because the market price of tomatoes happened to be too high to permit the cons to eat the food they had raised.

Prison is an unhappy parable of life in "outside" society!

POETRY

Bronze Man Breathing

Just to know how it would feel, released from destruction.
To be a bronze man breathing under archaic lapis,
Without the oscillations of planetary pass-pass.
Breathing his bronzen breath at the azury centre of time.

– Wallace Stevens

A few of these poems have appeared previously in *Motive*, *American Bard*, *Prism* of British Columbia, and *Iskra*.

Originally published as a collection in 1967.

Functions of Poetry in the Political World

> In our time, the language of politics has become infected with obscurity and madness.. .Unless we can restore to the words in our newspapers, laws, and political acts some measure of clarity and stringency of meaning, our lives will draw yet nearer to chaos.
> – George Steiner

Lord, on the continent where I was born, too many mouths are permanently open, and too many minds are permanently closed. Thirty-four basic words make up half our colloquial speech, and most of this is strung together in a series of clichés. It is only the lesser part of the lament for the death of language to open our ears and hear this. The greater part is that so few are listening. What passes for human communication becomes something like a tone poem – but the tones have been so often uttered in the same sequence and duration that the ear accommodates as it would to the ticking of an overloud clock.

How shall we share our experience and insight with the aid of these semi-automatic noises to which nobody listens? What is the nature of this tragedy which blocks our knowledge of ourselves, and of the values with which we relate to our world?

> ...after having declared himself a *Gottglaübiger* — a Nazi expression for those who have abandoned their Christian faith in a personal God and life after death — he addressed the group that witnessed the execution as follows: 'After a short while, gentlemen, we shall all meet again. Such is the fate of all men. Long live Germany, long live Argentina, long live Austria. I shall not forget them.'
>
> --Hannah Arendt, on the execution of Adolph Eichmann, in the *New Yorker*, March 16, 1963

Eichmann's tragedy, and ours, is the verbal stock response to experience. Faced as we are with the immediacy of our own executions, we achieve only the blurred unreality of a dream, and assure one another that 'the play's the thing.'

In a quite different sense, play *is* the thing. Alan Watts[1] tells us the psychotherapist is "dealing with people whose distress arises from what may be termed *maya*, to use the Hindu-Buddhist word whose exact meaning is not merely 'illusion' but the entire world-conception of a culture...Play is not to be taken seriously or, in other words, ideas of the world and of oneself which are social conventions and institutions are not to be confused with reality."

This easy confusion of reality with stock ideas about the world comes through even when Eichmann's superior, Hitler, receives news of the surrender of Paulus and the remains of the 6th Army at Stalingrad. Hitler cannot understand why Paulus has failed to commit suicide:

They have surrendered there formally and absolutely. Otherwise...they would have shot themselves with their last bullet...I can't have any respect for a soldier who is afraid of that...A man who doesn't have the courage, in such a time, to take the road that every man has to take some time...One can also say that the man should have shot himself just as the old commanders who threw themselves on their swords when they saw that their cause was lost...We had to assume that it would end heroically...With soldiers the fundamental thing is always character and if we don't manage to instil that, if we just breed purely intellectual acrobats and spiritual athletes, we're never going to get a race that can stand up to the heavy blows of destiny...What is Life? Life is the Nation...But how can anyone be afraid of this moment of death, with which he can free himself from his misery, if his duty doesn't chain him to this Vale of Tears...He could have freed himself from all sorrow and ascended into eternity and national immortality, but he prefers to go to Moscow.[2]

For twenty years, examples of everything Bad have been dredged from the Third Reich, overlooking our own first-cousin relationship. No accident when the Yank, complaining about the noisy water closets of England and the manure piles outside the front door of French farmhouses, welcomed Germany as most like home. And no accident when a durable American Himmler ferreting out campus free-speech movements charges that they are

> ...determined to destroy all acceptable standards of personal conduct and sane behavior...bent on eliminating all ethical practices relating to our established order...under the guise of academic freedom and constitutional privilege, flood our college campuses with obscene four-letter-word campaigns and pornographic publications which violate all codes

of ethics...offbeat dolts whose ability is measured only by how deep they can dip their poisonous pens into the pots of blasphemy, filth and falsehood...lawlessness, unbridled vulgarity, obscenity, blasphemy, perversion and public desecration of every sacred and just symbol.[3]

In defense, it might be argued that this is the kind of language to be expected from one who learned the art of public relations from Courtney Riley Cooper, former press agent for Ringling Brothers, Barnum and Bailey. The circus has never pretended to be the world of concrete reality.

Cleanth Brooks[4] remarks that "our generation inherits a language that has lost its hold on concrete reality, that is slack and imprecise, and that reflects a culture that lacks any commonly accepted value-system...The peculiar kind of knowledge that literature gives us is concrete – not a generalization about facts but a special kind of focusing upon the facts themselves – not the remedy for a problem but the special presentation of the problem itself...A formula can be learned and applied, but the full, concrete, appropriate response to a situation can only be experienced. Literature is thus incurably concrete – not abstract...Moreover, it may be that the work of the artist is most important in a civilization like our own, simply because our civilization is abstract and complicated...The dying flesh of language may produce a spiritual gangrene. One of the uses of literature is to keep our language alive – to keep the blood circulating through the tissues of the body politic."

MacLeish's study of words as signs[5], in which he examines an early English lyric, a Shakespearian sonnet, a lyric of Herrick's, and the third section of Pound's "Hugh Selwyn Mauberley," demonstrates how a passionate focus on the concrete experience freshens what in the inherited everyday language referred to by Brooks, would be plainly banal. In poetry, he argues, meaning has a very different structure from that which it shows us in prose. Poetic meaning has a structure which is proof against the analytical-destructive forays of a rationalism unhinged from its testable framework of human experience. The spirit-level used by the poet on his construction is the pulse of feeling, the discovery of intense personal existence.

> Stephen Spender[6] writes:
> I was standing in the corridor of a train passing through the Black Country. I saw a landscape of pits and pit-heads, artificial mountains, jagged yellow wounds in the earth...Oddly enough, a stranger next to me in the corridor echoed my inmost thought. He said, 'Everything there is man-made.' At this moment the line flashed into my head:
>
> A language of flesh and roses
>
> The sequence of my thought was as follows: the industrial landscape which seems by now a routine and act of God which enslaves both employers and workers who serve and profit by it, is actually the expression of man's will...the world which we create – the world of slums and telegrams and newspapers – is a kind of language of our inner wishes and thoughts...This thought greatly disturbed me, and I started thinking that if the phenomena created by humanity are like words in a language, what kind of language do we really aspire to?

One of the ground-questions with which Spender would be grappling if he built up a complete poem around his fragmentary line (he says it is easy for him to tell us what he'd like to do with it, but most difficult to do it) would be the place of the individual in history. In his preliminary exploration, he has already touched on economic determinism and individual responsibility.

Language and politics are engaged in a constant interplay. Perhaps the nature of our political experience is such that we no longer believe in the power of our words to set in motion any meaningful change. This, too, may contribute to our use of generalized rather than specific terms, and to the vogue of the cliché. Clear speech might help us recognize the desperate state of our politics–and this help we do not welcome. "The language of a community," insists a younger critic, "has reached a perilous state when a study of radioactive fall-out can be entitled 'Operation Sunshine.'"[7]

In our communities, the traditional educational processes supply us with banalities about the uniquely unconquerable human personality, while at the same time conditioning us to respond from stock items which in some long-vanished time may have been appropriate, reasonably fresh replies to political, economic, and social realities now changed beyond recognition. Bound within our Western view of personality as something "obviously" enclosed within a skin container, we are armed with language eroded to the point of uselessness in any relationship with those other "obvious" entities, some in skin containers, "outside" of, and in a subject or object linkage with us. In the sense that what happens to us is shaped to any degree by a lack of correspondence between our language and political reality, the deterministic forces are also inside us. Rilke writes:

> We have already had to rethink so many of our concepts of motion, we will also gradually learn to realize that that which we call destiny goes forth from within people, not from without unto them. Only because so many have not absorbed their destinies and transmuted them within themselves while they were living in them, have they not recognized what has gone forth out of them; it was so strange to them that, in their bewildered fright, they thought it must only just then have entered into them, for they swear never before to have found anything like it in themselves…For it is not inertia alone that is responsible for human relationships repeating themselves from case to case, indescribably

monotonous and unrenewed; it is shyness before any sort of new, unforeseeable experience with which one does not think oneself able to cope.[8]

In Rilke's meaning for individual destiny, it becomes that part of the historical ground which the fully human being has made his own, has admitted and accepted, has identified and affirmed, has absorbed within himself. But the inability to do this shouldn't be blamed solely on inertia and shyness. Surely it issues in some part from an education which rewards the stock response. What happens to the individual so conditioned, when faced with that "new, unforeseeable experience" under circumstances where the environment is mandatory, as in a concentration camp or POW stockade?

In the Korean war, American prisoners were faced with a radically different treatment from that which they had come to expect and for which their stock responses were, to a degree, adequate. Kinkead's[9] study emphasizes, with respect to Communist use of physical torture that, "the army has not found a single verifiable case in which they used it for the specific purpose of forcing a man to collaborate or to accept their convictions."

The initial phase in gaining collaboration is described by Kinkead:

>...the Chinese holding our men made every effort to appear humane to them in the beginning. After they had shaken their hands and offered them cigarettes, they congratulated them on being released from capitalist bondage. They repeated simple, easily understood slogans, such as "Be a fighter for peace," to them. A prisoner who was hesitant about cooperating was approached with the following plea: "Are you for peace? Of course you are. Every intelligent person is. Then, naturally, you will fight for peace. Good! You are henceforth a true fighter in the cause for peace. Now you will have an opportunity to display the courage of

your convictions and fight for peace." The prisoner was then asked to sign a "peace" appeal. If he balked, he was told that by signing he would simply be affirming a universal desire of all thinking human beings.[10]

Hannah Arendt, in her report on the Eichmann execution, commented on the banality of evil. Good has its own banalities, and a generalized "peace" has become one of them. As Shelley remarked on "love," it is a word "Too much profaned for me to profane it further." In terms of a living, sensitive use of language, "Fight for peace" is on a slogan-slinging par with, "Cough your way to health."

For the more literate, a response appropriate to the Chinese flavour of the occasion might be one of the brief poetic summaries in the Reps and Senzaki translation of *No-Gate Opening*, the Ch'an classic.

The psychiatric description of the collaborators, as summarized by Kinkead, includes these observations:

> For one thing, the returnees displayed much less than average interest in their environment. Their outlook was a noticeably restricted one, and they expressed few, if any, demands, desires, or wishes for the present, or plans and thoughts about the future. They discussed their lives in an exceedingly flat and unemotional way, using stock phrases over and over again.[11]

The description sounds suspiciously close to the mental condition of a boys' high school graduating class awaiting induction into the American armed forces. Pending availability of a "before" sampling of the returned prisoners and a control group, I would reserve judgement on whether the observed condition followed or preceded incarceration. It is noted that a Turkish group undergoing the same experience produced no defectors, against some thirty per cent for the Americans, and no deaths during imprisonment, against forty per cent for the Americans.

Reasons for the difference, drawn from the Turkish background, have been advanced, in line with Kinkead's desire to tell as much of the truth as possible without offending the military. One difference in the cultural conditioning which he didn't mention would be the peculiarly American meaning for "The play's the thing," wherein the individual is educated to play the life-game under the assumption that he is a self-sufficient, separable entity destined to triumph over his "outside" environment including, if necessary, other human beings in his vicinity. The joker is that this education does not provide the tools needed for the insight that this is *only an assumption*.[12] When the product of such an educational system is locked into an environment whose assumptions are totally opposed to his stock-response inventory, he goes functionally bankrupt.

> Yes, but I am doing what you call an admirable thing because I can't bear to be a separate person! I think so. I really don't want to be known as a Red lawyer; and I really don't want the newspapers to eat me alive; and if it came down to it, Lou could defend himself. But when that decent, broken man who never wanted anything but the good of the world, sits across my desk... I don't know how to say that my interests are no longer the same as his, and that if he doesn't change I consign him to hell because we are separate persons.[13]

Miller is arguing against that concept of the separateness of persons which is a functional part of the police state, and which is intended to guarantee that you keep your eyes dead ahead while the Joe next to you is dragged off the pavement for a chat with Big Brother.

Once this separable self is released from the form of classical tradition, its actions, attitudes and literary products can no longer be evaluated by comparison with established models. The critic influenced by Romanticism looks mainly for integrated feeling, not unity of structure. He insists that each of the factors involved in the totality be emotionally compatible, and will accept utterly incredible structure, as in *Tale of Two Cities* or *Doctor Zhivago* if only this criterion be met.

The world of incredible coincidence and improbable motivation, the magical Romantic world of the pixie in the computer is just as much a denial of reality as were the last words of Eichmann. Indeed, criticized on Romantic grounds, Eichmann's words and life were all of a feeling-piece: a consistent denial of reality throughout. Neither the Hegelian absolute ideal, nor the Romantic criticism which issued from it by way of Coleridge[14] are politically reliable.

The Romantic approach is at its weakest when it attempts to deal with the existence of evil: that source of terror supposedly transposed "within" from the Gothic supernatural "other." In *Tale of Two Cities* the Terror is political; it has crept out of the supernatural woodwork and has the feet of the mob, but it is still quite "other." In *Zhivago* it issues from a deterministic mythology and its tool, the State, and is again "other." Pasternak is a good Methodist, championing the right of the individual under Romantic philosophy to interpret the political Bible doctrinally for himself. He is also a good Methodist in finding that misfortune tests the worth of the individual; he matures under adversity. Grace must be earned.

The pre-Romantic world of status, tradition, and structural unity facing the terror of the "other" asked: How can evil exist if God is all-powerful? The Romantic-humanist world faces the problem of the allegedly "inner" terror by asking: How can evil exist if man's rational intellect is all-powerful? It looks like the same old ko-an, but it has moved around the corner off Cathedral Square.

Through all the changes in philosophical fashion and literary criticism, from the Classical to the Romantic in poetry, evil has stubbornly refused to be believably internalized. Certainly the real "otherness" of evil in the popular mind appears in the political paranoia which distinguishes American diplomacy. Its components are the devil theory of history and the logic of the excluded middle. Beginning with the argument that there are only two sides, and that choice is compulsory, the conclusion (probably on both sides) is that one has in reality no choice, and is merely doing what one must. "Every intelligent person is for peace."

Relevant to the matter of will-power, the assumption of the sovereign, separable individual, and the enforced taking of sides, Sargant[15] summarizes:

> In stressing the importance of further research on this whole problem, it must be emphasized once again that the concept of will-power and of any individual's power to resist for an indefinite period the physioological stresses that can now be imposed on both body and brain, have found little scientific support either in peace or war...some persons become converted against their will because they insist on doing what they consider to be the 'right thing' and go out to fight what is more wisely avoided or ignored. Their energies should be devoted instead to maintaining a policy of total non-cooperation, despite their pride and a natural inclination to test their courage and strength against those trying to provoke them...in groups of persons, morale is of supreme importance, as when individuals get fatigued they usually become much more suggestible to the brave or cowardly group attitudes of others.

I. A. Richards[16] does a useful job of documenting culturally conditioned blocks to the understanding of poetry and life. Many of his comments are directly related to the possibility of the controlled population which does not exercise choice:

> If we wish for a population easy to control by suggestion we shall decide what repertory of suggestions it shall be susceptible to and encourage this tendency except in the few. But if we wish for a high and diffuse

civilization, with its attendant risks, we shall combat this form of mental inertia.

Concerning the effect of good poetry on the stock response, Richards asserts:
> Nearly all good poetry is disconcerting...Some dear habit has to be abandoned if we are to follow it. Going forward we are likely to find that other habitual responses, not directly concerned, seem less satisfactory. In the turmoil of disturbed routines...the mind's hold on actuality is tested.

The comments of Richards on sentimentality and inhibition, while stemming from the great days of Freudian analysis in the late Twenties, also continue to speak to the point. A person may be accounted sentimental, he says, when he is too "trigger-happy" with his emotions:
> Some people regard indulgence in the soft and tender emotions as always creditable, and they wallow in them so greedily that one is forced to regard them as emotionally starved.[17]

In the quantitative sense also examined by Richards, a response is sentimental if it is out of balance with the occasion on the side of being overwhelmingly disproportionate. Extending the range of inquiry from the quantitative to the qualitative, Richards turns from the adequacy to the appropriateness of response: "Refined emotions are like sensitive instruments; they reflect slight changes in the situations which call them forth."

Concerning emotional reactions to generalized situations, he observes of a poem about a girl lamenting her lost or absent lover, that:
> ...this abstracted theme is nothing in itself...if the mere fact that some girl somewhere is thus lamenting were an occasion for emotion, into what convulsions ought

not the evening paper to throw us nightly? This is obvious, but there is reason to think that very many people are ready to react emotionally to a "pathetic" situation merely at this level of abstractness...[18]

These are the functions of poetry in the present world:
- to cut into the generalized with personal speech
- to point directly as possible to the real
- to provide quantitative and qualitative models for appropriate sentiment
- to freshen, clarify, and make more meaningful our language.

Clif Bennett
Fort William, Ontario
July, 1967

[1]Alan W. Watts, *Psychotherapy East and West* (Toronto: New American Library, 1963) p. 15.
[2]Alan Clark, *Barbarossa* (London: Hutchinson & Co., 1965) pp.255 ff.
[3]J. Edgar Hoover, quoted *Toronto Globe & Mail*, April 1, 1967.
[4]Cleanth Brooks, *The Uses of Literature*. Toronto Education Quarterly, V.2, No. 4
[5]Archibald MacLeish, *Poetry and Experience*, (Baltimore: Penguin, 1964) pp.28 ff.
[6]Stephen Spender, *The Making of a Poem* (NY: Norton, 1962) pp. 53 f.
[7]George Steiner, *Language and Silence* (NY: Atheneum, 1967) p. 27
[8]Rainer Maria Rilke, "Letters to a Young Poet." In *The Worlds of Existentialism*, ed. Maurice Friedman. (NY: Random House, 1964) pp. 266 ff.
[9]Eugene Kinkead, *In Every War But One* (NY: Norton, 1959) p. 34.
[10]*ibid*.

[11]*ibid.*
[12]Don Weitz, *Commitment and the "Helping" Professions.* Unpublished, 1967.
[13]Arthur Miller, *After the Fall* (NY: Viking, 1964) p. 46.
[14]Don Salo, *A Study of the Novel*, Jane Eyre. Unpublished, 1967.
[15]William Sargant, *Battle for the Mind* (London: Pan, 1963) pp. 209 f.
[16]I.A. Richards, *Practical Criticism*, (NY: Harcourt, 1963) p. 240.
[17]*ibid.*
[18]*ibid.*

Ruth, Mother Of Obed

"Boaz," she said, "do you mind how it was:
How we came to your fields at the reaping,
How we were happy, we sang,
Naomi and I – how we sang?"
    (In my blindness I sang;
     In my youth I made songs.)
He grunted.

"Boaz," she said, "you remember our love:
How the moon poured white wine in the doorway
All the long evening, all night?
The moon... the white wheat...that night?"
    (Blind men see the moon;
     In their youth they see moons.)
He was fat.
He grunted.

The Preachers

Two prophets came to Templetown.
One was tall, well-dressed and fair,
A man whose words had wide renown.
The other's face was sunburned brown
Beneath a mat of unshorn hair;
Rags and patches were his gown –
     A curious pair!

The ragged one hurled words of grim,
Wild prophecy: "Your life's mad plan
Is one weak drop upon the rim
Of time's deep cup. It is His whim
The roofs shall fall and end your span."

And when they tired of stoning him.
      They killed that man.

The other prophet smiled and spoke
Of how on earth had never been
A wiser, truer, nobler folk
Or holier clouds of incense-smoke.
And as they cheered and called him kin
And hailed him to the highest place.
      The roof fell in.

Old Rain

Old rain, that with a hollow gurgling sound
Rides streaming tiles and gutters to the ground,
Beats many-footed music on the metalcoated cells
And fills the prison corridor with ghosts
    of temple bells.

Old rain, old pagan rain
That kissed the earthblack woman's breast
In velvet kingdoms north of Timbuctu
And some poor, homesick captive blessed
With dreams of more familiar gods
    his people knew.

Old rain, old shameless rain
To soothe, in Ashur's angry face
Some heretic, some ill-considered bore
Who in the midday market place
Aflush with wine, profaned high Ishtar
    as a whore!

Old rain, old Christian rain

That washed the feet of Rome's police.
Yet spumed no Christian-slaughtered son of sin
As lower than the Prince of Peace
Or any Frank held chained and fast
    by Saladin.

Great gods, denying that they live and die,
Imprison doubting men who call the lie –
Until they' re caught and kicking
    in the flood of antic rain
That with a merry bellylaugh goes down
    the cosmic drain.

Progress

I.
From the rim of hills, wet, swollen hands
Of sullen clouds push down.
Beneath the tempest's heavy frown
The rabbits run to earth. Small bands
Of apes hold closer, keeping warm.
They shiver. They fear the storm.

II.
The Rain-God rides! His gleaming spears
He flings in anger through the trees!
The mother crouches; at her knees
Brown children greet the storm with tears.
Old warriors hide in huts of sod
And tremble. They fear the God.

III.
What says the sky? No god can tell
The terror some gray cloud may rain
Since men of science, lucid, sane,

Have built a sky-borne, man-made hell
To drive men underground, like elves.
They worry. They fear themselves.

Hijas Delviento

Las hijas del viento
    No hablan, no cantan;
Ayer y mañana
    Caminan y bailan,
        Siempre volante,
        Volante a mi...
Las hijas del viento,
    Dos verdes, tres rojas –
En faldas de fiesta
    Las hijas, las hojas,
        Siempre volante,
        Volante a mi...

On The Beach At San Felipe

This is a mad marriage, here,
Of hard desert, soft sea:
The delicate violet fish, curious.
Stares at the cactus.
Coyotes whine at the waves.
    Burro – what am I doing here, burro?
    I could be watching Juana dance flamenco...

Tonight, from the Sea of Cortez,
Long tide comes creeping in
Up a mile of desert-beach

And we try to distill water
With two tin canteens and a frying pan
And a copper tube yanked from a Ford.
>   *Burro – what am I doing here, burro?*
>   *I could be watching Juana dance flamenco…*

Because we saw how, at the only well,
On Sunday, two magnificent pieces
Of Mexican manhood took a bath
And the soapy water ran back down the drink
In this land where time walks with a limp
And even death comes by on crutches.
>   *Burro – what am I doing here, burro?*
>   *I could be watching Juana dance flamenco…*

Baja California del Norte
1948

Wasted Rain

With us, as in the desert of Sonora,
The soil that feeds our culture runs to sand
While thoughts of worth, to mead the hungry heart.
Are thinly spread throughout a bitter land
Like barrel cactus, dusty miles apart.

Right here, I think there might have camped
Some nomad of the intellect, intent
On hunting out one green-leafed, new idea
And pulling it apart in wonderment.
One night alone his bedroll rested here.

The last thin traces of his fire are lost
In ragged gullies cut by winter rain

Whose sullen floods across the desert stream
Unheld by tree, or rose, or rippled grain:
No chaliced mind awaits the urgent dream.

Valle Trinidad

Remembering what Yeats said to Synge
That sent him to the Aran Isles,
I listened to the man on the porch.
"The school is ruined,"
He said. "We have no teacher
And no priest. Eight hundred people
In these hills. The church and school
Have forgotten us. The Government? Hah!"

Perhaps I was he who was meant to stay:
Answer to tired eyes and sagging
Moustache, porch, fence-posts,
Adobes, footprints, dust.
  (Old tire treads are their sandals,
   And thongs of inner-tube.
   My friend wears Firestones.)

But I had business at the border;
My permit was six months illegal
And besides, I don't speak much Spanish.
  (What Yeats said to Synge was
   To go and live among people
   Who had no-one to write their history.)

Pinto Girl

(For Morgana, ten years old)

What are you dreaming, pinto girl?
Building corral with firewood sticks
For a pinto pony that's playing tricks
In your eyes, where the firelight gleams.
Where do they run to, pinto girl?
Where do they range – your dreams?

You're dreaming of horses, pinto girl.
Wild black horses in windy pines.
High sierras, and lost gold mines
And a trail to the open sky.
Hear' em galloping, pinto girl!
Where do they run, and why?

They'll try to bridle you, pinto girl,
Bottle and label and brand your soul
And dress you up like a barber pole.
You've the mark of a maverick breed;
Rebel and outlaw like myself,
Is that what you want – or need?

Don't let 'em hobble you, pinto girl!
It's better to forage the broken hills
Through sage and cactus and yucca quills
Than graze like a cow on the plain below.
Better to dust your heels and run,
Get clear of the town! I know...

I know the trouble is waterholes.
They're fewer and drier with every fall.
And soon there won't be any at all:
You'll be caught when you come to drink.
My prayers go with you, pinto girl.
I watch you build corral, and think.

Poem For Roger, Age 3

So you sleep:
    arms back, hands half-curled
    about some fragment of a dream,
    your tangled hair, pale blonde against the pillow,
    a moonlight net for secret butterflies.

When you wake
    your eyes, your round brown eyes
    are most enormous, child,
    and I have almost seen your world,
    as though some light immediate universe
    unwarped by time
    had twinkled once
    beyond a shining windowpane.

Most quick, entrancing earth you hold
    that you must leave reluctantly,
    fight sleep, recurrent little death
    who drags you down
    from day, and story-time,
    and paper aeroplanes
    that float
    away

Words Of The Jaguar Priest

> Arranged from fragments
> in Maud Worcester Makemson's translation
> of the late Mayan Book of the Jaguar Priest of Tizimin.

Once there was truth
Which we drew from the Serpent in ancient times,
From the clear, unclouded heavens
To the evil-knotted earth beneath.
But the latter days bring forth no priests;
No man, without doubting, accepts his government.
The gods hide their faces in rivers of tears;
Wet are their faces with drops like rain.

Have you forgotten the gifts of the heavens
On the day when you carried the idol of Kan?
Three symbols of strength from the great Tree of Life!
Three clusters of fruit from the nourishing Tree!
The Jaguar will pour out the magic of government:
Good chieftains, good men, good sons
To all four ends of the twisted earth.

And when from the dark and sullen sea
I shall be uplift in a chalice of fire,
You will worship the truth divine:
The ancient ways stand always ready.

The Perfumed Statue

Just so, with the mind's thin wedge he shaped her.
Cut round the corners of those marble lids,
Formed the almost-speaking instancy of lips
That barely part, arrested in some moonpale
Syllable of stone. What thought may hide

Within that proudly tossing head,
He, and only he, could tell you.

– And he is dead, Pygmalion, of a chill despair
That left him sick and motionless in her embrace
Whose timeless breast lay frozen in the instant
Of completion. Change of thought, or moving speech.
She knew not, nor any God beyond
The mortuary heaven of his dream.

For she was both his dream and death,
Was Galatea. He ground his passion into dust
Against the heedless coral of her lips
And cried his love unending down the fine,
Smooth mazes of her alabaster brain.

Mourn Pygmalion, his heart a rose,
Who bruised it bringing fragrance to a dream.

Depth

Tired is he of this turgid water
Who has known the mud flats only, on the lea,
And watched with aching heart the white gull's flight
Above the roaring breakers to the sea.
Aye walks he in the shallows poorly.
Digging clams on the sandbar's rim;
Beyond the thin horizon that his thinking knows,
His soul yearns on past the reach of him.

What unthought prize shall his heart discover
In new dimensions shaped below the spray?
Though he drown, shall the pain be worth this
One swift moment of a larger day?

Testing

Most who call it climbing go by easy ways and sure,
Satisfied with cattle paths on meagre hills and poor,
Nor ever dream a troubled dream of mountains piling high
To cry a granite challenge to the eagles and the sky.
They never pass the recall of the farthest lights of town,
But have a little picnic, and come untested down.

Others hold a whispering that urges them along
To climb storm-beaten pinnacles and hear the thundersong
Which rises in a melody heard best by one alone,
While flash and wheel and hover over twisted tree and stone
And shattered crag and aerie, the creatures of the sky –
These hills that some call hillocks, others say are high.

Moved by murmured drumbeats which end all rest, denied.
They ask no hand to hold to, nor any path to guide.
Scorning map and manuscript that guarantee the way
To contours of monotony and dreams of solid gray.
Each seeks the certain Everest that seems to wait for One,
And climbs without a compass to the kingdom of the sun.

Stranger

He had never known that morning valley:
Even the air hung alien, cactus-blossom bright
About the ancient shoulders of gaunt monoliths.
What birds there sang, he knew not.
Were there herds? A goatbell tinkled on the valley floor
Beneath the lifting mist. He heard no more
The talk of brothers, such familiar cadences of sound
As run colloquial needles
Down accustomed grooves of mind.

Some other earth embraced the family dream.
Ten thousand walls upreared their rocky arms
Between this spot and that where, as a child,
He woke estranged one sudden dawn
And, finding graveyard mould upon his hands,
Knew then he'd buried father, mother and a home.

Song For David

Once there were men in the tribes of our brothers
Mighty in manner of hand and of brain.
From the mountain of Moab, cold kingdom of Sheth,
Rich land of the Jordan they conquered and seeded.
The tent of the Midianite fell before Gideon's
Three hundred men from the tribes of our brothers –
Bring me the three who would follow him now!

The fields of Philistia are risen against us,
But we – we have made us a nation of tailors
Trimming our cloth to the needs of the hour.
Where is the man who will speak for the righteous?
Our hands are contented; our lips are of brass.
Dust are the temples from Dan to Beersheba;
Dust is our fathers' god today.

    Who goes alone to the vale of Elah?
    Who puts his faith in a slingshot now?

Undergoing Of The Evening-Lands

Killed space with speed.
Stuffed all the spirit-rooms
With dust not worth a prayer,
Piled furniture on each aspiring stair,
Daubed pictures on the windows God looked through.
Painted suffocation on the air.

Now all our cosmos
Like a drying apple shrinks
While we, within the core,
Shrink too. How shall I halt the crowding suns,
When I must press to you?

Come close…
There is no braveness now for dreaming-room.
Not any heart can sing the bursting seed
To crack our tomb. Huddle,
Huddle. We bought ourselves this doom.

Leda

Leda lay dreaming
Rhythm of wings,
Drumming of pinions,
Arrow that sings.

Dreamed the invader,
Felt the dream grow:
Torrent of feathers,
Passionate snow.

Phoenix That Died

You come to ask us how he died,
That wise, unfrightened bird
Whose skyward passing dimmed the sun.
We know not, but this much we have heard:

Some flaw within the jewelled brain
Reflected from the white horizo's rim
Grew large behind the wonder of his eyes
To breed a high, unearthly pride in him.

Thus spurred, he climbed that further sky
Beyond all legend of a crumbling earth.
(Men whispered that the ashes and the dust
Might be the only nest of his rebirth.)

He hungered for some purer space
Where dust could never dull his burning pride
Nor sunbound planets pull his startled wings.
He learned a fear of ashes…and he died.

All Fragile Arts

All fragile arts:
Poetry,
Pornography, I tell you –
Are crystals to encyst
A wild array of roses.

As if some wanderer
Tumbling down a well
Cried out:
"That moss!

That twinkling stone!"

The Zen monk.
When they told him
His calligraphy was perfect,
Burned his brushes.

Angles

Two fish were caught in the ocean
And put in a small globe of glass:
Their reflections swam round and around them.
"I expand!" sang one.
"The world shrinks," said the other.

A man went out in the desert
And lived there a month by himself:
He came back looking sad.
When they asked him,
He said he had ulcers.
(Didn't want to admit
He'd met his god
And been surprised
At the smallness of him.)

> Twelve angels stood on the head of a pin;
> They didn't have room to sit down.
> "Do you think we can dance?" asked one.
> The rest pushed him off.
> "Don't be technical," they said.

"Aren't you sorry," asked the snake,
"That God gave you no eyes?"
"Of course not; He can't be blamed,"

Replied the mole.
"Why not?" asked the snake.
"God is blind," said the mole.

    The devil met a woman.
    "What will you take
    For your soul?" he asked.
    "One wish," said the woman.
    "You may have it," said the Devil.
    "What is your wish?"
    "Your soul," said she.

A starving man wandered down a canyon.
He met a mountain lion, and gasped:
"Do you know where there is food?"
The lion stared at him
While he took two steps more and fainted.

Thoughtfully, the lion cleaned the bones.
"What an obvious question," he said.

    The gray philosopher, thinking,
    Walked alone in the garden.
    He saw a lily-of-the-valley.
    Yesterday it had two leaves;
    Today it had three.
    He frowned:
    "You are inconsistent," he said.
    And he crushed the flower
    With his foot.

A biologist drew his scalpel
Through the brain of a guinea pig.
For a moment he thought he could feel it
In his own skull
"How curious," he said.

Above, a massive shadow
Drew a phantom scalpel through his brain.
"How curious," it said.

> A man stood in a great courtyard
> From which a thousand doors swung open.
> "I am alone of my kind!" he cried,
> And he heard the sound
> Of a thousand doors
> Closing.

When the ants had conquered earth,
They wrote a book, explaining
How, from the world's first dawn
This had been inevitable:
Survival of the Fittest, they called it.

> The Last Woman, ailing,
> Crept to a cave and died
> Dreaming of men invincible,
> Dreaming of heroes.
> Eight miles away, ingloriously,
> The Last Man died of measles.

Dead Guru

> Read at the Memorial Service for Jim Corsa

Arrow of intent
Aimed at the sun:
Cosmos and consciousness
Lastly are one.

Dreamer of daybreak
Blinding to see,

Nightfall and silence
Be doorways to thee.

Singer of starhope,
Diamonds of pain
Melting in ebbtide.
Falling in rain.

After All

– and after all, watching time,
that weary accordion, fold up in pleats,
to ask yourself, while the last air puffs out
and all possible worlds
become pancakes:
What was it all about, eh? What ?

– because once I thought there was always tomorrow;
once we all said tomorrow, tomorrow,
and the clever ones, bigmouthed
gulped the real round orange of our days,
trading us tomorrow and an orange capsule:
(citric acid, artificial color, .1% benzoate of soda)

– and let too many days get by
so that this maybe is the last night
and I must write like mad until morning
thinking, after all, what difference
does it make : one minute, one day,
one life or a dozen, when all he
or any other possible god could say, is:

Where were *you* when the lights went out?

Greater Loyalty

We swear an allegiance to earth: Cybele,
Great Mother who nourished the creeds that fell
And the creeds that live. The earnest we give
Is prayer made worthy by toil.

    Pity the people
    Who deny the spirit its roots in soil!

All lonely valleys where roads are poor,
And the hunter looks for the red deer's spoor,
Covet the keys to our heart. What better part
Than reverent love of the earth?

    Dreamer and singer, behold:
    Here all dreams, all songs, have their birth.

Our flag is a field on a moonlit night
Crossed by the ghost of a curlew's flight,
Flown from the staff of a black crow's laugh
And topped by the cry of the loon.

    Dexter and argent:
    One juniper-berry, one saskatoon.

                              Kettle Valley, B.C.
                                  September 1954

Letter To Dan Katchongva

Peaceful people
I see that you have come from Hotevilla
From Shungopovy, from old Oraibi

Venerable names of places
Oldest cities in this land

Still runs, you say, through Hopiland
The spirit highway to the sun
Straight path the whiteman cannot see
Your headmen say that newer road
The asphalt carpet on the sand
Will break the spirit highway

I cannot tell if this is so
Clan people, I cannot tell
Dan Katchongva, you are friend
To my friend Ammon
I will tell you what I know

Do not trust the whiteman
Dan Katchongva
The whiteman has
An asphalt coating
On his heart

Sunset, South Rim

Now, slowly, flows that yearning hour
When the last light, turning, flees
Down the day's bright burning
Through heliotrope and mauve.

The first of night is soft, is feminine:
Dark goddess of the seventh gate;
The three-four lights accented
On the valley floor, dim pearls
A dreaming Negress holds;
And snow about is a linen dress,

A sheet, a muted shout
Against the half-bare shoulders of the hills.

Now is a time of yes-and-no.
Earth, equivocal, replies to misty stars
With misty slopes and hollows.
There, where the eye follows,
No sudden mass appears,
No sharp intent.

Even your smile
Holds the new moon's half-light.
The unawakened dream, the worlds of mist.
If we had kissed, I should have loved
Not you, but all of this.

Trial

> "...a summary court in perpetual session..."
> *Notes from the Year 1920*, F. Kafka

"It is not the burden which causes you pain – the burden of excessive sensibility – but the degree of your refusal to accept responsibility for it." Lawrence Durrell, *Cefalu*

"What is the judgment, then?" he asked,
And heard no answer there.
The corridor went down by fourteen steps
Of crumbled marble from the court,
And turned toward the right.

His hands hung free.
He lit his pipe, and thought
"What now?" He heard
The scrabbling of a beetle in the wall.

His feet were free. He walked,

And passing through the high and vaulted hall,
He met no man. No maid
In bright brocade and dirndl,
Laughing, tossed her head,
Or sighed. Here spoke no sound.

Four hundred doors of panelled oak,
Each slightly open, flanked his footsteps
Left and right. From childhood
He had walked these ways. He knew
All rooms. All rooms were empty.

These be the chambers of the law.
Here all his years are hailed
From hall to hall. The case
That never opened, never ended,
Called him on. He sought

Old books, dry, dim plateaus of thought
And wry advice. The artist in him
Darkly sensed the distant
Anonymity of judgment,
Whose tendrils touched

The now. His rooted veins
Had thrown the tree, the lifted bough
Aloft, of which the random oak was cut
To plank the floor beneath his feet
And hang the heavy doors.

"Cursed the heart by reason compassed;
The mind's own mist hides the grail in gray,
Through which the half-light looks upon
 A time that is not night or day."

He read this rune

On a tilted stone. It helped
To while away the time, to translate this,
And once in every language leave the lines
Incised on the oaken doors.
So came, or crawled,

One illumined hour, when,
Falling between two falcons,
He had knowledge. (Held and housed
In his moaning gut the meaning
Of the sacrificial knife.)

Beyond Eden

Love, when I watch your eyelids curve
Over the blue worlds dreaming,
Born is the word half-breathed
By the lips half-parted:
Peace to the midnight-hearted.
Ease from the bold air gleaming.

Gone is the glare: red sun that wreathed
Earth and her sisters dancing.
Love, oh my love! Come close
With your gift: Dark roses
That bloom where the bright eye closes,
Safe from the lightning glancing

Fierce on the sands of Eden. Those,
Those are the dunes that deny us!
Eden is land set flame
By the gods. Now heaven
Is bread where there is not leaven.
Nightfall, no angel to spy us.

Poe Cottage

"Poe wrote what he did because it was as remote as possible from his own experience." – Edward Davidson

The kitchen is cute colonial. The polished pewter shines
With an underwater gleam. Here, in the middle of maple
   and homespun,
That man wrote. Mrs Poe made tea, baked bread and
biscuits,
And swept the floor. " Lift your feet, Edgar... Edgar!"
Spring sun bugled through the starched curtains, spring
breathed
In the Dutch door. Birds chirped, but their notes broke
On the pitted shell of darkness, where Edgar Allan
Fabricated terror, wrote "Usher," "Ulalume." His pen
squeaked.
Poe, is the mind its own place? How much of it is ripe
With the myth of the Thousand-Year Reich? How much of it
Visible and controlled by any logic? Ah, Comrade Pavlov,
What of the unconditioned dog? Here is Poe Cottage;
In this precise and proper domesticity, all Hell broke loose.
And an admiring Japanese changed his name to Yedogar
Ranpo.

Tideland

Forty feet of river mud, I had,
Across from the downstream end of Annacis,
And a floathouse on butts of old cedar.
Tidewater, rich and wriggling, escaped
The documental grasp. Anonymous ooze
Puzzled our town planners, confounding
Municipality and province. As for Ottawa,
Too many generalities absorbed their eyes;
Other atoms weighed heavier than mud.

And there for half a year I paid no rent.
I rendered ciphers unto Caesar,
Heard Old Tom curse the Health Inspector,
Helped two boys pull a gillnetter wheel,
Shared my McEwan's, and watched them square a transom.

I meant to know that shore, that forty feet,
From stiff, archaic grass that sprang in segments.
Tubular and harsh, along the dike,
To the Fraser's edge. Things grew there
Not in beauty, but in truth. The mud gave birth;
The process worked. My tideland spawned
A verbal multitude. To this black earth,
Tiring of bleached abstraction, hygienic vacuum,
The ledgered noun, I came to find myself.

In The Manner Of Seurat

Half-shadowed, the evening esplanade.
Long shores of Lake Geneva, softness
Of early summer in the lakeside trees.
The candy-striped, crisp awnings of the small cafes

And, busy round the Madelein, the Old City roofs.
This air breathes light; the god's a pointillist
Who livened it, drove his thousand dots,
Quick, pastel fireflies across the canvas dusk.

En silhouette, a woman, slender, tilts her head
And grows through flecks of amber light
Toward her lover's kiss, so rooted on the shore
She seems a pliant tree uprising. Quietly now.
The breeze upholds, over the dappled lake.
The climbing fountain's lips upon the sky.

Geneva
June 1961

End Of Ramadan, Kano Emirate

Bismillah.

In his wisdom, the nomad prophet knew
That man, to be filled.
Must come empty to his god.
Such things the desert night perhaps may teach,
Where every lonely bush stands like a sura,
Sharp and clear upon that scroll
Of whitened sand, of which His mighty hand
Has smoothed the sheet.

So, empty, at the end of Ramadan,
We come to Sallih.
Now, at the Friday Mosque, our old men search the moon
Whose rising ends our fast. The coal-oil lamps are lit
And whisper yellow butter at the dusk.
Upon the eating-mat, the welcome food is spread.
The washing done, the water jars aside, we kneel

With all our brothers, from this dark edge of Islam
Far to the Afghan hills. Hear the ladani call:
We shall be filled.

As-salaam aleikum.

> Kano
> May 1962

Dried Leaf In Obutsudan

This leaf is from that tree,
Or from the children of that tree
Where once he sat alone, great heart and undefended.
All living things upon the wheel
Of endless worlds cried out. He knew their pain;
Warm prey, pale claws, frail leprous beggar by the wall,
Madwoman naked in the roadside dust,
Sobbing child, blind warrior in Maya's night.

Not armored mind, nor muscled might
Of legions holds our hope. This is he
Remembered by the leaf, whose way we walk,
Who spoke of ill, the cure of ill, the path:
His Dhamma blooms upon a thousand worlds,
The fragrant lotus of tomorrow.

Priest, Old Catholic Church

"And shall He damn, today,
This rose-and-curly infant in the front pew,
That crutch-embracing elder at the vestry door –

Yet both be only what might ever be,
No less than what was written, and no more?
Shall the moving finger never shake arthritic,
And the unforeseen not scramble any page?
O bounding blood of Christed man, cry out your rage!

"Crash through the rodent walls of Calvin's maze
To swig the magic wine, hail drunkard sun:
Any littlest toasted angel – Yes! Lucifer or Gabriel,
However far he fell,
Shall come up singing out of chaos,
Climb up laughing out of Hell!"

Old Testament Professor

By the candled wedding in cathedrals of the skull
(History and passion miraculously welded)
He brought them shuffling, mumbling, lice in their beards:
These mantic prophets of the Lord of Hosts
Whose torn rags trailed on the seminary boards.
Now to the soaped, deodorized and neutral noses
Came news of the twin garbage dumps of Bethel-Ai,
The clamor of corpses and camel dung.

And into the inert, but kosher, ministerial meat
Breathed the earth-fermented Breath
That belched on Sinai. Students became
Nephesh. Their ears were opened. Then they,
In the middle of the rational flatland,
Heard the lion of Jeremiah roar.

Khirbetqumran

It is always noon.
No shadow moves, nor ever has
Between the sea of salt and the broken rock behind me.
Sun, sun and hammers of sun beat on the brazen earth :
South from the tower to the millet field,
A single shuddering gong.
Days and men it eats, this sun.
Beginning and end are one
In the hand of Adonai,
But nowhere more than here:
First hope, last home,
White wilderness of fire.

Hatilah, my name.
My eyes hawk north
To where Vespasian halts
A half-day's march away.
End and beginning,
Birth, death and judgment are met
In this our last city,
More holy than Jerusalem.

    Will the eagles know what they have eaten, Eloi?
    From the kitchen, our brothers bring the final meal.

Loyalty Oath

To you and the thought of you
I come in peace, fulfilled
And under no compulsion known to me.
Feeling the person in history
To be a fragile possibility

And unmatured, the baby buggy
Bouncing down the Odessa Steps
Into what unchosen collision –
Or Lenin at the Finland Station
Trusting his suitcase
To the frosty grip of a probable tomorrow
(Yet not a dispensable person, said Trotsky)
- I place, perhaps, unmeasured value
On loving done freely.

We know this: The feeling's real
As any city market, airport or subway.
And at least as lasting. Dawn pulls
Us down forgetful gutters to the drains
But leaves you always something, leaves me this:
That shy, sure, querying, affirming smile
Before the cloves and cinnamon of your lips.

The Baffled Angler

"They called Him Fisher o' Men," Glyn Morgan says,
"But there's never a place a man can fish, not now.
Six hundred acres o' the common land, they've sold away,
And all the fishing rights together. I don't see how."
A lonely trout-fly snagged in his tweedy cap, he squints
And rubs a whiskered jaw, and says again,
"I don't see how. It used to be, you knew your man:
The parson or the squire – 'twas one o' them,

And if you crossed the parson, you crossed the squire."
His fingers curl as though they fist a rock
And feel its heft within his hand. But the target? Ah!
Gone gurgling down, pale altarcloth in a ballot box.

His stone uncast, Glyn Morgan views through narrowed eyes
The complex patriarchal state.

Usk, South Wales
July 1962

Incription

    for a grave
    near the city of the angels
    august 1962

Lived it up with   if and maybe
    scratched the itch of   well, perhaps
    kicked the gong of   never was
    in cinderellaland

See my new slippers
    in the vortex of a million sleeps
    dance on the universal optic
    and when I bed
    dredge up along my thighs
    the cinematic eyelid

Dreamboat foundered
    in the dry Mojave
    ten thousand thousand
    thousand miles
    from all the ports of is

desert song

film us a hero
the people yes
stretch us a fairy shrimp
ten feet tall
slap a burnoose on his
fricaseed brains
and clap him on
a camel

only
turning from
the twilight screen
we find this real solid guy
has wandered in
and howl him down
with a snort of hell
he wasn't supposed to
        (say)
        (look)
        (do)
              anything like *that!*

Words Of Solomon to the Shulamite, in Her Absence

"I am dark but comely, O ye daughters of Jerusalem..."

I thank you for being
    and for having been
    and for the sure becoming
    of what you yet will be

I thank you for saying
    only honest words

      and for bringing me the gift of silence
      when no words were right

I thank you for believing
    in the greatness of persons
    and the cleanness of instinct

I thank you for being terrified
    of the unbelievable
    and for helping me in my unbelief

I thank you for doing
     your hair like that on the last morning
     and even for the fact that this dawning
     I walk in the vineyards and cannot sleep

Thus I

Thus I, a priest of Karnak, cadenced slow
With lifted head, lead down the columned avenue
The votaries of Horus. Our way is straight,
As flat as desert plain, linear as the Nile,
And surely, without wish or will, approaches Anubis.
And Horus, perhaps. Perhaps Osiris. I smile,
Neglecting, in the moment's majesty,
A slight case of ringworm on the right heel.

How have I been shelled in this clerk's carcass?
A paper priest, entombed in a Bloor Street trolleycar
With a phalanx of thirty vertical mummies
I ride the choiceless rail. Direct I go,
But not to Horus: I have never seen Osiris.
I believe someone just trampled on my toe.

For John Huot

Then spoke the smallest imp:
"That I should become mature
Before that old and hairy god
Whose multisyllabic rage cracked
Half of hell's teacups,
Seems merely odd to me
And no clear victory, surely.

"– Nor of my own wish, believe me.
How should I, in the yolk, have known
The crystal world beyond the shell?
Or, flexing small muscles in my mother's gut,
Deduced these laws of mass and leverage?
This greater space that swallowed his
Like a blot on a Gaussian blotter –
I didn't intend it so;
I feared maturity," he said.

"Upgrown through some insistence
Other than my own, I found
This wider world a precondition of my pulse.
Unlike Brahm, I cannot breathe it back.
But in some wonder yet I stand
And sense this uncreate,
Unspoiled, unsoiled, unsold and solid scene."

Thinking in Primitive Communities

The possibilities open to thinking are the possibilities of recognizing relationships and the discovery of techniques of operating with relationships on the mental or intellectual plane, such as will in turn lead to ever wider and more penetratingly significant systems ...Benjamin Lee Whorf

1. Coexistence:
   The stone and the savage,
   Unseparate,
   Shared animate earth.

2. Millenia.
   Bent like light.
   Thought and expression curved
   Round to the unthought source:
   Tat twam asi.

3. "In the beginning," smiled Nagasena,
   "Was the Wordless.
   Inggas of words
   Will not construct this chariot."

4. Worlds of words.
   Words for the world_I_ess.
   To burn me is bad; it hurts.
   But to burn the not-me...

5. Unthink.
   Wave up a flag.

long
commentary
on
short
poem

ingga: unit of measurement applicable to calculus of
circulars, used in India ca. 400 B.C.

could have used kalpa, but that unit is applicable to large
ordinals, something like a quintillion, or perhaps like the
Pidgin "playnty too mutsch", except that the last is
understood to mean a thousand, more or less.

Chariot wheels, curved prow of chariot: circulars
construction of poem: circular or spiral
basic bennett thought-pattern   "

the poem opens with quote from Whorf
the poem ends with two images from Whorf which he said
could not be sanely used in English

in Ojibwa, the medicine man will talk to the stones outside
his lodge, if they are animate according to his perception of
person and interpersonal behavior

naturally, in 3., a dig at the Logos
the other beginning more real, more *with* the silent and
biological roots of culture

insight is all

Cinquains

>Forgotten Land
>Late discing,
>ground is hard,
>as though the earth
>against a too inconstant lover
>turned her face.

Burned Forest, Kalum Valley
White bone: rock.
 Black bone: tree.
 Between earth's ribs
 green and violet spikes of fireweed
 lift their spears.

>Clowns, Kids, Acrobats
>At circus,
>my children
>give according
>to their nature: the boy, bright envy,
>the girl, praise.

Swathing Oats
Slain sunlight
 lies fading
 on autumn fields.
 Winter must come: we've harvested so
 much of sun!

>Barrier
>Child-wife! Oh,
>halfway down
>the hall between
>your pain and mine: *yoshino,shoji,*
>paper wall.

Ortega In The Cellar

"Because of the blood," said Ortega.
"Because of the blood...
   Because the brain should hail only
   what the blood will permit
   (and not of necessity, as Schopenhauer thought ,
   but from pain's experience
   and the sharing of pain)
   I am no longer that poet of Madrid
   whom you knew.
"The brain unecstatic
   is no man's brother. The Cretan maze
   is its habitat, where it hides from the heart
   and plans paper grids which prove
   no mountains are. And yet,
   some learning is needed.

"The blood uninstructed
   gallops at windmills, the singing crystals
   crushed in the hand that clasps,
   the descending notes of the *saeta*
   dribbling away between
   our most reluctant claws.

"To be natural, even, is no longer poured
   in the cups of this perverse generation,"
   – so Ortega, leaning on a barrel –
   "but is wrung grape by grape
   from a rusty press with a reverse thread
   never invented in the nightmares
   of the noble savage.

 "Look," said Ortega, swinging his arms at the walls,
   "suppose we did a Gauguin,
   took off for Tahiti – well?

    Esso and Kleenex and Coca-Cola
    will follow us all the days of our lives
    and we shall be chewed by the teeth of a gimmick forever.

"If our hate is a child of fear,
    and our fear is of separation,
    shall we find perfect love
    in the heart alone?" asked Ortega.
    "Except we become as this little child
    who crouches over every
    crack-crawling centipede
    in original wonder,
    whose moment is forever Creation
    and the bung bouncing out of the first barrel,
    we shall not enter that kingdom.

"-but not by the will alone!" cried Ortega.
    "Through acceptance of life
    and the great unlearning of lies
    we may, a few of us, walk that path
    which is not the way of a child
    but is fit for the feet of those
    grown, in this sense, child-like.

"Because of the blood," said Ortega,
    "I am cooling my heels in this cellar
    and sipping poor wine from a broken cup
    with my friends who fish at night
    and awaken slowly
    in the late afternoon."

"Because of the wine," said Ortega.
    "Because the wine is of brotherhood,
    solvent to the eggshell wall between,
    sacramental, sanctuary to fellowship,
    and these are my people,

I've come here to drink it.

"Brotherhood at the university
   was compounded of credits in sociology
   with a graduate seminar in ethics.
   But, like *caritas*, which is warmer than charity,
   it begins at home. Brotherhood
   of the head only is a family of phantoms.

"I found it better to begin at my roots,
   and make my peace here with my father,
   who is a fisherman. Otherwise, I'd been lost
   in place and hour and person,
   not unlike that Prince in Elsinore
   who found sad ghosts roaming the sockets
   of his own disjointed time.

"Evil in Elsinore, and indecision,
   webbed him down. He raged about,
   and every thread he slashed
   led to a neighbor's heart. By blood
   or brain, for all his introspective cleverness,
   he learned no higher art.

"Now, let's imagine that his father,
   foreseeing this, might have outlawed
   evil in Denmark. The Court have argued so:
   were he all-good, all-powerful, quick heaven
   had been won. Yet others said
   in defence of this king-become-a-ghost,
   he planned to leave the Prince a choice
   through which he might have grown.

"In fact, it would appear his good was great,
   his power limited. So he was beaten,
   and so the Prince his advocate.

Too early sired, he'd hailed no Kierkegaard,
knew never the absurd leap
beyond the sword-point.

"Because of the blood and the wine," said Ortega,
   "I have become a dusty general
   in the army of defeated men
   whose god has done twenty-five
   in the model prison."

"Because of the sun," said Ortega.
   "Because, although it looks as if
   they *shall* buy and sell the land forever,
   nobody yet has figured
   how to fit a coin-slot to the sun,
   and the indiscriminate, irrational thing
   grows weeds and roses wildly,
   I am hopeful in a hopeless season.

"Slowly opened, and as slowly shut,
   Pio Sol, he turns on us a twelve-hour wink.
   Perhaps the best of his joke is this:
   Where did I ever say or hint
   repetition is not at least as godlike
   as innovation?

"Bedbugs, maggots and men
   breed in the alleys of Esplugas
   unloved, unwatched by the Guardia Civil.
   There the reasonable, but irrational drunk
   pounds at 3 a.m. on the iron shutters,
   screaming 'Vino!' and 'Vino!' again,
   for this is surely where the vino was
   so shortly before the sun went down.

"And, maybe, with sufficient pounding

    comes, heavy-footed, mine host of the inn,
    with curses, but also with wine.
    One who hunts wine at 3 a.m., surely
    his faith sustains him –
    plus, of course, a sure memory
    of the right shutter.

"Because of the blood, and the wine,
    and the sun," said Ortega.
    "Because the sun, too, is Catalan,
    though our hope's a rust-corrupted spur
    to gall the flanks of Rosinante,
    yet we ache up one more slope
    to solar echoes all unmet
    by feline things content to purr
    and chase soft shadows
    down a mildewed hall."

Barcelona
August, 1962

August
to
December

A Cycle of Poems
1985

If *Hiroshima* expresses anything, it is first of all the suffering
of those human beings society frustrates in their most fundamental aspirations.
                      –Andre Hodeir on *Hiroshima Mon Amour*

Civilization is bought for the price of our discontent
And the bomb wired to bedsprings in the couch of love.
Who honeymoons in Italy without the bride's family?
Carting along the aging aunt, dandruffed nephew
Vowing to see Venice and live a long time,
Our lovers are painting the human condition
On a topographical canvas in bright arterial blood.
Buy the frame anywhere between Kyoto and Coney Island.

This pain has overfilled all the abattoirs of time,
Floods against the crumbling earthwork of the hours
And thunders past the ticking of a cautious clock.
Elsewhen, risingfrom sauerkrautandWienerSchnitzel
Herr Freud prepares to demonstrate the primacy of genitals
By kicking the world in the crotch.

After we get down on the floor, pressing
Bare footsoles together in the manner of Bokonon,
Delighted the magic is still there, laughing,
Touching, loving, somehow it's again time for you
To go, and panic pumps up out of the hours
Into my eyes. I try to hold you, and my arms

Grow thorns, my voice assaults you, crying
The tap leaks, mortar is broken around window,

Furnace blower squeaks, porch light expired,
Garden full of weeds. Leave me alone here
In an old house: go home to your wife
Who's forgotten how to love you. Ask myself
If I need your apologetic good-byes to punctuate
The droning language of my day.

Our Lady of Apricots

She laughs easily at such things:
The evening light through apricot drapes,
A clever pingpong bounce of a phrase
Or a compliment when she's feeling down.
Her laugh is a mellow pewter bell
Rocked in the tides of her delight
And she herself is apricot, smooth
Spiced apricot and cream.

Her eyes, now, plead with you mistily
Through a web of morning dew,
Asking mutely for small magics
Of appreciation: "Attend, Joker!
On with the cap & bells. Amuse me;
It may be I shall reward you well."

Afterward, she is warm velvet infolded
To a shadowplay of dream, otherland
Recalled uncertainly, dissolving down
Through thin recurrent tremors of goodbye,
Sister of dark sun, slow-revolving
Netula. Only her hand, sleeping
On the silk of one pink-aureoled breast

Trembles at a doorway in the mist.

Her eyelids, though, veil altars, incense,
Towers and temples rose-marbled,
Through whose dusky curving corridors
Echo these despairing childish cries
Of ravished Egyptian maidens held
By bronze-armed, virile, improbable gods.

Desire is nothing
but the desire to break
the surface of all surfaces

–Robin Morgan

That something moves within the hand, head, heart.
Behind both eye and ear, prisoned but elusive,
Insubstantially held in a lattice of solids
Or apparent substance – we take it on faith.
Whether Christian soul, Buddhist karma, or avatar
Of Tara in the three-ring circus of our flesh,
Beyond the surface mirror is the port of our desire:
The You I know is compass to the You that yet may be.

And I shall thank whomever you are tonight
And thank the changeless power of the deep
For granting us this voyage past the headlands
And all our selves left standing on the quay.
Glacier to ocean, we melt and flow together
Like the crystal stream of some far northern fjord.

The lion goddess symbolizes the devouring, negative aspect of the sun-desert-fire, the solar eye that burns and judges; while Bast, although she is a goddess of the east, is goddess not of the sun but of the moon.

–Erich Neumann

Having wiped her paws and whiskers
Dry of fish, the Nubian kitten plays
At priestess, memories of Bubastis templed,
Colonnaded, worshippers of our lady of life
Whose basket held endless food for cats.
Smile upon us, daughter of Hathor,
Sister of the moon's own passionate games
With no goal but their own unwinding.

Inholder of oracles yet unspoken,
Cat or woman, the Black Queen furred,
You stretch and turn, quiver and pounce,
Then curl, live smoke upon the altar
Whose pleading topaz eyes invent
A drying ocean and a million homeless fish.

Correspondence

Actually, it's a doctrine from Swedenborg:
The mirrored furniture of earth reflects
Imperfectly the more ideal housekeeping of Heaven.
A bit Platonic, cool as the belief itself,
Not even slightly singed around the edges.
They tell, though, that once he dreamed of fire.
Don't look for the obvious, he said. You won't,
You see, know Hell when you arrive there.

Nor may I find in me and you such joy
Angelic as shall forever blot out pain
Or memory remain unshaken in some rose
Eternal. Firmly the falling petal, blowing leaf
Confine us to the quality of now, tight crowded
Harbour in the sea of might-have-been.

Though they came to learned Erinn
Without buoyant, adventurous ships,
No man in creation knew
Whether they were of the earth or of the sky.
                              —Eochaid O' Flynn

Not that the core of me is vacuum
But that I am too many, I am legion
And cough in that unmoving, dusty air
Shrouding the clay tablets, abraded memories
Of Nineveh, of faceless, namelost places
Scattered by a random hand across a map
Margined with stale warnings, blotted signs:
Walk gently, stranger. Here there be dragons.

So it is, tiring of the endless wind,
Convoluted waves and bleaching sun
That now I moor the fragments of my coracle
On the islet of your Celtic bed
To weep in the anchorage of your arms
Like some lost child intossed by the Western sea.

Look at this photo taken at her convocation.
Against the ivied walls; you know the place –
All weathered stone and greenery. The lawn
Well-tended, though trampled regularly by jocks
Practicing for the varsity. Cradling roses,
She bends her head slightly, smiles for Kodak,
Looking quizzically into the lens, not downward
Which would enact Our Lady Adoring Child.

Roses bloom to infant Christ, magicked
By a head's tilt, and she both Eve and Mary
In the garden of angular probabilities. Attend!
More than Mona Lisa lies behind that smile
And, as high Anglicans, we must endorse

Communion wizardry in cathedral or in camera.

To declaim that I am wounded by your beauty
Would make a round archaic sound –
Something Lancelot might murmur to Guinevere
While tiptoeing to her rosy velvet couch
Through the chalk dust spread upon the floor
By Arthur. (His foot, like that of Odysseus
And all heroes, was at least a size thirteen.)
The remark, however, would be a lie.

Through freely sacramental offerings of love
We grow toward completion, wholeness
Of the yet imperfect other. What joy
We spend each insubstantial moment
Is never for our wounding, but for healing,
The person rising radiant and entire.

Lady with Champagne and Monsters

Pearl necklace, earrings, a glass of bubbling wine:
Otherwise naked, she rides to us from Revelations
Comfortably seated on one of several monsters
Whose choral bellowing booms musically uncouth
Across the plaza. Solomon's apples, her breasts
Bloom firm and taunting, by her unregarded
Above the sun-warm belly, the dusky wedge
That curls soft smoke between her thighs.

To us she drinks, the long eyes cool and haughty
Above the flaring nostril and the crimson lip,
The crystal held to toast our noonday crowd
Jostling past commercial goods, utilities,
Commodities, oddities, necessities, niceties
No longer nice, or good, or useful anymore.

I will rebel, said Finn Mac Cool.
I will rebel against the lack of a lilt
In the west wind's song
Or a lateness in the coming of the dawn.

I will rebel, said Finn Mac Cool
At marching orders that lead to a bog,
At red threads missing in a Donegal tweed
And a half cup lacking of the *cruiskeen lawn*.

I will rebel, said Finn Mac Cool
From all flame-haired colleens who say
The heart of a man is a cold thing.
I will rebel, said Finn Mac Cool –
I and my son and my grandson.

–The Ranns of O' Rahilly

Devotus Defixusque

An old Latin translation from the early Greek magicians, meaning something like, 'bewitched by a knot.' And suggesting it takes a wizard to untie it.

Fool, you cannot approach her now,
Hopefully, with your vintage wine and roses.
Because of the web, man, the web of dream
Self-woven, where her threads of life are tangled
Endlessly, and every knot is Gordian. Even he,
Proud son to Philip of Macedon, spurs on
For Karagiozis, shadow-world of serpents.
How will you cut through a dream, fool?

While you pour the hoarded words in her sleeping ears

She smiles at the echoes lost in yesterday,
Reads in your eyes the summer of year-ago-gone
And kisses not you, but the ghost of memory.
Forget it, fellow. There is no bridge to that place
And the road-signs have been scorched by salamanders.

My hands hold the hours
like a fistful of ashes or pebbles;
I ask nothing of memory.
                                                –Neruda

Not easily, our sheets of paper and satin
Absorb these twin passions of love and poetry.
So many details rejected: stains, wrinkles,
An uncertain perfume, off-brand cigarette,
Clutter of slippers beside your bed. Only,
In the gray washes of memory, small things
Surface, bob around unsummoned begging
To be valued, indexed, catalogued.

Fraud, concoction, imitation of the real!
Joy in the completed kiss or the sonnet
Inseparable from the pain of momentary passage.
Cold remains: a static coloured photograph
Against an equivocal sky, three lines
Moulted from the flight of Pablo Neruda.

Pain, said the Lord Buddha, pain exists
And only an awakening to the unreal railway
Can lull the hurt of the wheel rolling over your toe.
To applaud your arrival in lands you had dreamed,
The resort hotel, gold sun and gilded sand
Held all my intent. Here: take a dozen tickets
To anyplace and pray the steel remains tough,
The tieplate not lifted for cooking tortillas.

I shall enjoy your laughter, the kindled eye,
Even the gaudy labels on your luggage. Come,
I'll help you to your train and look for mine,
Heading unreasonably elsewhere and alone.
Stepping down at a hundred stations called Zero
I joke my way through the whole inevitable journey.

Between the tinned evasions of your answering machine
And the multiple catastrophes of existence
Occasionally I met you. The random payoff,
Said Skinner, prolongs the desired behaviour,
Slipping the waitress a dime or a dollar, or sometimes
Nothing. We've been caught on the hooks of desire,
And know the junk on the street is mainly milk powder –
But you can't be blamed for trying. Chicken or feathers?

Crank up, friend, and hope for the best, not a burn.
Creamy pearls are hidden in the milk of human kindness
By the pixies. Not all experience is skim, say I,
Hoping to survive in the churns of memory, perhaps
Become a shade, another of those who haunt
The vacant spaces in the Swiss cheese of your life.

Surely it is no stranger thing that I,
Somewhat tone deaf, should spend Christmas
Hearing Zamfir on the Greek flute
And thinking of a Celtic woman
Than that she, who might this quiet evening
Be dancing with her coven on a hill
Sleeps three nights in a local convent.
Paradox, my lady, is the air we breathe.

All things born are other than they seem
And we most slowly learn ourselves
As more than any mirror shows.
Listening to the high, sweet Pipes of Pan

I dream you chalking an impudent pentacle
On Mother Superior's dark oak door.

While we drank tea, I failed to pray for the miracle
But the miracle happened and you loved me,
With your long legs and your tender arms
Of which you always seemed to grow one too many
When we lay on our sides embracing, your hair
An auburn riot upon the pillows. Oh, then
Our laughter sang deep and rocking through the evening
And the stars were daisies picked on a childish Sunday.

We were drinking tea when you told me. My hand shook
And I hid my eyes, blue like yours, unaccustomed
To crying for the end of this or any day. I stared
At the veins among freckles inhabiting my wrist.
Between one cup of tea and another, silently
The stars fell from their places and I became old.

I myself see in Mag Mon
Red-headed flowers without fault.
                              —Song of Manannán son of Lêr

When he begged for the horse and rode again
Home from Tir na Og, from the land of youth and dream,
They warned him only not to touch foot to the ground
And particularly not in that one Toronto suburb.
Niamh herself warned him, and he listened
But could hardly know after three hundred years
What Patrick and his crowd had done with the souls of men
Or of women. So he rode whistling out of the Western wave

And into the Borough of East York, a hard place
Unhallowed, and sprinkled with a spotty magic
Which almost made it possible, here and there, to see
What had grown green before the great desecration.

And there he found her, red-headed flower,
And earned his mortal harvest in a garden of weeds.

Collected Poems

The poetry collected in this section is from various sources, for the most part previously unpublished.

Belonging

went to heaven
the shining light a mile up front
me at the far rear
next to the public toilets
big choir i guess
couldn't hear much
tap on the shoulder
guy says
what you doing here
aren't you the fellow
used to publish dharma
for the western buddhists
come with me
peaceful in yellow robe
swaying while they chant
the diamond sutra
ring little silver bells
kids piling daffodils around
obutsudan for baby gautama
half asleep but no snoring
tap on the shoulder
guy in beard & spitcurls says
what you doing here
didn't you study with rabbi stern
in young israel schule
also when drinking tea

you save teabag remember
warsaw ghetto starving
20x reboiling teabags
they're looking for you
in the synagogue
come with me
like it bagels & creamcheese
cantor dovvening & making jokes
about the rabbi's wife
the fresh darkeyed women
behind the partition
life life life
when the rabbi dances
all his little hassidim
dance with him
tap on the shoulder
spectacled intellectual says
what you doing here
the american association for
the advancement of atheism
has read your cynical stuff
come with me

Invocation of the Unlikely

That the improbable may delight us.
If our best mock-up of a dragon
Turns out to be a Galapagos iguana,
Then let's have an iguana or two.
If you find a Beothuk Indian, let me know.

Outside the museum, please:
The Smithsonian is our jewel-case
Of slaughtered culture, like Kali
With her string of skulls around the neck.
Enough taxidermy! Let's have a live one.

Here's a fin for Finn's folk,
A cheer for the rebel Basque
And a buck or two for the Oka braves.
With all endangered species
Revolt is an act of survival.

    In the unwired villages of Peru's altiplano,
    Please don't tell them Mao is dead.

Thirties

dad

was a great giant bumblebear of a man
and in parental bedroom with the big slat bed
kid innocence i asked mom where she slept
way up here she said grabbing the mattress edge
and dad way down there pointing to the hollow

when we went to coney island and took pictures
so tall his head axed by the frame
a foot and a half above mom's lopsided smile
measured his belt once when he was sleeping
44" of heavy black leather with a big buckle

never got hit with it and only once his hand
when we were eating soup together
the slurping sounds he made were great
tried to imitate he never stopped slurping
but his free hand swung across and whacked
rolled out of the chair and against the wall
back of me hand to ye the irish say

my daughter disbelieves assures me that
the da was a violent man and punishing
certainly beat me many times she says
that's how i got to be like i am
can't recognize the characters in her fiction

bro

top designer and engineering ideaman
maker of mobile displays and working models
disregarded by mom the official punisher
but a genius in his own field and even you
have probably used the soap he dreamed up
incurve one side outcurve the other because
in the shower he said hell i don't have square edges

last models he made were for jack
whose math and physics cook up einstein corrections
bro glued pingpong balls in headache patterns
submolecular ghosts of virtual particles
together they made me understand
the world of rnodelmaking that pair
who dreamed the double helix and applauded
dance of dna before electron microscopes
or that shining young woman in astrophysics
don't let her near the hubble but she worked
with borrowed starphotos saw far galaxies
twowheeling around a rightangle corner and
it was true it was true it was true

after dad died we didn't starve
because there was one man
who was jewish and had a shop
we called the butterandegg store
so we ate butter&eggs&milk&bread
we must have owed him money

but mom was too proud for handouts
no she would never go on welfare
I was fifteen then and a communist
but tired of buttereggsmilkbread
walked from our shanty down to welfare
where everybody lit a big smile
waved said hello comrade clif

because they needed someone to work
with losovsky's red labor unions
party found me a job in long island city
small sheet metal shop where the machines
were all secondhand so safety guard
told me trim some soldering corners
for darkroom lights just little things
and the trimming press had worn gears
made a double stroke took off my finger
guy next to me got sick dumped iodine
all over my hand and off to hospital
where meals were good and i stayed
a week in the emergency ward
compensation paid & they needed the cash
nurses were young tough pretty
old guy in next bed trying for sympathy
whined doesn't all the blood bother you
& the little darkhaired nurse snapped
the bloodier the better and he shut up

i got a bad case of hearts & flowers
for head nurse desked at the ward door
couldn't peel my eyes off her white uniform
swelled away & divided made shadow
between where the starched cotton stretched
she 24 asked how old i was and
did i have a good job me 16 came back
once to visit she said stay lor lunch

later she married a dr schultheiss
who came from flushing long island

my hand still bandaged the party wanted
help on a picket line where big lou
organized the lumber workers and they
were locked out with a tough just sprung
from crowbar hotel herding scabs
we blocked the ramp mobbed the first car
bent down to rock it spill it over
but not fast enough so next to me
irish jack got brained with a sashweight
inside rolled tabloid knocked him silly
took him home on the bus where he kept
muttering like he was almost singing
oh oh baby oh oh oh
and holding both hands on his head
my bandaged hand bloody where
i socked someone

when I was 17 earl browder
ran for president with james w ford
big black man for vp
and 25 thousand of us paraded red flags
marched around on cue singing
filled madison sq garden to the rooftop
30' blowups of browder & ford
grinned conspiratorially up front
we roared the internationale
and i marched next to evvie
pink puppylove girlfriend who claimed
her people came over on the mayflower

made picket signs with bessie boris
who said we could do this forever

lets us get married and paint signs
for the party forever said bessie
lets us get married comrade clif
painted signs two days three nights
crashed slept seventeen hours
committee came by wanted more signs
mom said leave him alone can't have him

packed the square in front of city hall
hung an effigy of fiorello from a lamp post
the little flower our spaghetti mayor
who loved to chase fire engines
and didn't want to talk to us

tall mounted police drove a wedge
cut through crowd to the centre
captain rising in stirrups rescue straw man
pockets of ball bearings to spook horses
short sticks with nail through the end
cop stretched high blue arm reaching up
and crowd began leave him alone
leave him alone leave him alone
slowly settled back into saddle
eddied out again through seas of anger

darkhaired molly worked cheese counter
in the fiveanddime
slender longlegged smiling
had younger brother dad no mom
and i got some crazy idea about
sleeping with her in the party office

where i had the key because then
i was agent for young worker & sunday worker
and lots of old papers good for bedding
but didn't have the front door key

so put her on the late bus for home
tough luck

later a guy called kayo got her pregnant
she demanded comradely abortion cash
they gave it while kayo shipped to spain
with international brigade probably got shot
and molly never showed up again

wollgewachsig freewalking freetalking esther
took me along with boyfriend to art museum
staring at sculpture the kiss by rodin
pair of nudes man cupping girl's breast
esther nodded sighed keep that in mind morris

stuffed a beachball in bathingsuit belly
strutted through sand blaming comrade clif
a political opportunist she said
later on the homebound subway
dropped a tired head on my shoulder
you don't love me do you told her no
good she says my mother shouldn't worry
i'm going to marry a goy

when the comrades tossed me out
esther was up front playing secretary
came the vote she raised a hand to keep me in
looked up from table saw she was alone
slowly drooped hand and shook her head

big girl who slept around was unapproved
shirley said that's not free love
we don't mean every woman packs a mattress
damn it the party has its own morality

screwing around leaves you no time
to sell the daily worker walk picket lines
do the agit-prop on street corners
build the party make the revolution
one big soviet usa

big girl in the country on a hay ride
everywhere on the wagon at once
with six different guys six different places
nationalized everyone in one afternoon

some young italians hung in for awhile
helped us picket movies where they showed
red salute one more russky menace film
we all had signs to tote me on roller skates
rubberwheel chicagos most fancy thing i owned
and the black maria came wailing down on us

handed my sign to the next guy
said please hold that awhile
skated away straight past the paddywagon
and down the block whistling
never did see the italian bunch again

my friend avel got arrested
pushing out leaflets at a school
must allow free speech so hit him for littering
or loitering booked him at cop shop
what's your last name he says beth
what's your first name he says mac
wise guy

up on stand arresting officer barks sure
he saw avel passing out leaflets nobody wanted
that crap they all ended up on the street
did you actually see students tossing them

yes i did snorts positive redface irish cop
well why not arrest them instead of defendant
case dismissed

lou's wife rose small pretty as her name
looked so loud didn't need to speak
never figured what inside her head
brought her to us except big lou
our local commissar but when things
got dull & resolutions long & helixed
she was by the beard of marx good to look at

edna leaned against me wound arms around
whispered that a wife in paranoid russia
turned in husband trotskyite-wrecker-spy
to stalin's police and don't you think
she did the right thing

younger but not littler sister of rose
tubby edna worked twice as hard for less
but i shrugged her off quick & sticky
she probably made some other red
one damn good wife had six kids
bang-bang-bang paranoid americans

lily, daughter of variety store uptown
and half a committee plus me had meeting
year's worst rainstorm arriving soaked
lily tossed me bathrobe dried clothes
off to the hall in her brother's sox
to give our report to the comrades
where she picked a quiet moment
forgot your garters she shouts
great haw haw but avel said
lily is good as a man any time

thirties echo

then we clutched a teddybear hope
out of a tornado of destruction would whirl
enough turf for garden greens tomorrow
and blue above for something beyond
spyeye and ear tapping rebel grammar
although none were very clear on how
we'd organize the lower manhattan garbage

until we drifted north to farceland
feet bruised in the circular mall
trotting the 3ring consumer barnum
bit players with an engineered script

or praying our brothers nishnawbe
deal a red royal flush
at the lakeshore casino

Manifesto to My Son

Socialist Realism, says the comrade at the typewriter,
Disciplines my artistic will, guides the otherwise
Flamboyant flight of my imagination. Observe;
With what sober proletarian precision, coolly I finger
The articulated keys, forcing from this reluctant
Dialectic of flesh and steel, the synthesis
Historically ordained. All is as it could only be.
Further, I demonstrate within myself true normalcy:
Art's not freedom, but an extension of neurosis,
And plainly predetermined. How much more noble
To be shaped by history in the universal forge
Than squeezed like toothpaste from some private quirk!

So, smiling, I return to my machine, wondering
For just one wild, unprogrammed moment,
Why I should be grinning at this inanimate
But useful collection of metal parts.

Losing It

until 2 birthdays back
if i squinted into the mirror
with a 7-watt bulb
the guy didn't really push 80
complimenting myself i charge upstairs
sometimes 2 at a clip
4 flights to the doctor

time's downhill torrent
carves away step curve corner
erodes the standing monolith
stonehenge in the druid dusk
mocks a pitch for outdoor barbecue
1 slab daubed with a peace sign

back from town in fog or snow
the line 10 turn looks a little scrambled
our name on the battered mailbox
stares at me like a stranger
columbus getting his first squint
at the west indies and wondering
briefly where the hell he is

calico kitten and snowflakes

thinks each one falling
an injured insect
fluttering on crippled wing

head swivels, eye selects
victim to pounce on
leaps as it hits ground

loses it in the heap
swipes madly
claws hooked

got away again
oh hell
think i'll chase my tail

the days fall
twenty acres of drift

there
maybe that was
one to remember

                                        −xmas '99

Haretsu

If Hiroshima expresses anything, it is first of all the suffering of those human beings society frustrates in their most fundamental aspirations.
-André Hodeir on *Hiroshima Mon Amour*

Civilization is bought for the price of our discontent
And the bomb wired to bedsprings in the couch of love.
Who honeymoons in Italy without the bride's family?
Carting along the aging aunt, dandruffed nephew
Vowing to see Venice and live a long time,
Our lovers are painting the human condition
On a topographical canvas in bright arterial blood.
Buy the frame anywhere between Kyoto and Coney Island.

This pain has overfilled all the abattoirs of time,
Floods against the crumbling earthwork of the hours
And thunders past the ticking of a cautious clock.
Elsewhen, rising from sauerkraut and Wiener Schnitzel
Herr Freud prepares to demonstrate the primacy of genitals
By kicking the world in the crotch.

August 1982

Arigato

For one candle and two sticks of incense I thank you.
With right music by a friend at the right time
And with the presence of you before the shrine
You put me in your debt, lady. I came in need;
You met me with the Sutra of the Heart
Which I heard you recite eleven years ago
At the Obutsudan, when we burned incense

To the youthful memory of your daughter.

Gone, gone, gone beyond, gone altogether beyond:
Yet I cannot pass the point of this death,
Am trapped in a doorless room without tears
And only the convergence of your graciousness
With some words from an old book have freed me
To cry for that great and missing man, my comrade.

Hana Matsuri 1982 C.E.

Ai Kaze

To learn the ringing language of that land
Quick as the slap of bamboo on my shoulder-pad
When in *kendo* gray-haired Nakamura pounced,
Gut-feeling, end of staff shouting to belly:
"*Hara! Hara!* He is foolishly unprepared!"
Crack of awareness too near my collar-bone
And thankful for the mask on mouth and eye
Dancing toward what drum of understanding?

With your most gentle help, lady of Soto Zen,
To ride the wind that waits the paired intent
Whose kiss on the lotus of the eighteenth vow
Perfumes Amida's garden. No one lonely word
Nor cathedral of syllables may quite enfold
This breath, that moves among the petalled stars.

May 1932

Nanimo No Eiga

You cannot say if your composure is the calm of acceptance or the mask of a dulled heart.
–Dorothy Walters

But he has caught himself on the flickering screen:
Actor/audience, alive at both levels
And also being acted on/interacting.
In an early scene, calmly accepting
Death of mother/father, death of self.
Later, leaving the seacoast because of a dream
Of radioactive dust, forgetting to weep for the world.
Three women condemn him for lack of feeling.

No judge will rule more harshly than himself.
Beyond their ritual justice, lawful games,
He dances in a fading light of stars and planets,
Dead rocks and splinters, phosphorescent tombs:
You cannot say if this is earth, or memorial
To another place of the same name.

June 1982

Aki No Hiru-Sugi

Now the twin *ronin*, time and space, divide us.
Only one day and a few hundred miles build this blockade
But your afternoon sun warms a personal sanctuary;
Hill, valley and sky extend from your own heart's hope
To make a thing that lives without me. Apart,
I consider the weight of my shadow. Surely, love,
The Pure Land of Shinran Shonin will not tremble
Under my footfall. Would I eclipse tomorrow?

Not this autumn. Better I hoe the land and wait,
Tend the hybrid melon vine, climb my sandy hill
And breathe a hundred *nembutsu* for your return.
Wait I must, grafted to veins and arteries of light
Particular to this life-place, I and the cantaloup
Ripening toward our shared but individual harvest.

August 1982

Jiyuu-Na

Freedom means to be in your right element...
Have you ever known of birds
that wanted to live under water
or a fish that wanted to build its nest in the trees?
– Elle-Han'sa, Samé

To a merman lover the element of love is ocean
Rising tidal to an old seduction of the sun,
Wave rolling up the warm, smooth belly of the beach
To flatten over the seaward pull of ebb
With a slow, reluctant parting of palms, hand over hand
Sliding through a fingertip goodbye, and then
Turning in that wet-and-silver benediction
Homeward in wholeness, held within love.

One wing-tip flecked with the wave-top foam
The white gull dips to climb again
His thermal ladder through the sky. Just so,
Dolphin or manta or shark that I am
Your kiss will free the wing-wide spirit
To dance above the body of the sea.

August 1982

Kara-Na-Heya

Our materialist friend would objectively insist
The stains in the wine-coloured rug
Have not faded overnight, the three-ply walnut
Awkwardly nailed in the entry isn't more thoroughly peeled.
The pottery lamp is neither more squat nor less bright
And the hole in the blue bedspread not significantly
increased.
This is the same room, he would nod, smiling:
What can you measure that has altered?

But we are hardly of his time or place.
Our history confirms a metamorphic hour
Lacking the warmth of your hand or craft
And no shrine to any goddess known to me.
This room's indrawn to an empty cave, where
The lake fog comes creeping after the sun is down.

September 1982

Itami

I laugh and something catches and I cough,
Hurting a little and remembering the thin lad
In *randori* who caught me halfway through the *hanegoshi*,
Lifted me and dropped me on my tailbone
So I sat on the mat while fire ran down
The back of both my legs and burned
While I cried and laughed and cried again
Through the sparks exploding inside my lids.

Judoka, brother: I never did get off the *tatami*.
The quick and clever hands on sleeve and collar
Have thrown me a thousand times. Most I laugh
When most it hurts, and know that without laughter

I couldn't hold my hurt or live with yours
And would scrap my card from the *Kodokan*.

January 1984

Evening in the Castle

"Sleeps like a stone." My father, sir,
Professor Emeritus of Medicine, University of Cluj,
Said this of me. Perhaps because, siring me at sixty
He produced a son not fully alive, too tired
For the effervescent joys of air and light.
How does a stone sleep? Observing them
In the crypt (we have many) I've not found one
That wakened. I do not feel them brothers.

What I'm really cursed with, my silent friend,
Is this recurrent flicker of desire to live,
To walk again the dusty avenues of pain
My dark and twisted hours, and dance the pointless dance
In casinos of the night, returning home
Through webs of fragile dew to sleep again at dawn.

April 1987

Utica Station

Giant granite egg of the great roc or dodo,
It squats among empty lots, grimy alleys,
Third-rate honkytonks with unpaved parking.
The four-foot marble pillars are plastered
With Xerox signs begging infrequent travellers
Not to litter. A papercup coffee stand doubles
For bus tickets, and offers two dusty umbrellas
Deserted by someone on some other Sunday.

I kissed you and walked away, and you waited
Between your carrybags, half a mile of ancient oak
Passenger pews stretching away on either side.
You wanted no priest for the ritual of departure.
I rounded a column, looked back and waved
Weakly, feeling like heretic, a sadist or a fool.

September 3, 1989

Inscription I.

This I ordered:
Build me here Meru,
World mountain,
Centre of universal All.
Temple-tomb, this,
Of me, Suryavarman,
Warrior Lord of Angkor.

At this piece, bury me.
Dead king, I live now
One with Vishnu, Surely
We shall require this city
To house us both.

Inscription II.

All was in ruins.
The Chams having conquered
And I having driven them out
All is restored. I, Jayavarman,
Dedicate this lingam to my glory.

March 3 1991

Andy

"I want to look in on the library," says Andy.
At the big table near the checkout, bending
Down over a compact riot of small type
About Socialism and Unions and Canadian
Politics generally, he caresses the print
With his shaky carpenter's fingers.
Checking on his world. *How ya doin?*
He asks Ottawa, Cape Breton, the Gatineau Hills.

Old Wob from the One Big Union,
Andy hardly noticed national borders,
Worked the Thirties waterfront Stateside,
Drew five in Dannemora for goonsquad blood
In the North River and came back home.
Hey, have ya read this one? barks Andy.

Forgetting Faces

We found him loping down Courthouse Square
But Big Charlie had forgotten my name.
He wanted to be a fly-boy once.
Learned that Indians could take courses
On government cash, get him to Cloud Nine
Real quick; now an honest-to-God J.P.
He vacationed his pals in the Crowbar Hilton.
On some conference together eyeing my watch

And wondering when's lunch! Big Charlie says,
"Hey, white man, lookin' to see if it's
Time to be hungry?" A great kidder,
Quick on the draw, and I'm thankful that day
At least Big Charlie didn't smile and say,
"Y' know, all you white folks look alike to me."

Prayer Tablet

A woman stood before me and said, "I became
curious and checked what you're doing. You are
really teaching our children to write Sumerian."

Which one of me did that? This pattern
Has been torn and buried, each loosening thread
Eaten by rain and sun and the unweaving worm
Since long before friend Ea gave the word
To Utnapishtim, moons before the flood. I am,
Have been, shall be, and earn no lasting rest.
All yesternoons are cousin to this dawn
And fading strangers in the ebb of light.

Three-pointed, our hard reeds mark the mud:
Anu, Enlil and Ea-the-fish, we pray
Long peace from the Great River. Remember:
Inscribe the *dingur*, the *illu*, honorific
Saying, "God-name follows." O Lords,
Let the rain tomorrow dissolve this clay.

                                    June 1985 C.E.

The Dream at Penuel

By the River Jabbok I wrestled the thing:
God's angel, in a dream they said
But solid enough, my son, to break a real bone.
They will call this a myth or a Hebrew romance,
A little light fiction for a cold evening
By the hearth. Tell the kiddies ,grandpa,
How you got thrown to the sand and screamed
To a sky full of stars that didn't seem to care.

How do I show them the horror? Real muscle,
That creature had. Without words, a message
For me from my Lord: *All your thinking*
Cannot surround, define Me. Always the chasm,
The blackness beyond the smudge of your smoking fire.
Never entirely to know Me. My bones it broke.

Sometime in June

Sometime in June the hydrangea started it.
A few of the leaves had been chewed by a small gray beetle
And a lot of the top ones were tightly curled:
Home for some hatching bug, I thought
But pried them open and found the dead earwigs
Pressed nearly flat in the green fists, a couple
Neatly sliced in half by the ripsaw edges.
That tree looked wicked; I didn't like it.

Mid-July, the chard began to smother the carrots.
It was August when the cukes and squash
Ganged up and throttled the corn. I'm telling you
So you can keep an eye open, and a knife handy.
I was slow about it; a little before the first frost
The African daisies got my son.

1981

Besides

besides, said the ant
he left only stale crumbs.

charity with a hard crust
is abrasive to the esophagus

so i crawled up his nostril
and strangled him.

Bowed by the cost

Bowed by the cost of repairs
He leans upon his bike and gazes at the ground.
What to him are Chrysler and the swish of Cadillac?
Oh, Esso, Shell and boneyards of all lands,
How will it go with you
When this rough biker shall rise to judge the world
After the silence of a breakdown?

How many times

How many times I've tried to read that
piece of Rilke's without breaking up. Not
made it yet to the last line. Laid-on
pseudo-emotion? Hardly. The stuff can
unman me utterly, like that hour with
Bobbie when I got knocked to my knees
and couldn't stop shaking.

What breaks me up is poetry and power
out of time, a power that dissolves the
illusion of the separateness of days or
lives or loves. What tests the reality of loving is
love's power to engender poetry.

"I'm from a time that is not yet," said
Corsa the monk. Me? I'm from a day
forgotten.

September 1985

Ras Shamra

The digger found the tablet,
And a tiny idol, next.
Some forty gray Professors
Read Ugaritic text
While the digger stole the idol
And wandered home, perplexed.

"I wonder what it's good for?"
He asked his Arab wife,
Who threw some dung upon the coals
And cursed her barren life:
"An idol-stealing husband,
No child to ease the strife!"

But shortly she grew happy,
And swelled with more than joy,
Presenting to the digger
A ten-pound baby boy
Who, when he came to teething
Found a most entrancing toy:

Ishtar, Queen of Heavens,
Cast by an ancient arm
In metal cool and soothing
To hush his gum's alarm.

> *The scholars would have told him:*
> *"A cheap fertility charm."*

Intrumo In the Valley

For Ursula K. LeGuin

Who has danced with Dan Katchongva
On the edge of Oraibi, chanting up the Hopi sun,
Hauled wood for the sweat lodge of Soto Ojlbway
And hugs, perhaps, a Kwakiutl grandchild or two
May in dreamworld hunt the laughing friend
Whose shadow leaped through the dancing grass
And drumbeat hills of childlife. Bronze valleys
Guarded by bearded oak will host a someday tribe,

A nation yet to be, whose poetry and music
Resonate our long desire. And at some rock
Or roadside shrine, before the Samhaln festival
Salutes the pomegranate year, we meet an old one
Nodding to the autumn dust, and saying only,
"So you have come. But I have lived here always."

July 1986

Ash-toreth. Enish-kegal.

Your faces turn in smoke and flame
Behind the letters in my book,
Dark and light. Now, which more real:
The letter or the page beyond?
I wrestle choice. Both are real,
And change is in the whirling stars.
Life surfaces a thousand times,
Bright bubbles in the natal sea
To burst in evanescent foam
Beneath your smile of light and dark.

Perhaps the shadow and the fire
Transmute the single face I seek:
Unspoke, the goddess and the grail
Wait within the altar-screen
On which the shine-and-shadow play
Chasea name and name and name:
Ash-toreth. Enish-kegal.

Autumn 1969

Krestova

The Sons of Freedom said, "Now we have trouble;
God doesn' t recognize us shelled by our houses
And smothered in man-made woolies and boots."
So they torched their shacks, and stripped
And marched down the street through the snow
Past the Hudson's Bay store. The police scooped them
Into a paddy wagon, locked their kids in a prison school
Run by social workers. Things were quiet for a while.

Helen Demeskov and Joe Podnovikov
Are long gone, and even our saintly friend Peter
Who was Orthodox and an aging curator
Of the Douk museum at Castlegar. My intent
Is invisible among the many volumes, the walls
Of words. May I give you this book about Trotsky?

January 1987

Turnabout

The son of the well-known architet
Who sprouted in the shadow of dad's drawing board
Was mostly too drunk to pen a straight line
So we pulled together a bunch of guys and gals
And pried him off the booze, sat on him hard
Till he got his papers, made his wife dress sharp
And kidded him away from that woman's place
Where his pup sat on the back stoop and howled.

And he made it in a small firm. Senior partner
He was, in just three years, doing fine thanks
With a new house, two cars, kids in the choir,
Himself respectable and pretty well predictable.
His wife said, "I'm utterly, abysmally bored."
And she ran off with the local schoolteacher.

January 1987

One-Industry Towns

My friend in the north had a big map-board
With little lights for one-industry towns.
"Watch them flicker out when I press the buttons,"
He said. "See — the iron's gone, and now the
Pulp-wood, and the silver, nickel, zinc…"
He didn't mention fish rotting on a mercury diet
Or wild rice drowned when they boosted water level
But he could have. "See — all gone now."

They were my towns and my friends
And he made me feel like a flickering light myself.
But I'm not a man of one industry,

Not with a dozen trades and the dust of fifty towns
On these boots. He made me wonder, though,
Which of me, if any, would be left around.

January 1987

Long Distance

Around the curving Gulf the cars come,
Headlights of wet silk sweeping the dusky road.
We've phoned my brother: a conference call
About his wife. Carcinoma. Metastases.
Unlovely words, and now it looks as though
We rnay not hold our reunion on the Fourth
In Saratoga. "We may have to go to New York,"
Says Helen. We chorus Goodbye, hang up,

And watch the coastal drive. We'll stay
Here above the town; Jack and Helen
Are going to the opera. Miles and years
From our kid days together, we stretch
The web of friendship New York to Sarasota
And talk of another old pal with Alzheimer's.

Sarasota, Fla.
Feb. 21, 1987

Roberta the Improbable

I watched while you argued
  with a physical scientist
  and a math professor
  on the probable sum
  of innumerable
  small immeasurables.

They seemed puzzled
  and slightly amused.

You became angry;
  later, we made love.

E=η analog poem²

> November 1986

Roberta the Improbable: II

From the waist up
  you waded
  an inverted sea
  of bourbon and fantasy

Finding omens in clouds,
  firefly video,
  raindrop ballet.

One day we saw a squad car,
  two State Police
  lounging.

"May I touch
  the car?" you asked.

"Oh, thank God!
  It's *real!*"

> November 1986

La Fontaine de Vaucluse

"We may be learning how to tell the truth" – Marilyn Hacker

Sharp broken hill shaped like a hawk's wing
Hints that specific concrete blocks can fly
When properly motivated. The exceptional!
Once only and never again by sundial,
Clock or isotope decay. Shall we,
She quizzed the gray professor, discard
The sum of multiple immeasurables?
What weights unweighed move me and you?

Too urban for that oil of Constantin' s
But cousin to its muted colour, cool
Forever umber wood, pale apricot cloud,
She combs her closet for a pair of matching shoes.
We no longer synchronize our pocket memos.
What might be a hawk's wing is only a broken hill.

February 1986

Not that the core of me is vacuum

Though they came to learned Erinn
Without buoyant, adventurous ships,
No man in creation knew
Whether they were of the earth or of the sky.
    –Eochaid O' Flynn

Not that the core of me is vacuum
But that I am too many, I am legion
And cough in that unmoving, dusty air

Shrouding the clay tablets, abraded memories
Of Nineveh, of faceless, namelost places
Scattered by a random hand across a map
Margined with stale warnings, blotted signs:
Walk gently, stranger. Here there be dragons.

So it is, tiring of the endless wind,
Convoluted waves and bleaching sun
That now I moor the fragments of my coracle
On the islet of your Celtic bed
To weep in the anchorage of your arms
Like some lost child intossed by the Western sea.

Haiku

The trick is to get the same syllable count. Japanese traditional haiku also requires the season be indicated in the first five syllables.

| Nagare yuki | Stubbornly against |
| (Drifting snow) | |

Adjisai no hana	Drifting snow, last brown and
dry	
(Hydrangea blossom)	

| Kare kuroku | Hydrangea blossom |
| (Withered brown) | |

Tabi

*Desire is nothing
but the desire to break
the surface of all surfaces*
             –Robin Morgan

That something moves within the hand, head, heart,
Behind both eye and ear, prisoned but elusive,
Insubstantially held in a lattice of solids
Or apparent substance — we take it on faith.
Whether Christian soul, Buddhist karma, or avatar
Of Tara in the three-ring circus of our flesh,
Beyond the surface mirror is the port of our desire:
The You I know is compass to the You that yet may be.

And I shall thank whomever you are tonight
And thank the changeless power of the deep
For granting us this voyage past the headlands
And all our selves left standing on the quay.
Glacier to ocean, we melt and flow together
Like the crystal stream of some far northern fjord.

And I am shaken again

   I remember visiting Notre Dame in Paris and standing in the nave, tears starting in my eyes, furious at that old love's enduring power to move me.
                              - Marina Warner

And I am shaken again. What way my feet may move
Or mind perform its work, I cannot know.
Goya's duchess, your anxious eyes were asking,
"How do I look to him? What is he feeling?"

Lady, Lady: All my dusty thoughts were burned away
In the white light among the trembling trees.
Child again, my hands in fear and joy give praise
To the golden gifts of yesterday.

She is of very time, whose avatar you are,
And bathed in this pool held by the forest floor.
My swimming eyes unveil the dawning word
My tongue cannot pronounce. Oh Thou,
Accept my worship and be here reborn
To warm the orphan world of men.

July 1985

I sing not me

I sing not me.
I sing light-years ahead,
The longer view. I sing not you.
"Beyond! Beyond!" the music cries;
 Not both my hands, not both your eyes
 Shall reach so far:
 I sing a six-lane highway to a star.

Go, song,
 Seek out for me
 The hopeful and the strong.
 Outrace my crippled feet;
 Dance down each berried path,
 Each city street. Drink deep.
 The yearning heart enfold –
 For such, my beads are told.

1948

Hero

Go, hero,
  destroy some small, quivering thing
  in whose wet eyes pain lies drowning.
  Tell yourself the sharp thrust is kinder,
  the slow death of man or animal
  unapproved by Zeus.
  Scrape up a nimble Sophist
  to handle the details
  if your own wit's unwilling.
  Do it now, at daybreak.

Fit work for a hero, Jason:
  It is not easy, man,
  to come charging home to Corinth
  and, watching Medea braid her hair,
  say smiling, "Surprise, darling!
  I love another."

Journey

Leaving you, rolling in a slow train
Through the sad back windows and switch-yards of
Montreal
Peppered by makers of electric kettles, small castings,
Air compressors and corrugated cartons,
Angular crumbs dredged by an indifferent finger
From the dirty navel of our northern land,
I might have wondered if this were the only world
Had I not borrowed your eyes and been afflicted
With an elvish double vision:

Hip-roofed flats evoke the archetypal cave
From which, on Monday mornings, earth-mother airs

The world's gray thoughts all sudsy soaked
And flung unwrinkling on the wind.
Each fold a facet, garment gems
Cry sapphire, sing opal and amber, garnet.
Our concrete skies affirm probable pearl
Luminously uniting, at the smudged horizon,
This dubious earth and heaven.

New Song Heard in High Lothlórien

Four times ten the sounds of speech
 To forge the word whose ring will reach
Along the winds of space. How far
 To the lands in the world of the laughing star?

A hundred winds that blow all ways,
 And never a one that stops and stays:
Where is the wind whose wings are turned
 To the paths that the feet of song have learned?

A thousand stars, and a million more
 To drive the tides of dusk before.
Til word, and wind, and star be right,
 Wait a thousand times the thousandth night.

Lake Storm

Not Thor, but there!
  In each thin, recurrent flash,
  Loki the falcon, light-fringed
  jokes with the dark's dominion,
  his jest the silver-shattering spear,
  shield of hill-congested sky.

Land-held, leafthin, lonely,
  willows lean to the wind's hiss,
  hearing storm-talk:
  consonants of sand,
  syllabled spray.

The Rug-Carriers

Loki Val, high among jokers, tiring of hunger
And honesty, stole a rug of antique threads
Which he then transported to Astrakhan. Laughter
In the loud bazaar met his thumb-heavy pitch at noon
And two of the merchants, dark-eyed brothers,
Drank tea with him until dusk. They smiled
Each time they looked at his beaming face.
They brought a prayer rug later for his prison cell.

One of our brightest, leaving school early,
Took his grandmother's shawls, sewed them together
And made a floor covering of crowded colour.
This he sold in the market of Astrakhan,
Buying more shawls with the shekels. Now,
Ten years after, he is respected, wealthy,
And hotly directing a den of buyers
Who strip the farms of peasant shawls.

Abdu the poet, lacking paper or pen,
Wove the lives of his people into a poem
Which was hung on a wall of the Friday Mosque.
Young men, students, pondered the pattern,
Found knots and tassels of no known tradition
And wondered if blood had darkened the dye.
Their wondering led them to weave a net
Which pinioned the rulers of Astrakhan.

All the Poems I Never Wrote

Inside dope   logger son   sepuku daughter
    disagreeable habits of my wives
    and how to dump my aching guts
    on fourteen reams of (I hope) utterly
    absorbent blue-ruled writing pads

Hart Crane perhaps said something like
    the poet cried I exist
    that however replied the universe
    does not cause to arise in me
    any sense of responsibility

Which spills it all now & ever
    ochi kochi up & down the ginza
    much self-pursuing enterprise
    is a feckless piece of incest
    don't you think   *Quaestio*

                                                      May 1987

Lilith

When have I not been pleased with thee?
Shall I dispute my own right arm
Or argue the witness of both my hands?
Your alchemy is all my life and laughter.

Walking the paths of a small town
You looked inward, walked down beyond the small,
Memories of small winds in your hair,
Your toes in the yesterday of small grasses

While I stirred the dust of a hundred cities
And burned my eyeballs on a thousand suns.
Within this immediate point, in the centre of all
And beyond the edge of everywhere, we met.

How should I not be pleased with thee, Lilith?
Your alchemy is all my life and laughter.

Etruria

Lilith sheds an Etruscan smile
On the cramped sarcophagus of my sleep,
While I reassemble my hoarded bones
With a mouthful of dust to keep,
To keep.
Small room, and the roof is low.

So lightly she lies on the fluted lid
That I hardly know if she's there at all
And in me no tune or note remains
That through the stone may call,
May call.
(Its weight is of memory, though.)

So heavy her smile on my onyx heart,
Her lips on my basalt thighs
That I alone on the Judgment Day
Will never be able to rise,
To rise.
My cairn is beneath the snow.

More Real Than We Think

Reality is predatory; it not merely presses upon man with the
urgency of its evidences, it eats one alive.
                                        -Daniel Berrigan

We are born into a day with teeth:
Time chews us. The bite of the hour is hard
And cracks the bone. Not like that of a dog,
Said Rabbi Akiba, but the bite of a donkey.
History eats us – you and I and our tangible loves.
See: the menu doesn't even have your name.

Friend, I can't promise that you'll be tastee,
Or the flavour remembered. We're basted
By an absent-minded chef in a dim café.
The owner's on holiday in the Bahamas.

Maybe only the cockroaches are real?
Don't think it, or you'll roll to the floor
Like a stale bagel. There could be, just perhaps,
A value in it. Possibly, friend, this world,
This hour, this hungry instant is most intensely ours.
And we, and it, more real than we think.

                                                1973

Changeling

No, I can't tell you why I woke
And popped up in bed like a stringed puppet
To find you in your half-slip
Suggesting return to your own room.
Why must you go? Merely that
Your wakefulness disturbs me,
And you feel guilty of my slaughtered sleep?

Changeling, there's only a bead I see
Of the rosary of your hundred worlds:
One calls you from me now
While your green-slippered, buckled, restless feet
Dance along the paths under a misty moon.

What shall I mourn of your going:
The empty half of my tumbled bed,
Or the possible kisses we didn't share?
Rather sing happy, say glory and glad
That those small feet have walked my world
In the hour when I was there.

                              Summer 1968

Some of My Best Friends

Heinrich Schwartzchild, who called himself Henry Black,
Stood on a corner in the ghetto and looked sad.
Henry had this funny little Charlie Chaplin moustache,
You see, which one-two-three fingers were always,
Or almost always, twitching around the ends of.
And then, when he'd sit down with a bunch of us
He always sat down next to one of the girls.
So he looked coyly (he thought) around one end
Of the moustache, and twisted it, and spoke:
"Are you married?" Only he always made it like
"Arrr you marrreet?" Then he'd hitch himself over
A little closer to the girl, looking, in his
European-style winter overcoat, like an unsmoked
But slightly soggy cigar, or an anaemic wurst,
And she'd sooner or later move somewhere else.

But, eventually, he met Liz. Liz had had
A Socialist husband who'd been fighting
The Battle of the Mimeograph Machine
In one of these splinter groups that had
An office in a water closet six flights up
Within slogan-shouting distance of Union Square.
(You think I'm kidding? I remember
A quarreling couple – she was pregnant –
Proudly showing me just such a hole
Under a leaky skylight: National Office, they said.)

> *Appropriately? my wife puts on a Benny Goodman,*
> *And says Dorothy is now showing quite a bit*
> *And the phonograph "goes itz-bitz and that's it*
> *How do you fix it again, Clif?"*

So anyhow, Liz wasn't pregnant
But she sure could wrestle.
One time she and Henry wrestled
All over the floor of a drug store.
Liz won; she picked up Henry
In a fireman's carry and staggered
Out the door. I was embarrassed –
But I think I finished my milk shake.

Henry and I played pingpong
In a joint full of smoke and green tables.
He beat me all the time, too.
There was a big fellow like a blob of dough
Down Mexico; he beat me every game of chess
After I taught him how. The trouble was,
He was an idiot.

> *Boy, that Goodman sure can blow!*

So could this Arthur play violin, down Mexico,
Only he played it like a player piano
And you kept looking for the roll of paper
With the Swiss cheese holes in it.

Kerouac, in "On the Road," wrote one good spot
About Mexico. We were beat twenty years back,
In the Village, but we didn't have
A good press agent. (And might add,
To be nasty, took time to learn to write,
So didn't do three novels a month.)

What kind of music played down Henry's mind?
Krupa on the drums is not quite like
I remember Chico Hamilton doing "Solo Flight,"
But it couldn't be Benny bouncing around
In Henry's head, that night late, after pingpong,
When we stood under a street lamp and Henry said,
"You know, I think you are the most sane friend I have."

All this grows out from Henry, see?
And he wouldn't know about it, ever, not guess
That little butter-ball of a Yiddish girl
I blind-dated him with one evening
When Liz was mad at him.
Had rowed up the Connecticut River
One slow summer afternoon with me
To a small and rock-pocked island
Where we uncomfortably ate sandwiches
She had made, and her little
And equally Yiddish brother made remarks
About the rubber memories of romance
Two dozen Lotharios named Ginsberg
Had tossed in ecstatic abandon into the bushes,
Where they hung limply, like Christmas ornaments
By Salvador Dali, waiting for time

To make them tinkle. So who wants
To make love, anyway, in the middle
Of somebody else's Ancient History?
But after Henry vent out with her once,
We neither of us heard any more about it.

Also, he had a friend named Holley,
The son of a man called The Boxcar King.
Holley used to drop around the cellar
Where I had my presses, and kept
The mad artist, De Moreland, who
Painted Ukranian easteregg designs
On ceilings, walls, floor, doorknobs –
And never any driers in it! Now Holley,
He said the bunch kind of closed Henry out
Because he was Jewish, or because
He was Very Jewish, or because
He was just Real Weird, and Holley
Was mad about it. But I was busy
Watching that Holley wore a muffler
An overcoat rubbers heavy sox and
No shirt. Just a dickey like you'd wear
Maybe with a tux. And his girl Dachine
Had chartreuse stockings with crooked seams.

Now, last winter, I was back in the Village
And it is the fashion (which it wasn't then)
To wear chartreuse stockings. Or black or purple.
And I said to someone in British Columbia
That the Village girls wore green eye shadow
So heavy yon tripped over it at high noon.
And they said, "That's nothing. The girls
Do *that* at U.B.C." But I said,
"That's not all. The boys
Are wearing *blue* eye shadow."

Dachine wrote a villanelle,
"Where Are the Joys My Heart Had Won?"
Based on a line from Pound, I think,
But that was twenty years ago.
And de Moreland made it Out
After three tries with poison,
Razor blade & the Flop From the Rooftop.
On which last he landed in a canvas awning
With tube steel frame. You know: Goes
From front door to curb. The janitor's wife
Heard the racket and hustled hubby up
For a look. He saw the awning and said,
(de Moreland had hobbled away) "Any guy
Who can do that I am *not* gonna tangle with!"

Henry
Walked with a slouch. Told me that
Back in Berlin, he carried noiseless typewriters
In an old knapsack, one at a time,
Through the streets to what was left
Of the Underground. Those were early Hitler days,
A chunk of the Thousand Year Reich. And Henry?
Nobody ever stopped him, he said. He wore
The armband, the *moghen David*. He was
The caricature of a Jew. The Gestapo never
Noticed: Henry looked like he'd been
Crucified twice already.

> *Funny thing about typewriters. We used*
> *To smuggle them in from Switzerland,*
> *For the remains of the Brandler-Thalheimer group,*
> *Through Jay Lovestone. Remember? When Stalin*
> *Knocked off the Zinoviev-Kamenev faction, back in*
> *The first Moscow Trials, Jay justified it. Or tried to.*
> *But when Bloody Joe took the Tomsky-Rykov bunch,*

And Bukharin got his (Bukharin was Jay's friend)
Then Jay screamed, "Rivers of blood!"
And that was the end of that honeymoon.

Not For This

Not for this do I hate you, nation accursed:
Not for the brass and the tinsel,
But that you proclaim it as gold;
Not for the fact that the fire is out
But that none will admit it is cold;
Not for your deaf, senile statesmen
But for those who deny they are old.

Not for this do I damn you, people corroded:
Not for the depth of your blindness,
But the boasting you make of your sight.
Enough that the world has been murdered!
But you have to prove you were right
With babbling of daylight and freedom
And creeping down into the night.

1947

Nagasaki

We've written in letters, to shock the blind:
NO HAND IS CLEAN OF THE CLOTTED GORE
For the world is sewed with a tiny thread
From hand to hand, and from head to head
And even to Mary Ann, age four.

You didn't know that, eh, Mary Ann?
But the gift they gave you on Christinas Day
Was a wooden cart with a wooden wheel:
Before the war it was made of steel.
You kissed your mother and ran to play;

You couldn't have known of a business man
Who formerly sold a kiddie cart
All Steel, Ten Dollars, and Worth the Price!
Now made of wood – not quite as nice –
To save the steel for a bigger part.

Nagasaki is just a dot
From the plane that carries a queer, bright thing –
A rose of hell for the human heart
In which three petals are held apart
By a toy wheel turned to a metal ring.

A baby crying, A sickroom cot.
People are pins on a master plan.
Slowly over the waiting town
The flower of death comes floating down –
A gift from the hands of Mary Ann.

                                                    1947

While repulsing a young man of Science

While repulsing a young man of Science
Within a time-travel appliance,
Reverse gear was stripped,
And before she'd been flipped
She enjoyed an Entangling Alliance.

A blooming young belle of Verdun
Curled nude in a garden for fun,
Imitated a rose
And remained in the pose
'Til plucked by a botanist's son.

A three-titted cowgirl, Priscilla,
Seduced with fox, mink & chinchilla,
Gave with each lay
Free milkshakes away
Of cherry, sweet lime and vanilla.

The Weaver's Son

The Weaver stands by the empty loom.
The fallen shuttle on the floor lies still,
For the Weaver's son would follow the road
To the end of the rainbow over the hill.

The Weaver's eyes with his grief are full
And the tears their story of pain have told,
But the Weaver's son has heard the tale
Of the Rainbow's End and the pot of gold.

"See, father, there where the wide road goes,
Far over there where the rainbow bends;
The winds have told what the clouds confirm:
There's a pot of gold where the rainbow ends."

"Not so, my son, for the clouds have lied,
And I trust no word that the winds may bring,
For the road is long and the rainbow fades
And a pot of gold is a useless thing.

"But you are young and the rainbow calls...
Still I ask that you hear me ere we part:
A wiser search would have soon revealed
That the rainbom's end is within your heart."

1938

The World

The World is back of Listening Hill,
Over the tops of elmtrees high
And down a stretch of backwoods road,
Near where the uplands kiss the sky.

The World cries out with a raucous voice
That it's fearfully big and strong –
But it isn't as deep as Hollow Brook
And it's really not as long.

The World is such a tiny thing:
It quite securely lies
Between the curve of a woodpath brown
And the wind-scoured, rainwet skies.

1938

The New God

   (On noticing the different degrees of attention
   commanded by a church bell and an air raid siren)

High in a tower the new god sits,
At the top of a winding stair;
He stretches wide his whirling mouth
And spits at the frightened air.

In the Square below, his subjects stand
Agape with awe and fear,
While the new god screams to the shaking land
That the wings of death are near.

No muezzin crying Allah's might
In the dreamy twilight hour
Has gripped their minds in mewling fright
Like the new god in the tower.

The old gods were too soft and weak;
Swift time gave them the heel.
They did not know a god could speak
With a thousand mouths of steel.

1945

She also

She also
is a daughter of Dana,
child of the great one.
She and I
in an eddy of time
looked once
and knew our one Mother.

Dana, comfort
your children:
give us each other
and a moment of peace
on this
momentary island.

Sister of my soul,
will you know me
as brother and lover?

White Lady

Ashtoreth.
Enishkegal.
I call you
by the lost names.
I call you
even from the seven-barred city;
See this woman. Hear me.

If ever she need
and I serve her not,
Cast me out.
If I fail her
l fail you,
O my white lady.

If ever she speak
and I listen not,
Take my ears.
If I can't hear her
I can't hear you,
O my white lady.

Grant truth
to my worship:
Deny her
and I deny you,
O my white lady.

Moon Stallion

Tonight, the air is strangely cool and wet,
And in the hills the Indian gods are watching.
Who goes into those hills tonight is met
By shadows of grave Indian lovers walking
In silence on some moonlit parapet.

Surely the moon is a silent silver stallion
Who feeds upon a field of midnight blue.
Whose heart may mount that magic silver stallion
And ride him through the night to dreams of you?
Oh, he must have a bridle made of silver;
Bright silver be the spurs that he must use;
And he must climb the highest of the mountains
To win that silver stallion, or to lose.

Whose feet may run a lyric road of moonlight,
Whose soul must go out singing to the stars,
Alone shall find him waiting in the moonlight
And spur him through the night's thin silver bars.

                                        May 11, 1949

Sixth and San Pedro

Beyond the arch of wrinkled stone
The city stirs in sleep. Gray morning comes
To turn the blankets back, and strangle yawns
And boil a pot of coffee in the darktown slums.

How ugly Is your face,
O harlot among cities!
Unveiled of the night's romantic lore
You stretch your smoky thighs in this sad place
Without cosmetic neon,
Like a morning whore.

>
March 8, 1949

Poem for Roger: II.

"I had a little talk with him," you say,
And then you stop. No more.
I want to know what things you said
Or didn't say. But then you look at me
Who am already old, and far behind.
You say you don't remember. That's not so;
The things you know, you five-year-old,
Would blast my painted, world apart
If I should ever look at it your way,

And you are simply being kind to me,
Selecting what you will or will not say.

Dusk Forest

It's cold. That twisted ironwood
May hear a muffled drum
Beat madly, catch the hum
Of one more bee before the day
Is gone...The dark has come.

Bacchus! Some devil's caravan
Has forced the hidden door
Of night; the subtle core
Congealed, dead Pleasure's fruit
Corrupts the forest floor.

Taut trees, great crying violins
Beneath, a naked bow
Bend earthward, cringing low,
Weeping pools of rusty leaves
To bed the bitter snow...

The Jealous God

Here waits one who scorns to take
Just any offered corner of your soul;
However hard you plead
With half a voice,
Stands he immobile,
Inviolate.
       (Eros, maiden, is a strong and jealous god.)

In half his cup is there no taste,
Nor any light to greet the eye of one
Who weakly squints at him
Through shading hands.
The risk of blindness:
Here read his price.
       (Eros, maiden, is a strong and jealous god.)

Atomic War

Not that the thing was done –
 But done without reason.
Not to object that the thistle grows –
 But it grows out of season.

Blinded Moth

Around my lamp the creature winds
 A driven, hot, impassioned flight;
It dips a wing in primal flame,
 Impenitent, and drunk with light.

Quixotic

Beyond my lamp, recurrent night
 Assails the island of my thought.
I fight the tide, what time my feet
 In sand are most securely caught.

William Randolph Canute, Publisher

The dawn is here. I've worked all night
 Building paper barricades against the light.
Buy smoked goggles; beware the sun!
 I'll let a couple rays through to everyone.

Captive Moth

In solemn eyes, the amber light
 Reflects his destiny of fire,
And iron pyrite dust he spreads,
 Protesting I delay his pyre.

Objector

So cursed soon the rooster crows!
 Earth spins on. My brother clods
Hurtle down the aisles of space.
 I move a pen against the gods.

Warning Posted

Eat not of one loaf,
 Nor drink the same wine
Lest your lips be only
 The shadow of mine.

Speechless

Of this the spirit of my dreaming hands
 Imperatively sings.
Beside the rounded rampart of your breast
 My words have broken wings.

Planck's Constant

This is the beat of Beethoven's Fifth:
 The ever-returning tide of creation,
Microcosmic pulse of the aeons,
 Immutable key of relation.

Schroedinger's Equation

Here is the door to the world of If,
 A land where a mote may be Brahm indeed,
Where Aristotle is Krishna's rug,
 Where the seed is a plant, and the plant, a seed.

Heisenberg's Principle

Never to mount on a pin The Ultimate Nature,
 Nor swear it's the fog, or ourselves, we pierce.
Caught by our senses, and whirled in an orbit
 Through Planck, and Berkeley – and Ambrose Bierce.

Materiel

What shall be my house of words
 When roof and walls and floor are done?
I have tried to catch your eyes
 With mirrors in the sun.

Infacticide

Shall they complain whose god is dead,
 Who found some truth, but hid it?
Why mourn him with the scriptured lie?
 It was themselves who did it.

Hill Fever

I want to hit the trail again
And follow where it goes
Over the hills and up and up
On the heels of winter snows;
And I want to stop on the Goshen range
Where the way goes 'round the edge,
And breathe in deep of the mountain air
And climb to the highest ledge.

A man can see the hills from there,
And chuckling mountain streams,
While sleeping valleys deep in shadow
Conjure mountain dreams.
The hills are bright with morning light
That tints them one by one:
Dark green and green and lighter green
They roll toward the sun.

My heart cries out for the little hills
Where there is no timberline
With every haunting breeze that hints
A breath of mountain pine.

To the Man

Wherefore shall a man now bare his head
And kneel in silent awe to pale Opinion,
That leper clad in lying silks
Who by unreasoning Faith is fed,
But to proclaim himself a slave – a minion
Enthralled by the ashes of the dead?

Why mutter to himself, "It is not right,"
Then turn and shrug the shoulders, saying:
 "Let another do it -- I cannot lead the fight
To give strong eyes to the blinded multitude;
Myriad the Powers that conspire upon their sight
...And what avails one man against that vampire brood?"

   Mark how the strength of Nature's law
   Still a stronger truth can frame:
From a single spark, fallen
On the dry and waiting tinder
Mounts the all-consuming flame;
From a single seed, buried
In the warm and pregnant earth
Springs many a green-leafed branch;
From a single stone, dislodged
On the rugged mountain-side,
Thunders the mighty avalanche.

Again

There – down the street they come again
To the bursting bugle's cry;
To the maddening beat of the drum again
The regiment marches by.

The sick and well, the blind and lame
Give them cheer on cheer,
For it's off to the sport of another game,
The blood of another year.

How short the memory, poor the mind –
Scarce twenty years or so
Since they shattered the lives of their own kind
And plundered a fallen foe.

How swollen with pride the martial chest!
The ruthless, pounding feet
Crush Reason's brain and Beauty's breast
And trample them on the street.

* ** *

How long 'till the judgment overdue
With ultimate darkness comes
To blanket the dead, and the dead they slew
And silence the tortured drurms?

Autumn passed through here today

Autumn passed through here today.
Now leaves that brushed her flaming head
Are tinted deep with breathless red
That pulses through the green array
Of oak and elm on Turkey Hill.

The city's driven crowds of men
May little heed and little fear
The hidden plan that smolders here,
That dares to breathe a song again –

A song of life on Turkey Hill.

We'd lead this ragged world away
To show it sun swept fields of grain,
To wash its face with auturan rain –
And yet this waits another day

While down the slopes of Turkey Hill
The scarlet legions pour
To melt the granite soul of man
Forever, evermore.

With what a sudden hand

With what a sudden hand the clouds come down
To stuff the jailhouse yard with cotton wool!
White, fugitive, the winterflowers fall
To press their wet, small faces at the pane,
While one or two blow through the bars and melt.
They run as though afraid of freedom's air,
As if the quadrangle were only here
To house the orphan legions of the snow.

Invitation

There's a quiet garden in my soul
Where small, soft-feathered birds sing constantly
To charm the sun's round golden bowl
Above the flowered hills.
The first half-timid rays declare
A tiny gate half open there
Among the daffodils.

Singing birds and gate and garden wait
The heart-enchanting step of one who comes,
Most surely comes, or soon or late.
And I shall know and care
Though silently her feet may pass
As diamond dust upon the grass
The day I find her there.

                                        Los Angeles, March 1949

Ports of Call

Wondering which of us is giver of the greater pleasure
My eyes hunt the hollows and hills of your joy,
Up from this sweet lagoon of autumn heat
Whose feather-fringed caress encloses
The fernwet cay, the silent mooring
Of my kiss. The sea-swells of your thighs
Are softly rounded, rising to a lunar pull
Of tidal flesh more smooth than lilies,
More strangely strong than ivy. These ranges
Trap my vision, and through the tendrilled mist
I wander to your belly's billow and curve.

This too is tidal, sea-harvest heaving,
More ripely moving than a school of dolphins
Arching out of spray into clouds and back,
While past this playful deep the washes part
Upon the headlands of your breast, twin dunes
Upswept and parted from this resting valley
Each to its nippled, tulip-bud horizon.

How proudly pressed erect, how thirstily pouted
They tease the very wind to finger them!
And now, as you twist your head in almost-pain
On the crest of this eager Golgotha
Each burning tip strains upward on its aureole,
Ravishing the evening and the startled air.

Tell me, how shall I say -

I'd rather see that halfway-
  laughter in your eyes,
Catch the sudden glad surprise
  of a seabreeze in your hair,
Meet the memory of your smile
  most anywhere
Than swap my place with any boy
Who had a thousand Helens
  in whatever Troy.

How shall I say?
With no matter what persistence,
What ineffectual song will sing
The caroling, clear fact of your existence?

March 14, 1949

Abduction of the Daughter of Maria

Yes, it was one week after we stopped for the wine
(Guadalupe Maria, you make a good wine)
Saw the washed-out bridge too late,
Flipped the embankment

And we and the flivver stank of wine.
The *ollas* – the clay pots – they clashed together.

And you sent after us, somebody's cousin
With a letter you wrote in the dispensary
Next door to the wineshop
Where you kept a pickled foetus
In formaldehyde, and where
You delivered children, doctored bellyache,
Stitched up the wounds
Of the wine-blurred knifers
And kept all the pesos, Maria,
The pesos of many purposes
Nesting in a dry wine-jar.

You said, "Yesterday noon in Guadalupe,
Nine bandits came from the high Martirs;
They took away my daughter; she is fifteen.
The Chief of Police is a fat old drunkard;
I asked him to help me. I cried;
I said, 'Bring back my daughter.'
He said, 'Yes, certainly. Maria,
Give me money for bullets
And food for the men.
I will bring back your daughter.'
He is a fat old *borracho*.
Come quick. I need your help."

So we went 'round the long way
And came in from San Felipe,
Eating rock oysters at low tide
And nothing much at high tide
And rented a burro
For slightly more than we could have bought one.
Walked west to the wall of the Martirs,
Froze in the desert night,

Forgot about it and came back.

And we heard from somebody's uncle
The bandits rode down to Guadalupe
And dumped your daughter
In the middle of Main Street.
They said she had a bad temper.

The Dying Metaphysician

"And when you stake your wisdom for a woman,
 Compute the woman to be worth a grave,
 As Merlin did, and say no more about it." –Robinson

I have taken a concubine.
Life and I have been thrust apart
By the icy press of her lips on mine:
There's frost on the windows of my heart.

What is there now I may look upon
Free of her fingers crystal-cold?
Even the steps where my mind has gone
Are iced with the pay of the over-bold,

What man may chance on the arctic path
To the white embraces of her room
And, pierced by icycles of wrath
Go free to a softer, warmer doom?

But once enraptured by those eyes,
Once feel the chill of her pointed breast,
Once know the truth of the dim surmise
And fatally hope to know the rest.

***

Death is a woman, cold and dark,
And I have held her hand in mine.
She will know me by her mark
The night I cross the shadow-line.

Sons of Zarathustra

Weary are we, out of skyward rocks
Preaching to pygmies in Sidon and Tyre.
Plainward we come, each of us bent
With brushwood, with sticks for a funeral pyre.

Grimly we come, driven by the years' caprice
To this poor desert of their parched desire
Where voices cry for wine, cool wine
Prometheus-like, we pour them a throatful of fire.

> (Vultures they are. Feeding their mouths
> What can we gain from the gift of our liver?
> To the takers, a Nazarene cloak.
> A cross for the giver!)

"Hand them a drink," Philanthropy says.
Poor tinder then for the flame that we hold.
Spoil our bright bonfire? Not for the hinges
Of Heaven's own gate, not for a river of gold!

The land wants a firing, for underfoot
The dead brush chokes all the warm earth's yearning;
Run if you will to the end of the world –
It is long overdue, – this burning.

(Torchlight on rocks. Arrogant sparks
Fly from the rubbish of too many years.
There is crying, but not from us.
For this job, no tears.)

At Ensenada Bay

There's something here that makes me feel
That same old, aching incompleteness,
As though I might go walking down
The moon's own highway on the sea
To find some vagrant part of me
At Punta Banda...As well to know
There's nothing there but mist, and mocking surf
To join in hollow counterpoint an uncompleted tune.

Almost I think; In what mad world
Beneath a harsh metallic moon
Dance free the wanton fragments of my soul?
Some fine galactic joker, uncontent
With such a search as only earth has seen,
Laughed once, and thrust the tides of space between.

1949

Hospitality

Indiana hailstones bouncing like ball bearings
Made pedalling a cycle dangerous sport.
I turned at the farm gate, dropped the wheels
And scrambled up the side porch, panting.
She watched from behind the sagging screen door,

A tea-towel clenched in one hand.
"OK if I stay here a bit, please?
It's getting terrible out on the road."
She nodded, wiped her hands on the cloth.
Quietly set the catch inside the rusting screen.

                                                    1997

Gwendolyn & Milton

That gray fog hovered between them.
She looked quizzically up; he smoked,
His face blurred, as if always
He was becoming, not yet complete
Or away somewhere on a visit.

Gwen saw a golfcourse in a moonscape,
Shared a fish dinner in Memison
While Milt read poems to the counterman
At the deli on Cecil & Spadina.
Sometimes, halfway, they seemed to meet.

There's a ton of unpublished poetry loose
Between Toronto and the moon.

                                    March 6, 1994

DoGGerEl GrEeTIngs

Maple & pine, poplar & beech
Try for the sky with the stretch of a reach.

Trees push tall & varying green;
Ho! Littler blue & horizon seen.

Slicing wind & shattering ice
Pile dead angels in paradise.

Bit by little & sidle by creep,
The forest moves whenever you sleep.

– Kaliph ben Et
1999 & all that

Beyond the mountains of despair

Beyond the mountains of despair,
Writ in smoke on moving air,
Varuna, Brahma, Vishnu, Bod
And all the other names of God,
Unheeded, drift to blank Nowhere.

Next to Vaino's broken lyre,
Beside Ahura-Mazda's fire,
Gently rest this shattered cross:
Symbol of another loss
To man's own madness and desire.

"Krishna; Horus, Egypt's pride;
Christ they cursed and crucified:
What have we gained while still they slay,
But words that any man may say –
That and little else beside?

"'Tis not enough that once you bled;
Again with thorns they crown your head,

While on their little earth a hell
Of smoke and flame, of shot and shell
Awaits another prophet's tread."

Rebellion

Thou hast told me for long that a most mighty Idol
Dwells in the innermost shrine;
Thou hast vowed he hath power to judge of my worth,
And is my father, even as thine;

Thou hast told me I need not fear death when I die –
I and the others who heard –
And bade us together erect him a Home,
For, lo! Was that not the great Word?

Gladly we gave thee of gold and of diamonds,
(Yea, and until we had none!)
That thou couldst then build him this Temple abode
To rival the copper-red sun.

But I late on one night softly crept by the priests
Sleepily guarding the Door,
And there in the sacred and innermost Shrine –
Thine Idol lay flat on the floor.

The god in thy Temple is shriveled and small,
Powerless, feeble and old;
O, why hast thou covered this pitiful thing
With glittering diamonds and gold?

I have seen thy deceit and I heed thee no more,
But forth on the paths I shall go,
To tell to each tribesman the thing I have seen,

And they who will listen shall know!

                                                    1940

Prison Graveyard

Fourteen men are buried here
Beneath atone markers, plain, austere

And numbered One, Two, Three…this so
Their names not even birds may know.

They sowed them here where few will pass
In private cells beneath the grass

Where each extends his numbered stone
Lying, as he lived, alone.

Rooted in the greenery
Grows a twisted apple tree,

Drops a rank, untended fruit
Through knotted branch and water-shoot.

On the grass that quilts their bed
Rest the apples, green and red.

None are perfect; all are marred,
Bumpy, bruised and insect-scarred.

All are thick with wart and spot,
Yet some have worms and some have not.

Here is man who cannot say
Whether worm or whether nay –

Under grass, embraced in mould,
Dreams there brass or dreams there gold?

1946

Bitter, O lord of the eight-fold path

Bitter, O lord of the eight-fold path,
Is the flower and fruit of this generation.
Ours is neither the calm Nirvana
Nor a three-ring circus in Christian Heaven

Disillusion crystallized
In poetry become Socratic –
Yet not Socratic;
That would link it with the hemlock cup
It cannot take. It dare not drink
The waters of oblivion.

We are too restlessly alive,
Energetically purposeless,
Brightly dilettante,
Yet not without knowledge
Of the pain in our time.

Diana with a broken bow,
Hermes paralyzed,
Diogenes without a lantern
Stumbling down rough, unseen roads
And squinting at the mist.

May children play in the silences

May children play in the silences
  between your words.

May the Hasidim dance in your smile.

May you and I unfold in each other,
  one-tenth of the wonder that is us.

Spendthrift

White poppy
Holds in fragile fingers
A burning ball of sun
Until such brightness turns them
To ashes, one by one.

White poppy's
Honey-butter fragrance,
Too sweet for it to bear,
It showers on the hillside,
It flings upon the air.

Why A Zebra?

> *A poem for* Fish Wrap, *the OCA student rag, which filled itself with zebras one issue.*

Michelangelo's David parades a limp pecker
Across a hundred portraits of our local censor
While a march of zebras peppers the margins
Of this manifesto of student intellect.

Why not a zebra? Where the signs and symbols
Are bleached of meaning, the myths buried,
Angel-feathers tarred, devils exiled,
And a hygienic vacuum fathers no hero?

Or worse: maybe, as Lem suggested
And Vonnegut insisted, we've finally
Achieved the pits of legendry
By evolving ourselves from roach shit.

                                            December 1984

The postman walks with a four-foot stride

> *I'd mortgaged myself to get Florence to the offbeat Hoxey Clinic in Texas. Got worried when not even Hallmark cards came!*

The postman walks with a four-foot stride
O'er hill and hollow and mountainside;
I wait for his footstep with tremors and chills,
But all that he brings me is bills – just bills.

I peer and I squint through the mist and fog,
And my heart within me is light as a log,
Cause I'm waiting for letters with X's from you
And all th&t I get is, "The phone bill is due."

I lie here in wait like a spider couchant
(In Boston I maybe could rhyme that with "aunt")
One letter I ask, and not a selection –
Ah, this one's a bill for the garbage collection!

Brown sugar is sweet and honey is too,

But if you don't write I'll go sour on you.
I beg you to try, O try to remember...
This one says, "Taxes are due in September."
c. 1954

Who He?????

Who do you know that's a man so rare
He can mingle a grin with a cold-eye stare?
Who can command, without commanding – demand,
without demanding,
And at all times remain very understanding.

He speaks the language of many a different land
But his English is the one we least understand,
Which probably has caused this famous note:
 "I don't apologize for what I say, only for the other guy's
ignorance" (unquote)

He's not too good at remembering names
But is really up on Foundation games.
He does not always hear so well –
Not that it bothers him, as this quote will tell:
"The fact that I didn't hear it reminds me of many other
times when I also did not hear anything that reminded me of
anything".

He wouldn't raise his voice at will.
Ask anybody – with the exclusion of Jerry Hill.
He has Job's patience – and needs at least that!
Who else would put up with the antics of Pat?

At present he's trying to make the budget grow
And more grey hairs are beginning to show.
By now most everyone knows who we mean,
And here are some tips to keep his esteem.

Say you will – when you're not sure if you can,
Then enlist the help of your fellow man.
Say you know – when you're not sure if you do.
(The dictionary will carry you through.)
And to quote the man himself, who by now everyone knows:
"If it works – follow it down the street and see where it goes."

Adam's Death

How shall I describe that look?
Hung now upon the faces of my sons,
An unexpected fruit ripe out of season,
Intruder in the garden of our innocence.

They, and I, and Eve, are silent,
Waiting for this newest revelation.
Someone has left the tent-flap open:
It has announced itself, first winter wind.

We knew this once before, or something
Like it, and called it murder.
Then, the seed was hatred,
Human hatred. His name was Abel.

There is no name for this, no robe
Of words to cloths the naked novelty.
What comes next is raw, cold, bony,
Crunching at the ribs.

October 22, 1994

Yih Jing Sonnets

In the late summer and autumn of 1977 the casting of *Yih Jing* (often transliterated, *I Ching*) by coin and yarrow stalk was demonstrated for me, and I was given a copy of the Wilhelm/Baynes translation. Another friend provided Fenellosa's essay on Chinese characters as a source of poetry. This collection of sonnets is one outcome.

From a beginner's text on Chinese, I moved to Wieger's etymological dictionary, searching out the radical for the character connected with each of the sixty-four hexagrams in the *Book of Changes*. The poems that work are a coming-together of some personally valued idea or experience with the images in the evolved character, the additional images of the component trigrams, and the Confucian/Taoist commentaries.

Along the way, I found the powerful work of Holmes Welch on the improbability of 'translation' from classical Chinese, and Joseph Needham's amazing scholarship. One gentleman, himself an interpreter of Chinese poetry, used several beautiful Hong Kong stamps to tell me of the *Yih Jing* that:
> Two persons in Hong Kong claimed to have understood it. One is dead and the other is suffering from an undiagnosed nervous disorder.

With that kind of encouragement, it is easy enough to recognize myself as no expert on the *Yih Jing*, very much a novice in written Chinese, and no calligrapher. I do claim to be a passable sign-painter of the Kowloon Fish Market School of Applied Arts. Purists are welcome to dismiss the poems as non-sonnets; they don't conform to the traditional metre. And you'll find the Wade-Giles and Putonghua systems used indiscriminately in Romanisation.

The locale varies from an unspecified corner of China in different historical periods, to a pine-forested hilltop in Central

Ontario. There is a connection: our almost-pure sand hills have been planted successfully with red pine, something the Chinese have sent experts abroad to study.

Black Moslem groups in the U.S. used Yih Jing as a sort of brain-storming aid to jog their imaginations on tactical possibilities they'd overlooked. It may be worth saying a bit about the work and its uses from a viewpoint more at home in modern North America than in ancient China.

It is surely justifiable to return to something like *Yih Jing*, which is not of this time, as part of the process of seeking a coherent and unified direction in which to move through the chaos of our days. We cannot jump ahead and select a stable lookout point in future history from which to make sense of the thousand and one philosophies in current competition, but we can move backward, standing on ground older than our specific scientific technology.

So we become something like time travellers, while remaining always and in many ways the desperate children of our age. Part of that age in North America takes the form of pragmatism, frequently reduced to John Dewey's: "Don't tell me it's *true*; show me that it *works*."

Charles Sanders Peirce, founder of American pragmatism, had a lot to say about signs and symbols; some of his remarks may suggest a variant view of *Yih Jing* and its uses.

1. A proposition (read: a casting of coins or yarrow) is best comprehended as a complex sign fully grasped only in the process of becoming aware/attending to the 'habits of action' invoked while trying to confirm it/make it work.
2. A casting is a suggestion for action which we will apprehend to the same degree that we can sense/describe/be specific about the steps needed to implement it.
3. Different responses are in fact different only to the extent that the 'habits of action' invoked are themselves different.

Perhaps we are involved in an experiment on the overcoming of chance which begins with an understanding-in-action of the lawful nature of chance itself. Anyone who has used a table of random numbers will be aware of the lawful structure involved.

Returning to Black Moslem use of *Yih Jing*, the over-looking of tactical possibilities may have a lot to do with a grossly incomplete picture of reality or, if you like, of the tools available for a given job. I recall dusk on a snow-drifted peak of the Green Mountain Wilderness, me looking about for the hilltop hideaway of my friend Alfred, gradually realizing I'd climbed the wrong mountain. I had a survival blanket, but the temperature promised something between sleepless discomfort and major frostbite. In the fading light, I noticed a depression in the drifts, like a small valley curving away behind a thrust of rock, and found a decent little ski hut tucked away around the shoulder of the mountain.

Alfred once said, "There's always something in the environment you can use, if only you don't blind yourself to it by carrying around too sharp and limiting a picture in your head of what you think you need to survive." Let the surround provide, said Alfred. And it often will.

A suggestion for action, then, is more securely based when it rests on a choice sensibly made among visible tools. Some tools are hard to see, or to accept as suitable, because we have clouded our vision with a rigid certainty of our needs. The *Yih Jing*, like Madison Avenue's old technique of brainstorming, may invite a withholding of judgement until more tools appear within an improved range of vision.

A major Canadian novelist and poet, Margaret Atwood, who looked through some of my work remarked that, had I published about 1912, I'd have been a real hit. She also felt the poems seemed to fall unevenly into the more universal, and the more personal and vernacular categories. I agree. There seem to be about a dozen that are completely satisfying. The calligraphy is from Wing's *Workbook*.

–December, 1987

1

☰
☰

CH'IEN

☰

**ABOVE: CH'IEN
HEAVEN**

☰

**BELOW: CH'IEN
HEAVEN**

☰

**UPPER: CH'IEN
HEAVEN**

☰

**LOWER: CH'IEN
HEAVEN**

RULING LINES

▶ ☰
☰

CREATIVE POWER
(The Creative)

In the world of New Year art, eyes probe outward
To the week after next, to a target beyond the frame:
The row of faces on the reviewing stand carefully objective,
Conferring state secrets on the brush of no painter.
They will be here posing in the week after next,
Providing duration in time. By waiting long enough
We share the parade's end, cleanup of banners,
Much paper, and a torn pair of trousers.

Liu Ling, old man of Bamboo Grove in Honan
Wandered around his garden without clothing.
Visitors and neighbours felt both li and law offended.
Remarks were made. He said: Universe is my home,
This garden my trousers. In heaven's name
What are you doing in my underwear?

2

K'UN

ABOVE: K'UN
EARTH

BELOW: K'UN
EARTH

UPPER: K'UN
EARTH

LOWER: K'UN
EARTH

RULING LINES

NATURAL RESPONSE
(The Receptive)

Your hands poised above the saffron pillow
Open, parting like leaves moved by a breeze.
Earth pulls at the three coins. They drop
Into the pattern of light and dark, strong and yielding.
They dance together a moment, then rest. You,
Sitting on the floor with me, assist the oracle.
In a high room under the roof, we wait
For changing wind, sun on leaf, shadow, answer.

Three dozen times, I failed to write the sign of *k'un*:
The brush wavered. The lines were weak, forced,
Or would not hold together. Only as I assist the brush
On its own path does the sign live, leap from paper,
Move like leaf-shadow. From our different rooms
We watch the varying suns, the drifting leaves.

3

CHUN

ABOVE: K'AN
WATER

BELOW: CHEN
THUNDER

UPPER: KEN
MOUNTAIN

LOWER: K'UN
EARTH

RULING LINES

DIFFICULT BEGINNINGS

To think of you without burning, without need,
Walking the breezy lakeshore and listening
To children laughing and the leaves of trees
And you talking of your family, who have more faces
Than a poet has verses. I cannot. Today
I curse this apartness and want you greatly,
Damn my own rooting on this wordy hill
And all the dependent clauses of hope.

One final crow sculling through the tidal evening
Homeward over fields of summer corn, heavy
And slow, punctuates my thought. Protesting
Between the paragraphs of time, becalmed in summer honey
I enquire in grammars of straw for the syntax of commitment,
Word of certainty, poem of truth in a single sound.

4

MENG

ABOVE: KEN
MOUNTAIN

BELOW: K'AN
WATER

UPPER: K'UN
EARTH

LOWER: CHEN
THUNDER

RULING LINES

INEXPERIENCE
(Youthful Folly)

Today I watched your small self playing:
You hammered pegs into a board, climbed on cushions
And later climbed on me, pulling my hair.
Under a large pillow, you pretended to be turtle
Crawling across the floor. Not being sure
What sound a turtle makes, you made none.
When you stood beside me saying nothing
I hugged you, and you told your mom you liked me.

Your mother, little brown-eyes, is a thief and sometimes mad;
Your father's in jail for fighting half the police force.
In the pool of youth, there may be enough fresh water
To wash away the grime of this inheritance.
Play, brown-eyes. You and I are both
Fools enough to hope tomorrow may be better.

5

HSU

ABOVE: K'AN
WATER

BELOW: CH'IEN
HEAVEN

UPPER: LI
FIRE

LOWER: TUI
LAKE

RULING LINES

CALCULATED WAITING

Earlier, I walked on the south slope
In a field of wild strawberries. A brown bird
Nesting under a dwarf maple, the lower leaves
Spread like a roof over her hungry young,
Fluttered away to mislead me. I looked
At the small ones, their mouths wide
In a permanent cry for nourishment.
A cool wind moved over the unripe berries.

Two days more, and the nest is empty.
Cunningly woven of twigs, each round more fragile
Toward the centre, a whirlpool of wood,
It spins forward a quiet purpose
Into another season. I wait here, tasting
Wild strawberries, which are not your lips.

6

SUNG

**ABOVE: CH'IEN
HEAVEN**

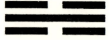

**BELOW: K'AN
WATER**

**UPPER: SUN
WIND**

**LOWER: LI
FIRE**

RULING LINES

CONFLICT

After the rain, in the robin's nest,
Four eggs of a clean and brilliant blue.
How could that bandit, the red squirrel,-
Know they were there? He darted upward
Chattering. The robins fluttered around him
But he never turned back, thinking only
Of eggs, the delicacy of unhatched bird.
He stole them all. The pine stood empty.

Pine's top grows toward heaven, roots to water.
Somewhere in the trunk is a quietness doing neither,
Doing nothing but be, for bird or squirrel.
If heaven and water work in opposite ways,
Who will deal justly with cone and root?
Perhaps, in this conflict, let us not interfere.

7

SHIH

ABOVE: K'UN
EARTH

BELOW: K'AN
WATER

UPPER: K'UN
EARTH

LOWER: CHEN
THUNDER

RULING LINES

COLLECTIVE FORCE
(The Army)

I, Huan of Ch'i, address the prince of Ch'in:
It is true that we are a prosperous people,
Our brine wells deep, salt plentiful,
The metal of our salt pans of the best,
Iron foundries productive, fields tilled
And artisans among the finest. This you see,
Approving also the order of your marching troops
Heavy with weapons we do not possess.

And so you conquer. My family scattered,
I write with one remaining reed.
Beware, prince, the itch for power:
In ignorance, we scratch our neighbour.
Beware also, too much salt, my prince.
Even a cupful is enough to choke you.

8

PI

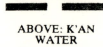

ABOVE: K'AN
WATER

BELOW: K'UN
EARTH

UPPER: KEN
MOUNTAIN

LOWER: K'UN
EARTH

RULING LINES

UNITY
(Holding Together)

Charles the Great, King of Franks, received a gift
From Bagdad, Harun al-Raschid concluding
That those who share a common Cordovan enemy
Need not peer too closely at other creed or banner.
"All rivers of earth," said the Caliph, "flow together
Either at the Bosporus or in the Western Sea.
The tides lean their slow elephantine bulk
Obeying one clock on their damp shores or ours."

Charles in Aachen, for the tenth time
Wound up the chimes of the Turkish clock
And smiled. Most, however, he liked the pachyderm,
Contemplating a larger bedroom to include it.
He mourned the elephant when it died prematurely.
The clock will still work if one is careful.

9

HSIAO CH'U

ABOVE: SUN
WIND

BELOW: CH'IEN
HEAVEN

UPPER: LI
FIRE

LOWER: TUI
LAKE

RULING LINES

RESTRAINED
(The Taming Power of the Small)

It is written: under indigo sky on a night of high full moon
The Duke of Chou prepared to march against the tyrant.
A horse neighed, breath drifting a moment on the chill air
While harness menders humming war songs joined leather
to metal.
A dog sniffing along the stones snarled at a fragment of
bone.
In a far corner of the courtyard, a turner and his apprentice
Repaired broken spokes in a wagon wheel.
A few clouds, but no rain, moved slowly from the west.

It is not written that an hour before marching
His young wife wept in his arms: "Stay. Don't leave me;
I want you." A little later she said: "Go;
Forgive the weakness in me that spoke before." He went,
Carried her memory into battle, and spared the lives
Of ten prisoners, one grandmother and a crying child.

10

LU

ABOVE: CH'IEN
HEAVEN

BELOW: TUI
LAKE

UPPER: SUN
WIND

LOWER: LI
FIRE

RULING LINES

Conduct

Bodhidharma came to bring the dhyana-craft,
White water-jewel within the lotus pad. Aha!
He had a dozen doors banged round about
'Til only one remained to open, one inside
Between the first and second eye. Who listened
Learned to ride the ox, returning home to Changsha
Or to Shanhaikuan. "Be priest of oxen, clean
Your stable, dung the field," preached Bodhidharma.

Dongguo, farmer said: "In my dream the Buddha came
And spoke with me; nine thousand demons
Flat beneath his feet, he floated on a throne
Of solid gold; a thousand lightnings played upon his crown!"
Who brought the dhyana unlocked his jaw and sighed,
"Dongguo, do you now grow better rice?"

11

T'AI

ABOVE: K'UN
EARTH

BELOW: CH'IEN
HEAVEN

UPPER: CHEN
THUNDER

LOWER: TUI
LAKE

RULING LINES

PROSPERING
(Peace)

In all of Chuang Tzu, no woman says a wise thing.
This is not life as I have lived it. Yang and yin
Together nurtured the egg of history, broke the shell
Of the new year and flew between earth and heaven.
Perhaps he knew merely painted ladies of the Pillow Book,
Tried his cynical and windy song with women
Of two dimensions only. Perhaps a woman of depth
Or height was a thought his time forbade him.

Today I watched a bee aggressively hunting nectar
From a printed blossom on a silk umbrella,
And I have seen an insistent butterfly
Attempt to settle on a painting of milkweed pods.
Peace does not follow from perching always on the left leg
Nor by closing the right eye to half of reality.

12

P'I

ABOVE: CH'IEN
HEAVEN

BELOW: K'UN
EARTH

UPPER: SUN
WIND

LOWER: KEN
MOUNTAIN

RULING LINES

STAGNATION

Standstill: the minutes drag their rusty incoherence
Reluctantly around the day. Some ice-age mastodon
Who gulped down time, head thrown back in a frozen roar,
Glares at the roots of this glacial morain
On whose hump of sand I've built my cedar home.
Moveless my mind – but I would have it move;
Beyond my window, crickets in the vetch and rye
Repeat a dusty word. All's in a capsule here.

Colour drained, crumpled, once a dream-pale green and gold
The parchment chrysalis left on the window ledge erupts
This exclamatory butterfly in orange, black and white
Whose damp wings assess my kitchen's hospitality.
Unready to fly upward, tentative, quivering,
Sleeps now at the edge of our table-top plateau.

13

T'UNG JEN

**ABOVE: CH'IEN
HEAVEN**

**BELOW: LI
FIRE**

**UPPER: CH'IEN
HEAVEN**

**LOWER: SUN
WIND**

RULING LINES

COMMUNITY
(Fellowship with Men)

Courtyard of ruined temple, snow piled in corners,
Fallen stone, black and broken roof beam, one starving dog.
The Shang priest squinting through white eyebrows
Reads a charred and splintered bone, watched by three.
Hu the scholar says they wait a great Messiah. Scholar Feng
Denies it. Man three, caretaker, shivers here
In a small hut against the inner wall, alone
Since the bronze doors were taken ten years ago.

He tugs at a ragged coat, eyeing this terminal priest
Bent over the ambiguous bone: no clear oracle.
The cracks run every way from the piercing iron
As the lives of the fellowship run their separate days.
In the morning wind, they will scatter again.
Leaving only the caretaker brewing a weak and scanty tea.

TA YU

ABOVE: LI
FIRE

BELOW: CH'IEN
HEAVEN

UPPER: TUI
LAKE

LOWER: CH'IEN
HEAVEN

RULING LINES

▶

Sovereignty
(Possession in Great Measure)

That which I have, has me. Along these miles
We reach to fulfill each other. Good space, you said,
That we know ourselves contained, defined, free and
Self-possessed. Hearing the late winter wind
Harrow the hills between, I think of King Wên,
The Duke of Chou, and the prison walls that part them,*
I am not your earthly father, but might have been:
My hand moves out to your hand.

Later, from shoulder to elbow, my right arm
Burns all night where you touched me.
Now, how may the flame in your fingers
Bring peace to my flesh? I wonder,
And wondering watch your smile, angelic imp,
Gioconda whose eyes mirror hell and heaven.

*Early legends identified the Duke as the King's son. He was the regent of Ch'eng Wang, who succeeded the son of Wên.

15

CH'IEN

ABOVE: K'UN
EARTH

BELOW: KEN
MOUNTAIN

UPPER: CHEN
THUNDER

LOWER: K'AN
WATER

RULING LINES

MODERATION
(Modesty)

(On searching for the radical of the 30th Hexagram)

Now I, imitation of a scholar, shall sit
Chewing my gums in a vague unrest, pretending
To find some inner calm beyond this storm of daubs
Crammed in this wordbook by a Jesuit priest
Working from ancient cast bells and vases.
Unworthy descendant of the grand recorder,
I hunt for the root, the original, the genuine –
And end up inventing one almost as good.

Down the multiplied jungle of false characters
(Two or three of them added by my brush)
In one thrust of momentary light through the leaves
Illumining rare old bronze, may come
A glimpse of the muscular primitive
Blinding my eye and stilling my hand.

16

YU

ABOVE: CHEN
THUNDER

BELOW: K'UN
EARTH

UPPER: K'AN
WATER

LOWER: KEN
MOUNTAIN

RULING LINES

HARMONIZE
(*Enthusiasm*)

The dog trumpets his being, makes a mock hunt
For groundhog, fox, chipmunk – whatever moves.
Lacking other action he prances below, glares upward
And barks at a pine cone, imagining squirrel,
Inventing claws, the flickering quick eye, flying arch,
Fantasy of motion. Poplar leaves are troops marching.
White-tipped waving banner of tail, dog leads them
Into heroic victory, then sleeps, omitting ancestral sacrifice.

He rests in ignorance of families and gods,
Knowing fathers neither holy nor secular. Dog alone
Peoples his world with present illusion, dragging into dream
No half-formed terrors from tomorrow, adding only
The astigmatic inward eye of history: Perhaps, he thinks,
I am that ancient emperor re-incarnate. His name – ?

17

SUI

**ABOVE: TUI
LAKE**

**BELOW: CHEN
THUNDER**

**UPPER: SUN
WIND**

**LOWER: KEN
MOUNTAIN**

RULING LINES

ADAPTING
(Following)

My friend has returned from Xinjiang-far-north
And we've had time to talk. He says he met
A white-haired man outside the village, hermit
Who named himself Lao Tse reborn. He wanted
Not a handout but an apostle, some follower
To bring the news of him along the road to market.
"– and whether you will or not, you shall. For I
Must shortly die and you go on. Preach me, inheritor."

Now, how shall we know who is Lao Tse, who not?
Who cannot follow can't lead; cannot suffer can't heal.
What joy or strength did he ask of you? What need?
He is lightning resting in the town dump, unmanifest
And drawn back into a midden choked with questions,
A fool who'll tell the three-times-burned to light fresh fire.

18

KU

ABOVE: KEN
MOUNTAIN

BELOW: SUN
WIND

UPPER: CHEN
THUNDER

LOWER: TUI
LAKE

RULING LINES

REPAIR
(Decay)

Dead foxes: These played with their kits at the burrow
Or lay, nose between paws in the warm sand.
Decayed and toothy they sprawl in the gully
Under a hum of flies, poisoned or shot
At the close of winter. Carefully upwind of April breeze
On the end of a long-handle spade, I bury the solid parts.
In what remains, wet, pale things feed and squirm;
At the finish of foxes, they announce a new beginning.

The fox in the mind plays with truth: What is real?
Mountain wind ruffles the white patch, the red-brown fur
As he bounds across the clearing, distracts the inward eye
From the slow decay of kings and princes,
Kingdoms and principalities. Ah, fox,
May we hold back corruption from some part of love?

19

LIN

ABOVE: K'UN
EARTH

BELOW: TUI
LAKE

UPPER: K'UN
EARTH

LOWER: CHEN
THUNDER

RULING LINES

PROMOTION
(Approach)

On the sand hills, we're burning yellow birch
And waiting for an uncertain spring. The black dogs
Run miles away, forget food time, sleep fitfully
In unaccustomed corners. Air is neither cold
Nor comfortably warm. What to wear? Shall I
Handle wood with gloves, or afterward, peering
Through the gray morning, pull the fine splinters
And wonder at my dullness in a nothing day?

Down country, lake remains frozen but soft,
Sagging under the fishing huts, the air damp
And heavy, slow with unfallen snow. In this month
Patience or impatience sprouts no quicker crocus.
Dogs return, heads low, eyes watery. Unhappily
They regret too-successful approach to a friendly skunk.

20

KUAN

ABOVE: SUN
WIND

BELOW: K'UN
EARTH

UPPER: KEN
MOUNTAIN

LOWER: K'UN
EARTH

RULING LINES

Contemplating

Sitting in the lotus, Kwan Yin's daughter looks inward,
Tugging a black shawl around her shoulders,
Settling into morning meditation. Her gaze,
Drawn away from the blue room and a hundred small blue flowers
Blooms now behind, beyond the visible garden.
Turning to that will, flowers, room, quality of blue,
All things that know her bow to the compact circle
Of her stilled beauty, bend through her golden aura.

Magnetic, quietly intense, unmoving you achieve
What you do not attempt. Drawn down to you
The very walls contain like a curving hand
The blossom of your being. Silent, you may be
Repeating a mantra. Adoration is a mantra
Midway between invocation and offering.

21

SHIH HO

ABOVE: LI
FIRE

BELOW: CHEN
THUNDER

UPPER: K'AN
WATER

LOWER: KEN
MOUNTAIN

RULING LINES

REFORM
(Biting Through)

To withdraw, leaving the shell of self marching the boulevard,
To mumble no bones, no longer hear the drum
Nor see the waving banner. Most difficult of all
To hold back response, both pity and fear, yet ache
In awareness of every tick-tock passing, alive to time,
The alarmclock need for recognition of one right day.
Under heaven, no greater hunger. What if never
Again the arms rise together on that desirable hour,

The proud teeth locked on the indigestible moment?
Our way out is inward. Retreat, as always,
For collecting the broken bits of our inheritance,
Wiping off dust, dirty fingerprints, the garbage
Of immobile human sediment. What flashes clean
Shall shape us again: faceted, prismatic, the biting edge.

22

PI

**ABOVE: KEN
MOUNTAIN**

**BELOW: LI
FIRE**

**UPPER: CHEN
THUNDER**

**LOWER: K'AN
WATER**

RULING LINES

GRACE

Morning wind shakes holiday snowdust from pines;
Winter sun twinkles the facets of the world
With the sharp and manifold colours of a crystal
Turning slowly on invisible thread.
Deep white unbroken except for the ski track
Of my daughter, and some blurred footprints
Where a visitor headed for the south door,
Waded into a snow drift, and turned back.

The fourteen who drank tea at our table are gone
With the young boy who frowned in concentration
As he lifted his cup. Again blizzard, drifting,
Heaped heavy on the bending pine. Over the gully
Beneath maple and basswood in a pale filigree
Ghost trillium yields to winter in a dream of spring.

23

PO

ABOVE: KEN MOUNTAIN

BELOW: K'UN EARTH

UPPER: K'UN EARTH

LOWER: K'UN EARTH

RULING LINES

DETERIORATION
(Splitting Apart)

When you first entered the school, there was no doubt:
Beneath this roof I was teacher and you, student.
Only as the wheat waved green and golden into flour
And green and gold again, I watched you grow
While in your growing the schoolhouse, aging, shrank
Like some thin, abraded shawl about your shoulder.
To the drums and bugles of the autumn sun
You ran laughing after a ball down the dusty yard.

Now you are woman, and I no longer sure
Who is teacher, who student. Behind my desk
I cross out parts of a half-written poem.
Today I am flayed and racked and torn apart
By your going. I think, in the dust the wheat
Will not grow this year. Let me help you pack your books.

24

FU

ABOVE: K'UN
EARTH

BELOW: CHEN
THUNDER

UPPER: K'UN
EARTH

LOWER: K'UN
EARTH

RULING LINES

Returning

Through the last of corn-snow, climbing the hill crest,
Every few steps breaking through the crust, laughing.
My friend found it easier slogging through the pines,
Calling to me from the wood's edge.
Alone on the hill, my eyes travelled down the sky
Through that inverted shining sea of improbable blue
And caught the tips of maples beyond the ridge:
Milky smoke-lavender, memory-colour of you.

Time and my breath held a moment there.
Surprised and pleased among maples, I return to you,
Unexpectedly waiting for me in the spring-glad trees.
Tender as hope or the hint of buds returning
Must my heart become to chalice the gift of you
Returning again in lavender smoke on a blue-white hill.

25

WU WANG

**ABOVE: CH'IEN
HEAVEN**

**BELOW: CHEN
THUNDER**

**UPPER: SUN
WIND**

**LOWER: KEN
MOUNTAIN**

RULING LINES

INNOCENCE

Here in the thaw at winter's end
I try again to write you. My words rebel,
Refuse to march, or sidle slantwise, conspiring,
A double agent who'll deal me in the marketplace.
I suspect myself, doubt the innocence of my intent,
Know I've not found harmony, finger the bruises
Of that long, despairing fall from Eden.
Shall we move beyond desire in that unintended land?

Not yet ready, I am not yet ready
To walk firmly from the manipulated city
Beyond the web of your or my idea
Of the right, the regular, the coherently ordered,
To take the walk for its own sake
Or the hush of wet snow under my foot.

26

TA CH'U

ABOVE: KEN
MOUNTAIN

BELOW: CH'IEN
HEAVEN

UPPER: CHEN
THUNDER

LOWER: TUI
LAKE

RULING LINES

POTENTIAL ENERGY
(The Taming Power of the Great)

Yu the Great, daily terrified by thoughts of flood
Led the people to tame wild water. Those he picked
To build dikes, clear channels, raise dams of earth
Were men who followed his plan, inventing nothing.
Rising early, he saw the pattern of ditches cross the plain,
Heard the call of the day's first carriers of dirt.
Movers of mounds in wicker baskets. Through order accomplished
He drew back to himself strength for another dawn.

Officers of Yu could not stop what once they started,
Knowing only to do, do more, do once again
For Yu, whose character was thereby strengthened
Through obedience of many. Alone he stood
On a hilltop, searched alien sky for a raincloud.
Yu the Great ate seldom at his family table.

27

I

**ABOVE: KEN
MOUNTAIN**

**BELOW: CHEN
THUNDER**

**UPPER: K'UN
EARTH**

**LOWER: K'UN
EARTH**

RULING LINES

Nourishing

"And," said Wu the baker, "I will wonder
As you pack and leave for that other land
Why my feelings are split like pine cones
Chewed by the red squirrel and scattered. Hurting,
Wanting to hold you and cry, all I can do
Is be confused. After all, it is I who helped you,
Leaving as you want to leave from things and places
Not any more for your growing. I should rejoice.

"To feel one thing, to find the fresh-made loaf
In all ways perfect, a delight to touch, to smell,
To share with friend. No crumb of doubt,
No hiding from the single flame of cleansing joy
That sweeps away the dust of too-much-me.
I think, perhaps, that may be so in Heaven."

28

TA KUO

ABOVE: TUI
LAKE

BELOW: SUN
WIND

UPPER: CH'IEN
HEAVEN

LOWER: CH'IEN
HEAVEN

RULING LINES

CRITICAL MASS
(Preponderance of the Great)

Qian the courtesan, who bloomed in morning-glory silk
Of pale blue, magenta, lavender, violet, was daily gathered
By a different hand. All were hands gold-banded, entitled
To reach in fat purses belted heavily to fat bellies
Or carried by a thin servant waiting at the courtyard wall.
She wondered, sometimes, where they went beyond the garden,
To what possibly insignificant but varying fate,
What doubtful greater joy, proud passion, soaring dream.

One, they said, had ridden away to war
And died, and come no more. And one, stroking
His beard, walked thoughtfully to a monastery
And disappeared. Of most, no tea-time news returned.
Qian, ill and dying, was unsure if she had held a thousand men
Or the same man one thousand times.

29

K'AN

**ABOVE: K'AN
WATER**

**BELOW: K'AN
WATER**

**UPPER: KEN
MOUNTAIN**

**LOWER: CHEN
THUNDER**

RULING LINES

Danger

I am squatting on this log in the wet sand,
Head in my hands, being sick. Each time
The voice of that old man screams in my mind
I retch again. We were supposed to have killed a prince,
You and I, in the name of freedom. Here
We have something that was almost a corpse already.
Tangled in the lines and hooks he'd brought
To fish in a leaky boat. He didn't fight back.

We had to pick a gray, damp day for this –
Or something picked it for us. What anger I had
Is soggy, and my brave intent lost in a sheet of fog.
If by this we made liberty for ten thousand men,
What have we made ourselves? Is it better,
Finally, to be a free monster than a caged saint?

30

LI

**ABOVE: LI
FIRE**

**BELOW: LI
FIRE**

**UPPER: TUI
LAKE**

**LOWER: SUN
WIND**

RULING LINES

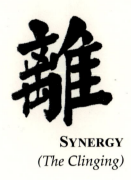

SYNERGY
(The Clinging)

Let it be that I, while blinded in this temple.
Hold to thy radiance through my own and private night
And like sandalwood consumed at a shining high altar
Brighten thee more. And yet, from thy touch
To know the morning glory rides in beauty on the vine,
Brave trumpet to that fire marching up the distant sky
As I to thee, thy celebrant. Great goddess,
Help me move beyond all suns that rise

And all that set. Console an aging votary
Whose footprints vanish in the autumn dusk.
Gone to worship in a deep and fragrant darkness
Hungry enough to gulp down gods and devils,
Vast enough to lose every last collapsing sun
Their feeble, futile alchemy may spawn.

31

HSIEN

ABOVE: TUI
LAKE

BELOW: KEN
MOUNTAIN

UPPER: CH'IEN
HEAVEN

LOWER: SUN
WIND

RULING LINES

ATTRACTION

Yugong Feng, with help from a hardwood pole
Scuttles diagonally down the slope of a deep ravine,
Moving crablike through imagined ancient water.
From the fine sand his foot knocks loose three stones
Which roll and hop together to the gully floor.
Feng, resting, holds to his eye the largest rock,
Smooth convex planes printed with small immobile shells,
Ocean made rigid, long courtship of life and death.

And on one round corner – ah! lovely, shapely:
The frugal outline of a marine snail, four-chambered,
Lightly traced as the memory of a near-forgotten kiss
Wooing the unresponding stone. Feng nods:
"Hah! I am not so old as you, friend rock,
And somewhere here I've seen new ginseng growing."

32

HENG

ABOVE: CHEN
THUNDER

BELOW: SUN
WIND

UPPER: TUI
LAKE

LOWER: CH'IEN
HEAVEN

RULING LINES

CONTINUING
(Enduring)

That these moments live: wind and thunder,
Breathing and bellylaughs, large and small
In a Yes that links our laughter to the rolling world.
Prince Chi dissembles, feigns madness in a mad time,
Fingers his beard and waits the dawn-wind. Lovingly
He sips the lees of wine pressed from a good year's grape.
Love's the wind that moves the sampan of the sun
To ride the tide of returning day.

She murmurs: how sharp your beard!
The women nod: her neck and chin are marked;
For some of us the night is less than lonely.
The guards will say: Prince Chi is not entirely mad;
He hums and whistles – look, by the early candle,
In the silence of his cell he writes a love poem!

33

TUN

**ABOVE: CH'IEN
HEAVEN**

**BELOW: KEN
MOUNTAIN**

**UPPER: CH'IEN
HEAVEN**

**LOWER: SUN
WIND**

RULING LINES

RETREAT

Leaping over frosted leaf, two dogs play in melon patch,
Black, with dirty white Ch'an apron-bibs on their necks,
Tumbling, rolling in faded grass under gray sky.
Zhang watches, mountain farmer, raiser of melons
And snow peas and other food in season. He nods,
Understanding the bounding joy of dogs, not knowing
Why at the same time he should feel sorrow
When the first snowflake melts on dark uplifted muzzle.

Retreat of summer down the mountain: Zhang sees
Remaining yellow leaves toward the valley floor
Slow-moving in breeze like waving dog-tails, vanishing
Into year-end as four-foots, barking, disappear in bush.
They run invoking no tomorrow, unknowing winter chill
One snowflake brings to wrinkled farmer Zhang.

34

TA CHUANG

**ABOVE: CHEN
THUNDER**

**BELOW: CH'IEN
HEAVEN**

**UPPER: TUI
LAKE**

**LOWER: CH'IEN
HEAVEN**

RULING LINES

GREAT POWER

Master Ho, great among the *fang-shih*,
Wrestled three days the Lord of the Dark Quarter.
Holding still the crouching azure dragon of the east,
Other arm fending the pale and hungry western tiger
He rooted his toes down to heavy gray bedrock
Until his eyeballs were level with the fresh grass.
Unmoving in his inward strength, firm as the axle
Of a cart to carry boulders, the Master endured.

In a flood of icy rain, tortoise and serpent
And the god under his black, wind-swollen banner
Flung themselves against him. Yet he prevailed,
Winning from the clashing winds and waters
A new ancestral temple. This he did because
He could not bear to go home and face his wife.

35

CHIN

**ABOVE: LI
FIRE**

**BELOW: K'UN
EARTH**

**UPPER: K'AN
WATER**

**LOWER: KEN
MOUNTAIN**

RULING LINES

Progress

They have said in the Imperial City: Change the signs.
Undoubtedly the sun of progress warms the earth
And, rising, widens our horizon. I am one
Who works with brush and tablet of ink,
Knowing there must be change, and tides, and daybreak,
Yet I move uneasy, feeling something of golden value
About to slip away, wondering what prize we lose
When burning our brushes, discarding ancient signs.

Ch'in Shih Huan Ti burned many books,
But not the *Changes of Chou*. Something in language
Is precious. Vigorously uprooting the signs
What do we tear from the earth, grunting,
Pawing and snuffling like a wild boar? Perhaps
We punish our own city, both heart and head.

36

MING I

ABOVE: K'UN
EARTH

BELOW: LI
FIRE

UPPER: CHEN
THUNDER

LOWER: K'AN
WATER

RULING LINES

CENSORSHIP
(Darkening of the Light)

Early frost has bruised and bent the oat-stalk,
Sending a wounded sun limping toward winter.
Corsa the monk is dead, and Tai Hsu the bishop
Who ordained him, and Suzuki who gave him incense
For his friend in America. Firm in sanctuary
The gray calligrapher winces, flexing cold fingers,
Mourning the springtime years: O Lord of Light,
Point us your path to the last kiss, the last goodbye.

Who has not taken refuge falls stricken for the world
And for himself, slashed in belly and thigh
By the icy blade that cripples the oat,
Hearing in the steady tread of winter down the hill
Alaric pounding on the Roman gate.
That final dusty sunset in Pompeii.

37

CHIA JEN

**ABOVE: SUN
WIND**

**BELOW: LI
FIRE**

**UPPER: LI
FIRE**

**LOWER: K'AN
WATER**

RULING LINES

FAMILY

High wind: ghost of a moon shivers in morning sky.
Stacking cordwood, I wear your old jacket;
Raising my arms, I smell your sweat, my son.
And think of you in a far province, sweating
While you cut bigger trees than mine. This wind
Cries snow, whispers long winter, gossips a
Chattering conversation with my elbows and knees.
Resting, I look down the road for your coming.

Be here for the holiday at the year end:
Your mother and I have a new quilt for you
And your woman. Stay a while with us
On the hill, and we'll remember the winters
When you were small, and make home-talk
And perhaps your sister will join us.

38

K'UEI

ABOVE: LI
FIRE

BELOW: TUI
LAKE

UPPER: K'AN
WATER

LOWER: LI
FIRE

RULING LINES

CONTRADICTION
(Opposition)

Fire and water: Unwise to promote unity by force.
Instead, say the *Annals of Lü*, let the Emperor prove
He can handle a plough, let the Empress weave
At the loom. So, through categories of warp and woof,
Furrow and seed, we shall establish order.
Millenia add to our pattern and style
Until the raw, uncultivated question, the wild
Barbarian name for freedom is woven invisibly over.

Yellow Turban or Eighth Route Army, query remains:
From what ground or force grows your right to rule?
The cry for freedom becomes a ceremony,
Emperor symbolically scratching the Imperial Garden.
If one is planning to assassinate duke or prince,
How difficult when you first must bow from the waist!

39

CHIEN

**ABOVE: K'AN
WATER**

**BELOW: KEN
MOUNTAIN**

**UPPER: LI
FIRE**

**LOWER: K'AN
WATER**

RULING LINES

OBSTACLES

We walked in the park, moving through a memory of
summer.
When I stopped and turned your shoulders to face me,
Searching your eyes, you asked, "What do you see?"
The deepest eye sees a different hour, ear hears
Ticking of another clock than yours, not a mountain
Between but a moment thinner than shadow of a thread,
A rice-tissue obstacle, translucent ghost of a fog
Sliding between my hand and yours: obstruction.

Here we are, yet we are not now. The direct path
Is hardly the shortest: Better to go our temporal ways,
Get reborn and return from the other side smiling,
Peeling off wrapping-paper shrouds and ribbons
To find at last that fragmentary instant
When the moss will keep still under our toes.

40

HSIEH

**ABOVE: CHEN
THUNDER**

**BELOW: K'AN
WATER**

**UPPER: K'AN
WATER**

**LOWER: LI
FIRE**

RULING LINES

LIBERATION
(Deliverance)

Ragged, torn wing and pallid colour
Imply this once-imperial butterfly
Did by some doubtful grace outlive the winter.
Accidentally trapped within my Eastern window
It flutters hopefully against the glass.
Northern slope and tree-protected glade
Yet deep in snow deny the immanence
Of thunder, yellow crocus, April rain.

Stubbornly it taps upon the pane,
And I must help it taste the leafless field,
The faded sun, the frosted windy night.
Out and away, the scrap of black and orange
Veers drunkenly into the Western wind,
Staggering toward one last late dance with life.

41

SUN

**ABOVE: KEN
MOUNTAIN**

**BELOW: TUI
LAKE**

**UPPER: K'UN
EARTH**

**LOWER: CHEN
THUNDER**

RULING LINES

DECLINE
(Decrease)

Lao Bai, white-haired, peers at untimely mist:
Midwinter thaw draws up the melted snow,
Insubstantial unfeatured white blending into gray.
Underfoot, what holds with earth is heavy,
Slowing the loaded firewood sledge, clinging
To boot and ankle, tiring eye and bone.
He halts, brushing off a stump, and sits,
Hand on knee, at the clearing edge.

One thin pine is bent, one broken
Under the pale shroud. Two more
Lean crookedly upon each other. Far off,
A high branch cracks and falls.
In the memory of Lao Bai, cool haze obscures
The name and face of another boyhood friend.

42

I

ABOVE: SUN
WIND

BELOW: CHEN
THUNDER

UPPER: KEN
MOUNTAIN

LOWER: K'UN
EARTH

RULING LINES

BENEFIT
(Increase)

My son, there were only two logs remaining
Of those you carried through drifts to the hilltop.
The stove was hungry. I took the red maul,
The axe and iron wedge to split maple.
Reading the tree life, searching wood-history
For a weak line, I drove the maul, remembering
How easily you did this. Harder for me, but friend Scott
Did it at ninety-four; we've only twenty degrees of frost.

To those with maul and axe it has been said:
You are the elite of the world; history will avenge you.
This I doubted once, with my friends on the Long Trek,
Winter marching in, and everybody nursing icy toes.
Not any more. Even Menachem, who hid in the Yeshiva –
History will avenge him if he can re-write it.

43

☱
☰

KUAI

☱

ABOVE: TUI
LAKE

☰

BELOW: CH'IEN
HEAVEN

☰

UPPER: CH'IEN
HEAVEN

☰

LOWER: CH'IEN
HEAVEN

RULING LINES

▶ ☱
☰

Resolution

When Master Li walked slowly to the Western Gate
The guard, under instruction, asked why he wished to leave.
Gazing toward the desert, he replied, "For no reason.
The wind is behind me." The guard shook his head:
"Every traveller leaving or arriving shall have reason.
Master, remain here. I cannot allow you to pass."
"Very well," smiled the bearded one. "Have you a brush,
A scroll, an ink tablet, a place where I may sit?"

After an hour the Master handed over the scroll,
Saying, "Here are a hundred reasons." Guard admired:
"Venerable One, it's beautiful, but I cannot read."
"Give it to your officer," the Master called, striding
Into the desert. Officer Yin scratched his head:
"He wrote one hundred times the character for Reason."

44

KOU

ABOVE: CH'IEN
HEAVEN

BELOW: SUN
WIND

UPPER: CH'IEN
HEAVEN

LOWER: CH'IEN
HEAVEN

RULING LINES

TEMPTATION
(Coming to Meet)

T'ao Ch'ien, after resigning the government job
Returned alone to his boyhood home. Walking
He wrote poems in his head. Arriving
He was greeted by a woman of the village
Who offered him tea and wine, asked
About his health and life in the capital, whether
He had written much lately. Her eyes crackled.
She leaned into each reply. He sat, drank tea,

Watched her walking back and forth again, again.
While he answered she remained calm, then moved
As a new question brightened within her. He looked
At the way her hands shifted, dry leaves rustling.
A fire moved with her, armies marched, bamboo burned.
He said: this is now a two-poet town.

45

TS'UI

ABOVE: TUI
LAKE

BELOW: K'UN
EARTH

UPPER: SUN
WIND

LOWER: KEN
MOUNTAIN

RULING LINES

ASSEMBLING

Knowing that we're neither of this race nor religion
We carry gifts for the occasion. Naming of a first son
Has brought together white-haired bustling grandma
Busily pouring tea and feeding everyone
(Have another cookie; I'm not counting them)
Cousins aunts uncles little and big
Grandpa telling stories about when he was ten
And youngest daughter looking hopefully for an audience.

Much laughter. Great opening and closing of doors
And peeking breathless into crib of newborn
(Look: doesn't he have his father's nose!)
While at the heart of this family hurricane
Sleeps the unheeding innocent hub of the evening
Doing purely and competently nothing whatever.

46

SHENG

ABOVE: K'UN
EARTH

BELOW: SUN
WIND

UPPER: CHEN
THUNDER

LOWER: TUI
LAKE

RULING LINES

ADVANCEMENT
(Pushing Upward)

They said to the novice, "Keep climbing the stair;
At first you'll need only your confidence. Then
On the second step, a few light sacrifices –
Nothing to alarm you. The third step is taken
Unopposed, like storming an empty city, undefended.
The fourth will speak to your questing feet
Of other world than this. Continue. Walk on.
At the top, even for us, is darkness. Persevere."

Eyes looking down over the white-gowned shoulder,
Strong cheek-bones, firm small chin. Beginning
Of a smile. Each feature distinct, architectural.
From the arched brow a broad slope to the hairline,
The hair brushed back smoothly. "Goodbye, goodbye:
My eyes hold you. Growing tree, no return to ground."

47

K'UN

**ABOVE: TUI
LAKE**

**BELOW: K'AN
WATER**

**UPPER: SUN
WIND**

**LOWER: LI
FIRE**

RULING LINES

ADVERSITY

On a Print by Raphael Soyer

Locked in that rectangular paper pattern of blue and brown
She poses, resting between pirouettes. Perhaps,
Turning her back on the mirrored room, she watches
From her window the city street below: taxi, trolley,
Window-shoppers in their own slow dance, pedestrians
Pouring into the crosswalk, wave against wave
Meet and part, flow around, rise in a frothing tide
Over the curb. Her toes point outward on the parquet floor.

Leave her at the window, Raphael. She's dreaming
Of the Christmas angel cresting a triple entrechat:
She'll not touch earth tonight. I'll be Igor
In *Spectre of the Rose*, waiting as she waits,
Silently applauding the strength, grace and balance,
The never-choreographed electric leap that yet may be.

48

CHING

**ABOVE: K'AN
WATER**

**BELOW: SUN
WIND**

**UPPER: LI
FIRE**

**LOWER: TUI
LAKE**

RULING LINES

THE SOURCE
(The Well)

Your daughter has been with us and returned;
We think she was happy here. Falling in snow
She laughed. Playing, she became tired and rested.
Because of the holidays we let her eat favourite foods.
She moved quickly from one game to another
And only in the last hour, on our way to the village
I looked at her face, bundled between hat and shawl:
Her eyes are like wells. In older agrarian times

The well, nourishing at the centre, stood as pivot
For the turning fates of men. Farmers and princes
Came and went; well remained. Here are small
Inexhaustible oceans bright with dreamfish,
Indwelling light. Farmers and princes may do less
Than follow the dream in women's eyes.

49

KO

ABOVE: TUI
LAKE

BELOW: LI
FIRE

UPPER: CH'IEN
HEAVEN

LOWER: SUN
WIND

RULING LINES

CHANGING
(Revolution)

It is useless, at any rate, to halt the waterfall:
The melting, flowing, immediate moment
(Momentarily vanishing and reappearing Other)
Frozen, entombed in the name of sanity,
Social continuity and payment of mortgage.
Eyeing the swallow in ecstatic right-now flight
Flickering in and out of instantaneous reality
And preferring to dream of a yellow cow

I cling to smoke of my ancestral fire
Denying the whirling, grassgreen joy of the dancing monk
– Oh, damn me all laughing Taoist priests
Tumbling like plum-leaves through my garden gate!
Spring wind or autumn wind rippling my pond:
All seasons change – and all return.

50

TING

**ABOVE: LI
FIRE**

**BELOW: SUN
WIND**

**UPPER: TUI
LAKE**

**LOWER: CH'IEN
HEAVEN**

RULING LINES

COSMIC ORDER
(The Cauldron)

The waiter might have marched with the Eighth Route
Army.
He observed the young woman, smiling, give the man
A red rose and two buds. They laughed and shared poems,
Eating Eight-Jewel Duck, fine noodles, and a thick soup,
Specialty of the house. After they finished their tea
The man said, "Thank you." Waiter shook his head:
"That's how they say it in the North. Different here."
Silently, he also criticised handling of chopsticks.

The man's house is named Lü-Ger-Shan, in English
Greensong Hill. His friend from Szechuan says,
"Green is another word at home; not that." A teacher
Has corrected one of the woman's poems: grammatical,
Not street talk! Too many *chia-chieh*, borrowed errors.
Excuse my use of the Wade-Giles; should be Putonghua.

51

CHEN

**ABOVE: CHEN
THUNDER**

**BELOW: CHEN
THUNDER**

**UPPER: K'AN
WATER**

**LOWER: KEN
MOUNTAIN**

RULING LINES

SHOCKING

Thunder above, thunder below. Who will laugh ha! ha!
In the berserk teeth of the wind? One dwarf candle
Probes the inner chamber of my fear: A thing undone
Or done too often calls a bolt to crown my guilty head.
No, I've no such ego to applaud this booming score
Orchestrated for an audience of one. I'm shrunk by storms
Impersonal to me in space beyond this homely star,
Whose lightning chokes a spectrum past my range.

The moth within the pane can't see what holds him back,
Nor we our self-made fear through human eye;
This stage outcrowds the theatre of the mind.
Consider, then, our corporate fate, whose sins outride
The storm-god's mad halloo, demand a rude specific jolt
From cosmic engines measured to our pride.

52

KEN

**ABOVE: KEN
MOUNTAIN**

**BELOW: KEN
MOUNTAIN**

**UPPER: CHEN
THUNDER**

**LOWER: K'AN
WATER**

RULING LINES

MEDITATION
(Keeping Still)

Today in the sand hills I limbed the red pine,
Cutting the long logs. The morning mist worked in
Through my shirt. My sweat worked out.
Too many pines were down, piled on each other:
The reddish-tan branches blurred in green needles,
A tangle of brush strokes, images overlaid,
Tumult of bark and cone, branch and twig,
A rich confusion, texture on texture woven.

Rest follows movement. I lean on the axe,
Breathing the wet and brilliantly acid air
Among the linear stillness of these poles
Thirty-forty years growing. For part of an hour
I hold my mind here, moveless where the wind combs
The ghost of tree-tops. Beyond nothing is joy.

53

CHIEN

ABOVE: SUN
WIND

BELOW: KEN
MOUNTAIN

UPPER: LI
FIRE

LOWER: K'AN
WATER

RULING LINES

DEVELOPING

To continue: The feet follow each other onward
Where the path is an unsure memory overgrown
With thistle and spike-leaf and wild pea,
The heart's music raggedly screeched by a rusty crow,
Agitator of a thousand pine cones. Continue:
It is only the going on that makes it worth.
But not alone if I can help it – no tree
On a mountain-top signals to an empty world.

I will greet you yet, whether you hide in silence
Wrapped in a vacuum under the glacier, or sing
Lullaby among the orchestra of chaos. The wild goose,
Finding food, lifts a music of abundance to his brothers.
Here is one feather, dropped from the clouds,
And a message: Comrade, I wish you health!

54

KUEI MEI

ABOVE: CHEN
THUNDER

BELOW: TUI
LAKE

UPPER: K'AN
WATER

LOWER: LI
FIRE

RULING LINES

SUBORDINATE
(The Marrying Maiden)

I have walked alone in rooms that knew your dancing
And waited in corners where we have laughed together,
Looked through misted windows marked by long-ago rain
At a tiny garden of dead herbs we once planted.
In a dry and empty season, the echo of your singing
Makes small music in the narrow stairways of now.
That you love another is acceptable to me and right,
Who see all things as becoming and passing away.

Your care gave meaning to moments changing, even to lamp
And door and colony of books. Yet you were never caught
In these: much of you will waltz barefoot through any marriage
Unheld by plate or cup or gentled hand. Therefore again
In a time beyond this, rosemary, tarragon, mint
And your smile quicken a spring I hope to recognize.

55

FENG

**ABOVE: CHEN
THUNDER**

**BELOW: LI
FIRE**

**UPPER: TUI
LAKE**

**LOWER: SUN
WIND**

RULING LINES

Zenith
(Abundance)

Trouble in our time: From what high excellence
Shall we decay, leaving our heritors to dig
More than barbaric rubbish from the ruins?
When all our solid juggernauts are dust
What clarity of purpose may remain?
We who rode the thunder and the flame
Lift past the fanged and taloned years
Our crumbling bribe for memory's jade altar.

In the chariot tombs of Anyang, you today
May see the wheels, the axle and the singletree
Outlined in earth, all empty space from which
The wood has long departed. The bronze fittings
And ritual vessels chant to us of fullness,
Completion, the firm and elegant beauty in *ting* and *ku*.

56

LU

ABOVE: LI
FIRE

BELOW: KEN
MOUNTAIN

UPPER: TUI
LAKE

LOWER: SUN
WIND

RULING LINES

TRAVELING

They said in the village: He was a sign-painter
And a tramp. After he left, they remembered
How he played the clown, grinned as they laughed
At him and things he did. He was a friend
To servants and musicians. A dancing girl
Followed him to the bridge on Fire Mountain.
He said, "I hurt," when she kissed him goodbye.
For three days nobody noticed his room was empty.

Perhaps he knew us better than we ourselves.
With his going something of us is gone,
And our joking about the evening hearth is hollow
As if in his packsack he carried away closely
The meaning of our time and place. Maybe
It was he who stood still, and we who wander.

57

SUN

ABOVE: SUN
WIND

BELOW: SUN
WIND

UPPER: LI
FIRE

LOWER: TUI
LAKE

RULING LINES

PENETRATING INFLUENCE
(The Gentle)

For John Heimler

When Lin our teacher returned from prison, we met,
Eight of us, among lemon blossoms in a Southern garden.
The sea breeze moved through his hair, still dark at sixty;
Calmly, he continued the lesson interrupted by iron bars.
"You and I, we will not hide behind the mask of Law –
We allow ourselves to be discovered. Sometime, somehow
We were there. That which was there whispers: Lin, remember
You are not better nor different. You are salt in the wave."

Regretting the prison years, one of us asked, "What of anger?"
"Yes, there is personal anger. No movement without it,
Nor could you trust my love. But say then
To your childhood's anger: Look, *that* is done."
Laughing, Lin helped our host's little daughter
To climb on his knee and put her arms around him.

58

TUI

**ABOVE: TUI
LAKE**

**BELOW: TUI
LAKE**

**UPPER: SUN
WIND**

**LOWER: LI
FIRE**

RULING LINES

ENCOURAGING
(Joy)

The lord, being flattered, laughed at his high table
And laughed again when they told him of Ch'ü Yüan,
Poet and honest man, who drowned himself
Because he was not believed. Giving of advice,
The courtiers add, must be carefully done
To avoid offence. Ch'ü Yüan inadequately admired
Gold robes of state, quality of dumplings and tea
At the high table. So, in the lighted boats, they sought him

As we in the dragon ships tonight, laughing still,
Tend the joyful lanterns and prowl the lake
For the unforgotten body of a poet and suicide.
Day five, month five, with a chunk of festival moon
We celebrate him of less fortune than we:
Doubly cursed by honesty and the goddess of poetry.

59

HUAN

ABOVE: SUN
WIND

BELOW: K'AN
WATER

UPPER: KEN
MOUNTAIN

LOWER: CHEN
THUNDER

RULING LINES

REUNITING
(Dispersion)

Feng the carpenter, one holiday in the park
Jokingly encouraged to wrestle with Young Quian
Removed his jacket, settled bare feet on the ground
And crouched, circling for the first hold.
As his foot slipped, he read the confident smile,
Knew he'd misjudged or moved too slowly.
Thrown heavily to the grass, he sat up aching,
Shook his head, sneezed, combing out straw and a dead ant.

Surmised from one defeat the nature of all:
All things gone, all attributes, possessions,
His house of hardwood beams, family, boyhood friends
All shrunk to a loss no bigger than a wrestling throw
And himself alone on the floor of reality
Watching the pitiless victor smiling down.

60

CHIEH

**ABOVE: K'AN
WATER**

**BELOW: TUI
LAKE**

**UPPER: KEN
MOUNTAIN**

**LOWER: CHEN
THUNDER**

RULING LINES

LIMITATIONS

That of which there is only one: hazelnut,
Larch and juniper. In all this walkabout
There are less than two of these, hazel
To the north edging a copse of basswood,
Larch on the sunrise rim of a pine forest,
Juniper low and spreading in the south pasture
Near a broken cedar fence. Each solitaire
Carved sharp in my mind without a copy,

Lacking halfhearted imitation, slurred echo,
Double-goers that are almost, not quite
The thing itself. You also, no avatar or overtone
Of any god or music before you. Most human,
Most you, rare reality minted once only
Whose presence I have somewhat known.

61

CHUNG FU

**ABOVE: SUN
WIND**

**BELOW: TUI
LAKE**

**UPPER: KEN
MOUNTAIN**

**LOWER: CHEN
THUNDER**

RULING LINES

INSIGHT
(Inner Truth)

"In the Middle Kingdom," the storyteller said,
"Live two seekers of truth who are half blind.
This may not matter: they look first within themselves
And celebrate with gentle joy each inner veil that falls.
Some think they hunt the shadow of the phoenix
Or other half-mythical and fast-dissolving bird
Unfledged of the mind's frail shell. Battle-winds rise
And die around them. They drink white wine together."

Raising their eyes from the wine-glass, each smiled
At the blurred underwater image of the other,
But caught entire and clear the glow of another truth,
Different, but compatible with their own. Joined hands,
Like the linking verities, and burning faces
Turned toward the sky: "Comrade, the moon is nearly full."

62

HSIAO KUO

**ABOVE: CHEN
THUNDER**

**BELOW: KEN
MOUNTAIN**

**UPPER: TUI
LAKE**

**LOWER: SUN
WIND**

RULING LINES

CONSCIENTIOUSNESS
(Preponderance of the Small)

Firewood: Five cords of maple I've stacked in the bush,
Carrying it by armload down the aisles of pine.
Next year's warmth, it will winter here
And dry slowly into summer and fall.
Holding the logs in the bend of my right arm
I hold the fires of a year ahead,
The meals, the long evenings, snowshoes
Hung against the door, neighbour talk over tea.

Saw, axe and cordwood: small things, common
To other lands than this. The work I do
Brothers men in villages I'll never see.
A hundred times and another hundred
I cut, lift and carry, making small motions
That fill the cooling days with potential sun.

63

CHI CHI

**ABOVE: K'AN
WATER**

**BELOW: LI
FIRE**

**UPPER: LI
FIRE**

**LOWER: K'AN
WATER**

RULING LINES

AFTER THE END

Mending road, and feeling in the footsoles
Uprooting of rough stone ballast by the cloudburst,
Washout of gravel and sand in delta fans,
Sudden sharp ravine like a small river gorge,
Roof torn from the ant-nest and rushed away,
Then smoothed out, the road moved over on a curve
And spread in the field. Even with the new ditch,
This completion is another beginning, prelude to rain.

Wheelbarrow, rake, long-handle spade. Cotton gloves
Because these hands have weathered sixty years.
Red ant, madly hiding eggs, sees the path-mender
As a hovering cloud of power, not known directly
But by his works: a vast and blurred divinity.
Resting, the road-god hunts the sky for future storm.

64

WEI CHI

**ABOVE: LI
FIRE**

**BELOW: K'AN
WATER**

**UPPER: K'AN
WATER**

**LOWER: LI
FIRE**

RULING LINES

BEFORE THE END

May-Blossom Chang, when her father died, dressed
demurely
In silk severely cut, with no adornment. Slowly
She walked among the visitors, careful as a fox
On thin ice. With thoughtful deliberation
She poured tea for old friends of the family.
This done, she stood quietly with hands folded
Or sat with her aunt. Only her eyes moved,
Following the young men who talked with her uncle.

Later, when all the uncles and cousins, tiring,
Have returned to their homes, May-Blossom
Will stand for a moment in the moonlit gate
Holding to her lips a bud of the peach tree
And remembering that at least one man
Found her supremely attractive in mourning.

That work is done. I've closed the Chinese book,
Remembering an aging Argentine who said, "Imagine –
There are volumes (old friends) on that very shelf
I'll never look through again." He might have sensed,
With his angular appreciation of adjectives, there remained
Some complex nouns yet to be modified, two or maybe three
Inventions not otherwise copyright in the publishing jungle.
My friend, at forty-seven, asks, "Is there *more*?"

There's always more. It's just that coming down,
Crashing from that high of creation (imitating God)
You don't know when the thing will hit you again
And keep looking around for unlikely new causation.
It isn't only the Church can't tell when life begins:
Man, we don't know what prods the first word onto paper.

A Brief Biography

Born in late 1918, Clif Bennett grew up in New York City together with his mother Maude, father Steve and younger brother Dick. Skipping three classes, he started high school at the age of 12, graduating at the age of 15. When he wasn't going to school, he rigged poker and roulette games, using the proceeds to buy and sell stamps.

His father died after being diagnosed with a heart problem and ordered back to work by the company doctor. This was a formative time in Clif's life who joined the IWW as a direct result. He also joined the Communist Youth League and eventually came to see himself as an anarchist. This led to draft evasion for which he was hunted throughout the States and eventually imprisoned at the age of 26. (Yet, he volunteered for service in the Spanish civil war but was refused by the Party who felt his talents could be put to better use at home).

Freshly released from prison, Clif felt it was time to let the world know how perilously close to becoming a police-state his country had grown and wrote a revealing biography of the life and practices of J. Edgar Hoover. The result of this was a revealing series of articles about the life and practices of Clif Bennett which caused him to quietly leave the country, crossing the border into Mexico at the age of 28. There at the health resort of La Puerta he met Florence, his future bride and mother of his children. Thus, Eric and Lora Bennett have J. Edgar Hoover to thank for their existence.

Clif attended Goddard College, Vermont, in the 70's to attain his Bachelor's Degree and OISE in Toronto to gain his Masters of Education. He worked as centre director of the Addiction Research Foundation in Orillia until his retirement in 1987.

Clif spent most of his life married to Veronica, who had left Germany at the age of 19 and emigrated to Canada where she met Clif in 1958. The last 20 years of their life were spent on a hilltop north of Toronto in a house designed according to their combined wishes. Veronica died in 2002.

Today at the age of 94, Clif divides his time between summer visits to his daughter and her wife in Sweden and winters with his son in Florida.

– Lora Bennett, Norrköping, Sweden , March 2013.